SEA OF TREASON

Also by Julian Stockwin

Kydd
Artemis
Seaflower
Mutiny
Quarterdeck
Tenacious
Command
The Admiral's Daughter
Treachery (US title: The Privateer's Revenge)
Invasion
Victory
Conquest
Betrayal
Caribbee
Pasha
Tyger
Inferno
Persephone
The Baltic Prize
The Iberian Flame
A Sea of Gold
To the Eastern Seas
Balkan Glory
Thunderer
Yankee Mission

JULIAN STOCKWIN

SEA OF TREASON

HODDER &
STOUGHTON

First published in Great Britain in 2023 by Hodder & Stoughton
An Hachette UK company

1

A CIP catalogue record for this title is available from the British Library

Hardback ISBN 978 1 399 71671 0
Trade Paperback ISBN 978 1 399 71672 7
ebook ISBN 978 1 399 71673 4

Typeset in Garamond MT by
Palimpsest Book Production Limited, Falkirk, Stirlingshire

Printed and bound in Great Britain by Clays Ltd, Elcograf S.p.A.

Hodder & Stoughton policy is to use papers that are natural, renewable
and recyclable products and made from wood grown in sustainable forests.
The logging and manufacturing processes are expected to conform
to the environmental regulations of the country of origin.

Hodder & Stoughton Ltd
Carmelite House
50 Victoria Embankment
London EC4Y 0DZ

www.hodder.co.uk

Safely in harbour
Is the King's ship; in the deep nook, where once
Thou call'dst me up at midnight to fetch dew
From the still-vexed Bermoothes – there she's hid

William Shakespeare, *The Tempest*

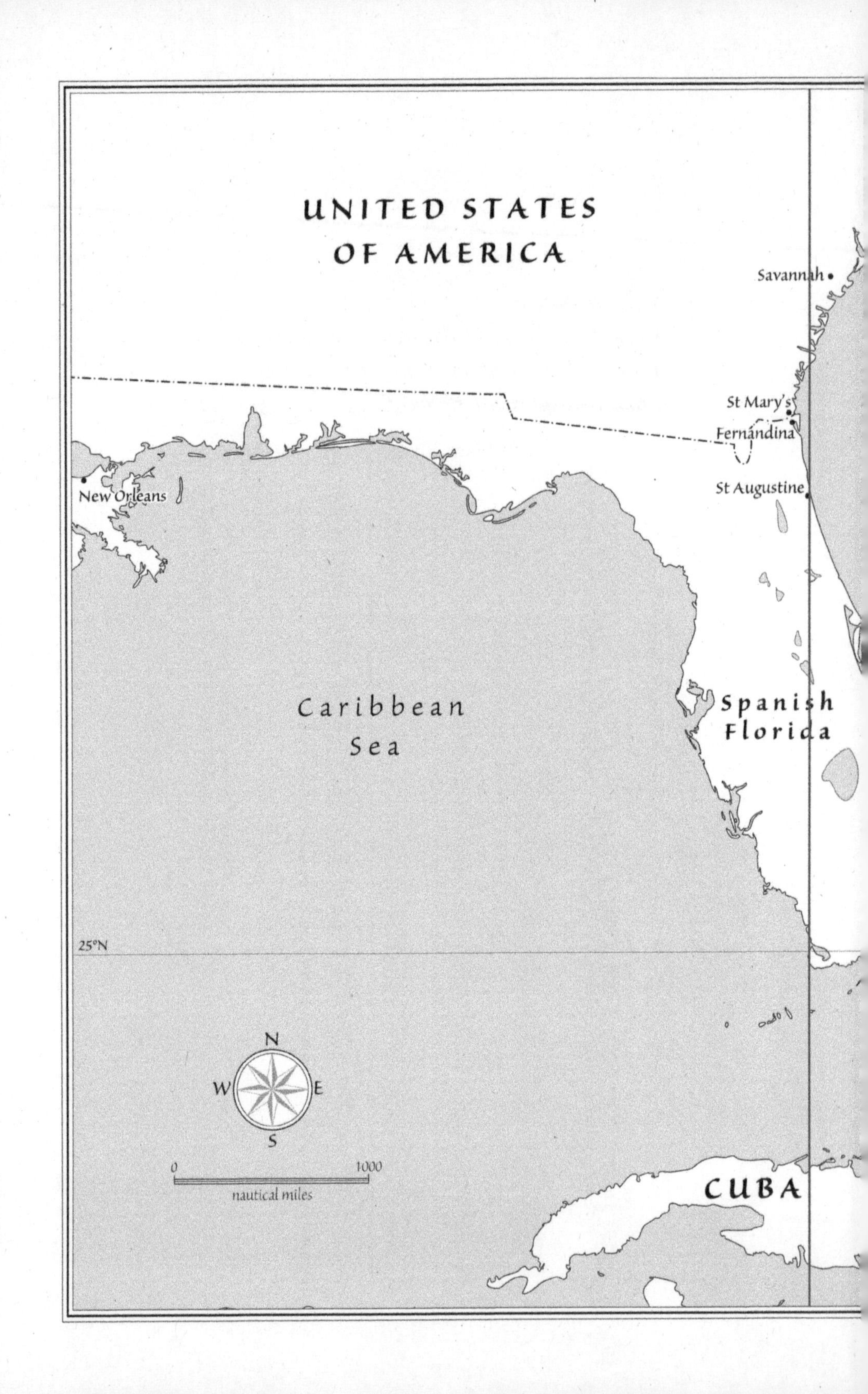
UNITED STATES
OF AMERICA
Savannah
St Mary's
Fernandina
St Augustine
New Orleans
Caribbean
Sea
Spanish
Florida
25°N
N
W
E
S
0
1000
nautical miles
CUBA

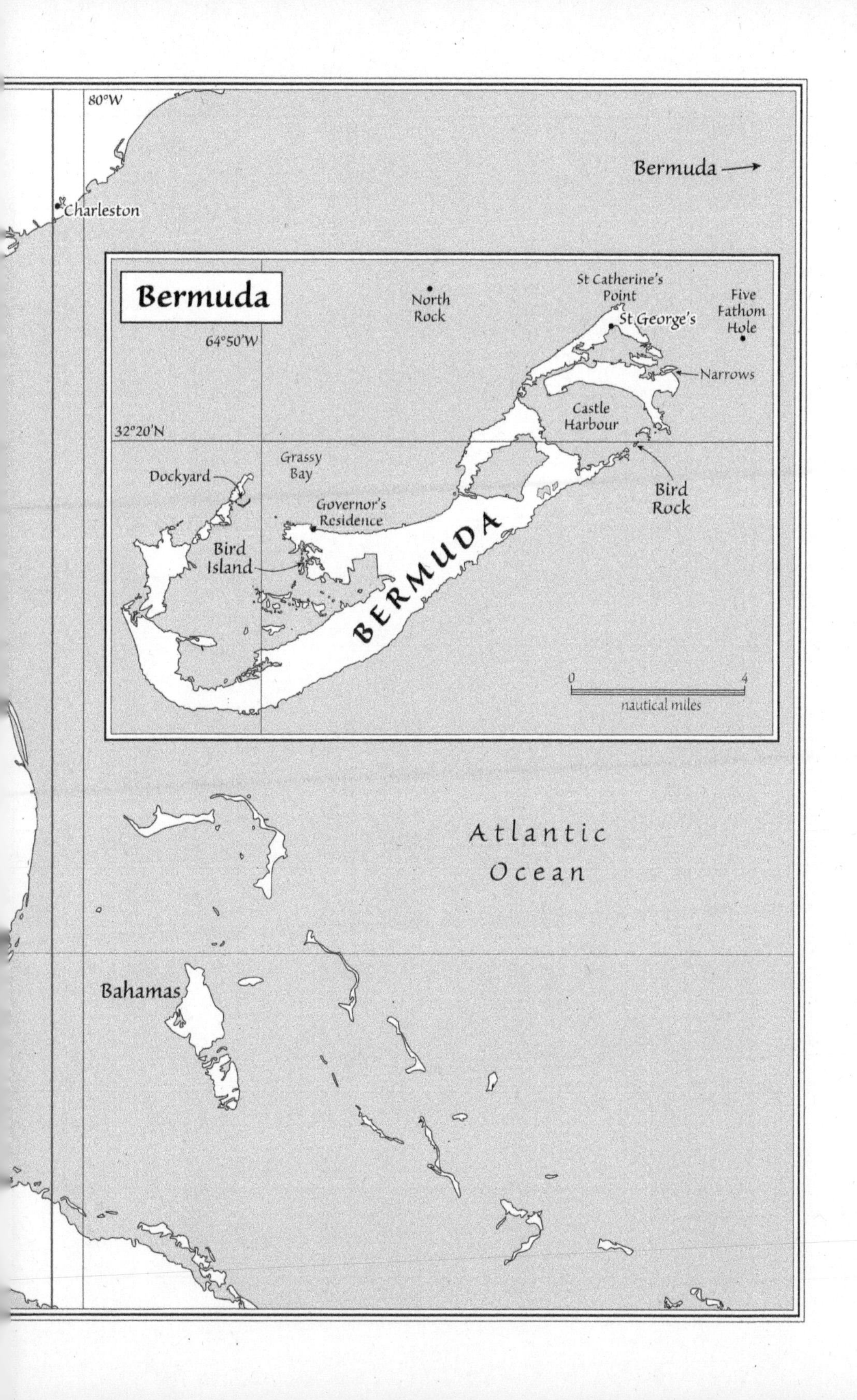
80°W
Bermuda
Charleston
Bermuda
North Rock
St Catherine's Point
St George's
Five Fathom Hole
64°50'W
Narrows
Castle Harbour
32°20'N
Grassy Bay
Dockyard
Bird Rock
Governor's Residence
BERMUDA
Bird Island
0
4
nautical miles
Atlantic Ocean
Bahamas

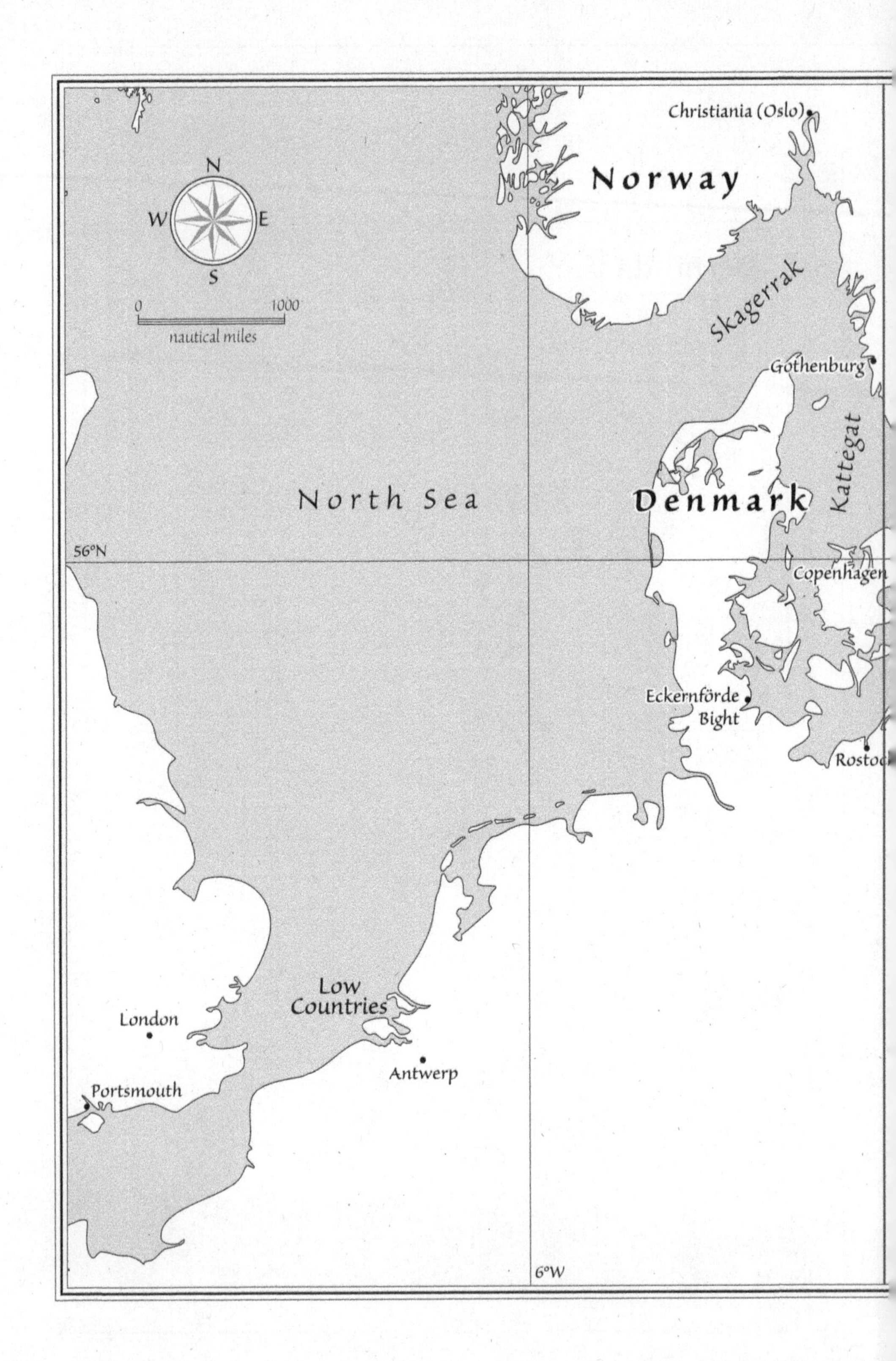

Christiania (Oslo)
Norway
N
W
E
S
0
1000
nautical miles
Skagerrak
Gothenburg
Kattegat
North Sea
Denmark
56°N
Copenhagen
Eckernförde
Bight
Low
Countries
London
Antwerp
Portsmouth
6°W

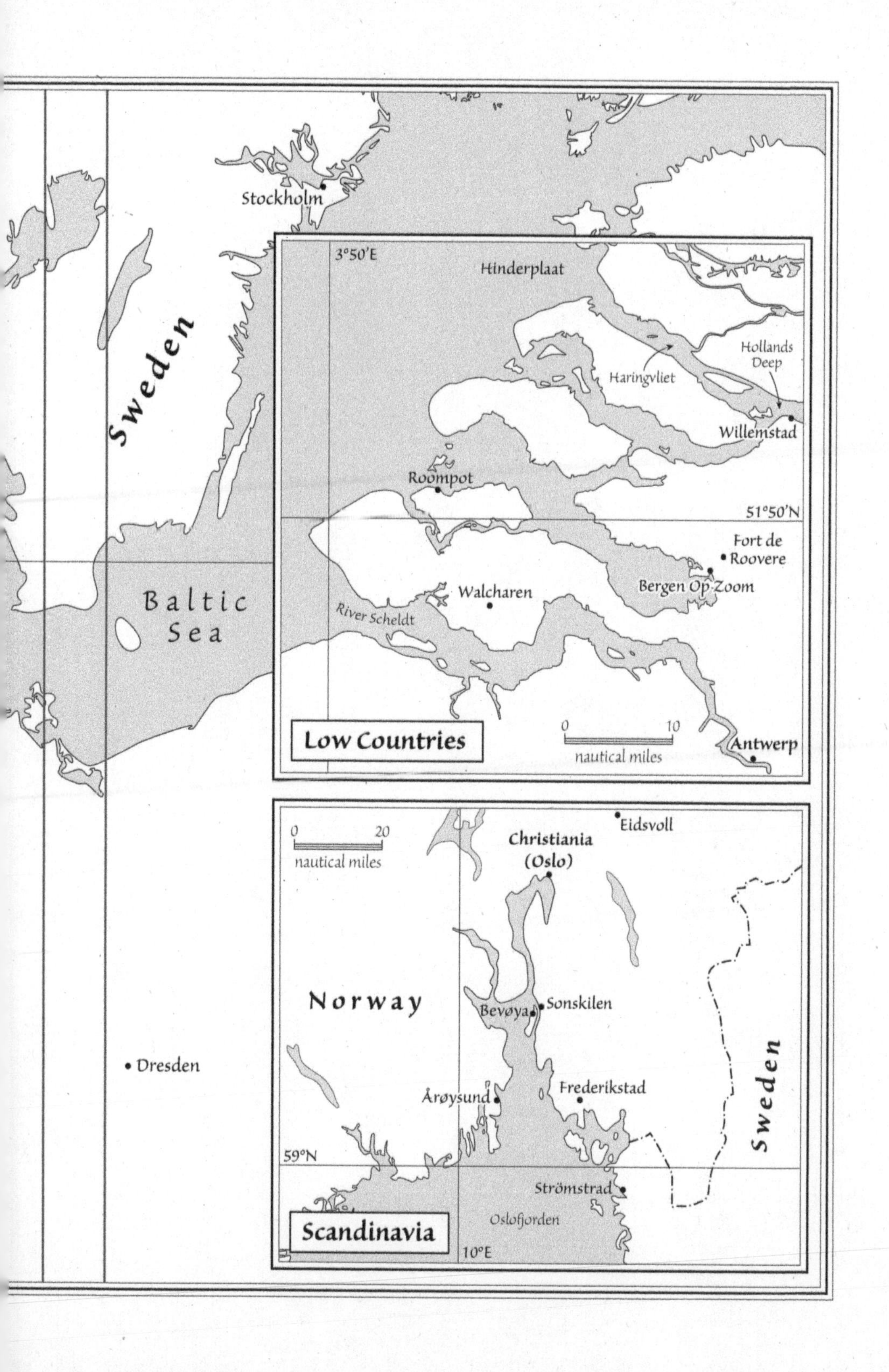

Stockholm
Sweden
Baltic Sea
Dresden
3°50'E
Hinderplaat
Hollands Deep
Haringvliet
Willemstad
Roompot
51°50'N
Fort de Roovere
Bergen Op Zoom
Walcharen
River Scheldt
Low Countries
0
10
nautical miles
Antwerp
0
20
nautical miles
Eidsvoll
Christiania (Oslo)
Norway
Bevøya
Sonskilen
Årøysund
Frederikstad
Sweden
59°N
Strömstrad
Oslofjorden
Scandinavia
10°E

Dramatis Personae

**indicates fictional character*

*Sir Thomas Kydd	Captain of HMS *Thunderer*
*Nicholas Renzi	Earl of Farndon, former confidential secretary to Kydd

***Thunderer*, ship's company**

*Ambrose	Second lieutenant
*Clinch	Fourth lieutenant
*Clinton	Captain of Royal Marines
*Craddock	Kydd's confidential secretary
*Doud	Quartermaster's Mate, friend of Stirk
*Gubb	Purser
*Halgren	Captain's coxswain
*Joyce	Sailing master
*Lawlor	Gunner
*Martyn	Third lieutenant
*Opie	Boatswain
*Pinto	Petty officer, friend of Doud
*Roscoe	First lieutenant

*Stirk	Gunner's mate, long-term acquaintance of Kydd
*Upcot	Carpenter

Others

*Avery	Mate, *Mary Miller*
*Bazely	New-made frigate captain, previous close friend of Kydd's
Beauharnais	Prince Eugène de, general and stepson of the Emperor
Bennigsen	Russian field marshal, head of military
Bernadotte	Marshal of France, changed sides against Napoleon
Berthier	French grand marshal and chief of Imperial Staff
*Bingham	Wife of Bermudian shipowner
Blücher	Field marshal, Prussian military leader
Borlase Warren	Admiral and commander-in-chief, North American Squadron
*Bowden	Commander, captain of *Weazel*
Brown	Admiral, Jamaica Squadron
Buckner	Landowner of Eastern Florida
Cochrane	Legendary but controversial frigate captain
Cockburn	Governor, Bermuda
Cole	Admiral in charge, northern element of North Sea Squadron
Colston	Rear admiral, Baltic squadron
*Congalton	Shadowy secret service dispatcher
*Costin	Elijah, American merchant
Cotton	Rear admiral, in command of the Texel
Croker	Able and influential secretary to the Admiralty

De Estrada	Governor of St Augustine
*Esther	Persephone's maid
Evans	Commodore, Bermuda dockyard
Ferrers	Captain Royal Marines, aide-de-camp to governor
*Francis	Kydd's son
Frederik	Danish crown prince, also governor of Norway
Frederik VI	King of Denmark-Norway
*Gavery	Bahamian smuggler
Graham	Lieutenant general Sir Thomas, leader of Antwerp expedition
*Gundersen	Yngvar, blacksmith
*Gundersen	Øyvind, son, Björn, another, Dagmar his daughter, Kirsten his wife
*Harris	Contributor to the *Bermuda Gazette*
*Holt	Rebecca, young admirer of Kydd
*Hoskins	Sergeant of foot
*Jago	Under-steward to the Earl of Farndon (Renzi), secretly an accomplice
Jarlsberg	Count Wedel, influential Norwegian businessman
Karl III Johan	Johan Bernadotte (q.v.), king of Sweden
Laforey	Admiral, Leeward Islands Squadron
Madison	President of United States of America, 1809–1817
Mathews	War veteran and adventurer, leader of Florida Patriots
McIntosh	Military leader of the Florida Patriots
McKee	Colonel John, United States commissioner
*Meares	Lieutenant colonel, staff at Horse Guards

Melville	First Lord of the Admiralty
*Mercer	Bermuda widow
Monroe	Secretary of state in Madison administration
*Moreau	Adjutant commandant on Bonaparte's staff
Ochoa	Teniente Coronel, Cuban colonial military
Overton	Colonial secretary
*Prinker	House of Commons lobbyist
Reeves	Lieutenant, platoon commander in assault on Fort de Roovere
*Richards	Lieutenant-in-command, *Curlew*
Schwarzenberg	Head of Army of Bohemia, part of thrust against Bonaparte
*Simon	Stowaway, young lad wanting to fight Napoleon
Smith	Lieutenant Colonel, US 8th Infantry, federal assistance
Sverdrup	Professor and president of the assembly
*Tracy	Lieutenant in command US gunboat
*Turner	Lieutenant, *Weazel*
*Villar	Fishing boat skipper
*Wilkins	Shipmaster of *Mary Miller*

Chapter 1

1813, London

On arrival back in England after his successful encounter with an American frigate, Captain Sir Thomas Kydd, Bart., had been promptly summoned to attend on the First Lord of the Admiralty. Alighting from his carriage in front of Admiralty House, he felt a frisson at the sight of the august surroundings, hallowed by centuries of Britain's wielding a victorious trident in the long sea wars.

'Do sit, old fellow! A tincture of the right sort, would you say?' Viscount Melville offered genially.

Kydd had never seen the admiral in such an elevation of spirits. He had expected a measured approval of his conduct, or some classical allusion to laurels from this careful and reserved individual.

Melville leaned forward in concern. 'The wound is troubling you less, I trust?'

Kydd had been seriously injured in the thigh at the hands of a Yankee sharpshooter several months before. 'A twinge at times only, my lord.'

Melville nodded and sat back. 'Well now,' he continued, 'and what shall we do with the hero of the hour, hey?'

Kydd gave a cautious smile. Could it be that the First Lord wanted him to know that the unpleasantness over his recent unsuccessful support of the adoption of steam power in the Navy was over and done with? Also that if he'd made enemies because of it, they were powerless to harm him now, and he was being welcomed back into the fold at his previous standing?

'If truth be told I'd be more than happy to feel my own deck under me again, sir.'

Melville gave a hearty chuckle. 'As so you should, so you should – no other way to win your flag, now is there?'

Kydd flushed in pleasure. This, from the very summit of the Admiralty, was the broadest of hints that he was in favour for the ultimate distinction of all – an admiral's flag. Post-captains could be made admiral without ever serving in that rank – a yellow admiral, as it was termed – but Melville, it seemed, was referring to an active sea appointment, commanding a squadron or fleet and sailing against the enemy.

It would have to be at some later point, the political winds set fair, the war grinding endlessly on, the interest from on high remaining his – but he had been led to believe he was in good odour with those who made the vital decisions, and might well, in time, be granted the felicity of a real flag.

The First Lord continued warmly, 'As it happens, two circumstances happily coincide: your availability for command and HMS *Thunderer* now completed her great repair. How does that satisfy?'

'Right well, sir!' Kydd said fervently. He was more than ready to renew acquaintance with the graceful sail-of-the-line he'd taken through the worst that Neptune could throw at her. It would no doubt be blockade duty along the French or Spanish coasts, but also a chance to let the healing complete.

'I rather thought you would,' Melville said, with a mischievous grin. 'And are you not interested in which station?'

'Sir?'

'In respect of the wound you suffered recently, a post in reach of the Biscay gales would be a trial, I believe. More to be desired is a fortifying and salubrious spell somewhere in the sun – how does the Bermudas appeal?'

'In a 74?' Kydd replied, in amazement.

'Certainly. They have an ancient 56 as guardship but in view of the American war it's desired to make a flourish off their south with something of more respectability. Not that we expect anything in the nature of an alarum in those quarters, it merely being an augmentation of force for the time being.'

Bermuda – the winter quarters of the North American Squadron and one of Britain's oldest colonies. He'd never been there but he understood it to be the quietest station of all – and the most pleasant. There would probably be no distinction to be won but from what he'd just heard he'd no need of such, for the time being.

'A fine prospect, sir.'

'Good. I'll instruct your orders be made up accordingly. Now I'd wish to let you know more of why you're being sent. Don't be misled – Bermuda is a sovereign possession of ours, lying as it does off the American coast and in the approaches to the Caribbean. It's well guarded by quantities of wicked reefs that make for a near impregnable situation for the defenders. Thus whoever possesses it will stand astride the sea lanes and dominate this part of the world. God forbid, but if our Yankee cousins lay hands on Bermuda we will be in a pretty pickle. You're there to show that any motion towards a landing will be met with insuperable force. I rather feel it will be enough.'

'A single ship?'

'I would think so.'

The Americans had nothing larger than a frigate and would never risk an assault at this stage, so life on station was set fair to be an uninterrupted tranquil cruise.

'As to your line of responsibility, you'll be on detached duty from Sir Borlase Warren and the North American Squadron, but as they'll soon be returning to Halifax, it's unlikely you'll be having many dealings with them, apart from books of account. Should the occasion demand, you'll be reinforced, of course, but given the current showing of Cousin Jonathan I'm doubting you'll still be there when they return at the end of the year.'

Kydd knew that, in other parts, the war with Bonaparte was still raging and, with a pang of guilt, he asked about the latest news.

'Boney? At his most dangerous, I'd have to say. Returned to Paris after Moscow and an appalling retreat, yet the devil has the gall to demand of his people they give him a fresh army, which they have, in the amount of a quarter-million – so far. He's about to strike back and I fear we're to be in thrall to the villain for a long time to come.'

Melville came around the desk and offered his hand. 'I do sincerely wish you good fortune, Sir Thomas. Commanders of your stripe we're in grave need of, both now and in the future.'

Chapter 2

It was a pleasant post down to Portsmouth dockyard where *Thunderer* lay. Kydd was sharing the coach with a fellow captain of a ship-of-the-line on his way to the Mediterranean and Admiral Pellew.

At Hindhead they took time to enjoy a very acceptable beef pie in the company of a London-bound colonel headed the opposite way, but they were soon back on the road, speeding on.

The last approach, Portsdown Hill, with its fine view of Spithead and the sea, provoked the usual stirrings of excitement for Kydd and he alighted at the George Hotel with eagerness. He hauled out his fob-watch. There was just time to clap eyes once again on his beloved ship.

Still in plain clothes, he made his way through the well-remembered streets to the golden spheres at the dockyard gate. He was recognised by the porter who, blank-faced, directed him to *Thunderer*, newly emerged from her docking and in an alongside berth. Her bare masts towered above the jumble of buildings as a course to steer.

She was not in commission and wouldn't be until the

formalities had been enacted at the mainmast. He therefore had no right to go aboard but nothing could stop him now. She looked in remarkably good fettle, given her many months under dockyard care. There was activity everywhere and he approached the brow in anticipation.

He took in her no-nonsense, uncompromising British lines that spoke of defiance of the waves rather than a craven gliding over them.

An affronted dockyard matey saw him come aboard and made to stop him but shrank back under Kydd's glare.

And then he was standing once more on *Thunderer*'s quarterdeck. There were curious stares from the riggers and a figure in worker's garb stopped and hastened across. 'Sir Thomas!' he called. It was Roscoe, his former first lieutenant who had been put ashore at the de-commissioning.

'Roscoe, old fellow. Are you . . .?'

'Received word out of the blue, on half-pay in Yarmouth, from their lordships, that *Thunderer* was to commission, and as her premier before, was I able to resume at short notice?'

'And I'm main glad to see you,' Kydd said, happy to have the young man where he belonged. 'Even not knowing her new captain?' he teased.

'Well, er, I was hoping that . . .'

'Then indeed know that I shall be her captain, and we shall see through the next commission together.'

There was a broad smile and a hesitant, 'Er, and what waters will that be in, sir?'

Kydd smiled back. 'We'll hear about it when I get my orders. Can you tell me what state the ship is in?'

Roscoe had obviously taken his appointment seriously and had done what he could to priddy the ship in readiness with only dockyard workers to chivvy.

'Let's have a look at what they've done for her,' Kydd said, hearing that, beyond provisions for a sudden flood of crew coming aboard, *Thunderer* was to all intents and purposes ready for the life that would then infuse her.

Her wounds, mostly below the waterline, were now healed with oaken strakes of unimpeachable strength, and the few blemishes above board had been neatly and elegantly made right.

'Er, no other officers have made their number to you?'

'No, sir.'

So *Thunderer* was going to start her next adventure with an unknown team at the top and a ship's company largely provided by the press-gang.

'Standing officers?' The boatswain, gunner, carpenter, purser, cook. Those tasked to stand by their ship as she was brought back to fitness as a ship-of-war – and the only faces he would know from the old days.

'All present, although I suspect that Mr Lawlor is desirous of smelling powder as soon as he might.' The gunner had had the least to do in the long months of her repair as *Thunderer*'s guns had been landed during her docking.

Much still lay ahead for the ship before she could set sail for Shakespeare's still-vex'd Bermoothes.

Chapter 3

Knowle Manor, Devon

'Yes, dear, but it's leagues from anywhere and—' Kydd tried to reason.

Persephone was having none of it. 'Thomas, I'm coming and that's an end to it.' She pointedly closed her atlas. 'If it's as quiet as you say, what's your objection?'

'Francis?' he replied. Their infant son obliged with a snort of delight at being referred to.

'I have a maid, and the boy needs good fresh air, which I can only believe exists in the deeper parts of the ocean in which Bermuda swims.'

'Well—'

'You've got a big ship now, which allows me to pack all the necessary apparel.'

Kydd sighed. It was a quiet station, why not indulge her? 'Then you shall come. With Esther, of course.'

'Thank you, my brave sea warrior. It'll be so heavenly to have you to myself for once.' She frowned. 'Oh dear – there's a complication. Mr Craddock called to see you before but declined to take a room here while you were absent. He's staying in Plymouth.'

Lucius Craddock, Harry to his friends, had ably served as Kydd's confidential secretary after the previous holder of the post, Dillon, had died at the hands of the French. As far as Kydd had known, he was still back with the family business in the north.

She gave a wry smile. 'It's just that he's had some sort of falling out and has resigned his post, thinking to stay with us while he considers his position.'

In a short while Craddock was in the drawing room giving out his plight. It seemed that his more active and far-seeing manner of business was not appreciated in Manchester. The collective wisdom of the family was that, in view of the renewing of the threat to world commerce from Bonaparte's rebounding, caution was to be recommended. His situation on the board was no longer tenable.

Kydd saw his chance. 'Harry, dear fellow, only if it answers, but your old situation in *Thunderer* is open to you – a cruise to the Bermudas?'

Chapter 4

Portsmouth

Thunderer had been taken to the fitting-out wharf and was well under way to being ready for sea. With the first draft of volunteers settled in, and three of the four officers having arrived, Kydd decided it was time to set the ship's heart to beating. 'Mr Roscoe, we shall commission at ten tomorrow, do prepare for such. And ask my officers to attend on me in one hour.'

The new second lieutenant, Ambrose, was a quiet but intelligent individual. His previous service was in a light frigate, ending in a wrecking, various ships-of-the-line and a last voyage in a gun-less transport to Cape Town. Steady and reliable – the best kind of officer in Kydd's estimation.

The third lieutenant, Martyn, was careful, possibly too respectful, and somewhat retiring. Having served in nothing larger than a brig-sloop, this was understandable and in Kydd's eyes even laudable. In a small ship, leadership and the rapid, faultless exercise of nautical skills was essential for everyone's survival.

Fourth Lieutenant Clinch was another matter. His appearance was curious. A markedly older man, his uniform was near threadbare, the lace of cheaper pinchbeck and his blue frock-coat faded. His features were hard, however, almost resentful. As soon as he spoke it became clear. He was a tarpaulin officer – one who'd worked his way aft the hardest way and believed he was of another tribe to the well-educated society favourites bred to the quarterdeck.

Hearing his service Kydd understood more. Lately snatched from being lieutenant-in-command of a cutter and finding himself most junior lieutenant in a battleship, his world had shrunk from being lord over all in his little command to being at the beck and call of many above him. Kydd sympathised but he expected loyalty and dedication from him in just the same way as the others.

He greeted the standing officers formally: the one-eyed Bull Opie, a boatswain of the old school, utterly staunch and dependable; the crotchety gunner, Lawlor; the pinch-faced but shrewd carpenter, Upcot. The purser, Gubb, was ready as always with a hill of papers; and the cook moaned about the quality and quantity of the victuals being haled aboard.

One of his papers requested an exchange of Royal Marine officers from a 98-gun ship bound for the Baltic and *Thunderer*. It seemed a Captain Clinton was unduly anxious to ship out in a vessel headed westward rather than the more lucrative Baltic station. Kydd smiled softly. It would be good to have William Clinton with him once again.

Later in the morning the sailing master made his appearance.

'Mr Joyce! Am I to understand you're . . .?'

'Aye, sir!' The jolly features of the old master creased in

pleasure. 'I'm t' take up m' place as is right 'n' proper for the barky.'

The wily individual had heard of Kydd's appointment and had lost not an instant in petitioning for a warrant to *Thunderer* as being known to the captain – and immediately available.

'So happy to see you, Mr Joyce. I believe we'll have sore need of your services where we're going.' Before Joyce could get a word out, Kydd gave a slow and meaningful wink. In the event the master would be the first to know, needing to lay in the chart folios involved. Perplexed but happy, Joyce stumped off on his wooden leg, now a lighter and stylish cork article.

Craddock quickly had the books in order, and when further drafts of seamen came aboard, they were duly mustered and entered. They were just numbers now but within days of sea-time the individuality of each would emerge and Kydd would have a measure of *Thunderer*'s ship's company.

And then as the vessel neared readiness for sea there was a hesitant knock at Kydd's cabin door. Martyn diffidently leaned in. 'Sorry to disturb, sir, but we have a volunteer who won't have it 'less he sees you.'

Kydd's hopes rose. It had happened this way before and he had a good notion of who it might be.

'Mr Stirk!' he exclaimed, with genuine pleasure. 'So good to see you! Thank you, Mr Martyn, I'll see to this man.'

After the lieutenant had left he came out from behind the desk to greet the mariner whose influence on his forming as a seaman would never be forgotten.

'Toby – you're shipping with us?'

The piratical gleam in Stirk's dark eyes had not diminished in its intensity and the lithe, muscular figure had lost nothing to the years. 'Heard you was the owner agin,' he growled. 'Like as t' take us in the way of some sport.'

'Yes,' Kydd agreed. 'As can see you snugged down in a gunner's mate berth this hour.' The gunner would be more than content to see his old mate restored to him.

Stirk hesitated. 'Depends.'

It was not like the bluff old seaman to make conditions and Kydd waited, allowing a slight frown to cloud his features.

'As I don't fancy a v'y'ge without I has shipmates I c'n trust.'

'Well—'

'You'll swear on it as if I put the word out to m' friends you'll find 'em a prime situation if they volunteers for the barky?'

It was more than Kydd could ever have hoped for!

'You mean, Doud, Pinto—'

'An' the others as who can be found – aye, sir.'

'We sail in a few days.'

'Leave it t' me, sir, if y' please,' Stirk said firmly.

True to his word, *Thunderer*'s company was made complete by the addition of some of the most deep-dyed seamen to be found anywhere on the high seas. To see the hulking Swede Halgren nonchalantly mounting the brow with his sea-bag slung over his shoulder by his left-hand hook not only solved the question over who was to be his captain's coxswain, but guaranteed that if it ever came to any kind of close-quarters fight his back would be safe.

And the others – their features were older but there was no mistaking the easy lope of the prime seaman. Shipmates for years, their staunch friendship and trust would spread to others, an unspoken example to the rest of the hands, raw and fearful as many would be.

As their departure drew near it was time to embark the passengers. The passage would take weeks. He had Persephone and Francis, with her maid, accommodated in his bedplace, while he rigged a comfortable hammock in the great cabin. Craddock gladly found sanctuary in the captain's clerk's larboard side cabin.

Kydd was assailed by quantities of doting parents who, having heard of a voyage to Bermuda, desired their sons to be set on his quarterdeck, for he was both a legend and bound for a station in a place reputed both quiet and safe. He took three as midshipmen.

Soon it was the final hours, with bundles of newspapers to be stowed, chests of specie struck below, awkward spars laid along for the new dockyard, and a garrison-bound detachment of the 52nd of Foot looking about in bewilderment.

And then, almost guiltily, *Thunderer* set forth from a wartime Portsmouth heading for the sunlit seas of the south, her little flock of transports and lesser naval craft obediently taking station on the two-decker, her passengers gazing back pensively on the fading blue-grey of England.

Chapter 5

Thunderer, at sea

'As I were quartermaster's mate in *Minotaur*, right after we gave 'em best – the Americans, that is,' the sailing master puffed importantly, 'an' we has t' fall back on Bermuda, all as is left to us from Nova Scotia right t' the Caribbean.'

'Really? Then you're no stranger to these waters,' Kydd replied politely, his gaze steadily ahead.

'Not as who would say,' Joyce agreed modestly. 'Didn't have time t' note it all down.' Kydd hid a smile. If Joyce had been a quartermaster's mate, as he himself once was, it would never have been his business to do so.

'I remembers it as what sent Ol' Jack – our master as was – near lunatic.'

'Oh?'

Joyce looked at Kydd with pitying eyes. 'Y' hasn't seen a hell-place f'r mariners like it, sir. Near thirty mile across o' rocks an' reef, most land no higher'n twenty-five feet. Means from seaward ye've no sighting and then it's two fathom shallows and a wrecking.'

'So how . . .'

'By exact attention to y'r four Ls only.' Kydd knew what he meant: latitude, longitude, lead and lookout – all prudent position-fixing measures. So a Bermuda landfall was to be made by immaculate navigation.

'And I didn't know Bermuda was that big.'

'It ain't,' Joyce said positively. 'Guernsey is larger by miles, an t'would fit in the Isle o' Wight eight times over. All islands in one place.'

'Then how best to approach?' Kydd knew the answer but wanted to hear Joyce as a measure of his knowledge of the waters.

'Right at the norrard edge o' the reefs. North Rock. A wicked bunch o' rocks, all of 'em together up sharp, like crocodile teeth. We lays these t' starb'd and claims a pilot who takes us through the channels t' the inner lagoons. A fearful navigation.'

'Have you returned to Bermuda since then, Mr Joyce?'

'Er, no, sir.'

Kydd, however, had made it his business to secure the most reliable word on this remote outpost. 'Well, I have it from the latest rutter as takes advantage of a great survey a dozen years ago by a Captain Hurd, saying as the best way to St George's, the main harbour, is from the eastwards. We raise Five Fathom Hole to the east and from there if we're a lesser draught vessel we can go direct into St George's or if a sail-of-the-line we take up on a channel around the north and we find a dockyard and an anchorage fit for a fleet. And buoyed all the way.'

'Hmmph. Only takes one rock out o' place. Can we be sure on the reckoning?'

'I rather think we can. Captain Hurd spent nine years on his survey.'

In the event it was even easier. They simply ran down the latitude of 32° 23' until the low blue-grey of Bermuda firmed ahead. The small squadron heaved to at a marked buoy, *Thunderer* in the van. The red and white flag at her mizzen peak signified the need for a pilot and before long a slim cutter was on its way out.

Used to the usual hoary brass-buttoned mariner in sea-boots, Kydd found this pilot of quite another sort. A young, barefoot and grinning Black man introduced himself as Jacob, king's pilot, with an assistant Jeremy, and a grubby paper to prove it. They got to work immediately. Jacob loped off and took position right forward on the fo'c'sle, while Jeremy remained by the helm, careful to keep the pilot within sight.

'Under way, Cap'n,' he said. 'An' bear away larb'd.'

'What course?'

'I don' know, Cap'n,' Jeremy said cheerfully. 'We go where Jacob says.' The distant figure raised an arm, crooked it downward and waited. 'Easy all – a touch t' starb'd.'

Kydd could see what was happening. The pilot was gazing into the limpid transparency of the water ahead to spy out the mysterious dark patches against the light sea-bed to piece together an underwater picture that would provide direction to the desired channel. It was masterful, the result no doubt of years' conning ships of all kind through the maze of sub-sea crags.

The land resolved into distinct islands, and as they drew nearer Kydd could make out the conical red- and green-painted channel-marking buoys pacing away around the modest headland to the fleet anchorage, and was comforted. The run-of-the-mill entrances and exits would be straightforward, thanks to Hurd's hard work.

As they came closer it was possible to make out a fort – two, three. These would be guarding the narrow passage to the inner St George's harbour and capital. But for them, the helm went over and they passed north and sharply around St Catherine's Point to head in a direct line to a broad anchorage with an island sprawling across their bows. The chart indicated that this was Grassy Bay.

Kydd's little squadron had reached its destination.

There was no welcoming fleet of line-of-battle ships at anchor. Admiral Warren had left for Halifax and the larger war and they had the anchorage to themselves, and the freedom that implied.

Who then did he report to? His hasty instructions indicated that the Bermudas had a governor and commander-in-chief, whatever that meant in practice, but his true line of responsibility was to the absent Warren. To confuse the issue he could clearly make out a commodore's pennant lazily flapping among the dockyard buildings. If he was to make obeisance first to the senior naval officer it could well be seen as a slight by the civil authorities and—

'Boat putting off, sir.'

It bore a naval ensign, indicating an officer on board, and shortly Kydd was made aware that Commodore Evans would appreciate knowledge of who they were and what they were doing in his anchorage. That is, after he'd first presented himself to the governor, Sir James Cockburn. Dilemma solved, Kydd was informed that the governor's residence was only a mile or two away on the heights of the southern shore, from which, no doubt, he was observing them at that very moment.

Chapter 6

Sir James Cockburn, 9th Baronet of Langton, greeted Kydd loftily, his manner reflecting his feelings at being obliged to acknowledge a mere sea-captain, however noticed by the powers-that-be.

'You've visited the Bermudas before?' he opened.

'No, sir,' Kydd answered politely. The house was in cool stone and the reception room well furnished – but something was not as it should have been and he couldn't put his finger on it.

'Then you should be aware that this is a remarkable place, not to say peculiar in its peoples and ways. Yet do bear in mind they've been here since the year 1612, our oldest colony, and may therefore be suffered a trifle of forbearance.'

They, not *we*?

'Nevertheless, I do account your presence a distinct asset here, an access of strength to my defences of immeasurable value to me.'

Kydd's hackles rose. If the governor thought that *Thunderer* was under his orders there could be troubles to come.

'Sir, my orders are to act specifically as a deterrent. To this end I intend to cruise the American coast from time to time as I see the need and—'

'Quite so. We shall speak later of my extensive plans for the defending of these islands and until then I make suggestion that you do become familiar with Bermuda, don't you think?'

That was it! The room, possibly the main one in the mansion, had no fireplace. The social focus, the natural centre of attention in any English drawing room, was missing, probably in deference to the climate.

'I will do so, sir.'

'Most naval officers of a certain quality do maintain a presence on shore, Sir Thomas. I shall direct my aide to make advice as to how this might be done. A fashionable lease would probably answer?'

'Thank you for your consideration, sir. As it happens I'm accompanied by my wife and young son and would be contented to see them accommodated well.'

Cockburn reached for a bell-rope.

A pleasant officer of the Royal Marines appeared and bowed to Kydd.

'This is Captain Ferrers. He is available to consult as his duties will permit.'

The governor abruptly moved towards the door, then hesitated and said in an odd tone, 'I do wish you well of your stay, Sir Thomas. If there is anything I can assist you with, then pray do not hesitate to ask.'

Outside, the amiable Ferrers suggested they make enquiries in the right quarters concerning lodgings and meet on the morrow to inspect prospects.

Kydd had every trust in Persephone's ability to make a

suitable selection and, not over-keen to spend his day looking over houses, found it convenient to call upon the commodore superintendent of the dockyard.

The new dockyard was growing apace on the long island marking the end of the anchorage. Kydd could make out a spar yard, blacksmiths and a quantity of storehouses, but only one building yet of stone, set among a luxuriance of cedars. The commodore's pennant flew from a simple mast in front of an equally modest cottage.

He was welcomed not by a flag-lieutenant but a beaming lady who ushered him into a comfortable living room.

'Thank you, my dear,' the occupant said. 'Do leave us with a noggin and we'll be content at that.' It had to be the commodore, but his comfortable plain dress did little to indicate it, or the steel-rimmed spectacles, which, with his round-faced, genial countenance, put Kydd in mind of a bookish don.

'And we see . . .?'

'Sir Thomas Kydd, sir.'

'As?'

'Captain, HMS *Thunderer*, 74, for the nonce attached to Bermuda to act the deterrent.'

'And?'

'A number of smaller vessels in replacement, as requested.'

'Ah. I see. Then you owe your duty to Admiral Warren, the others ours to dispose of as we desire.'

'Um, that seems to be the case,' Kydd replied. There was a sharp and penetrating mind behind the humble appearance, he realised.

In the next few minutes he was treated to a lucid overview of what Bermuda should mean to a sailor: while the miles of encircling reefs were a death-trap to the unwary mariner they were at the same time its impregnable defence. None without a thorough knowledge of the few channels into the inner lagoons could think to mount an assault and this was, in the form of the majestic survey by Hurd, kept strictly secret. Only approved and well-defended channels were marked on the charts. Therefore the islands possessed defending soldiery only in the hundreds manning scattered forts overlooking all such strategic approaches.

Seeming inclined to talk, Evans disclosed that the governor might well be forgiven his short manner in light of the hard time he was given by the propertied and privileged classes in the form of a House of Assembly and his council, not necessarily of his own views.

Kydd was surprised to discover that their very competent king's pilot was in fact a slave, one of some thousands in Bermuda. Even as the slave trade was effectively banned, there remained some still in bondage, paid for originally at the auction block and therefore legal property. Many trading ships were manned by slaves, and smugglers had all-Black crews for they could not be made to testify against their owners.

As yet the dockyard was unable to undertake repairs of anything like a major nature but the island was blessed with groves of cedar, straight and true growths. It had the property of resisting shipworm and, because of its resinous nature, did not need seasoning for long periods, ideal ship-building timber. All around the colony were slipyards, large and small, their crowning achievement the Bermuda sloop, said to be the fastest craft afloat.

More interesting details were disclosed but Kydd had to call a halt. *Thunderer* was still in sea watches, awaiting her captain's dispositions for everything from liberty to the hands, to setting up for sea service in these waters, and he had to return.

Chapter 7

Roscoe was waiting when *Thunderer*'s captain stepped aboard. 'Stand down the men, sir?'

Any new arrivals were expected to conform to routines in force at the anchorage, not so onerous in this case. Kydd had the rules and regulations and fell in with them quickly. It would be 'river discipline' – both watches of the hands at work in the forenoon, leave to one watch in the afternoon. The anchorage ran a liberty-boat after midday, its destination St George's, the older town at the other end of the islands, and Hamilton, the up-and-coming township just the other side of the land that faced them.

'Please,' Kydd replied. 'Larbowlines may step ashore after midday as you see the state of the ship warrants, officers at your discretion, Mr Roscoe. And I'll be off myself.'

A note had just come aboard that Persephone had found a prospect at St George's and would be delighted for his opinion.

She and Esther were at the jetty talking excitedly, with two men in attendance. Kydd joined them and learned that a most desirable residence was awaiting his approval. It was close by, in Duke of York Street, at a discreet elevation above the sturdy buildings of the Customs House and other waterfront edifices, some with modest towers of a military cast.

The house was not palatial but well-suited to the semi-tropical conditions. With a shady veranda and stone walls, it was cool and restful. Inside, its high ceilings and spacious rooms were tasteful and practical.

It had until recently been the *pied-à-terre* of the flag-captain of Warren's fleet and it seemed his larger items of furniture could be included in the lease to be passed on to the next occupant, with the services of the domestics lately in employ at this address. The large dining room and decorous entertaining to be had in the assembly room decided it for Kydd. Their new residence was styled Monte Rosa.

Later, with Lady Kydd on his arm, strolling along the quaint but colourful street in the velvet warmth of an evening wreathed by tropic fragrances, he pondered the fates that had brought him to this serene paradise while the rest of the world was plunged into endless war.

'Such a fine place for Francis to take his first steps in the world,' Persephone said later, as the maid briskly finished her ministrations. 'And such a lot of good people to admire him.' She paused a moment, then added, 'As will be a perplexity how to meet them all, I fear.'

Kydd put down his *Bermuda Gazette* and looked fondly at her. 'Which I fancy will not tax you overmuch – an entertainment of note will bring the great and good flocking, I'm persuaded.'

'No doubt to see and make acquaintance of my handsome and distinguished husband,' she teased.

'As it may be, but you must do without my presence for a time, my dear. I have to get *Thunderer* earning her bread before long.'

Chapter 8

Thunderer, *at sea*

Kydd's orders were clear – by the presence of his ship-of-the-line he was to let it be known to the Americans that it was risking too much to set one of their formidable frigates loose on the valuable trade routes to the Caribbean.

Standing astride the quarterdeck of a battleship, he knew he need have no misgivings about any possible outcome, even if he was sailing alone but for *Weazel*, the little brig-sloop gamely following in their wake.

The issue at hand was how to convey that *Thunderer* was in these waters to stay, not a passing member of Warren's squadron.

The populous north of the continent was drawing the attention of the admiral's powerful squadron in Halifax, so therefore the southern coasts were Kydd's. Extending the line of latitude of Bermuda to the American seaboard touched the states of North and South Carolina, and further south, Georgia. Further still lay Spanish territory, Florida, which did not concern them.

As far as he knew there was no United States naval presence in these waters but there were significant-sized seaports, Charleston and Savannah. The first was responsible for many of the privateers that plagued this side of the Atlantic. The other was the chief cotton port of the south. A sudden appearance off the coast of a mighty two-decker of-the-line with a disinclination to leave would have a gratifying effect.

With the fine north-easterly trades fair for their objective, it was only days before they raised the hazy line of the American continent. Kydd cautiously shortened sail. Their inshore charts were old and he distrusted them, so he set a leadsman to work in the bows.

A shocked 'By the deep – four!' told him there was less than a fathom under their keel. This far out to sea?

He soon had the answer. The south-east of the continent was lowland and often marshy, threaded through by innumerable waterways, all of which had been endlessly depositing silt and mud to seaward for centuries. Little wonder that treacherous shallows reached out so far. There would be deeper channels known locally but no way of spying them out in the drab, discoloured offshore waters. It made any thought of a threatening flourish close off the port out of the question.

'Heave to, Mr Joyce,' he said heavily, and ordered, '*Weazel*'s pennants and captain to repair aboard.'

He waited at the large table, what charts he had spread out before him. When a well-remembered soft knock sounded he eased into a smile.

It was good to see Bowden again, the timid midshipman of years ago transformed now into a commander. His own ship was tucked in under their lee and a confidence in his manner showed he was taking well to the dignity of command.

'Sit yourself down, Captain,' Kydd said breezily, aware his use of the honorary rank would please the young man. He'd heard the officer, by simply being on hand in Halifax when the Tygers were being shipped back to England, had been plucked from the ranks of needy lieutenants to fill the place of a promoted sloop commander.

'Sir. And a particular pleasure to meet you again,' he responded shyly.

There'd been no opportunity to meet in Bermuda during the few short days Kydd had been on station, and Bowden had only recently arrived, deployed on the station's defences by Warren. Kydd had claimed *Weazel* as an escort and they had corresponded briefly before sailing.

'A mort of pother in my planning,' Kydd opened. 'You'll know my orders require me to linger close off Cousin Jonathan's ports to top it the ogre. Yet I find the waters hereabouts shoaling and foul to a degree.'

Bowden murmured sympathetically.

'How much does *Weazel* draw?'

'Oh, er, at the moment a touch less eight feet.' As the implications of the question penetrated there was a flicker of dismay on Bowden's face, quickly followed by a lift of the chin. 'But if you desire I should perform that duty in your place, do not hesitate to order it so, I beg.'

Kydd had no intention of asking this, for the little brig-sloop would be a laughable menace to flourish before the Americans.

He hid a smile and laid out his plan. 'Rather than a species of threat I rather fancy the Yankees will look on you more as a most desirable prize-of-war. What I require is for you to trail your coat as near as you may to them, and when the villains put to sea to spring upon you, be so good as to lure them out to me.'

There were means to stay out of sight for as long as possible, which would be considerably helped by light conditions being in their favour.

'And if you should contrive to allow this to happen near dusk I should be obliged.'

Chapter 9

After Bowden returned to his ship, Kydd's conscience pricked. He was sending the young man not only into hazards of nature but into an unknown hostile situation. As a principal port, Charleston would have cutters, gunboats and others to shepherd in blockade runners taking a chance with the privateers. If he was overwhelmed by them in light winds there was nothing Kydd could do for him.

But if it worked, the Americans would know they'd been lured into a trap and from then on would never know if chasing a lesser British warship would end with them squaring off to a battleship. And the primary purpose of his cruise would be more than satisfied, especially if he repeated the trick in Savannah, further south.

As *Weazel*'s sails diminished into the distance Kydd took up position. Bowden would make his run directly out to sea, at right-angles to the coast. He, Kydd, would go to one side to allow hunters and the chase to pass, while he would lie quietly out of their sight before lunging in to cut them off from their lair.

It was asking much to disguise or conceal a hulking ship-of-the-line but he had some ideas up his sleeve.

Until Bowden appeared, hopefully chased by the enemy, it was a matter of waiting.

Evening drew in and an offshore breeze began wafting elusive fragrances of magnolia and jasmine, with the unmistakable reek of swamp and marshland.

The sun lowered imperceptibly over the distant land, and shadows lengthened towards what promised to be a spectacular sunset. Still no activity. Roscoe, standing with Kydd, fiddled with his cuffs, clearly wanting to give vent to an opinion not necessarily in Kydd's favour. Thinking better of it, he stalked off to annoy the boatswain.

Kydd's mind turned over possibilities. Perhaps the recovering reputation of the Royal Navy meant that an engagement had been declined. Or they'd been seen by a fishing boat. Or that—

'Gunfire!' Faint flat thuds carrying far on the warm evening air.

Kydd strained to see into the eventide shades but could make out nothing. Only the masthead lookout had the height-of-eye to spot anything at that distance.

A hail came. 'Deck hooo! I see sail – all together like, two, three – five. Two on 'em square-rigged.'

'Where headed, you looby?' Kydd bawled back irritably.

'Standing out directly!'

It had to be Bowden. With as much patience as he could muster Kydd ordered *Thunderer* to quarters. Probably only the smaller guns on the upper deck would burn powder if it came to an altercation but exercise at the great guns would not be wasted time.

'Strike all sail, Mr Joyce,' he ordered. Now, in the growing dusk, there would be no betraying pale patches – the ship in bare masts would be difficult to make out against the darker regions to seaward.

'I see 'em!' Roscoe grunted. A scattered collection of lighter blobs had come into view, resolving into individuals too distant to recognise.

After a while it became clear. *Weazel* was leading the pack by a short head, closely followed by another square-rigger with a cutter and lugger on either beam, and coming up fast from astern was a wickedly raked fore-and-aft craft.

Now for Kydd's move. Cautiously the fore and main courses were set. *Thunderer* had been positioned to the wind such that when full and drawing the edge of the sails she was end on to the gaggle of ships issuing out. These would not yet be visible from their decks and the higher topsails and topgallants were carefully doused. The smaller class of warships did not possess masts and yards capable of setting lookouts on high as a full-rigged vessel could.

Thunderer gracefully swung under the wind's impulse, heading in the opposite direction into the land. In a very short while she would slew around and cut across their wakes, and they would know they had been tricked.

The outnumbered *Weazel* was trading fire with her pursuers but she was by no means the fastest of them and her pop-gun six-pounders were never going to be battle-settlers.

Thunderer unveiled her presence in a dramatic, surging swing that took her across the last of a blazing sunset.

The cutter and lugger fell away from the chase, uncertain what to do, while the elderly brig tried to make off to leeward. In a masterly display, *Weazel* in an instant hauled her wind and went after her.

Only the last vessel showed fight, now recognisable as a war-schooner of the feared Baltimore breed. Astonishingly, she didn't go for *Weazel* but, in a graceful pirouette, flung herself back to face *Thunderer*.

Taken by surprise Kydd tried to make sense of it. A ship-of-the-line could blow the handsome but far smaller ship of war to splinters in one broadside. What was she doing?

Slashing past *Thunderer* in a fine show she rounded to off *Thunderer's* elaborate sternworks. Then, brailing up her main, she proceeded to open fire with her tiny four-pounders.

Stung by the effrontery Kydd found there was little he could do. The only guns that bore astern were a pair of nine-pounders that could not depress sufficiently to return fire.

Then he understood. The daring and intelligent captain was causing sufficient annoyance to demand his attention, allowing the others to flee the field. And it was working. The relatively ponderous manoeuvring of the big two-decker could easily be matched by the fine-lined and agile schooner, whose puny guns, while unable to inflict much in the way of damage, would sooner or later begin taking life.

Gratefully picking up on what was happening, the cutter and the lugger spread every scrap of canvas to run for safety shorewards. The brig was not so lucky – *Weazel* had come up with her, and as Kydd watched, her boarders began swarming on deck.

Its colours came down in short, savage jerks to rise again, surmounted by a British ensign, at which the schooner, knowing it would now have the undivided attention of the two men-o'-war, wheeled around and beat a retreat.

Chapter 10

The cruise had started out splendidly, Kydd mused smugly, contemplating his whisky glass in the spacious splendour of his great cabin. Even as they laid their bowsprits for the run south to Savannah, dismaying news of the unstoppable menace off their ports must be spreading far and wide.

The cargoes of this chief cotton port went to the Manchester textile mills and elsewhere around the world, funding the war for the United States.

This time the chart was more informative. The waterfront lay a good fifteen miles above the entrance to the Savannah river, unable to take sight of a lurking ship-of-the-line to seaward. Should he send *Weazel* in, right up to the port?

Then he realised something. Deep-laden cotton ships with a draught not much less than *Thunderer*'s were obviously able to reach the docks. Why not make sally themselves up to the town? The appearance of a battleship so close and ominous would cause panic and consternation on a monstrous scale.

Feeling the effect of the whisky spread pleasingly, he realised that, with the awesome power of the decks of guns at his command, he could loose a wasting devastation on the seaport that could put it to ruin and therefore out of the war. But at the probable cost of many dead.

The whisky glow faded as another thought took hold. What if, in a deadly repeat of *Tyger*'s end, he went aground and *Thunderer* too was lost? Madison, President of the United States, would make certain the world never forgot it – the vaunted Royal Navy now losing a ship-of-the-line to the Americans.

No, it was not necessary to take such risks in the achieving of his goal. Why not simply lie off the river for a few days and intercept the valuable commerce passing to and from Savannah? Seize and destroy – confusion, dread. It would have the same effect. No need even to put *Weazel* to hazard.

Bowden was enthusiastically in agreement. With one capture on its way to the Bermuda prize courts, even if shared with *Thunderer*, there was now every prospect of more.

At the pre-agreed place athwart the entrance to the Savannah river the pair ceased their southward track. They were now in the position to be able to cut the sea-lane that led to Savannah. Any vessel inward- or outward-bound must pass within sight and would be duly intercepted.

This required no particular plan – it was what was happening all the time off French ports like Brest. Reducing to topsails, it was just a matter of opening the distance between them but remaining within sight of each other while straddling the approaches, *Weazel* close in and *Thunderer* standing off.

The morning wore on, the low, hazy coastline just visible, the wafting odours much the same as previously but no sail anywhere. By late afternoon it was becoming a mystery. A busy port like this and no shipping?

Night fell but they kept alert for furtive blockade runners, helped by a gibbous moon. By break of day the conclusion was obvious. They were victims of their own success. Word had reached here of the unanswerable threat that prowled the coast and Savannah was in a state of siege.

Kydd was not disheartened. It had only confirmed the effectiveness of his deterrence and he could now move on. The whole American seaboard must now, and for some time, be fearful that somewhere he would be lingering, lost to view, waiting to pounce.

Chapter 11

Kydd thought he would next proceed past Spanish Florida and show himself in the gateway to the Caribbean, where it was known both privateers and French frigates were roving. He'd then make his number with the Jamaica Squadron at Port Royal, and afterwards sail to the larger Leeward Islands Squadron in Barbados before returning to Bermuda.

As they tracked south the sub-tropical warmth began turning into the well-remembered languid heat of the Caribbean, and with the Bahamas slipping by unseen to larboard, they entered the glittering sea.

The length of Cuba lay across their course to Jamaica. The usual route was to round the big island to the east, the Windward Passage, but Kydd was going by the much less frequented west-about way. It was Spanish territory and therefore not hostile, but flaunting his presence would do much to make privateers and their ilk a trifle thoughtful, for which the Jamaica Squadron admiral could only be grateful.

Making the southern coast of Cuba, it was then only a straight beat to Port Royal, three or four days away, enough time to set the ship to rights for the inevitable admiral's visit.

Heaving to in the shelter of an island they set about the task, but then against the ugly grey of a gathering rainstorm, a tiny sail was spotted away off, heading urgently towards them.

It was not to be expected that the lordly *Thunderer* should take notice and, without being ordered, *Weazel* shook out canvas to intercept. Kydd saw the two converge, then after a space, both made to come up on them.

'Rather think you might hear this man,' hailed Bowden, pointing into the smack bobbing about. There were three aboard – two Black men and an individual in a ragged officer's uniform looking up pleadingly.

Kydd waited patiently while a midshipman slid down to help him up the man-ropes. Then, with a reserve becoming the captain of such an imposing ship-of-war, he returned his bow.

'Teniente Coronel Ochoa,' the man said, clearly awed by his situation. 'Of His Catholic Majesty's Colonial Service.'

So he had English. What was a disreputably dressed lieutenant colonel, presumably of the Cuban colonial military, doing in a boat seeking to board a British warship?

'Sir Thomas Kydd, captain of His Britannic Majesty's Ship *Thunderer*, sir. And what might I do for you?'

He looked about and, seeing the knot of seamen around the wheel regarding him with open curiosity, replied, 'I beg privacy, sir, if you will?'

In the great cabin the man sat gingerly in one of the armchairs and Kydd smiled encouragingly.

'For your knowing, sir,' Ochoa began, and took a deep breath, 'Cuba at this time is in a state of rebelling, a revolt of the radicals. The forces of our king are sore pressed and if we do not prevail the country will follow Hispaniola into grievous misrule.'

Kydd had heard of the recent uprising that had ended in the independent ex-slave state of Haiti. 'I see. Do carry on, sir.'

'I come from the important island of Viñuelas nearby here, where lies a fort. Unfortunately it has been captured by the *renegados* who will use it as a means of subduing the country-side. Sir, if this happens, it will turn the island into a base for rebels, who will spread to the rest of Cuba and cause us much harm and ruination.'

He paused and fixed Kydd with a look of dramatic appeal. 'Your country and mine are linked in a great struggle against the tyrant Bonaparte. I ask you from my heart to come to our aid in putting down this peril to our lives.'

'Coronel Ochoa, you realise that this is a ship, not an army? I really cannot see how we can assist in any kind of action of a shore military kind.'

'You can! You can, sir! When I saw this mighty warship stop so close to us, I knew it was a sign from Heaven that help was at hand. Should you sail to the fort they will shake with fright and run at what they see!'

With the mother country fighting for its life in Iberia it was not surprising that colonies were taking the opportunity for independence. Kydd was sympathetic to this far-away servant of Spain trying to maintain the peace, almost certainly with nothing in the way of troops, funding or other support from home.

'You say, um, Viñuelas is not far?'

'The large island next beyond this,' he said eagerly.

'Then I will call by it if you remain aboard to show me.'

Kydd led him back to the quarterdeck.

Whatever his feelings in the matter there were problems to resolve. Spain was not a formal ally and he had no duty to go to their aid in what amounted to a colonial disturbance.

But this was possibly a slave revolt, and if the English plantation owners heard that no effort had been made to stop it spreading, there'd be trouble.

How much time could he spare in doing whatever was being asked? His cruise was the paramount cause and he had no business to jeopardise it.

And there was no getting away from the fact that this was in the command area of the Jamaica Squadron admiral, only a few days away. Rightfully, he should submit the request to the higher authority, instead of taking it upon himself to act.

Kydd decided at the very least he could go and see the situation for what it was.

Chapter 12

They reached the island of Viñuelas in a matter of hours, and a small township of the same name tucked into a sweeping bay. On steep slopes above, dominating the bay and the town, were the grey stone walls of an old-fashioned fortress.

Some sort of engagement was in progress. Odd puffs of musketry gun-smoke appeared in desultory play along the parapets and from the surrounding scrubby rocks. It was clear the fort was being closely invested but not with the usual panoply of formal siege-works, massive guns, ravelins, trenching.

'And, you see, they fly the banner of His Majesty,' Ochoa said miserably, pointing out the flagstaff with its dash of colour, 'claiming they act in his name.' As he'd predicted, the firing petered out at the sudden appearance of a ship-of-the-line entering their field of battle.

What was the meaning of it all? Whose side was being reinforced? There was no more firing – but in a show of defiance the fort ran up a string of flags, meaningless to *Thunderer*'s signal crew.

If this meant they were treating for surrender before the

wrath of the great ship was known, then their contribution was complete, and they could sail away in satisfaction.

But Ochoa sniffed in derision. 'They defy us to do our worst. And that we shall do, will we not, Capitán?'

Kydd knew he was being dragged into the conflict against his will but for the same reasons as before he couldn't abandon the scene.

The fort wasn't grand or intimidating but Kydd took in the bastions, casemates, prodigious walls. They might be old but were thick and square, massively set into the volcanic rocks on the slope in a dominating position. This also acted as natural bared ground, revealing any attempt at a stealthy approach or to mount heavy guns.

He'd been at many sieges and investments involving the Navy and almost without exception they'd proved near impossible to succeed, even with heavy artillery to command.

If he was wise he'd offer his regrets and be on his way. He was not about to waste the lives of his men on a faint hope that was by no means a vital issue in the struggle with Napoleon.

The ships lay together and Kydd returned to his cabin with Bowden.

'A hard thing, Charles, to quit our situation without firing a shot,' he murmured.

Bowden said nothing but it was plain he felt the same.

'I remember the fight we had at Rosas Bay, Cochrane and I,' Kydd mused, 'so many barbarous ideas he had for discommoding the enemy. I wonder what he'd conjure in this pretty moil?'

They sat together in silence, bringing to mind those fearsome times on the Spanish shore.

Bowden gave an apologetic cough. 'Sir, forgive if you think it a foolish notion but it does cross my mind . . .'

'Do go on, Charles, I beg.'

'The fort is halfway down a slope, an incline,' he began hesitantly.

'And?'

'All the fortifications on some sort of hillside that I remember – even including the Russians in the Arctic – have their facing side tall and grand, thick and stout. On the other hand, their uphill side is low and never so great.'

'And this is why it contains the fort's gate, I'm supposing,' Kydd added, rubbing his chin.

'So I make conjecture – from a place of safety above could we not send down casks of powder with a fuse that will roll down the incline and, being stopped by the wall, detonate there?'

'Ah – well done, sir!' Kydd chuckled. 'A right noble plan.' With the sovereign advantage that casualties would be minimal and the subsequent storming of the fort would be the business of the Spanish themselves.

It had difficulties but what plan did not? The most challenging was that as the barrels picked up speed they would finally impact violently with the wall and shatter, scattering the charge into harmless powder grains. Another was that, as he knew after his experience with Fulton's torpedoes, unless an explosion was tamped down its fury was largely lost. And the rampaging barrels would bounce and glance off the uneven ground, however bare, and could end up going off course entirely.

Before spending valuable time setting about these obstacles he'd have to make sure the notion had substance by going ashore and seeing for himself.

With Bowden, he took Halgren and *Thunderer*'s gunner's mate to eye the ground. If Stirk was not happy with the adventure it would be called off.

He had Ochoa to handle the Spanish and refused Craddock's staunch plea to come – this was a job for professionals.

The firing had resumed fitfully, taking up the to and fro of before as if there was no giant ship astride the approaches.

As they set out in his boat he directed Halgren past the fort and on to a small beach, which appeared to offer a pathway up onto the scrubby summit of the slope, but as they drew near there was ill-aimed musket fire from a scurrying band of men gathering at the water's edge.

Ochoa screeched out an objection, standing to show himself, and the firing died away.

'*El estúpidos!*' he exploded and, when they landed, fisted the nearest, snarling his anger. 'Don't concern, Capitán. I will bring a company fit to be your guard. Stay here for a time as I will get them.'

'An' a shonky lot they looks t' me too,' Stirk muttered scornfully, taking in the scowling figures. They were in unrecognisable scraps of uniform, deeply sun-touched and with an odd assortment of weapons. But the Spanish Crown could ill afford better.

Ochoa was back with a group of about thirty, loping along like seasoned men, even if yet more threadbare and scruffy.

Kydd led them off up the path but before it levelled out into a plateau Ochoa stopped dead and pointed ahead. 'Sentry!' he hissed, and snapped out orders that had each man drop to a crouch. Then, without hesitating, he gestured to a dark-faced individual who wordlessly hefted a knife and darted away. He was back within minutes, wiping his blade.

'He says the fort is now in clear sight below.'

There was no possibility that the tons' weight of any kind of cannon could be wrestled up from the beach or cliffs to a position that would allow a bombardment of the rear, and mere infantry could never stumble across the bare rock in full view. Therefore all attention would be on the other side.

'What do you think, Toby?' Kydd whispered to Stirk, who with pursed lips was looking down the slope at the rear wall.

'Not s' good, I'm thinkin', sir.'

'How so?'

'Y'r casks are goin' t' roll down well enough, but they needs steerin' or they'll be all over, like a pig at the fair.' The big seaman turned to regard Kydd seriously. 'An' that there in the middle is their gate. Won't have t' push too hard to knock 'em over. But . . .'

'I heard. Only if we have steering.' Was the idea to be rejected so soon? It had to be if it was seriously thought that they could control and aim a clutch of barrels bucketing down a hill.

Stirk's dark eyes glittered. 'An' I didn't say as how we couldn't.'

'Steer a barrel?' Kydd asked in disbelief.

'Aye, sir. As every gullion in the trade knows how.' The wiles and skilful ruses of smugglers were legendary: why not in the steering of wildly pitching barrels?

It turned out to be simple. To haul a cask up a steep rock-face parbuckling was needed. A long rope held at the top of the cliff by its middle, the two ends let down to the base and, after being passed around the cask, led up to the top again. By hauling on the ropes the cask was duly rolled over and over to the summit, steering achieved by tugging on one rope or the other.

In this case it was even easier, for it was in reverse, the cask starting at the top and being eased away down the gradient. It would be under perfect control the entire time with no chance that it would career down and smash itself to fragments. And to target the gate itself was now more than possible.

'We do it, Toby!'

Chapter 13

Ochoa was admiring and respectful and kept his band together ashore while details were concluded in *Thunderer*.

If it was the gate, then a couple of water leaguer barrels should do the job, the interior lined with stone to tamp the explosion and a fuse let into its head to protrude sideways, clear of the rolling.

A false bush was constructed, behind which the operation would be conducted, and very soon other preparations were in hand for an assault timed for sunrise.

Like many a smuggling venture before, casks were landed in the shadows of the night. They were parbuckled up the steep bluffs and carefully manoeuvred to the chosen spot above the fort.

As the soft light of daybreak stole over them, the four men of Stirk's crew readied themselves. He and another were on one cask, Doud and his assistant on the other, all no strangers to furtive doings by night.

Ropes laid out in seamanlike coils, slowmatch alight and tested – and round about some hundreds of Spaniards lying, waiting.

Kydd could see no advantage in delay and gave the order. It was the most fantastical start to a battle he'd ever known.

Match was blown upon and touched to fuse and the bulky barrels edged out from under the false bush. With a light push both were started forward, the ropes being carefully paid out while noiselessly they began their last journey.

They'd quietly progressed more than halfway down before there was any sign of attention – faint cries of surprise, disquiet. It would be near impossible to understand, a pair of cook-house barrels slowly advancing down the hill for no reason.

Before long the rear parapets became crowded with excited figures gesturing, free with their opinions.

The barrels drew nearer, guided by the invisible hands above, until with a swirl of activity it became evident that an officer had arrived. The pop of muskets began but it was too late. Carefully shepherded, the casks ended their pilgrimage firmly against the heavy gates and the job was done.

At precisely the time dictated by the fuse length the gunner had cut, the charges went off. In a gout of flame and consuming smoke, the detonation echoed loudly, and when the confusion had cleared, the toppled ruins of the gate could be seen in the centre of the gap where it had been.

Incredulous shouts burst out and with whoops and battle cries the Spanish rose up and rushed the opening.

'Stand down, Mr Stirk,' Kydd said, with satisfaction. 'I do believe we've done our part.'

Chapter 14

A sultry tropical heat lay low and humid for the few days' sail to Jamaica.

Kydd was aware that it was unusual that a full-blood ship-of-the-line could individually make a difference; the commander-in-chief of the Jamaica Squadron, Admiral Brown, would no doubt have reason to commend their cruise.

He recalled the shimmering sights of Port Royal, from those years ago as a young seaman and again as a light frigate commander. Now he was making arrival in the majesty of a battleship.

There was Drunken Man's Cay, Gun Cay and the low sandy peninsula of the Palisades, beyond which the pirate city of Captain Morgan's day had so disastrously slid into the sea.

Thunderer made her way past the Middle Shoal buoy and into the inner harbour but the naval anchorage was near deserted, a single sail-of-the-line and two frigates, so there was no difficulty in finding an anchor berth.

Kydd did not bother to look for an admiral's pennant aloft on the two-decker – the commander-in-chief would be inland, in the Admiral's Pen in the cool of the hills above Kingston.

It meant a boat trip to the jetty opposite and then a ketureen, a light trap with a sunshade, and a brisk trot along dusty roads to the interior.

It was agreeable to be here with no pressing threat of war. Virtually all the French sugar islands had fallen into their hands and the age of pirates had long passed. A pity he had to move on for he remembered how enjoyable life could be here.

His only duty was to advise the admiral of his continued presence in Bermuda and his suppression of the slave rebellion. He was not expected but no doubt some impromptu entertaining would eventuate in the evening.

Admiralty House was as he remembered. Glorious frangipani blooms, along with the stern sight of a blue ensign and the blank-faced Royal Marine on entry on guard.

The flag-lieutenant seemed flustered and, judging by the relaxed disarray, it was probable that visitors were rare, the Jamaica station no longer with the importance it had once had.

After a decent interval Kydd was shown in and announced. 'Sir Thomas Kydd, captain of *Thunderer*, 74.'

Admiral Brown was making ineffectual attempts at tidying his desk, but looked up, distracted. 'Sit yourself down, then, old fellow. A cordial, or sherry – I've a half-decent amontillado?'

'Thank you, sir, the cordial.'

'Then what the devil brings you here, Sir Thomas, dare I ask?'

'To make my number, and acquaint you that I exist – as *pro tem* reinforcement of Bermuda while this disagreeable American war carries on.'

'Well, apart from privateers, there've been no threats of size hereabouts.'

'I'm ordered by their lordships on a cruise of deterrence off their coasts, which I've been conducting these last few weeks.'

'Any sport?' he asked hopefully. The admiral's prize share these days would not be great in this part of the world.

'Not really, sir. They seem disinclined to engage with a sail-of-the-line. Oh, one piece of amusement. I came by Cuba west-about and discovered the island in some sort of rebellion against their Crown. One of their colonial officers came out in a boat from Viñuelas and begged for assistance in putting down the rising.'

'Which you refused to give, in course?' Brown snapped, suddenly sharply attentive.

'Sir, I was about to sail on when I realised that, should I neglect to bear a hand with the restoring of lawful authority in a slave rebellion, I would incur much odium from our own plantation owners for fear of a possible spread of same to their holdings.'

'So what was the outcome, pray?' Brown's tone had become hard, menacing, his look a dangerous glare.

'Why, bearing in mind the need to avoid casualties and the expense of a bombardment I reduced the fort by other means.'

'You . . . reduced . . . the . . . fort?'

'I effected a breach by means of casks of powder rolled down the hill upon the walls. The officer, Ochoa, it was, took his men in and—'

'Stop! You've said enough, sir.' His head dropped to his hands and a muffled groan escaped.

Kydd could hardly believe what he was hearing. 'Admiral, would you kindly explain—'

'Why, sir? Why did you not seek me out for my approval? Don't tell me – because you were on detached duty and didn't feel the need, hey?'

'No, sir! I judged the imminence of the situation . . .' He tailed off at the venomous look he saw.

Then unexpectedly it fell away to be replaced by a sagging despair. 'No, Kydd, I'm supposing you're not to know.'

'Sir?'

'An officer at the first rank of achievements at arms, you're not to be blamed for moving against the foe wherever he presents. In this case it proved . . . unfortunate.'

He drew a deep breath and gave a sad smile. 'You see, old chap, what you did was to allow yourself to be gulled. When Ochoa declared himself, what proof did you ask that he was who he claimed to be?'

Kydd's expression gave his answer and Brown continued. 'You reduced the fort – where the last Spanish Crown troops on the island were defending themselves. Ochoa was an Aponte rebel. He needed to take the fort and so seize the island as a base to spread his rebellion on mainland Cuba. Now he has it.'

'I'm sincerely sorry for my error, sir.'

'The pity is that I was merely waiting for *Juno* frigate to return before mounting a landing of my own in aid of the Spanish. Hah! They must have thought their day of deliverance had come when you hove into view.'

'Sir. Any expedition in relief I should be glad to join,' Kydd said stiffly. There was little else he could think of to say.

Brown slumped back. 'That will not be necessary, Sir Thomas,' he said wearily. 'It would content me should you weigh and be gone with the least possible delay.'

Kydd kept the news from *Thunderer* and her crew – he'd done what he'd thought right at the time and didn't feel answerable, and they had loyally carried out their duty. It would be sorted out in time but served as a caution to all of the fragmented situation in the Spanish colonies while the motherland was fighting for its life.

It was a tranquil, pleasant week's passage across the Caribbean to Antigua, the well-found dockyard at English Harbour and the naval base at St John's, the other end of the island where he briefly paid a call before heading off south.

The fabled sugar islands that had proved a river of silver to the great powers of the region now lay before him, fought over and seized by turns until the British had finally triumphed and possessed them all.

His purpose would be to sail past each, flaunting the presence of the Royal Navy to any who might think to rise up, the further meaning of deterrence as he saw it in his orders. And in the process having a most diverting cruise at little risk.

Having passed the length of the Leeward Islands, *Thunderer* shaped course through and seaward for Barbados, the home of the Leeward Islands station and the largest force in the Caribbean.

The admiral here was the renowned disciplinarian Laforey, one of Nelson's ship-of-the-line captains who'd taken on the French van at Trafalgar nearly alone and thereby saved the day.

Carlisle Bay opened up as Kydd remembered, the earthen gullies and bright green cane-fields with their windmills overlooking Bridgetown below, but nowhere did he see any sign of Laforey's squadron.

Thunderer's anchor plunged into the transparent depths, decorously followed by *Weazel*, and then the bum-boats were on their way out to them. There would be no liberty to the hands, however, for he had no intention of delaying more than he had to before returning to Bermuda.

He sent Roscoe ashore to discover the circumstances. He was back before long with word that the squadron was out to sea on exercises and not expected to return within the week.

It was vexing but not serious – his primary objective was American deterrence and he'd completed that.

Time to return.

Chapter 15

A cheerful, wafting south-easterly kept with them until they squared away for the Five Fathom Hole buoy and the Narrows, the entry point for Bermuda's naval anchorage. Persephone and his son were in this Eden and Kydd couldn't think that life could offer anything more delightful.

With the fleet gone he had the whole of Grassy Bay to himself. *Thunderer* settled to her rest. He and the sailing master had been able to dispense with a pilot, the buoyage being so clear.

It was odd, having no admiral or commander-in-chief requiring him to report. The governor and civil head didn't really count and it only remained for him to prepare a voyage report for inclusion in the next dispatch to Halifax.

But that could wait and he left the ship to Roscoe and took his barge under sail with a crew of earnest midshipmen to St George's, from where he would have been sighted as he entered the anchorage.

Monte Rosa was waiting for him, a squeal of welcome from a vigorously squirming Francis and a look of the utmost love from Persephone.

'A fair voyage, my dearest?' she enquired fondly.

'A mort vexing it must be admitted but that makes a return the sweeter,' he declared, with a kiss.

Helped out of his uniform, he settled down to hear of her discoveries and new friends, hugging to himself the knowledge that this beautiful and talented woman was his to love and cherish. Having so recently passed through the gates of Hell and now given the chance fully to mend, he had everything to live for.

He found that her particular friend was now one Arabella Bingham, wife of some kind of ship-owner, and another was Fanny Mercer, a widow of means, both of whom he would meet at an assembly on the Thursday.

The governor he already knew, but he would meet Charles Overton, colonial secretary that evening. At the same time it seemed Kydd should know the social distinction to be made between the native Bermudians and those in civil authority appointed by the colonial office in London.

He sat back and let happy prattle flow over him – the loquats and pawpaw for the picking in their garden, the quaint plaited palmetto hats to be worn against the sun and the graceful pigeon-berry tree coming along so well in the corner plot.

Plans were laid for a picnic, given the multitude of lovely spots to be found among the many islands, and there were rumours of a ball to be given by the governor to mark the King's birthday.

It promised to be a most congenial situation while the rest of the world was locked in its titanic conflict. Kydd tried to dismiss the thought, for he had been given his orders on the highest authority.

The next few days passed happily. They enjoyed the delights of an evening boating expedition among the islets of St

George's Harbour, and the picnic at Paynter Vale with its crystal caverns was a great success.

The reefs and lagoons were enchanting and Persephone quickly had her easel out and soon splendid romantic views were being daubed for posterity while Kydd sat at his ease next to her, taking the sun with an improving book.

Craddock, with little need for his services in the absence of a demanding admiral, and his captain, found the beauty of the realm irresistible and spent much time in a hired boat visiting the islands one by one.

One evening he announced that for the immediate future his being would reside in splendid isolation on a small, uninhabited islet with a spectacular view of the ocean, there to contemplate life and existence.

Kydd recalled the hideous experiences in the Adriatic that had brought them together. His presence here was as the result of some family disagreement and he understood why his eminently rational friend might desire to step aside from the world and its cares for a while.

Chapter 16

It would be some time before *Thunderer* need make another flourish off the American coast, and rather than spend his time in idleness, Kydd decided to try to satisfy his professional curiosity as to how Hurd had surveyed so meticulously the countless isles that made up the archipelago.

Commodore Evans seemed gratified that he was showing interest and made time to share the details. In an extraordinary feat of hydrography, Hurd had completed his heroic task in 1797, having plotted the position of every one of the hundreds of tiny islets and the thousands of sub-sea rocks, unseen channels, swashways and deeps that made up the fearful nautical challenge that was Bermuda.

Such was the vast sprawl of the reefs that it was possible unexpectedly to pile up on the first hidden rocks when far out of sight of land. It was Hurd's genius that by providing safe routes through the frightful maze he'd made Bermuda such an invaluable base for the Navy.

'I regret we don't have his chart in *Thunderer*,' Kydd said. 'Or will it be many in a folio?'

'Neither could you, Sir T,' Evans said flatly. 'As being in the nature of a grand secret.'

'Oh?'

'You came into your anchorage near fifteen miles through coral reef, skerries, the rest. And without a pilot.'

'I did – the buoyage is excellent, may I say.'

'You would find it quite impossible without our buoys, you'd agree.'

'Well, yes.'

'The Americans know this and realise that the first thing we'd do should they make sally against us is that we'd remove them.'

'I'd think so.'

'But if they had Captain Hurd's chart they'd then be empowered to plot carefully ahead of time any approach they choose conformable to safe navigation – any, we cannot know which, and clearly we can't defend from every direction at the same time.'

'Quite.'

'Therefore there are only two charts suffered to be in existence and both under lock and key. One in the care of the Hydrographer of the Navy in London and the other . . . hidden.'

Kydd was suddenly consumed with a desire to see for himself the extraordinary work – how, for instance, was it possible to scale down the colossal numbers of individual rocks and sea hazards to the dimensions of a standard Admiralty chart? 'A pity. I'd give much to take a sight of it,' he murmured.

The commodore hesitated. 'It might yet be arranged. Shall we say you have an appointment with the governor at his residence tomorrow night at eight?'

It was an odd time, neither dinner nor supper, or even that for a cards evening, and Kydd compromised with plain clothes and a cane.

He was greeted not by the governor but by the commodore, accompanied by his flag-lieutenant. 'Sir James is not at home,' he explained, 'but we have the run of his study.'

The sizeable book-lined room, dominated by a large polished mahogany table, was discreetly watched over by a hawk-eyed major-domo.

'You know where it is, David,' Evans said, handing over a key on a tally.

He returned with a roll of charts under his arm – never seen in naval service where all charts, for practical reasons, were stowed flat. It soon became obvious why: these were not standard-sized charts.

When spread out they were immense. In two sheets together they covered all of fifteen feet, overlapping both ends of the large table. One mystery was explained: every one of the thousands of rocks was noted, but at a giant scale. And as far as Kydd could see they were all there. He craned to survey it all but wherever he looked there was minute, infinitesimal detail. Soundings, heights, hachured topography, even individual buildings and seamarks.

'A work of . . . of much distinction,' he stuttered, unable to take his eyes from the spectacle.

His gaze strayed to one side, to St George's, and there along the lower street he was able to pick out what had to be Monte Rosa in the street above the naval establishments.

'Quite so,' Evans said smugly.

The detail was towering in its complexity, but the scale was more than adequate.

'Six inches to the mile,' the commodore said, as if reading his thoughts.

No wonder it was held here for safe-keeping. There was no secret of Bermuda that was not laid bare, and any who could take in what he was seeing would be in a position to trespass where they may.

'I do thank you, sir, for this experience,' Kydd said sincerely.

The commodore nodded politely, adding that perhaps he would see him and Lady Kydd at the governor's ball the following week.

Chapter 17

The ball was held in the Court House, the legal trappings in no way dampening proceedings but serving to limit invitations to the select few.

The governor and his wife led out to polite acclaim.

When Kydd and Persephone took the floor there was a general frisson of excitement: they made a pair not often seen in these islands. A noted baronet of proven fame in the wider war and his high-born lady of evident quality.

Kydd was careful to pay the utmost respect where it was due as the introductions were punctiliously made by the flag-lieutenant. He mentally noted the more important. The leader of Bermuda's House of Assembly – distinct from the Bermuda Council, which acted as an upper house. He'd already met the colonial secretary, whose supercilious manner made Kydd, who'd had the ear of the King himself, suppress a retort.

A judge of the Vice-Admiralty Court ponderously acknowledged him and a colonel of artillery was most effusive at the honour done him.

There were others to seek out – like Persephone's

Mrs Bingham's husband. Said to be in shipping, it seemed that its nature was more in the line of privateering, out of Hamilton.

And he noticed one or two jolly sorts who might provide reliable invitees at any sort of regular get-together.

At refreshments Persephone showed him off to some of her new friends. He responded gracefully to each. Then she reached into a small throng and brought forward a young woman of probably some eighteen years in a prettily ribboned muslin dress, who curtsied shyly, looking up at him with huge blue eyes.

'My dear, please meet Miss Rebecca Holt. She expressed to me an ardent desire to see a real sea hero and in this I can most certainly oblige her.'

Kydd was aware the young lady was remarkably attractive, with an artless innocence that was most appealing.

'Sir Thomas!' she blurted. 'As I heard led your fleet to victory at Lissa. And now is captain of a mighty battleship. I'm so honoured, sir!' She beamed at him, impulsively curtseying again.

'Why, you flatter me so, my dear,' he said, caught off-guard. 'My duty only,' he added awkwardly.

'Poor thing,' Persephone murmured from behind her fan. 'Lives with a cantankerous father who's lost much in trade since this American war – hates to see her in society.'

'They say you chased a Yankee frigate all over the Pacific to put an end to it. So exciting – so brave!' she blurted, clearly overcome.

Kydd saw a way out. 'Er, might I be permitted to introduce my officers?' He'd noticed Roscoe nearby and called him over.

'Miss Rebecca, this is my first lieutenant, Mr Christopher Roscoe. Mr Roscoe, Miss Rebecca Holt.'

'My honour indeed,' he declared loudly, giving an elaborate bow, quite evidently much taken with her looks.

'Oh,' she said, unsure. 'Then you're . . .?'

'HMS *Thunderer*, her premier,' Roscoe said, with a brilliant smile. 'Next under Sir Thomas and takes care of the ship for him.' Roguishly, he took her hand and pressed it to his lips. 'And one day I shall be happy to be the one to show you over her.'

She blushed prettily, her eyes downcast, but her hand remained in his.

Kydd spotted a figure at the back of the gathering. 'Ahoy there, Mr Bowden,' he called. 'Pray do join us. There's someone here you should meet.'

Bowden threaded through until, with something like a shock, he noticed Rebecca.

'Miss Rebecca Holt, do meet Commander Charles Bowden.'

With a stiff bow, Bowden stuttered, 'S-So p-pleased to m-make your ac-acquaintance, Miss Rebecca.'

She laughed delightedly. 'Then do you serve Captain Kydd in his ship too, sir?'

'Not Mr Bowden,' Kydd said firmly. 'He's captain of his own ship, *Weazel* brig-sloop,' aware that the young man had also been smitten.

Roscoe came back instantly. 'As is not quite the same weight of metal as a battleship, in course.'

'But you are a captain, Mr Bowden?' she asked, puzzled.

Before he could answer, the master of ceremonies formally announced the next dance, with a flourish, and Roscoe fell to one knee.

'Should you refuse me this dance I swear you'd leave me truly devastated, Miss Rebecca!'

'I will dance with you, good sir.' She laughed and allowed herself to be swept away.

Chapter 18

Monte Rosa

Kydd was in his drawing room devouring an English newspaper only five weeks old when there was a knock at the door. The maid came back with a card on the silver tray, which she proffered to Persephone, who picked it up curiously.

'A Mr Edwin Harris, my dear. From the *Bermuda Gazette*, I see. I believe I'm at home to this gentleman, Esther.'

Kydd laid down his newspaper and rose to meet his guest.

Harris turned out to be a pleasant, open-faced man in comfortable but well-cut dress and carrying a small satchel. 'Sir Thomas Kydd? So kind in you to see me.'

'Do sit, Mr Harris. Refreshments?'

'Thank you, no. I won't take up more of your time than I should.'

'Then what can I do for you, sir?'

Harris took out a sheaf of notes. 'Sir, I write occasionally for the *Bermuda Gazette*, a respected organ of record. Your appearance in our midst is an event worthy of note, I'm persuaded. And it's in my thinking that an article concerning a sea hero of our times in more of a biographical vein would be of much interest to our readers in this decidedly maritime society.'

'A biography?' Kydd said in alarm. 'As touching on my infant days and so forth? I really can't imagine any being charmed by such, do you, Seph?'

Persephone smiled fondly. 'One or two, my love.'

'From what I've learned of your successes at sea, Sir Thomas, I would wager more than a few.'

'At sea . . . the clash at arms – not a scene for the tender-hearted. Or the readers of your journal, I believe. Upon reflection I'm desolated to feel obliged to refuse you, sir.'

'Oh, Thomas! You have so much to tell.'

'This must be true, sir. Principally how you do feel, facing the malice of the enemy and the perils of the deep both. This you must concede is the very fundament of a story.'

The man's sincerity touched Kydd and he weakened. 'Sir, if I grant you my time, what shall be your lay, or whatever the business is termed?'

Harris leaned back. 'Why, sir, this depends entirely upon the nature of our connection. Should it prove fruitful, the regular appearance of an article progressing your life would be more than acceptable.'

'Sir, I find talking of myself disagreeable in itself and—'

'It is for that reason that I propose my interviews be in more diverting settings such that Bermuda can provide.'

Persephone brightened and broke in, 'Quite so, Mr Harris. Thomas understands and is delighted to comply.'

Chapter 19

The brightly painted little ferry snubbed into the planked landing stage after a diverting trip across Castle Harbour and Kydd helped Persephone out. It was remarkably dense in vegetation with pathways and trails radiating away.

'I rather think you'll be gratified to discover this little hide-away, Lady Kydd,' Harris said. 'And at the end we shall dine on our famed Bermuda rockfish.'

'Your recommendation is all we will require,' Persephone said, and twirling her parasol prettily, she and the little party set off.

A limestone cave drew expressions of admiration as did several more, but then they came upon a truly extraordinary sight. A large pool of the most alluring intense blue, set at random in the wild growth, surrounded by small mangroves.

'A mysterious creation,' Harris said quietly, as if to divulge a confidentiality. 'No one knows how deep it is or why it's here.'

Persephone instinctively recoiled. 'And are there creatures that live in those depths, pray?'

'If there are, they've not devoured the unwary. There are

those who declare that the swimming here is the coolest to be found anywhere in Bermuda.'

The delicate pink sands a mile or so to the south were a spectacle in themselves. Fishing boats were drawn up in rows and men glanced up curiously at the strangers.

As they strolled companionably back along the trail, Harris turned to Kydd and asked politely, 'You've heard of Tom Moore?'

'The Irish poet? A mort too fierce in his verse for my liking but I believe he's a rare hand at pleasing the ladies. A writer of squibs for the Whig interest, as I recollect.'

'A radical, I'll grant, but I forgive him all for his "The Last Rose of Summer",' Persephone put in.

The path widened and they emerged before a clearing beside a sheltered inlet. A quaint two-storeyed gabled house of uncertain origins nestled among the cedars, oleanders and wild sage.

'Can you imagine how old this is?'

Persephone pondered for a space. 'I really don't recognise the style but it seems of an age, Mr Harris.'

'Edwin, please. Well, it may surprise your English soul to find that it has been here continuously inhabited since 1652.'

'Remarkable.'

'And if you were here under ten years ago you would find our very same Tom Moore staying in what was by then a snug tavern, composing his immortal works.'

'Ah – there I have you, Edwin! I have it on excellent authority that a calabash tree was his favoured locus of creation.'

'You are undoubtedly correct, Lady Kydd. And over there you will find the said article.'

A lone tree of pendulous tufted leaves stood at a distance with a rustic bench beneath it.

Here it was he wrote this for his true love, Nea Tucker – who in the event was not free to return his addresses:

'The day-light is gone – but before we depart
Here's a brimmer of love to the friend of my heart.
To the friend who himself is a chalice,
A bowl in which Heaven has pour'd a rich bumper of soul!
Twas thus, by the shade of a calabash tree
With a few who could feel and remember like me.'

Kydd muttered a polite appreciation but it was not really to his taste.

'Edwin, you must tell me more of Bermuda. Why is it that—'

'Dear lady, I think it time that Sir Thomas earns his repast. Over a local rummer of course . . .'

Chapter 20

Aboard Thunderer

'The captain has not left specific orders about visitors.' *Thunderer*'s first lieutenant snorted. 'I take it to mean that any officer in favourable standing may invite who he wishes to view the ship.'

'It may perhaps be prudent to await his return, expected hourly,' Ambrose, second lieutenant, said carefully, adding that the captain of *Weazel* was in the great cabin with a dispatch.

'Damn it, all I desire is to show my guest the curiosities of the barky!' Roscoe snarled, raising his telescope to focus on an approaching craft.

Bowden appeared on deck. 'The captain?'

'No.'

'So . . .?'

'A guest of mine,' Roscoe ground out.

'Oh? Then shall we be introduced?' Bowden said lightly.

'She wishes to observe for herself the intricacies of a line-of-battle ship,' Roscoe said, in icy tones, 'which I doubt you will be in any position to satisfy.'

The boat, a shore wherry, came alongside. In it sat Rebecca and her maid. Both were wide-eyed, staring up at the great ship, nearly as long as a town street.

'Rig a chair,' Roscoe snapped importantly. The watch-on-deck sprang to obey and the two were swayed in, helped to the quarterdeck by the solicitous first lieutenant.

'There, my dear. You are now aboard His Majesty's Ship *Thunderer* of 74 guns and—'

'Why, Captain Bowden! You are here as well. Do thank your men for their efforts in bringing me in, will you?'

Roscoe cut in instantly: 'They are not his men to command, Miss Rebecca. He has no authority on board *Thunderer* – this is my ship and they're under my orders.'

Bowden's face set as the first lieutenant offered his arm and they progressed together forward past the martial row of gleaming cannon.

Ambrose, telescope under his arm, resumed his duties of the deck. It wasn't long before he was warned of the approach of the captain. He'd stepped ashore in plain clothes and therefore there was no need for a piping party.

'Anything?' Kydd asked after he'd boarded.

'Very quiet, sir. We do have Commander Bowden on board with dispatches for you.'

The captain of *Weazel* appeared with a satchel of the kind used to convey important 'hand of officer' communications.

'Where's the first lieutenant, Mr Ambrose?' Kydd asked, with a touch of impatience. Surely Roscoe would interest himself enough in his captain's return to be at the ship's side to greet him?

'Ah, I believe he's below, entertaining his visitor, sir.'

'Then I must wait upon his convenience, I find. Very well, we shall all remain here to admire the view.' He folded his arms and gazed seaward with a thunderous expression, carefully not noticing the midshipman sent in a frantic scurry to find the first lieutenant.

'Oh, sir, I wasn't aware you had returned aboard,' a breathless Roscoe said, as he erupted from the after hatchway, his bemused visitor following a little more decorously. 'You weren't piped on board.'

Kydd let the weak excuse go, taken by the bright picture of youthful innocence the girl and her parasol made in the martial austerity of a man-o'-war.

'Did you then pay your respects to the grand old lady HMS *Thunderer*?' Kydd asked her teasingly.

'Oh, sir! Such a splendid structure – so sublime in its particulars.' She took in the rows of guns, the shot garlands and massive bulwarks. Then her eyes strayed up, following the ratlines that mounted each naked mast, up to the fighting tops. Then more ratlines to the barely perceived celestial reaches at the very tip of the mast, hundreds of feet aloft.

'It cannot be possible for your sailors to climb the ladders and then . . . and then reach to the very top,' she breathed, wide-eyed, her hand to her mouth.

'I rather hope they can,' Kydd said, suppressing a grin. 'Else when the ship puts to sea she'd be in a pretty moil.'

Bowden stood quite still, his expression blank, his eyes unreadable.

Roscoe stepped forward briskly. 'Mate-of-the-watch,' he barked, 'one hand aloft, atop the mainmast.'

The grinning watch-on-deck had edged aft to watch the fun and, being under the eyes of a pretty woman, volunteered to a man, but Kydd held up his hand.

'Stay. Mr Roscoe, this is not a task for the duty watch who have more important tasks. I rather think that you should show Miss Rebecca how we do it.'

'S-Sir?'

'Come, come, Mr Roscoe. Your visitor wishes to see how a tarry-breeks sailor mounts the rigging. Can you not find it in you to show her?'

'B-But . . .'

For some reason a giddy madness took hold of Kydd, born of his years at sea as a young and daring seaman. Flinging his hat at an astonished Ambrose, he bawled, 'First t' set hands on the mainmast cap!'

He pushed through to swing around and into the main shrouds in one lithe movement, the sure sign of a prime seaman. With a quick glance across he saw that Roscoe had roused himself to perform a workmanlike similar move and now it was the rapid ascent to the tops.

With the ship at anchor in calm waters the journey was far easier than the usual swaying, heaving progress in the bluster of the open sea but Kydd felt a searing pain up his leg which told him that his action at this time might well be termed ill-advised.

To some extent he could favour the other leg, for climbing the rigging was more a matter of hauling up and settling the feet ready for the next move but he was definitely slower than he had been.

He glanced across at Roscoe, whom he saw pause momentarily. With a chuckle he understood. It was nothing to do with the man's nauticals: he was unsure whether it was wise to beat his captain in a manly contest.

Paradoxically it goaded him on. The ratlines narrowed and they drew nearer to each other on opposite sides, nearly equal in height from the deck, but then it was the futtock shrouds. Without thinking, Kydd effortlessly transferred his grip to the outward hanging traverse and hauled himself up and around into the maintop.

Roscoe's somewhat later appearance now owed nothing to deference but to Kydd's desperate times aloft off Cape Horn, the Bay of Biscay and a thousand other occasions around the world.

He continued and found his rhythm again. Haul and grip – one foot, the other – one hand up, grip, the other hand – haul again. His old sea skills were more than making up for his wound. His natural agility was not shared by Roscoe, whose movements were becoming laboured and awkward.

In rising glee, Kydd pulled ahead and took the last distance in steady heaves until he was up with the cap, a round disc at the finality of the mast. With one hand fiercely grasping he slapped the other emphatically on the top of the cap, then clenching his fist punched triumphantly, the traditional gesture.

He glanced down: Roscoe was a good forty feet below, looking up ruefully at him. He'd been beaten fairly and squarely, probably affected in these rarefied heights with an urge to cling harder, move more deliberately.

The real sailor knew that he could suffer a death fall even from the first tier of shrouds onwards and therefore there was no point in fearing these regions where what he encountered was of the same kind as below.

For another dizzy moment Kydd toyed with the idea of reaching the deck again by the vertiginous sliding down a backstay like the careless young seaman he'd been, but stifled the thought and descended in a dignified manner the way he had come.

Avoiding the look of hero-worship from young Rebecca, he turned to Bowden and said gruffly, 'Shall we now have a sight of your dispatches?'

*

Under the admiring gaze of the watch-on-deck and officers he took refuge in his great cabin, wondering uncomfortably what Persephone's reaction would be should she hear about it.

He read the confidential dispatch, which set out the essence on just one page. It seemed that from loyalist information received by the North American station it had been determined that an American spy or spies were known to be active in Bermuda. All steps should be taken to deter and apprehend the same. No further intelligence was at hand regarding identification or other facts concerning them.

What the devil? Was he expected to comb the islands until he found a spy or . . . No, it was not that. This was merely the clearing of a yardarm, the need to show that some kind of action had indeed been taken on receiving a direction from a higher authority.

He'd bear it in mind, but with local forces to hand far better placed to spot a stranger or odd activity, he wouldn't take any particular measure of his own.

Chapter 21

Monte Rosa

'Well, darling, how is your stout barky that you've spent so long on board?' Persephone said, after he'd found his chair and paper, a whisky ready by his side.

She paused, then frowned. 'Now look at you – your second-best clothes and you've got some marks all down the front. You really should be more careful.'

'Ah, now, there's a good reason for that.'

'Tell me, Thomas.'

'Secret dispatches,' he said flatly.

With an incredulous look she begged him to explain.

'You're not to tell anyone but I've this day received word from the commander-in-chief, no less, that he's intelligence of an American spy, or is it spies, who are now abroad in Bermuda.'

She blinked uncertainly. 'The marks?'

Kydd gave a convincing wince of annoyance. 'Well, in course we must search the ship stem to stern in all kinds of unpleasant places.'

'Oh, I see,' she murmured, awed. 'A spy!'

'Keep it to yourself, Seph. We don't want the population to panic.'

'Thomas will be joining us shortly, Edwin,' Persephone explained, several days later. 'He's with his ship still.'

Esther came with cool drinks and the two relaxed into comfortable chairs as she hovered discreetly to one side.

'I do hope we impress with the conch stew. Cook has been busy all morning.'

'I'm sure I shall, Persephone. Saving that in truth I'm here with the express object of discovering just what a certain lieutenant was scheming ashore in Minorca.'

She glowed with pride. 'A story not many know. But I dare to say it will be all the more thrilling if told by Thomas.'

Making play with the jug of cordial, she went on to ask politely, 'Then how have things been at the *Gazette*? Have you an interesting nugget of news you may share with me?'

'Not so many, dear lady.' He sighed. 'Bermuda is not to be noted for its criminal classes. The talk now is all on the dispatch just in from the authorities warning of American spies.'

'That's supposed to be a secret!'

'As cannot be. If the common soldiers of the garrison and patrols must be told of the danger how long can it so remain?'

'Yes, a spy! How dreadful. At the time I was born we had the odious American incendiary Jack the Painter, who tried to burn down Portsmouth dockyard and all its workmen by a secret device.'

'Ah, yes. But your common spy I venture to say is of a much less threatening character. He's more concerned to discover information for passing to his masters and will not desire to perform acts of such desperation.'

'Edwin, that's saying this spy is less dangerous?'

'Not at all. In fact the possession of the enemy's dispositions must be of the utmost value to a general as will give him the means to evade their defences. I'm not a military man but to me this makes for a gratifying advantage.'

'I suppose it must.' She pondered, then added, 'Then to root out our spy do we look to the stranger asking questions, sinister figures in the night . . .'

'Not necessarily, I fear. There are still some here in Bermuda who for their various reasons do support the American cause. They're the most dangerous of all, knowing what they do of their native soil.'

'Still?'

'Let me give an example. In the American war for independence there were those here in Bermuda in correspondence with George Washington who undertook to steal for him a hundred barrels of gunpowder from the magazine in St George's and smuggle it out. They succeeded with ease.'

'How dreadful.'

'Quite. And it's not too difficult to suppose what our spy will be doing.'

'Edwin, are you seeking to frighten me, pray?'

'Not in this case, for his objectives will be as naught if he comes before the public. I see the fellow quietly pacing about, determining the angles a gun from a fort may bear in an assault, for instance. This will give a priceless indication to a commander as to what direction to mount his attack.'

'And if he enquires into the provisions being delivered to the same forts he'll gain knowledge of the numbers inside it.'

'And when the descent finally comes we'll no doubt see him furtively signalling the best places to invade.'

Both fell silent at the implications.

'How then shall we lay the villain by the tail?'

'Unless he makes a mistake, I rather suspect we cannot.'

Chapter 22

St George's Harbour

'My dear, it's all too much for my nerves,' Arabella Bingham declared, her fan in an agitated fluttering. 'A parcel of spies in our midst, it's not to be borne.'

Fanny Mercer nervously looked out over the sunlit reaches of the harbour from the porch of her home where the ladies were taking morning tea. 'Why we don't see the soldiers turn out, march up and down and so forth I cannot imagine.'

'I rather think that all possible is being done,' Persephone said firmly. 'More tea?'

'It's all very well for you, my dear. Your husband stands ready with a great ship to carry you safely away but mine is, well, the registrar of lands and doesn't command such a one.'

'I've instructed the servants to shutter the house completely after dark,' Fanny said gloomily. 'Better to lie stifling in the heat than be murdered in my bed.'

'And Reginald insists on keeping a pair of hunting dogs in the drawing room as will greet any who seeks to invade.'

In a morbid silence their eyes strayed to the waterfront

below where in the warm sunlight the ebb and flow of the town's business carried on.

'It's awfully quiet,' Fanny ventured, looking about fearfully.

'Well, you don't expect the rascal to parade before us,' Arabella said witheringly.

'He . . . Well, he could be any one of 'em walking about down below there.'

'I do think we've not a lot to be frightened of,' Persephone said brightly. 'After all, what secrets do we ladies know that he should threaten us?'

'Well . . .'

By the landing stage, a sudden shouting erupted and a crowd quickly gathered. Abruptly the ladies' conversation stilled. They heard strident voices carried up as a sergeant from one of the outer forts urgently called for an officer.

They hurried down to discover what was afoot. Above the excited babble Persephone pieced together the reason for all the fuss. An alert sentry at the end of his beat late the previous evening had happened to look across at an uninhabited island opposite and had spotted a movement. He'd called the corporal who had the big watch telescope and they trained it on the spot.

It was a figure that moved across their vision, between the arc of fire of the guns of the nearby fort, then back again. In the bad light, however, it was too indistinct to make out.

The guard was turned out but there was some delay in finding a boat and the figure vanished into the gathering darkness. This morning it was decided that if a full search party was mustered it would leave the small fort temporarily weakened so they had called for help from the garrison headquarters up the hill.

As a crowd began swelling, the ladies decided it was prudent to return to the Mercer residence.

*

The hubbub died away at the appearance of the commanding presence of Captain Sir Thomas Kydd striding down from his house, drawn to the sound of the disturbance.

'What's this hullabaloo about, Sergeant?' he demanded.

The soldier saluted smartly and rapped out the situation.

'You've got the island under observation?' Kydd asked.

'Sir.'

'Then the scoundrel is still there. No time to be lost, I believe.' He thought quickly. They needed men, dozens at least. 'Sergeant, take your men and make visit to every taphouse and inn hereabouts. In the King's name take up every soldier and seaman you can find and bring 'em here.'

'Sah!'

At the jetty the island ferry was nosing in to discharge its passengers.

'You sir!' Kydd bellowed at the man by the tiller. 'I take your vessel under command by authority of the Crown. Lay alongside, if you please.'

The haul from the taverns was considerable, swelled by those wanting to be in the front row of the entertainment. 'Stand aside,' Kydd ordered the press following the spectacle – they were preventing men boarding the ferry.

After a fast passage, sail was brailed in and the men pushed ashore to the fort jetty where a young subaltern greeted Kydd.

It was this officer's prerogative to take charge of the affair and Kydd stood back. 'Your men, sir. Any movement or boats?' he added politely.

'None, sir. He seems to have gone to ground.'

'Then I wish you good hunting, sir.'

There was a hasty issue of arms and the fort's boat put off to land the search party. Kydd saw them off, undecided whether to wait for them in the watchtower of the little fort.

It was a serious affair. A determined spy loose to do his worst was no trivial matter and his capture would do much to restore confidence with the local population. On the other hand he'd promised to inspect the midshipmen's workings, a necessary device to indicate his interest in their existence. And in the final analysis it was an army matter.

'Sir. Sir?' It was the young officer, breathless but clearly exultant.

'Um, yes?'

'We have him! Led us a merry dance but now he's ours. Rum-looking cove, foreign and with a beard but perfect English. Says that—'

'Well done. Where is he now?'

'Oh, he's still on the island. We need to chain the monster but . . . er, overlooked to bring any with us.'

'I'm sure you'll find a way. I desire you shall transport the wretch back to St George's and I'll be up with you there presently. I have business to attend to in my ship.'

St George's was in a ferment. A burst of applause greeted Kydd as he stepped ashore and the air rang with shouts of 'Finish the job – hang the bastard!'

The garrison commander was summoned to express appreciation of Kydd's prompt action.

'As fine an example of service cooperation as ever I've seen,' he said importantly. 'Very satisfactory.'

'You have him secure, I trust.'

'But of course! Do you wish to view the fellow?'

'Not really, sir.' The man was as good as hanged and he had no wish to gloat.

'Very clever, this one. Had his story well conceived. Claimed to be ship's clerk or something on your very own ship, Sir Thomas!' he guffawed.

In a flash of horror Kydd saw where it was leading. 'Er, perhaps I will clap eyes on the brute.'

'Oh? Well, it's not pretty where we have him, but if you must.'

There was a flourish of keys and the padlock over a nearby pit grating was opened. Kydd moved over to see down. There, in the gloom, a figure in chains was looking up resentfully.

It was Craddock.

Chapter 23

Washington

'We shall not be disturbed here, I believe, General,' James Madison, President of the United States, said pleasantly, leading the officer into a modest but comfortable office.

His visitor was an improbable vision of another age. Elderly and attired in knee breeches, his long coat of military style was set off with a colourful tricorne hat, suggestive of the stirring days of 1776.

Accompanying him was a well-dressed and dignified citizen of some years.

'Mr President,' the old general said expansively, 'may I be permitted to introduce my good friend Mr Henry Buckner, who is here to add what he will.'

Buckner, a wealthy landowner in Florida, was there for his own reasons. First, he believed that the questionable scheme on the table was in the best interests of his country. And, second, he recognised that here was an opportunity that came only once in a lifetime and he would do all it took to bring it off.

'Leave us,' the president instructed an aide, then added quickly, 'Oh, and desire the secretary of state to join us if you would.'

James Monroe entered cautiously and took the remaining chair. 'Mr President.' The tone was questioning. In the room there were none of the usual functionaries – clerks, secretaries and others. These proceedings were apparently to be off the record.

'Ah. These gentlemen – General Mathews and Mr Henry Buckner – are here to acquaint us with certain considerations in respect to the Florida question.'

'Yes, sir. East or West?'

West Florida was a Spanish possession abutting the Mississippi delta and claimed by the United States as naturally forming part of the Louisiana Purchase of a decade previously.

East Florida, on the other hand, had no such relationship and was held as a territory of the Spanish Crown. It had one most desirable quality for any possessor: at the south-eastern corner of America, it was the strategic gateway to the Caribbean. And Monroe had made no secret of his ambition to see the entire continent under one flag – that of the United States of America.

'East Florida, sir,' General Mathews answered briskly. 'As is seethin' with desire to be one with their brothers to the north.'

'Is this so, sir?'

The question was pointedly put to Buckner, who shifted uncomfortably. He was one of the considerable numbers of American landowners who maintained a plantation in Florida by favour of the Spanish and who were required to enter an oath of fealty to the Crown and demonstrate residence in the colony.

'Mr President. In these strange times all my compatriots are united in the view that, given the victories the French have lately had over the Spanish, it's likely that they will shortly complete their conquest so that Spain and her colonies will fall into the hands of Bonaparte.'

'Or worse,' Mathews threw in darkly. 'The dogs could invite their English allies in to save 'em and next thing we'll see crowds of redcoats massin' on our borders ready to strike up into our heartlands.'

Pained at the interruption, Buckner resumed, 'You will perfectly understand that they do fervently crave an existence under the benevolence of the flag of the United States of America rather than any other.'

Madison gave a thin smile. 'This I can see. As to your situation you will no doubt be aware that we've already made approaches to the Cádiz Regency in an offer to buy the Floridas, but without result.' The smile disappeared. 'And I'm informed that a more delicate approach to their administration directly, in the nature of a pecuniary inducement, has also failed. Remonstrations and notes have no effect, and then what else do you expect of your government?'

'Sir, the situation can't be allowed to continue,' Mathews protested energetically. 'Slaves in Georgia are seein' Spanish Florida as a place to run to, throw off their chains. Soon there'll be enough of 'em armed by the Spanish to threaten our planters from the south.'

'Quite so.'

'As is only one of the scares makin' the good citizens of America in Florida pine for deliverance.'

'Understood. But what can you suggest? Make war on Spain? Send in an army on a peaceful neighbour? The prize is great but the people would never stand for it.'

Buckner's spirits rose. The president was recognising that

the stakes were not the relief of expatriate Americans in Florida but the much larger issue of securing the lands for the United States.

'There is one course that commends itself, Mr President.'

'Pray continue, sir.'

'Should there be a general rising of the people, those in fear of what the future holds for them in a weak and doomed colony of the Old World, might they not be allowed to beg that the great nation to their north do come to their aid, to stand by them in their hour of need?'

The barest flicker of interest was all he could detect, but he went on strongly, 'I have the names of so many who have pledged their all to this cause, wanting only that Washington does not spurn their beseechment.'

Madison reacted coolly. 'Should the feeling of so many be as you say, I see two difficulties. The first, that it asks that as subjects of the Spanish their oath of allegiance will necessarily be broken – this is treason and they will be branded traitors.

'The second, that this administration shall not be seen by the world to be aiding a rebellion in a friendly state. You will understand the reasons why.'

'Surely can, Mr President,' Mathews broke in breezily. 'But this'n is not a rebellion. It's naught but our citizens in fear of their lives, the Florida Spanish having not so many troopers in the country as can protect foreigners.'

The secretary of state leaned forward. 'Sir, I must remind you that—'

'Thank you, Mr Monroe,' Madison said sharply. 'And I'll remind you that this meeting is *sub rosa* and entirely without record. We are here to discuss possibilities only.'

He paused briefly, then said, 'Am I to understand from you gentlemen that a species of defiance, if not insurrection, in East Florida will ensue should I indicate that the government of the United States will in some form pledge its involvement?'

Monroe winced and looked away.

'You has my word on it,' Mathews replied firmly. 'I m'self will be returning with the good news and will raise a battalion of like-minded—'

'If such is our decision, which is by no means assured.'

Cynically, Buckner wondered how it would be done. Clearly Madison was eager to take up any scheme that promised to make him and his administration responsible for adding such a large and strategic territory to the Union, but how was he to reconcile this with appearances?

Remarkably, within days, there was an answer.

Ushered into the drawing room of the Mathews mansion strode a slight-built man, wary but confident.

'Good day to you, General,' he greeted. 'Colonel John McKee, and I have for you something that'll keep us busy for a spell, I believe.'

He handed over a document with a seal of the secretary of state.

Mathews carefully opened it. 'Well, an' I'll be hung as a polecat!' he exclaimed. 'Sets me up as a United States commissioner, powers as granted below to treat with the Spanish in the matter of the Florida question.'

He read on avidly, then blurted, 'Ha! I've authority to draw on military forces along the frontier. And not only that . . .'

'As have we both,' McKee said drily. 'Myself being appointed jointly.'

'Let me see that,' Buckner said tightly. It was as he suspected, impeccably worded with nothing to indicate an involving in any subversion or clandestine activity.

The shape soon emerged of what was actually expected

and it was all that he could have hoped for. Revealed in the strictest confidence by the secretary of state, it became clear that the administration was determined on acquiring the Floridas by whatever means.

While not committing anything to paper, instructions were passed on as to how it was to be done, if an outright concession by the Spaniards was not on the cards.

Mathews and McKee were to return to East Florida and set up some form of secret leadership around whom the disaffected could rally. Inducements in the form of future lands and offices could be offered, and for their expenses they could draw against funds to be made available, provided always that the utmost discretion was observed.

The objective was clear. Should the Spanish be confronted by a situation of turmoil and disorder arising in their thinly populated and defended Florida colony, they might well consider that ceding the territory – for a suitable degree of compensation – would be the more profitable option.

And finally, should for any reason the Spanish governor or local authority agree to amicably surrender their rule, they were empowered to accept it on the spot in the name of the United States of America.

Now it was their task to provide the agitation and anarchy.

Chapter 24

St Marys, Georgia

'Y'r right t' go inside, Gen'ral,' rumbled the big man by the door of the grog-shop, after a careful spying outside.

Mathews nodded importantly, surreptitiously scanning the grave faces sitting about a table, trying to gauge the mood. The room was crowded with his acquaintances, all by personal invitation, and all for the purpose of hearing what he had to say on his return from Washington.

St Marys was the furthest town south in the state of Georgia, of the United States in fact. Just across the river was a foreign country – the Spanish lands of Florida.

McKee sat near the door, wearing a constant frown as if in distaste at something. To one side Buckner quietly took notes, but it was Mathews in his showy revolutionary garb who held the attention.

'I thank you, one 'n' all, for attendin' this meeting. I've to tell you that my discussions with the president were very fruitful an' – dare I say it – rousing.'

He paused impressively.

'Get on with it!' echoed from the back.

'As I was sayin', we talked long 'n' hard and what he comes up with should stir the blood of every man here. He says as if there's trouble an' upset involving American citizens in Spanish Florida he's not goin' to stand for it and will send in the military.'

'He can't do that – it'd be an invasion!'

Buckner silently agreed. It would be war with Spain, just as they were facing the greatest naval power in the world.

'Ah, there he's ahead o' you, Jeb. He allows that if the people cry out for liberty, the freedom of the American flag, who's he to deny 'em their rights?'

'I ain't a-going to be part of it!' growled a sun-touched elderly man, evidently a landowner of sorts. 'The Dons have always treated me right. Why, when I—'

'What do you want of us, Gen'ral?' a hard-faced character to the side wanted to know.

'We declares as one our sworn intention to aid and rally behind those who demand their liberty, who stand up for 'emselves. Join up in a band o' patriots as will seize their destiny.'

Before the rumbles of disquiet could turn into shouts he raised his voice to add, 'And when we succeed against the forces of tyranny and raise the flag of freedom an' justice – as we've done before – then there'll be land an' high offices for those who answered the call.'

Cringing inwardly, Buckner let it go. For the stakes of an America made whole, anything that stirred the people was permissible.

'If this means joining some rag-tag rebel army, count me out,' snarled another.

'Hold y'r tongue, Elijah. We all know you're makin' a pile o' coin free-tradin' with the British under the Spanish flag out o' St Augustine. Leave us to get the job done ourselves.'

In truth there were few plantation owners Buckner could say would be whole-heartedly on their side. East Florida was well-placed to provide the cotton that England so needed for its northern mills, and fortunes were being made.

'A band o' patriots,' the fashionably dressed individual next to Buckner drawled. 'As will be paid an' recompensed for his trouble?'

'I've authority to draw on stores an' funds from federal sources, sir.'

'Which you won't object to we seein' such?'

This could be a finisher. Deliberately there was nothing in writing that could implicate Washington in an insurrection, but without such a proof of official backing and support in kind, how could Mathews's promises be believed?

'How dare you, sir? All proceedings concerning the President of the United States of America are not for the common gawking. Pray recollect yourself.'

It was not going well. There were no joyous cries of patriotism, no rush to enlist in a dedicated band of heroes. How were they alone to stand against the Spanish empire?

Chapter 25

Bermuda

'A most agreeable situation,' Kydd murmured, smothering a sigh. 'Do you not confess it, my dear?'

Persephone, enjoying the novelty of a comfortable reclining chair set in the sand under gently waving palms and within yards of a sparkling sea, felt obliged to agree.

'So kind in you to invite us to your picnic, Sir James.'

The governor, in his chair next to her, inclined his head in acknowledgement. 'There are, as who should say, compensations to find oneself rusticated at this remove from the noise and frustrations of London,' the governor admitted.

The first of the picnic dishes was brought: chilled eggplant soup, spiny lobster, tropical salad. Kydd helped himself generously. Victuals as splendid and fresh as these were seldom to be encountered aboard ship.

'Most agreeable,' Kydd mumbled guiltily, accepting a second helping of lobster. He knew *Thunderer* to be lying just out of sight to his left, at this hour the hands hard at work on her decks.

'You appear to find circumstances to your liking, then, Sir Thomas.'

'I do indeed, sir, being lately wounded and in need of respite.'

'A change, no doubt, from your usual harum-scarum young Navy officer, cast down without he has a smell of powder from time to time.'

'Quite so,' Kydd said seriously. 'As without same a man may ponder the reason for his existence. Bermuda is serene and delightful but nary a motion from the enemy to set the heart a-beating.'

'I do apologise that I can't oblige you, dear fellow. Nothing in the offing – unless there's any substance in some rumours I've recently been privy to, of Cousin Jonathan up to mischief in the Floridas.'

'Oh? They're still Spanish, aren't they?'

'Yes. But it seems the Americans want to snap 'em up while the Dons are distracted by Bonaparte at home. If they succeed it'll directly threaten us here, of course.'

'The Spaniards will ask help, I'd think, we being so near,' Kydd said hopefully.

'Not so much. They're a mort touchy about their colonies, thinking us rivals and ready to pluck 'em for ourselves.'

'Then . . .'

'Perhaps it might be a good idea the next time you go cruising to pay a call on St Augustine, their capital. See what's in the wind as you'd say.'

'Have you any intelligence on the meddling at all?'

'Not really. It could be all tavern talk. There's always been disturbances of a kind in East Florida.'

'Nonetheless, I believe I'll do as you say. Er, is there any more cheese, do you think?'

*

Kydd returned to *Thunderer* and consulted the charts. St Augustine was a town well situated some thirty miles south of the border and sheltered from hurricanes by a number of interlocking peninsulas.

He studied the chart more closely. One thing became evident – there was nothing like the depth of water to allow *Thunderer* to thread her way through the winding waterways to the inland seaport. To make a presence there would require a lesser breed, like *Weazel,* for instance.

Bowden could do it – he had only to find the Spanish governor and, without any suggestion of intruding, desire to know of any recent developments in the province. And if the official proved anxious about some matter he would offer Kydd's assistance. Otherwise he'd withdraw.

Chapter 26

Aboard Weazel

A week's sailing in this near-perfect north-easterly would do it, thought Bowden, as *Weazel* made her way seawards through the well-buoyed passage.

It had been inconvenient, but he would never admit it – not to Sir Thomas Kydd. He and Miss Rebecca had reached an understanding concerning their attendance at the soirée to be hosted by Mrs Bingham.

Their acquaintance had reached a delicate stage, but when he'd been shyly introduced to her father at the Hamilton market, he'd instantly snorted his disapproval and sharply taken her in hand.

If the odious Roscoe heard of his absence from the field he'd have no hesitation in clapping on all sail to head her off. Bowden clenched his fists in a helpless fury.

Bowden's meticulous navigation saw them raise the monotonous sandy flatness of the outer dunes of St Augustine. He was met by a distrustful Spanish harbour authority boat, which required him to anchor upon further advice.

Some hours later he was ashore, entering the stolid grey stone Castillo de San Marcos, a massive fortress centuries old. With a professional eye he saw that it was placed directly facing the maze of headlands and dunes that formed the entrance to St Augustine and its waterfront. With a smaller fort at the edge of the marshes, it was a formidable defence against any assault by sea.

'*Excelencia, Capitán Bowden de la marina real de gran bretaña,*' intoned an equerry, and the man at the desk raised his eyes – dark and cruel to Bowden's English soul.

Another, in broken English, cried, 'This, he Excellency Juan José de Estrada.'

Irritably, Estrada waved the man aside. 'Why are you here, Capitán?' he demanded, in barely accented English.

Taken aback, Bowden answered gently, 'Why, sir, to call upon your own good self.'

'Very well. We have made the acquaintance, you may leave.' His expression was hard and forbidding.

'Sir, I do not comprehend why you do not—'

'Capitán, I will not pretend that you and your vessel of war are in any way welcome in the Floridas. We took it from you in the year 'eighty-three and do not expect your return in any wise, still less the flaunting of your colours before my people.'

Despite the hostility Bowden saw in the man, he pressed on: 'I, as well, bring every expression of respect and comradely regard from my commander, Sir Thomas Kydd, who wishes to remind you of the warm accord that now exists between—'

'There is no formal alliance agreed between us, sir, and

therefore there are no grounds for any assumed pose of amity. You may water and victual, and then depart. Agreed?'

'Sir, might I point out that in these troubled times it may prove advantageous to both our nations if we remain friends in the face of belligerent motions by unfriendly states.'

Estrada remained mute and hostile as Bowden persevered. 'Particularly in view of the rumours we've lately heard concerning an insurrection of sorts incited by the Americans.'

'There are always rebellions and defiance to be expected from those *sabandija*. I have heard of no particular outbreak, but if I do, they'll be dealt with as they deserve. We need no help from the English. Good day, sir.'

Chapter 27

St Marys, Georgia

Mathews snatched the packet from the courier and, shouting for McKee, stormed into the room where Buckner and a merchant, Elijah Costin, were taking tea.

'Washington,' Mathews grunted. 'An' damn quick, too.'

Inside were several papers and a covering letter, which he read with growing astonishment.

'What's it say, Gen'ral?' Costin wanted to know.

Mathews slowly looked up. 'They've gone 'n' done it, friends,' he said, in lingering reverence.

'What they done?'

'Not jus' the president – but Congress, House an' Senate both – their resolution endorses the right of the United States t' take temporary possession o' the Floridas under certain contingencies.'

'What's they, then?'

'Er . . . "Authorised to take possession of, an' occupy, all or any of the territory lying east o' the Perdido river and south o' the State of Georgia, in case an arrangement has been, or in the event of an attempt to occupy the said territory, or any part thereof, by any foreign government."'

'The British,' Costin said with relish.

'Doesn't have t' be,' Mathews replied, with a wry grin. 'In these here instructions it goes on t' tell me as if I discover an inclination in the governor of East Florida, or in the existing local authority, amicably to surrender that province, I'm to accept it under terms below.'

Buckner saw where it was leading and couldn't help a smile of satisfaction. If a rebellion of the disaffected resulted in the fall of a town, then which was the local authority? Not the hapless Spanish.

'An' it says here, straight after the resolution, a bill was enacted there an' then t' pass it into law.'

'Well, I'll be . . .'

'An initial allocation of a hundred thousand dollars against expenses, presidential authority to create a territorial government once under American jurisdiction, and the province retained by the United States of America pending subsequent sovereign negotiations with Spain.'

A breathless silence fell, broken only when Buckner murmured, 'This changes everything, of course.'

'Certainly does,' Mathews grunted. 'Here we hold proof that President Madison and the whole government o' the United States of America is right behind us in our cause. A right pity we can't tell the world.'

'Why not?'

''Cause it was all in closed session, secret legislation as Congress does prohibit publication.'

'We can secretly show our recruits those papers you're holding.'

'No good. They ain't signed.'

'Doesn't matter,' Mathews pronounced. 'They wouldn't believe we'd be foolin' 'em as we'd be found out later. We gets busy – right now!'

General Mathews rose from the table set up in the front of the tavern. 'Meeting will come t' order,' he intoned importantly. 'As temp'ry chairman o' the East Florida Committee for Redress o' Rights I declare this meetin' open.'

It was a fair-sized gathering, many obliged to stand, some spilling out of the doors, all agog with excitement. It was common knowledge that Mathews had the ear of President Madison and was about to disclose plans for direct action to secure American interests to the south.

'All those not taken with a burning desire for liberty and justice come what may has no business here.'

A rumble of comment built to raucous shouts, which died away as he raised his hand. At stake, rumour had it, were lands, titles, riches – all going to those who stepped forward in the next hour.

'The first point o' discussion. Our loyal band o' brave an' true – I say it's to be known as "The East Florida Patriots". All agree?'

'Aye! The Patriots it is!'

'An' now who is it t' lead us to glory? I nominate John Houstoun McIntosh. Stand up, John.'

By late evening the Patriots had their being. A rebel leader, promises of fifty acres of land for every man who took up arms in the Patriot cause and a declaration of freedom of religion and continuation of rights and titles assured for Spanish subjects who became American citizens.

Buckner, however, was not carried away with it all. He couldn't help but see that the prosperous landowners and merchants of Spanish Florida were noticeable by their absence. They were doing too well at the Atlantic trade with the British to want to join a rebellion.

Looking about, he saw that most of those present were riff-raff – fallen tradesmen who smelt easy money, labourers mesmerised by the pledge of land, and a colourful scattering of pioneer frontiersmen. This was quickly turning from a rebellion of the aggrieved to a freebooter's adventure and he shied at the prospect.

It was left only to devise a flag. The Patriot colours under which they would march – a quorum of hard-drinking volunteers would see to this.

After the elated throng had spilled out into the night Mathews grew serious. It was clear to all, and especially to the new commander, McIntosh, that it was easy enough to raise the flag but quite another to plot out what next to do to bring their battalions to readiness.

McKee, whose enthusiasm was noticeably less as the prospect of action approached, was assigned the task of making demands of the nearest military post against the president's earlier pledge of federal support.

Powder, shot, muskets, clothing, mess kit, tents – there was no end to what was needed before they could form up. And, more to the point, would there be men? A detachment of regular troops that would not only stiffen the ranks but demonstrate legitimacy in their actions?

McKee came back from the Point Peter cantonment after a sympathetic hearing from the commandant but with mixed results. The perplexed officer had no orders in the matter from a higher authority but knew of Monroe's desire to add to America's borders and would do what he could for those who were attempting just that, certainly in the matter of supplies.

As for a detachment of troops, this was another matter. For the government of the United States to be seen furthering their interests in a peaceful neutral with military force was a step too far.

General Mathews made a personal visit to Point Peter and came away with an ingenious solution. Rank and file in the camp would be allowed to volunteer on the same terms of recompense as the Patriots but in the guise of deserters. They would be publicly charged, only to be pardoned and restored to rank after it was all over.

They were near battle-ready – but what was the plan?

It was barefaced impudence to think to take on the empire of the Spanish with such a rag-tag horde. And if they did, where would they strike first?

Mathews was not down-hearted – he knew what was needed and had his objectives finalised.

Florida was vast, thinly settled, and had only two towns of any consequence, Fernandina near the border and the capital, St Augustine. They would undertake a rapid march south, avoiding entangling actions to set the capital under siege. It would all be over in a week or two. Then, with the Patriot flag flying high, they would take possession and become the 'local authority', which would the very next day cede the town and the territory it controlled – Florida – to the United States of America.

'So where's your siege artillery, then?' the peevish McKee wanted to know.

'Who needs it when the townsfolk find 'emselves surrounded on all sides, no help in sight,' Mathews said caustically, 'seein' they hasn't heard a shot fired in their whole lives?'

McIntosh scratched his head. 'Askin' a bit much of us t' make it fifty miles or so through marsh an' swamp, alligators an' all. What shape will we be in when we pitch up outside the walls? That there San Marcos fortress is a big 'un, right enough.'

Buckner had a better idea. 'What do you say to this – that we move out and first take a smaller objective? The Spanish realise we're in earnest but, more important, Washington sees we're worth supporting – with more funds, maybe with soldiery.'

'Fernandina,' McIntosh agreed. 'Only just across the river, a new town, no forts. We can do it!'

Chapter 28

The day the Patriots crossed into Spanish East Florida under arms was not a particularly glorious occasion. A straggling line of men waded ashore from the St Marys river on to Rose's Bluff, an open stretch of ground, not far from a small plantation owned by one of the rebels. There was no sign of Spanish opposition and they established an encampment in tranquil surroundings, setting up fires and rousing out mess kettles for a first meal in hostile territory.

Mathews joined them and, with McIntosh, immediately set to preparing a manifesto, laying down their grievances and reasons for their treasonable rebellion.

The next day the general mustered his band, the manifesto was read out, and at its conclusion, ranks of United States infantry formed up in full uniform, very nearly outnumbering the Patriot irregulars. The 'deserters' had come to join the fight.

Fernandina was small but it was prosperous. To the fury of the traders in the sea-ports of Georgia it was taking energetic and successful advantage of its Spanish status to make fat profits from the timber and cotton trade with England. To remove it as a hated rival would make the Patriots heroes of the hour – and volunteers from Georgia were soon mustering.

Having colours aloft on foreign soil was encouragement enough for an unexpected ally. A trim little sloop hauled into view from the bend to seaward in the river. It flew the ensign of the United States Navy and from it stepped the impressive figure of a full commodore.

'General Mathews? M' name's Campbell, and I'm here to offer support to m' countrymen in arms who've thought proper to declare themselves independent – and here's m' hand on it.'

This was the senior naval officer, Charleston, who had heard of the rising and was going to do what he could for the rebels. It amounted to five gunboats only, each one mounting a heavy gun in its bows. But they would be the only artillery General Mathews had at his command.

The town lay not far away, at the north end of Amelia Island at the sandy estuary of the St Marys river. But between the Patriots and that place there were swamps, marshes and an infinity of creeks, watercourses and rivers.

Within the day Commodore Campbell had a solution. A flotilla of flat-bottomed cattle transports embarked the Patriots and delivered them to a commanding position opposite Amelia Island – and Fernandina. The gunboats, riding guard, then took position about the approaches to the port but held back, letting the situation become all too clear to the inhabitants and defenders.

Evening drew in and General McIntosh made his move. The military commander of the East Florida Patriots issued an unequivocal ultimatum to the undefended and unprepared town. Put themselves under the protection of the United States or suffer ruination by bombardment.

The answer was delayed but final. A boat under a white flag came out with an emissary of the Spanish Crown. A Patriot boat rowed out to meet it and words were exchanged. The emissary returned, and a short time later the Spanish flag fluttered down in capitulation.

From their position in Bell's river the rebels on their flatboats emerged into full view, landed on Amelia Island and marched into the central plaza. Before a stunned and silent crowd the Spanish military commander unbuckled his sword and surrendered it.

The Patriots had won their first victory, the second largest town in East Florida – and had set alight the flame of rebellion.

Chapter 29

Monte Rosa, Bermuda

'. . . if you would at your earliest convenience . . .' Kydd crumpled the note in some irritation. Recent pleasant social occasions notwithstanding, if Cockburn, the civil governor of Bermuda, thought to summon him, the ranking officer afloat when he felt like it, he would be swiftly disabused.

Even if it were an important operational matter, his line of authority still required him to consult the commander-in-chief, Warren, now in Halifax. Nonetheless, due to the peculiar command situation in Bermuda, he had some sort of duty to come to the aid of the civil power when called upon.

Looking down from the balcony he glanced at the prospect of his well-stocked front garden with its graceful pigeon-berry trees and curiosities such as the now slumbering night-blooming cereus. In this beauteous summer it was hard to think of the entire world locked in an endless struggle for conquest and survival.

He rose from his cane chair and caught Persephone's eye. She guessed that he'd been called away and went to see him dressed appropriately.

Cockburn greeted him politely, invited him to take a chair, then signalled to an aide. After a slight delay a short, unshaven individual with a hunted look was shown in.

'Sir Thomas, would you kindly hear what this gentleman has to say?'

There'd been no introductions and Kydd had a good idea why not: the man was probably an agent.

'The Americans. They've invaded Florida,' he blurted.

'What?' Kydd sat bolt upright. This – if true – was a grave development. As far as he knew there was no state of war existing between Spain and the United States of America. Therefore it was an unprovoked invasion of the kind Bonaparte had made his own.

If it were true.

'Er, what evidence have you for this, pray?'

'Why, my own eyes, Cap'n. Saw 'em landing 'cross the St Marys direct into Spanish Florida. There they sets up a camp an' a flag an' all. Talk was they'd be marching on the capital afore the Dons could get their wits together.'

'They had guns, cavalry, wagons?'

'Not as I saw any,' the man admitted. 'Had t' keep outa sight, like.'

'Well, how many soldiers did you see?'

'Some hundreds – could be others but the size o' camp says not too many more.'

An invasion without heavy guns, a supply train?

'Tell me – what uniform did they wear?' Maybe they were French regulars.

'Um, none I could swear to as I could recognise – 'cept a

whole bunch who kept together, an' they were in regular United States togs.'

Kydd looked across at Cockburn in consternation. If this was just a raiding party in retaliation for some imagined slight, what were US federal troops doing there? Why now? What was their object?

It was a mystery – but a dangerous mystery, which promised to turn into a direct threat to the Royal Navy's situation in this part of the world. Or was it a meaningless distraction that could be ignored?

'I should take a look,' Kydd muttered. 'Doesn't sound right.'

'Not in your great wooden wall, sir. The English are not welcome in Spanish waters.'

'As my sloop captain discovered in St Augustine,' Kydd murmured.

There was every reason for the Navy not to make an open visit. Their presence would not be appreciated and any intelligence to be gained would be murky at best. With the Americans tipped off as well, there would be little point to the exercise.

Kydd left without a solution, but a plan came as he walked along the waterfront. Asking casually of the ships' masters, he discovered that they had not heard of any invasion and were carrying on their trade as usual with Spanish Florida, as they were quite entitled to do.

He pondered his next step. For an agreed fee he would arrange to hire one of their ships, complete with the usual cargo, and pose as its master to give himself credibility in the garrulous local shipmasters' taverns. There he could hear the latest news as it affected them – the trading heart of a land always reflected the true state of affairs.

But could he send someone in his stead? Roscoe? Too

inclined to heroics for this quiet mission. One of the junior lieutenants? Not well-informed enough to take in any subtleties in the intelligence.

So it would have to be himself. But it was not in any way a difficult or hazardous affair so he'd be back in a week or two.

He broke the news to Roscoe, who seemed to relish the thought of temporary command of a battleship, but the necessary details to be attended to ensured that it was all around the ship within a short time that their captain was going on some kind of discreet reconnaissance.

As Kydd entered his barge Stirk, in his striped jersey and red bandanna, was standing there with a wolfish smile.

'Mr Stirk! And what do you think you're about, pray?'

'Why, sir, an' who's t' carry yer bags, then?'

With no further ado they headed for Hamilton and the merchant-shipping berths.

Chapter 30

Mr Wilkins was a mild man for a shipmaster and readily fell in with the plan. A straightforward voyage in cedar for cotton, Kydd in nominal command but the mate, Will Avery, in actual and commercial charge. In effect, a perfectly normal passage with all earnings accruing to the owners in the usual way.

Mary Miller was a plain but stout brig of the smaller sort, lively in anything of a sea. As ever in a merchant ship, she smelt of all the cargoes she'd ever carried.

Kydd didn't expect anything in the way of comfort and took the precaution of bringing a naval hammock, a fine refuge in a blow. He'd extracted as much information as he could from the agent and learned that the invaders had crossed the St Marys and made camp opposite the American town of the same name, well inland. He saw no reason to vary their port of arrival – Fernandina, a busy seaport on the Atlantic coast, the nearest to Bermuda in Spanish Florida.

The passage was uneventful and, with fair winds, Kydd spent his time in agreeable conversation with the respectful mate, learning much of the way the merchant service had changed since his experience as master of a Botany Bay convict ship.

He'd grinned to see Stirk holding court with the crew off-watch – who knew what salty yarns were being told to the attentive seamen?

As they neared the coast there wasn't the customary handful of sail converging on the port – unusual but not impossible, even given the prevailing fair trading winds.

They raised the outer reaches of Amelia Island, a drab, utterly flat terrain for endless miles in each direction.

'Port workings on t'other side,' Avery confided. Kydd had heard of savage hurricanes coming up in hours and a harbour protected from seaward by a large island was to be valued.

The *Mary* was well used to these waters and didn't need a pilot, shaping course easily between the white sand-fringed river entrance. Oddly, a small blockhouse opposite had no colours at its single flagstaff but inside the entrance as they bore away to the left there was the reassuring sight of various fisher craft at their trade.

'Strange,' muttered the mate. 'Should've had out the *despacho de aduana* for his squeeze afore now.'

At the quayside, however, there seemed to be ships and freight landing and they shortened sail ready to come alongside.

And then it became clear. From somewhere inland, among the thickly clustered buildings, a flag floated free, that of the United States of America.

Kydd stiffened. His mind raced – in one instant things had changed disastrously. The agent had been right: America had invaded Florida. They had proof now. He'd blundered into the middle of it. And, worst of all, as a British naval officer disguised as a harmless merchant captain, there was every excuse to see him hanged as a spy.

'We has t' go in, else we'll look fishy,' Avery muttered. They had no alternative. Ashore they were even now yelling for the lines that would be used to heave them into their berth. To refuse would draw attention.

But waiting for them was all the usual bumbledom of official notice. Would they be seen as a British flag vessel in a neutral harbour, or a captured ship in an enemy port?

Kydd turned to Avery. 'Take us in, Will – I'm a master who's had to take to his cot on account he's betwaddled in drink.' He hastily disappeared below.

Avery came down to the cabin some time later. 'Here's the story, an' it's a good 'un.' The invasion was in fact an insurrection against the Spanish authorities, but the rebels were being reinforced by United States of America federal forces. Fernandina had only just capitulated and was still coming to terms with the situation.

Kydd was puzzled. 'We're British flag. Why aren't we taken in prize?'

Avery gave a thin smile. 'The rebels gave out with a manifesto to get the citizens on their side. Says as how there's t' be the same trading as before for th' next twelve months. Includes British, as y' must believe.'

'So we get the wharf-lumpers to work,' Kydd said, without enthusiasm.

'I don't reckon on it,' the mate said heavily. 'All the British merchants ran when they heard the Yankee rebels comin' so we've got none t' take our lading.'

But with a sudden leap of spirits Kydd saw it as his way out. 'Will. It's supremely important that we get away quickly – I've got to get the word out. Now, as I understand it, our cargo's untouched?'

'It's still under hatches.'

'Then you won't have paid duties on it because you haven't

broken bulk. As long as that's true we can get clearance without pother. What if we claim we can't get a good price on it, and we're off to somewhere we can? We can quit Fernandina as soon as we may.'

Within the hour *Mary* was leaning to the same off-shore breeze and making good time for the dreary harbour mouth.

Kydd considered what next: he should clap on all sail for Bermuda in order to have dispatches sent by the fastest possible means to Halifax outlining developments.

He was interrupted by a vehement 'Damn it to hell!' Avery pointed out to fine on the larboard bow. A small lug-sailed craft was creaming along on a course to cross ahead with a wicked long black shape on deck forward and the Stars and Stripes at its peak. A United States Navy gunboat set to intercept.

That this rebel manifesto carried any weight with the commander of the boat was questionable. Helpless under its monster gun they would be taken in prize, and this small crew – and Captain Sir Thomas Kydd – would be made prisoner.

If it was recognised they had a chance of being let go if *Mary*'s master could talk his way through it. But as soon as Kydd opened his mouth he could give himself away, and the straight-souled Avery might trip over some detail. That left . . .

'Toby!' Kydd called briskly. 'You're now captain of *Mary*. Tell 'em what they need to know and I don't care how polite you are.'

He stripped off his frock-coat, cravat and waistcoat. 'Wear these – you'll look more the part.'

With a broad grin Stirk tore off his own striped jersey, light canvas trousers and even his well-used red bandanna.

In his new rig he looked quite the master, but his brass earrings and gnarled, well-tanned features were more those of a pirate captain.

Kydd had little option but to pull on Stirk's cast-offs, ignoring the muffled chortles coming from the watching crew. It was essential for him to blend in with the seamen until it was all over.

The gunboat crossed their bows, put about and a swivel gun cracked out to send up a modest splash ahead of them.

Stirk didn't glance at Kydd as he bellowed, 'Back fore-topsail – brace around, y' sluggards!' The brig hove to.

He folded his arms and, with a thunderous scowl, stood back to watch proceedings.

The gunboat, flaunting an oversize ensign, fussed alongside and a young officer hauled himself over *Mary*'s low bulwarks, followed by three armed seamen.

'Ship's master?' he demanded, looking about.

'Aye,' Stirk growled, not advancing to meet him.

Kydd eased to the back of the small crowd of seamen who stood by.

'Lootenant Tracy, cap'n of the United States gunboat one-six-three. Y'r papers, if y' please.'

'Get 'em,' Stirk snarled to Avery, who touched his hat and went to fetch them.

'Well, what are youse standin' about for?' Stirk threw savagely at the group of seamen. 'Nothin' to do? You 'n' you up forrard, re-hank them falls. You,' he glared at Kydd, 'up an' get rid o' that Irish pennant!' He pointed high up at the fore-topgallant sail, the weather outer yardarm displaying a loose line pattering down on the canvas.

'Aye aye, Cap'n,' Kydd said, knuckling his forehead deferentially before making a faultless leap into the shrouds for the climb up.

It was a smart move by Stirk, getting him safely out of sight, and he deliberately played for time, stolidly stepping up instead of with the lithe flow of a good topman. The little brig's spars were slender, her lines whip-thin compared to the brutish proportions of *Thunderer*'s upper rigging and he moved carefully, trying not to look down to where the act was playing out.

The neat but tiny curved foretop loomed and he made a business of hauling himself over and 'resting'.

'Get a move on, y' useless wharf-rat!' The roar came floating up and he made much of shuffling out on the foot-rope and to the offending line, which he made sure was seen to be fouled in a block and required tiresome freeing.

He dared just one glance to the deck and glimpsed the ship's papers handed back to Stirk, who roughly shoved them at Avery.

To his intense relief he saw the American officer hold out his hand in farewell, Stirk pointedly ignoring it, and the man turn to go back over the side.

Making his way warily back to the deck he heard Stirk bawl, 'Braces – sheet in, let's see some heavy in it!'

At Kydd's presence he turned his back and stalked off below as the brig took to the wind and resumed her voyage.

'A gran' job,' Avery said, awed. 'Saw off the Yankee in handsome measure. Seems they can be held t' their poxy manifesto.'

Still under the spell of the moment, Kydd hurried off after Stirk.

He was in the master's cabin, taking a deep swig from a bottle of whisky. Looking up, he said defensively, 'Didn't want 'em to see you change y'r kicks in the open, like.'

'Carry on, Toby.' Kydd smiled. 'Anyone says as how y' hasn't earned it has t' be dicked in the nob.' The foremast lingo slipped out as if the years between didn't count.

Chapter 31

En route to St Augustine

General John Houstoun McIntosh drew himself up impressively, looked around once, then raised his hand and bellowed, 'Patriots . . . *yo!*'

The untidy column of men tramped off expressionlessly, their gait ranging from the lithe mile-eating stride of the frontiersman to the awkward lope of the field-hand and the hopeless shuffle of the drifter.

Buckner took in the purposeful swing of the US Army detachment following on well behind. These, a 250-strong detachment of the US Eighth Infantry commanded by Lieutenant Colonel Smith, had been dispatched from the Point Peter military post under the provisions of Mathews's commission, to take possession of the newly won US territory of Fernandina. Subsequently, they'd volunteered to a man to join the assault on the prize of them all. Ahead lay a march of small weeks to the capital St Augustine, with no sign of either Spanish or even British interference to deter them.

Given all the fuss, misunderstanding and rivalries, they were at last on the move and, unbelievably, it looked as if all was falling into place. Florida was destined to become one with America.

After the first mile or two there was singing in the ranks. Some of the old Revolutionary ditties, later more earthy glees. Drenching afternoon cloudbursts, however, quickly led a dispirited band to trudge on in a sullen silence until a bivouac was called. Falling out of the line of march, they foraged for kindling and firewood, and then the welcome fragrance of an evening meal eddied about.

It had to be admitted, Buckner reflected, cradling his pannikin of rum, that there were more attractive prospects to be had than the present. Shimmering in the heat there was only flat scrubland – to the point of tedium – ill-defined thickets of pine-barrens and always the monotony of hard-scrabble grassland.

The scouts had been told to avoid settlements in their thrust south and this meant that shortly they'd be in the swamps and marshes he'd always avoided: humid and rank with stink and midges, a low-lying maze of endless streams and ponds. He was not on horseback, and must suffer chiggers and the like with the others, but hopefully their very numbers would discourage the alligators that, near submerged, were lying in wait for prey.

Their menacing night-time bass roar did nothing for sound sleeping. Neither did the nearby snarls of the Florida panther, the screeching of hawks and howls of the black wolf.

Buckner was never going to be an outdoorsman and the next days were a miserable, squelching trial until they emerged into the drier flatwoods approaches to St Augustine. The first outer settled population, occupants of farms or isolated homesteads, emerged to stare in astonishment at the slowly wending muddy figures.

Mathews was correct in the particulars of his plan. They were advancing from inland and the formidable stone fortress of Castillo de San Marcos lay on the opposite, seaward side of St Augustine. Nevertheless, there were lines of defence that must give pause even to forces well-equipped with siege weapons.

'Camp and doss down f'r the night,' decreed McIntosh. There was no need for haste – it was unlikely that the lazy Spaniards were even aware of what was in store for them.

'What do y' reckon, John?' Mathews mumbled, over his meat and biscuit.

The general threw a glance to where the regular US soldiers were lying up in disciplined rows, stacking their weapons clear of the mud and slop, posting their pickets.

'I would say no more'n three, five days. We've got numbers now.'

Satisfied, Mathews leaned back. Within a very short time it would all be over, saving the politics and the division of spoils.

Chapter 32

St Augustine

'Get out! Get out of my sight, *zoquete*!' raged Juan José de Estrada, the governor of Spanish East Florida and St Augustine.

His aide, Menéndez, shrank but held his ground. 'Excelencia, if we do not meet them in the field they'll be free to plunder and ravage the country like the dogs they are.'

Rumour of the planned invasion in aid of a rebellion had long been forwarded by loyalists in the north but Estrada had never believed they would carry it out. Not an unprovoked armed attack on friendly Spanish territory. And now extraordinary news had broken that the rebels had braved swamps and alligators to arrive at the gates of the city accompanied by a force of the US Army, which together outnumbered the defenders.

'So you'd want me to go out to face the traitors and their confederates, to be cut to pieces and leave the capital undefended? No, we keep our small numbers behind the walls of the fortress to stop them knowing our weakness.'

'Very good, Excelencia. Er, we have demanded reinforcements from Cuba?'

'Yes!' snarled Estrada. He didn't say that he'd been turned down without hesitation by the colonial headquarters, given the fight for life the homeland was enduring, drawing away all the resources of her colonies.

Florida was not a rich colony, like the silver-bearing South American provinces, existing on trade with whoever would take their timber, cotton and skins. There was little local tax revenue to devote to defence.

He was essentially on his own, and if they were to survive, it would have to be solely by his efforts.

'And can we call on our allies?' Menéndez said delicately. 'If they—'

'The English?' spat Estrada. 'You want me to throw open a royal road to the devils to take this colony for their own?'

'No, sir. I was more thinking of our Indian friends.'

Hardly friends, Estrada reflected, but he knew what he was thinking. Chief Bowlegs of the Seminoles had every reason to resent and distrust the Americans who were stealing the land of his fellow Indians across the border and the last thing he would want was for them to enter Florida and do the same to them. The Spanish treated them in the same way as other citizens: that if they held title to their land it was theirs, and Bowlegs was doing very well under this regime. But the canny chief did not want to be faced with a forced choice to take sides in a war between white men.

'Not regular troops,' he said dismissively. 'Hare-brained young tearaways of the tribe only.'

But it was worth considering. The British had Indian agents over to the west and were inciting the Creeks to rise against the southern states with some success. Who knew? If a good enough offer of alliance was made . . .

A murmur of voices sounded outside and a British naval officer was shown in. Estrada recognised him immediately. 'Sir Capitán Bowden. Why have you returned? I am most busy.'

Bowden bowed elegantly. Kydd had impressed on him the urgency of his mission – it was all very well for the Spanish to refuse assistance, but if it resulted in an American seizure of lands opposite the Bahamas and within reach of Bermuda, it was very much their business.

'Your Excellency, we're much concerned for your safety, the rebels so close.'

He'd only managed to reach Estrada because the invading army had not yet begun to encircle the town prior to the main assault – he only hoped they would hold off until he'd been able to return to his ship.

'You're offering to send in armed men?'

'Er, if this is what you wish, Excellency.'

'It is not what I wish, Capitán,' he barked. 'You'd then be no better than the rogues who are outside our walls. I advise you to make your way back to your ship before you're taken up by those treasonous scum.'

'Sir, you will understand that Captain Sir Thomas Kydd has the gravest—'

'I said I was busy. If you are not gone in the next minute I will find some who will be pleased to help you go.'

Hesitating only a moment, Bowden took his leave, fearing that any further talk would send the man into a fit of temper. He'd tried. Now Kydd had the responsibility.

Outside, surprisingly, his carriage still waited, the driver fidgeting nervously. The master's mate, who'd accompanied him, had a barely concealed cocked pistol.

The streets were increasingly thronged and they made their way to the docks with difficulty where they were delighted to catch sight of *Weazel* still alongside. Her bulwarks were lined with kneeling marines armed with musket and bayonet steadily trained towards the crowd clamouring to get on board.

A detachment of seamen was sent to clear a passage for the little party and, without further delay, lines were cast off and the brig-sloop warped out to catch the wind and sail away.

'The Yankees are on the move, sir,' *Weazel*'s lieutenant told Bowden. 'Saw 'em at the trot around t' the north.'

Chapter 33

Aboard *Thunderer*, Bermuda

'Damn it, Charles. You know what's at stake. Why didn't you—' Kydd spluttered, frustrated.

'I tried. The man is a pig, begging your pardon, sir.'

'So what's the current state, given we know they're before the city now?'

'I'm supposing they're deploying to attack when they're ready – I didn't hear of guns being dug in, so they must be coming on behind in a siege train.'

'It means that it's a matter of time only. And if the capital falls, so will all Spanish East Florida.'

'And then we'll have a hostile shore in our lee,' agreed Bowden.

Looking up cynically, Kydd added drily, 'And being the only commander of force in these waters who do you think shall be blamed for not preventing it?'

'Sir, this is grossly unfair,' Bowden protested. 'You're to inform the commander-in-chief and his is the duty to move against it.'

'Well said, old fellow. But Admiral Warren is in Halifax, a thousand miles distant. I've sent urgent dispatches but we'll get our response in weeks, if not months. The Florida affair needs motions of some kind in days, if not hours.'

'Sir, you cannot move without you have the blessing of the Spanish governor and that is unlikely to a degree.'

'I know. Besides which *Thunderer* is not rated for inshore work of any kind and could hardly be counted on to lend support to an army.'

Bowden pushed away his glass as though in disdain of solace in the face of such perplexities. 'Sir, should I—'

'No. Not a reflection on the puissance of your stout barky but I rather think it would be of little value in assisting a fortress ashore.'

'Then?'

'Just between us, I'm driven to desperation, dear chap. I cannot bear to remain at idleness in this Arcadia while matters come to a head.'

'So you'll . . .?'

'I do believe it's time for another cruise of deterrence. I can therefore see that I shall be offshore to St Augustine in the near future. Who knows what I shall find? And by then our Spanish friend might be inclined to accept a helping hand of sorts, who can know?'

Chapter 34

The outskirts of St Augustine

'You . . . you . . . Do I understand that you find it inconvenient to join the assault, sir?' rasped McIntosh, working himself up into a fury.

Lieutenant Colonel Smith, at the head of his regular troops stood tensely before him.

'I said, sir, that my orders are explicit. And they are to render such assistance to the Patriot forces as enables them to press forward with their plans . . . but this does not see me leading my troops in a direct attack on a neutral Spanish fortress, for reasons a child must realise.'

'Have a care, Colonel!' McIntosh blared into his face. 'I'm the general officer in the field for this expedition an' outrank you by a country mile. And my orders t' you are to fall in your troops as will see 'em lead the assault on the gates of the San Marcos fort.'

'Sir, you may call yourself what you will but this I cannot do.' He stepped back a pace and folded his arms.

'Damn you t' blazes!' choked McIntosh, his fingers writhing

on the hilt of his sword. 'I'll see you crucified for y'r arrogance, d'you hear me? Even if I have t' go to the president himself.'

'My orders do bear the signature of President Madison, sir.'

Speechless with frustration McIntosh turned on his heel and stormed off, back to the Patriot camp, which was carefully separate from the federal bivouac.

Buckner saw his temper and quietly enquired its reason.

'Won't stand wi' the colours!'

It was a setback but not a calamity.

'Then our way ahead is clear.'

'Oh? It's not clear to me in any wise, sir!'

'A full-scale attack on St Augustine may produce quicker results, but now we must resort to a slower and surer method. We starve 'em out.'

Smith could stay in his encampment, if that was what he wanted. His presence, however, would be sufficient to deter the defenders from issuing beyond their defences while the rebels kept up a hostile proximity.

Estrada, the governor, would not have gone to the expense of victualling and storing for what amounted to a siege: there had been no threats of that magnitude on his horizon.

For some reason he had seen fit to put all his defending troops behind the walls of the citadel. Buckner was no military theorist but could see that this would have the effect of making the attackers cautious, obliged to think the worst of the numbers – but then again, might it be because the rebel numbers were equally unknown to Estrada and he was keeping his own back?

Or were reinforcements on their way and he was simply husbanding his resources?

Either way, this could take longer than was planned.

McIntosh detailed off his men – cleverly, Buckner thought. Not in fixed positions in a ring about the town but as moving patrols, never in one place long enough to be marked. Other parties ranged at a distance into the countryside, discouraging any appearance by unfriendly forces.

It worked. St Augustine was small enough for their meagre numbers that exits could be covered, and at dusk one by one the bodies of riders thundered in to report, the first of who knew how many days of waiting. Holding himself in with patience, Buckner shared the tedium of the siege.

One evening he became aware of shouts and noise issuing from the barn that gave service as a mess-hall. It was beyond the usual night-time bedlam, angry cries and hoots betraying real anger.

Buckner hurried up, seeing McIntosh emerge from his nearby hut, a napkin still in place around his chin.

'What's this ruckus, y' bunch o' gooneys? See what the fuss is about,' the general ordered his dogsbody.

'We'se fed up o' these rations, Gen'ral!' whooped one, holding out a tin plate of difficult-to-identify stew.

'Perfectly edible,' grunted McIntosh, turning in puzzlement to the mess sergeant.

'We're runnin' out o' the doings,' he mumbled. 'Has to cut down on the servin' like.'

It was inevitable, Buckner realised. To starve the Spanish out implied they had enough supplies of their own to maintain the choke-hold over time. But there was no supply train for the Patriots of East Florida.

'Stap me!' exploded McIntosh. 'You're soldiers – go out an' get some for y'selves!'

*

Buckner was a native, born in East Florida, and his own plantation was some way to the south. He knew most of the owners, both loyalist and revolutionary Patriots, and was aghast at what ensued. In three days the Patriot camp had its meat. A herd of beeves, property of his friend Willard Tudgman and every one a prize breeding specimen, was driven in and slaughtered on the spot.

The soldiers had blundered in, armed to the teeth, and stampeded the herd out of its stockade. Tudgman had tried to object but he and his family had been threatened and, irrespective of their allegiances, had been forced to watch as their livelihood was destroyed.

It got worse. One evening, while out for a constitutional walk, Buckner was startled by a sudden disturbance in the undergrowth. He fumbled for his small-sword.

A Black man, dressed decently but with his clothes torn and mud-spattered, came towards him. It was Jemmy, a domestic slave at a nearby plantation. 'Sah. I beg o' you – come wi' me! They're murderin' the master!'

In the gathering dusk they plunged through the scrub until they reached an approach road. Ahead, Buckner could see the flickering of torches and a barn in flames.

He heard faint noise – hoots and shouts of jubilation, angry menace, drunken laughter. And then the scene unfolded. At an adjacent corral men were crowded about a fence post. A figure, head drooping, was bound to it. Buckner recognised the leader, Bucko Sam, a fellow landowner.

'Sam, what the deuce are you doing?' Buckner cried.

The big man turned, a knife visible in his fist. 'What d'yer think? This here's a scumbo who's taken the Spanish oath, an' he's now going t' tell us how many soldiers his friends ha' got hidden out in the San Marcos fort.'

The knife hovered suggestively below the man's throat.

'No!' came a shriek from a woman held back by three others. 'He's not! They're after where we hid our silver an' we ain't got any, I swear.'

Buckner, near speechless with rage, strode over and knocked aside the knife. 'You're a damned disgrace to the Patriot cause. These are American settlers, the ones we're handing freedom to – and you're going the tyrant over 'em.'

He wheeled around. 'And you men should be right ashamed of yourselves. Get back to camp this instant or General McIntosh will be getting up a pack o' court-martials as will see you all in chains as quick as you like.'

Without waiting for a response, he stalked off.

Chapter 35

A few days later came a new turn of events.

A small party approached McIntosh leading a horse with a blindfolded man dragged along behind at the end of a rope.

'General, we has a shabbaroon claims he's got a message from the Spanish big man hisself.'

'Gen'ral Houstoun McIntosh in command o' the army of the Patriots of East Florida. An' you?'

'Don Hidalgo Montez, and I have come – to offer peace.'

He was quiet, well-spoken in English and, despite his degraded position, held himself with dignity.

Buckner, standing nearby, felt a wild surge of hope. If they were offering terms for capitulation at this point, things must be well in the Patriots' favour. Mathews was absent, securing support in Washington, but if McIntosh was wise he would accept anything that could result in the flag of the United States raised in St Augustine's main plaza.

It was now inevitable. The Floridas would soon be American.

'So what then is your offer, *señor*?' McIntosh said in lordly fashion.

Montez winced, whether at the belittling of the *caballero* of his title or the exchange of terms being referred to, in a commercial style, as 'offer', Buckner couldn't tell.

'General, I'm privileged to extend to you the clemency of His Excellency Juan José de Estrada, governor of East Florida. He declares that, despite the provocation of the incursion without just cause of your armed party, he will allow their departure without hindrance to go back to where they came from.'

A rumble of incredulity spread, but in the same even tone Montez continued. 'Furthermore, he is aware that many of those who have sworn loyalty to the Spanish Crown in the past have been forced into acts of treason against their will and desire. These he forgives and specifies that, should they swear an oath of fealty once again, their lands and titles will be fully restored to them.'

The incredulity turned to an uproar.

Buckner guessed that Estrada was acting out of weakness, this a bluff but with enough attraction in it to lure the less committed in the Patriot cause.

'So that's the offer,' roared McIntosh, throwing his hands into the air. 'An' we're supposed to bow down an' skelter off. We, the Patriots who have St Augustine by the throat! Which o' you men wants to down arms and ride off, jus' when we've nearly got Florida in our hands?'

There was a jubilant roar but it was underlain with a sinister snarl. 'Scrag the bastard! Any who goes wi' the Spanish gets what's comin' to him.'

Buckner had to look on as it was generally agreed that not only would they stay in siege until the town surrendered but as of this night they would fan out over the countryside. Any who did not side with the Patriots – and swear to it – would suffer eviction and the destruction of their property.

With infinite sadness he saw that the cause was still before them. Florida would no doubt in time become American – but not by the hands of this sorry crew.

Chapter 36

St Augustine, administrative headquarters of the governor of East Florida

'Council will come to order!'

Juan José de Estrada looked up dully, regarding the corpulent figure of his aide with distaste. They were all here – all those with a stake in the continued existence of the town and its dominions for which he held the last responsibility, and he had to get on with the final act.

'I've summoned you here for one purpose – to discuss a proposal for capitulation.'

There were gasps and murmurs but no cries of defiance or consternation.

'The chief reason for which is that I have to tell you that all my demands and pleading for reinforcement have not been met. As a result we're outnumbered and cannot defend ourselves in the field.'

Absently fiddling with his quill the governor added, 'And that's not to overlook the grave, if not disastrous, victualling situation. Only Indian corn and the last of the salted beef, grain near gone and . . .' He tailed off.

An indistinct murmur from the end of the table he recognised as that of the *alcalde* of an inland settlement much harried by the rebels.

'. . . and worst of all, the marauding and thievery that is turning my dominions into a wasteland. Revenue is now so withered as to be near vanished and desertions are common. *Caballeros*, now is the time to consider the last sanction.'

He drew a paper closer and tested his quill. 'What then shall be our terms?'

Chapter 37

Aboard Thunderer

'Sail, sir. Thought you'd like to know.' Roscoe was apologetic, his face almost comical with concern as he leaned into Kydd's cabin. He knew, as they all did, that their captain was struggling with just what could be done with the mightiest ship on the ocean when forbidden by the Spanish to interfere, and when the threats were all on shore.

'I see. Of a size?'

'Oh, no, sir. Lug rig, from the coast to the south and holding course.'

Some kind of fisher-folk going about their business in these waters, determined not to notice a lone, hulking battleship? 'Thank you, old fellow. Let me know if there's any change.'

It was getting to Roscoe too, Kydd saw, this helplessness when history was unfolding under their lee. He had Bowden and *Weazel* inshore, keeping an eye open, but he, too, was constrained by the haughty Spanish.

Shortly it became evident that the little craft was headed

towards them but not making much way with this slight, hot and humid breeze.

Curiously, as *Thunderer* backed sail to heave to, it deferentially tacked around her stern to come neatly alongside in trim naval manner. The reason was quickly revealed. One of the two who boarded was Turner, Bowden's lieutenant in *Weazel*, who it seemed desired to impart intelligence.

In the great cabin Turner introduced the other man. 'Commander Bowden asks you to hear this man who's to be trusted, he believes.'

'Well, then, Mr Pauling.'

'Sir, I'm an English citizen, a merchant factor in cotton and hides in St Augustine, and may I proudly say have been so since well before this unpleasantness.'

His bearing was that of one used to affairs of significance and he was dressed fashionably.

'It therefore pains me to confess that I'm lately fled from the port for reasons I will be open with you about.'

Kydd was told of the events leading to the investing of the capital by rebels who it seemed were acting in concord with the United States Army with a view to taking all of Florida.

'Sir, the situation now?'

It was as bad as he'd feared – perhaps worse. The rebels circling the town had gone rogue, pillaging the countryside for food and plunder while the Spanish governor was outnumbered and unable to defend St Augustine. It was widely thought that he was about to capitulate.

'To surrender!' Kydd said, appalled.

'Indeed, sir. It is why I and my family sought sanctuary in the nearest British ship-of-war, your sainted bark *Weazel*. What can happen when the capital is taken leaves me in despair.'

If conquest was imminent it had reached a terrifying climax.

Admiral Warren's fleet in relief would be much too late to intervene. There were no immediate British forces in aid, they were far in the north, and in any case, in the face of Spanish obstinacy, they wouldn't be allowed to land.

'This I don't understand, Mr Pauling. Why is it that the Dons are refusing all help from us? We can find soldiery enough in Bermuda to make a difference, which must be better than a surrender.'

'Captain,' Pauling said heavily, 'Estrada is a Spaniard of the old breed, back when we fought together over our colonies. He's of the belief that once you set foot on their soil they'll never be rid of you.'

He gave a sad smile. 'He'd rather let the Americans possess the territory than the *inglés*, believe me.'

To Kydd the condition was far beyond the simple taking of a town, involving strategics of another dimension – and he would be held to account should he do nothing while the capital fell. But if he forced the issue, landed marines or some such in defiance of Spanish sovereignty, he would be held liable for a breach of international law.

It was a stalemate of the harshest kind and time had finally run out.

'Thank you for your information, Mr Pauling, and good fortune to you and yours for the future.'

He waited until he was alone in his princely cabin then held his head in his hands. How much easier it was to sail into battle where the challenges were those of courage and skill under fire, elements that the Royal Navy held the most precious.

It was no comfort to realise that if ever he raised his flag as admiral he would be no stranger to responsibility for solving such quandaries.

A whisky had magically appeared by his chair but he needed

all the clarity of thought he could muster – and then, out of the blue, it came to him.

The musing on an admiral's flag, then the idle thought that followed of what salute would be due to his flag were soon dismissed, but had returned in a different guise – and with them, his plan of battle.

Forgetting he now had a prim silver bell for summoning attention he roared for the cabin sentry as he would in the old *Tyger*. 'Ask Mr Turner to attend on me.'

It was passed on and soon the young lieutenant stood respectfully before him. 'Sir?'

'The lugger you came here in, what's its nature?'

'Er, a fisher-craft of sorts. I'm afraid I can't say more than—'

'Its skipper?'

'A local fellow, his name I forget.'

'Hale him aft, if you please.'

The man was of an age, with an accompanying dignity. 'Capitán Villar, your service.'

So, blessedly, he had English.

'You fish around St Augustine?'

'*Sí*. We fish *huachinango* off the shore.'

'So, in the entrance to the harbour?'

'Of course.'

Kydd sat forward eagerly. 'Can you tell me the depth of water as you close with Vilano and your Conch Island?'

'That near? I don't think it can take your great ship, sir.'

Kydd detected a hesitation. 'Why not, pray?'

'The sands. From the three rivers, they bring out shoal an' bar that change all the time.'

'But you know them, I think.'

'Each day they—'

'Today. You can know the depths?'

'We must, to know where the *huachinango* are, but, sir, for you—'

It was enough and there was little time.

'Pass the word for Mr Roscoe.'

Kydd waited impatiently until his first lieutenant stood before him. 'We're going in, Kit,' he announced, in a tone that defied contradicting.

Thunderer was at the moment comfortably offshore, the shallows off Florida left well a-lee, and the low-lying St Augustine was far out of sight.

If his plan was to work he had to set eyes on the town through the narrow entryway to its inland location. For this he needed to risk all the shoals and sand-bars that Villar had mentioned, but he was going to trust a professional whose very livelihood depended on knowing their ever-shifting lurking places.

Men were told off to man the chains both sides with lead-lines, others posted in the fore-top to scan ahead for tell-tale kelp beds and darker rock ledges.

It was early afternoon and they had little time if they wanted to catch the tide. But if they hastened too rapidly an irreplaceable ship-of-the-line would be hard and fast on the estuary flats, much like Nelson's old *Agamemnon* at the river Plate.

With Villar at his side Kydd stood by the helm as *Thunderer* shaped course for the St Augustine inlet.

Roscoe had his orders, however incomprehensible they must appear, and the big ship stole in under small sail, Villar's eyes picking up on the flat, brindled shore as it came into view ahead, on both sides, casting about for sea-marks to fix his position.

Kydd flicked a nervous glance over the side, a lighter tone of the water coming from a reflection of the sand not so many fathoms below.

And then . . . the barest hint of land across his vision

ahead. It firmed – and he saw the unnatural stippling of buildings on the pale blue horizon and to the right the unmistakable mass of the San Marcos fortress. St Augustine, perhaps another half-mile . . .

'Stand by!' he bellowed. The fo'c'slemen attended at the anchors, the tiersmen below, and, most importantly, the gunners stood to their massive iron beasts, each poised for instant action.

Well inside the entrance Kydd set his plan in train.

'Slip!'

In seconds an anchor at the stern was let go and plunged into the shallows. Under the impetus of the rivers flowing seaward, *Thunderer* rotated about it until, broadside on to the current, the length of the ship, with its rows of guns facing the town, a bower anchor forward was let go.

Now for the final act. 'Hoist!'

Simultaneously from the fore-, main- and mizzen-mast floated out the proud colours of Spain.

'Fire!' At precisely the same time the gun salute began – not the puny crack of six-pounders but the mighty bass roar of the biggest guns afloat.

One, two, three and more. The smoke of a full ten-pound charge from each of the lower-deck thirty-two pounders quickly rose in a towering cloud and the staggering blast of sound echoed back from the foreshore.

Fourteen, fifteen, sixteen – this was going to be the full twenty-one guns of a royal salute, and it went on and on.

Kydd gave a savage smile. No one could accuse him of a war-like act – wasn't he merely respectfully acknowledging with salutes the royal suzerainty of Spain? This day was sure to be some kind of saint's day, after all.

What he had in mind, however, was to achieve quite another effect.

*

Estrada pulled on his jewelled gloves, token of his position as *El Soberano*. In old-fashioned breeches and gold-buckled shoes, a feathered cap and delicately ornamented rapier, it would be the last time he would wear them. At the main plaza he would render up the city and its dominions to the godless American rabble outside.

His servant flourished a rag on the already spotless shoes and he was ready.

Then, from out in the bay, he heard the heavy thunder of guns.

Crossing quickly to the balcony he looked out and saw a great ship, enveloped in gun-smoke and closer to where no large ship had any right to be.

It continued to fire its huge guns but already there was a growing commotion in the streets below. Screams and shouts – and running feet.

More guns, and by now the ship was hidden behind fast-rising billows of smoke, which made it impossible to know what was going on behind it. An invasion? Preparation for a bombardment of the town?

The brutal crash of the heavy guns was causing real panic and Estrada couldn't think what to do. If there was—

'Excelencia – sir,' his aide gulped in excitement, bursting into the room. 'Sir, we are saved!'

'What are you babbling about, you idiot?' he snarled, badly rattled by the unreadable events unfolding.

'The Holy Mother has heard our prayers and has delivered us!'

'What? Get on with it!' rasped Estrada.

'Sir, the rebels – they're giving up, running! They've seen the great ship and know it to be English, but it flies Spanish colours in amity with us. They say that it is even now landing a tremendous force of redcoats to come in aid of us, and they swear they will not stay to be taken by Englishmen.'

For a moment Estrada stared at him then fell to his knees, his aide beside him, as they fervently offered up prayers of thanks for a timely deliverance.

Chapter 38

Bermuda

With the glittering seas and pellucid green in a breath-taking show, the hired lugger completed its crossing of Castle Harbour. Large, but rock-strewn, it was set in the centre of the north-eastern reaches of Bermuda, well placed for the important St George's settlement.

Edwin Harris had promised a wonderful spectacle for their second outing, but was mysterious as to the details. Kydd knew in general that they were headed through the jumble of islands that guarded the south-east entry point to the harbour, through to the open Atlantic. Was that their destination?

'There – you've taken bearings on 'em often enough to enter the harbour, but have you stopped to think what they mean?' Harris pointed to a well-weathered grey stone fort perched on one of the islands they were passing. 'King's Castle,' he said, in something like reverence. 'Goes back to our earliest days, the first Charles. It's the oldest English fortification in the whole New World, and the commandant's house the oldest English house in all the Americas.'

'There's another on the other side of the island,' Persephone murmured.

'Yes – Devonshire Redoubt,' Harris said quickly. 'There's more still – Bermuda must have above fifty forts in all, as I haven't counted them. These are here to deny Castle Harbour and St George's to the enemy, and we have to say, in all the centuries past, no infidel boot has ever defiled our soil.'

Once the open sea was won the lugger's helm went over in a sharp turn to the south, down the coast. After passing an island a deserted beach hove into view.

'How wonderful!' Persephone breathed, as they approached. It was the prettiest spot imaginable, the emerald pure seas lazily swishing into the delicately toned beach sand, untouched by a human foot.

'Not so many know this spot – there are no roads leading to it.'

The skiff delivered them ashore, around them on all sides the soft grey serried rocks of Bermuda limestone as if in an enfolding privacy.

Persephone set Esther to putting out the chairs and cloths for the happy party.

'Miss Rebecca, have you ever been here before?' asked Roscoe, as he casually rearranged things to set his chair next to hers.

'I do declare I had no idea it was here,' she said sweetly, but she turned to her other side where Bowden was making much of fixing her parasol just so in its bracket, apparently requiring his own chair to be conveniently on hand. 'Why, thank you, good sir. I find the sun is at its most ardent at this time of the year.'

As it happened, the day had been well chosen: a soft south-easterly off the water brought a delightful coolness and a sky veiled in a white haze took the edge off the sun's brightness.

Craddock stretched out, his loose-laced shirt and bare feet token of his recent castaway experience, his eyes closed in something like rapture. Kydd was relieved to see the lines in his face were easing.

'Cassava pie, anyone?' Persephone invited, and the guests tucked in to a splendid repast.

Harris chatted amiably about the remarkable history of Bermuda, so much of it still to be seen, and Kydd was content to let the champagne and lobster work on him. There was, at the moment, nothing on his horizon that he need concern himself about. The Florida invasion had been turned back, the West Indies was quiet, and apart from a flurry of ill-tempered dispatches from Admiral Warren, there were no further demands from Halifax.

There was every reason to enjoy the day, and he accepted a slice of rum cake in a distinctly mellow mood.

'Oh! Look – down by the sea!'

'Where?' demanded Roscoe and Bowden at the same time, Roscoe leaping to his feet in manly concern.

'Well, just over there,' Rebecca said uncertainly. 'It's, well, if you'll allow it, a sandpiper, of the spotted variety,' she added more confidently. 'They're quite rare for Bermuda.'

The men eyed the little bird doubtfully, but it was Roscoe who was quickest off the mark. 'The sandpiper, spotted? I rather think it the brown-rumped of its kind, my dear.'

She frowned. 'Are you not thinking of the common whimbrel, sir?' she said shyly, shading her eyes.

'Not at all.' Roscoe harrumphed. 'You'll note, er, how the little beggar hops along rather than walks, a sure sign it's your brown-rumped.'

'Oh. Captain Roscoe, I had no idea you were in the bird-watching line at all. As in my small way I am myself.' She looked up at him with a dazzling smile.

'Or it could be a nought but a white-bellied, um, curlew,' Bowden broke in but was ignored by both.

'Perhaps we could make exploration together to the more remote places – to discover even rarer birds, that is,' Roscoe went on smoothly. 'Do you have a favourite rare bird at all?'

'Well, I have an egg collection that some do say stands with the finest in these islands. It's always been my desire to acquire that of the phalarope – but this is so seldom seen in these days that perhaps it no longer exists.'

'We shall do it!' Roscoe exclaimed grandly. 'I wonder where . . .?'

'The pity of it.' She sighed. 'Not far from here, on a bare rock called Bird Island. As I said before, I've never been there but it's said to be the last place it was sighted, four years ago. It was favoured as a nesting place because without greenery the poor mother phalarope was able to see beasts stalking in from any direction.'

'Bird Island?'

'She's right, you know,' Harris said, leaning over. 'Not more'n half a mile to seaward from there,' he said, indicating a rumpled island not so far off.

Bowden was quicker this time. 'I shall find you one, Miss Rebecca. Do save a mort of that paw-paw for my return.'

He ran to the skiff sitting hauled out of the water further up the beach with a boat-keeper taking his ease on the further side.

'Out!' he commanded, pointing to the waves.

Astonished, the man obeyed, hauling the boat around but then Roscoe arrived. 'You're not contemplating taking this boat out alone?' he demanded.

'I'm perfectly capable of taking a pair of oars, sir!' The rum punch was having its effect.

'For reasons of common prudence I'm to be with you. Let's get her launched – two, six, heavy!'

Unless Bowden resorted to fisticuffs he couldn't stop Roscoe, and they clambered aboard, taking an oar either side and pulling valiantly for the first island.

'You wish me to ease away?' Roscoe said irritably, his showy tug and heave out of synchrony with Bowden's more studied long, powerful strokes.

They skirted the first islet and there ahead was a sea-washed rock that barely qualified as an island.

'We have to land – but where?' Roscoe said, as they lay on their oars.

'There's a tide scour around the far side, bound to be a gyre of sorts in its lee,' Bowden replied, remembering the fearful waters around the Channel Islands.

Not answering, Roscoe gave one or two tugs to align the skiff and they headed in.

Bowden boated his oar and was first ashore but glanced back and saw Roscoe holding the bowline with a pained expression. He took it but then realised Roscoe was free to scramble ashore while he held the painter.

There was a heavy boulder close by and fashioning a bowline-on-a-bight he quickly had the skiff bobbing securely at moorings.

But Roscoe had the advantage and was somewhere at the other end of the rocky islet. Bowden took stock. There were nests, cavities, pools, birds lifting and screaming at the disturbance: what did it all mean? Which one was a phalarope, for Heaven's sake?

'Got one!' Roscoe's triumphant cry came.

'Where did you find it?'

'Be damned to it – get the boat in, we're going back.'

Cradling the egg in his kerchief, Roscoe waited, and Bowden was obliged to get aboard and take up the oars by himself.

'You'll have to take us back. This egg is too precious to risk.'

It was a long pull to the beach, the seas unaccountably rising as they made the distance. Roscoe gave a fine performance of stepping into the shallows and heading straight to a delighted Rebecca.

'Milady – your egg of the phalarope.' He proffered his prize carefully in cupped hands.

She gingerly reached for it. Then her smile vanished. 'Mr Roscoe? This is your jest?'

'I don't understand.'

'That, sir, is no other than the egg of the common lapwing.' She sniffed in disdain. 'How you might think to confuse it with the beautiful green-flecked article of the phalarope I'm persuaded must speak to a less than shining acquaintance with the art.'

She sat back scornfully, taking up her cordial and sipping daintily.

'As I tried to tell him,' Bowden said sorrowfully. 'It was never that of the phalarope. It would seem we would do better to go in search of it ourselves. Er, I find I am at liberty later in the week. Should we—'

'That is so kind in you, Captain, but I've accepted a private tour about the Paget Fort in that time. Such a sweet man, Algernon promises to show me just how the army lives as it prepares for the worst the enemy can bring against them, brave fellows.' She gave a pitying smile and Bowden fell back, defeated.

Chapter 39

Later in the afternoon Kydd stirred and opened his eyes. As happened often at sea, something out of the ordinary had alerted him. What was it?

The beach was quiet, most sleeping off the splendid picnic. He raised his head but there seemed to be nothing untoward. Puzzled, he concentrated – and then he had it. The languid surge and playful swish of the incoming waves had been replaced by a more fretful crump and drawn-out hiss.

He sat up. The seas were by no means threatening but his years in Neptune's realm led his gaze immediately to the horizon. It was obscured by a thin, sullen band of darker grey. From the south-east, the breeze had backed to steady, even if still cool and pleasant.

'I'd give much for a sight of the glass, Charles,' he said, in a low voice, so as not to alarm the ladies.

Bowden opened his eyes and seeing where Kydd was looking gazed out too. After a short while he replied quietly, 'And I've seen its like often enough in the Caribbean.'

Kydd leaned over to Harris. 'Edwin, old fellow, do you think we should be worried at all by that blashy weather upwind?'

'Do I think it a species of hurricanoe, or some such?' He sat up, staring hard. 'I wouldn't have thought so, the season being not yet with us, but a wise Bermudian never trusts the weather.'

Kydd nodded and, after hesitating only for a moment, stood up, brushing himself down. 'Well, I'm sorry to spoil our rest,' he said loudly, 'but the afternoon moves on and I've just recollected some work that I must do. Shall we pack up?'

Leaning to the breeze, as they re-crossed the bright waters of Castle Harbour it all seemed a little hasty, particularly as Kydd was a stranger to these parts. Nevertheless, he'd never been one to take chances merely on the whim of the moment.

St George's harbour was unusually crowded with shipping, a convoy recently arrived and a number of thinly manned American prizes sheltering while they victualled and watered for the next leg of their voyage. They were all taking measures against a possible blow, laying out cables, another anchor and so forth.

Rebecca, it seemed, was anxious to be home if there was to be any kind of a storm and Bowden took his leave to return to *Weazel.* Kydd felt it only polite to invite Harris in for a snifter in appreciation of an entirely enjoyable picnic. Blessing the fact that his residence was so near the waterfront, he paused to give orders to Roscoe to repair immediately to *Thunderer* and take precautions consistent with conditions until he arrived on board later.

Back at Monte Rosa, Harris opened, 'I know you've duties aboard, Sir Thomas, but it would gratify me if you could say something of your various encounters in defiance of Neptune at all. Readers in this part of the world are especially interested in such.'

Kydd happily obliged. It was not difficult to bring to mind

several occasions that had thrust him into the centre of the majesty and violence of a great tempest at sea.

In the forefront of his mind was the near-lethal hurricane that had beset the tiny cutter *Seaflower*, with his sister Cecilia aboard. He'd shared the last extremity with her, but was spared by a miraculous grounding on a remote island.

And then there was the fearful chase of the French predators in his dear frigate *L'Aurore*, only saved from inevitable tragedy by top-class seamanship.

There were other occasions—

'Thomas! It's getting worse – should we do something?' Persephone's voice penetrated and he became aware of a fractious rattling of the windows, which he had not noticed, so immersed had he been in his conversation with Harris.

Looking out he saw the harbour was now white-flecked, wind blustering under grey, thunderous clouds.

He snatched at his trusty grego, and driven by every captain's worst fear – that he would be out of his ship in its time of trial – he hurried down through the gusts to the little jetty. There was no boat: the vicious choppiness of the water had sent them off to find shelter.

In a lurch of dread he knew there was no possibility of getting out to *Thunderer*.

There was nothing in his power he could do for his ship. He must see out the blow, however brutish, ashore. He'd never done so before.

Glancing at the rows of merchant ships, jibbing and restless with their crews hard at work, he was wrung with worry. What if Roscoe omitted to lay a kedge to windward, just in case? If he forgot that keckling was needed with a coral bottom – if it didn't occur to him to cross-lash the heavy guns against the inboard side of the gunwales?

Wet through with sudden gusts of rain Kydd made his way

back to Monte Rosa. Was he to see through the man-killing drama from the comfort of his own armchair?

Choking with frustration, he threw off Persephone's wifely ministrations and sank into his chair.

Harris, sensing his mood, kept his silence. The wind's moan now turned assertive, aggressive.

Refusing to look out, Kydd knew the progression. If this was a full-blown hurricane it would be fast-ascending screaming blasts before long, and a hideous fight for the life of the ship, then the sharp change of wind direction and another fight. Would *Thunderer* emerge alive?

The afternoon light faded into the murk of dusk and, as it always seemed, the storm approached its height as night clamped in.

Finally, he could stand it no longer. He crossed to the window and looked out into the chaos. It was difficult to make out but his instincts took hold and he saw what was going on.

The drama outside was bathed in a ghostly luminous glimmer, which did much to reveal the wild scenes of streaming seas and wind-torn spindrift in which ships were struggling for existence. A full moon, riding high and serene far above the madness of storm wrack, gave mere mortals sight of their fate.

By it Kydd saw inner St George's harbour, crowded with ships, white with breakers and speckled with the lights of vessels trying to warp themselves clear of each other. The waves were not the huge and majestic thundering rollers of the open ocean but confused, vicious and from all directions – almost impossible to predict. This was not only an enclosed harbour but it was set in the middle of twenty miles of reefs, which had the effect of disrupting such seething monsters.

Hours passed, furious winds shook the house and the harbour passed into a misty welter of craziness and confusion.

Chapter 40

In the early hours Kydd was still in his chair, tormented by thoughts of *Thunderer* being pounded to a ruin – but she was out in the naval anchorage in Grassy Bay, the seas moderated by the width of Bermuda and in a more open, regular fetch.

Here in the harbour the very thing that mariners craved – a shelter from the storm and anchors down – was working against them. There was no longer any real haven: the wind's blast was merciless and, with a rock and sand seabed, their anchors were not holding.

With so many vessels crowded together the result was inevitable. Outer ships began dragging anchor, others parted their cables. All were carried unstoppably downwind to collide with those still holding to their ground tackle, in an agony of splintering and shrieking timbers. First one, then several were driven helpless inshore, their pitifully few crew unable to do a thing to stop them until they struck with a heart-breaking finality. More followed – some in a death embrace with another, all to end the same way as a dark mass of tangled wreckage torn to pieces.

Kydd's attention was caught by a larger vessel out further, deep laden and with anchor down but clearly being driven to her inevitable doom. Through pricking eyes he saw movement, lanthorns brought on deck. They were going to make a fight of it.

One light made its way along the bucking deck forward, leaving a cluster remaining on the after deck – and then he understood. These were playing dimly over a group huddled together, unnaturally small figures. It was the captain's family taking passage with him, terrified for their lives in the insanity raging all around.

With a lump in his throat Kydd watched as the drama played out. Unless this captain could perform some miracle every one of them would be in either Heaven or Hell within the hour.

He caught the first move. The passing forward had been to cut the anchor cable. Bounding like a horse given its head the ship immediately slewed about, driving downwind bows first towards the shore. The captain was using the wind's force to pick up speed to send the ship hard up over the shallows to give his precious souls a chance to fling themselves ashore.

But before that happened, Kydd saw a fatal betrayal that would condemn them. The ship was being driven into the shore further along, beyond the limits of the harbour proper with its wharves and jetties, into a seafront that was a sprawl of rock beaten to a white smother by the wild seas. But the vessel was deep-laden. Its fat belly ensured that it grounded, lurching to a staggering halt well short of the shallows. Between it and life was the frenzied crashing of seas on the rocks, a frightful death waiting for any taking to the water.

Kydd looked again. The bowsprit was a stump: in the maelstrom there would be no crawling out over it to the landward side. It was too hard to take, here in his warm and safe haven, his loving wife and family securely with him, while out in the wild madness just yards away others faced their end.

The lanthorns moved, carried down to the foredeck, figures jerkily following. This captain was going to play it to a finish.

Two lanthorns detached and moved to the base of the foremast. In their light the glint of metal appeared briefly and Kydd grasped what was happening. If the lofty mast could be felled like a tree over the bows there was a slim chance it could be their pathway to life.

Roaring like a madman, Kydd raced to the door, thrusting out into the darkness without even his foul-weather gear on.

Savagely collecting his thoughts, he paused, then sprinted over to Aunt Peggy's, the nearby tavern much favoured by boats' crews standing by. Bursting in on the battened-down customers, he bellowed, '*Thunderer* – captain's barge!'

Stunned, the men nevertheless roused themselves. If their captain felt it necessary to put out into a full-blown hurricanoe, who were they to object?

His coxswain, Halgren, scrambled to his feet and stood before him, ever loyal.

'With me!' Kydd ordered, and set off in the darkness down the road to where the last act of the drama was under way.

The lanthorns were all about the foremast where several men were hacking and hewing at the feet-thickness of the mast. Others set to on the shrouds and lines that normally held the sturdy spar proudly erect. The huddled figures did not move, seemingly mesmerised by the ferocity of the gales.

'When the mast comes down, get out on it and bring in those bantlings,' Kydd instructed, an impossibly dangerous order but understood by those seasoned seamen.

They were just yards from those who would be going back to a stiff grog and hammock and those whose life was now drawing to its close.

Suddenly the foremast gave a preliminary shiver and sway. Ungainly, but in unfaltering inevitability, it teetered, then swung down to crunch to a stop over the foredeck, unbelievably protruding over the rocks to the scrub beyond.

'Move!' roared Kydd, the first to launch himself at the rain-slick spar. Scrabbling for a hold he became conscious of the familiar rough touch of rope. It was one of the halliards normally soaring vertically aloft but now serving as a common foot-rope under a yardarm.

He flung himself along, feeling through his feet. His arms fell over the mast, gripping another line the other side. Others saw what he was doing and followed.

It was only when the broken timbers of the beakhead emerged below that he realised they had got aboard. He looked up to see the agonised features of a woman kneeling beside the mast. She was thrusting a child towards him. Kydd babbled some words but they were carried away by the wind's scream. He reached out and took the infant, with huge staring eyes, in his hands.

He held it close, feeling its terror, then pivoting awkwardly gave it to Halgren behind him, knowing it would be passed along the line to blessed safety.

The woman's face was still contorted with horror and dread as she handed another child to him. The little girl whimpered, looking back at her mother, and Kydd tried to comfort her before he passed her, too, down the line.

Next it was the woman, who paused, piteously looking back to where the figures around the foremast stump were there still, watching.

Then the men aboard came forward, gruffly ignoring the helping hands while behind them the ship, hammered by the rampaging combers, broke up into pieces.

Chapter 41

Even as the crepuscular light of daybreak stole in to infuse the madness, the hurricane continued, but as if in pity it began a fitful reduction of the hard blasts. Kydd pulled on his grego and ventured out into the murderous bluster to spy out the night's destruction.

It was appalling. As far as he could see into the intermittent rain squalls, every one of the ships anchored out had been swept to ruin against the shore, crushing and demolishing those tied up alongside, which had seemed safe.

He counted them, trying to ignore the pitiful scenes of destruction and death. At the same time his heart filled with dread at what he'd discover of *Thunderer*'s fate.

He had a duty to advise the governor of the extent of the devastation and what it meant to the colony. At the residence he would also be able to look out over the Grassy Bay anchorage and see if *Thunderer* still lived.

It took much of the day for the relentlessly rain-lashed two-horse diligence to struggle through by the North Shore Road to the governor's residence and when he finally arrived it was to a dismal scene.

Men were at work removing furniture and decorations sketchily covered against the weather. Portraits and paintings, a vast Turkish carpet he recalled seeing in the governor's living room, rolled up and secured, odd articles of apparent value in chests, other objects carried out reverently.

'Sir James?' he enquired, not sure what to expect.

'Front reception room been blown in,' the man puffed. 'We'se gettin' these under cover. Dunno where His Nibs is b'gob.'

And then a vision flashed before Kydd of the infinitely precious Hurd. 'Is the chart safe?' he asked tightly.

'Chart? Ye'd better ask him,' the man said, thumbing over to the major-domo, who Kydd remembered from his earlier visit.

'Oh, the chart. Don't concern yourself, Sir Thomas, it's still in its water-tight and locked chest, perfectly sound and well protected from this bedlam.'

Cockburn, he learned, was to be found in a mansion further inland and was not in any mood to be told of disasters and calamities. Having done his duty, Kydd left, desperate to get out to *Thunderer*: he'd seen her at a distance, riding at three anchors, and, as far as he could tell, still in possession of all her masts and spars.

Outside the building, he drew his grego close. An elderly gentleman, whose intensity was unsettling, immediately confronted him. 'Captain Kydd?' he demanded.

'Sir Thomas Kydd, captain of His Majesty's Ship *Thunderer*,' he answered tightly.

'Then, sir, you are the one I must see.' His gaze to Kydd seemed bordering on unhinged and the knuckle around his walking cane was tense and white.

'Sir, do observe that I'm closely engaged and cannot possibly—'

'You must – you will!' the man hissed, the cane banging on the ground in emphasis.

Kydd glared, uneasily aware that he was not wearing a sword or any other weapon to defend himself against a lunatic. 'Good day to you, sir,' he said decisively, and made to go, but the man moved to block him.

'Sir – my name is Holt and you'll find I'm not unknown in these parts.'

Holt? Wasn't that . . .?

'And I desire you to know that my daughter Rebecca . . .' his voice tailed off and then continued thickly '. . . is even now in the course of eloping with her fancy man.'

The slip of a girl who had been playing his officers for fools had run off with—

'Who is the gentleman concerned?' Kydd asked quickly.

'Does it matter? They're at this moment aboard one of my trading brigs, which is now preparing to put to sea as the weather moderates. Sir, there is no time to lose! I demand that you act to intercept it with all the force at your command.'

'Mr Holt. This hurricanoe does preclude any move under sail on my part and, in any case, is this not a civil affair? Do you expect me to arrest them both out of hand? No, sir, I will not act in this matter.'

He pushed the man aside and stormed off, his mood dark. If Roscoe had abandoned his post to race off with the girl he'd have him crucified – or if Bowden had lost his head over the maid so much as to turn his back on *Weazel* his fate would be equally dire.

Thunderer was safe – that at least was a blessing and, controlling furious thoughts, he set off in the bluster of the storm back to his residence.

Harris was still there. Kydd told him and an engrossed Persephone about the amorous flight.

'That would be *Providence*, one of their bigger sail,' Harris said. 'New, two masts, about three hundred tons, armed against privateers. I've heard she turns in good times on the Caribbean run so can be considered fast.'

A thought struck Kydd. 'Where does she dock?' he asked. If it was either Roscoe or Bowden it was probably still not too late to lay hold on the love-struck officer.

'Oh, that would be down from here at the other end of the waterfront, where Holts have their warehouses.'

'I'm going there to seize the wretch. Shouldn't be long.' A bemused Harris begged to come too, saying he would be able to point out their objective. If this was anywhere within St George's harbour they were very likely to be ruefully sitting on a pile of wreckage, however.

Chapter 42

Kydd and Harris drew into the back of the warehouses in a hired trap. A group of men were heaving at the rain-soaked remains of a collapsed roof, the contents of the godown being piled up next to it. A bored supervisor in foul-weather gear stood by them.

Kydd went over to him. 'What happened to *Providence* at all?'

An eyebrow lifted. 'Who's askin'?'

'Navy.'

'Well, ye won't find her here, Admiral. As they sees the blow comin' they gets clear, goes to Hamilton t' ride it out, I hears. Him 'n' her both,' he added, with relish.

'What was that?'

'Ye didn't get the drum? Course, ye're Navy, no idea what's goin' on longshore like.' He lowered his voice and confided, 'Well, the owner's dear daughter runs off with her fancy man in his own ship, leaves him ragin' like a bull.'

'Er, who was the gentleman involved – a naval officer, perhaps?'

'Course not! Everyone 'cept Holt hisself knows it's Abe

Gavery, the sly dog. Runs a smugglin' gang t' the Bahamas. Y'r Navy coves been given the right royal run-around by yon Miss Rebecca as gives us our laughs, I c'n tell ye, Admiral.'

Kydd gave the ghost of a smile. 'I see. So you wish the lovers a *bon voyage*?'

'Not as I sees it. He's a two-faced beggar who knows the Americans a mort too much, an' she's naught but a regular thief.'

'Thief?'

'I was in Hamilton an' watches while they loads for Nassau, an' there with the other lading was a lumpin' big rich carpet which I recognises. It's from the governor's ken, his own, which she must ha' looted in the hurricanoe.'

'Well, thank you for your information.' He slipped across a silver shilling.

By now Kydd had no intention of being further involved and they returned to Monte Rosa in silence.

Just as soon as the door opened a lieutenant of marines thrust forward. 'Sir Thomas? Urgent news, sir, of the utmost importance.'

'What?

'Sir. From the governor. He cannot understand it but the Hurd chart is missing – no longer in its chest or anywhere he can search. He can only assume it's been stolen and is at the present moment being conveyed out of the colony – even to the United States.'

Kydd froze. This was the worst possible news. Whoever possessed the chart had the means to plot a secret path to land an assault anywhere they chose, and Bermuda's only defence was to guard every ingress – quite impossible with the forces it had.

It had to be stopped. And this was a purely naval burden.

He knew what had to be done – clamp a hold over every

point of exit: at all costs stop every vessel that was putting to sea and search it thoroughly. Given the tempest still raging they had a chance of interception at the dockside with the aid of the army garrison but once put to sea the likelihood fell off considerably.

But with what naval vessel could he chase any departing ship? With *Weazel* somewhere still out at sea the only sea-going ship locally available was *Thunderer*. The thought of a battleship in stern chase of a trading brig was ludicrous – but just possibly very necessary.

He tried to visualise how the precious chart would be smuggled out. Its chest was stout and large and could not be disguised: word of it could be relied on to reach the frantically searching officials. If not, then how?

The chart – or the two halves – was of immense size, far bigger than a ship's chart, and would be damaged if it were folded down. There were standard leather tubes for conveying normal charts but they were far too small for the Hurd.

How the devil had it been spirited out of the governor's residence without anyone seeing what was going on?

And then came a stab of insight from something the wharf-lumper supervisor had said. The governor's carpet . . . He could see it happening. A corrupt official pocketing coin to divulge where the key to the chest was. The thieves, seeing a perfect opportunity in the chaos of the storm, simply rolling up the carpet, the broad width of the chart snugly interleaved within it and quickly removed. He'd actually witnessed it himself, he realised, with embarrassment.

Then on to the ship, a reasonable acquisition for a couple about to set up home – except it had been seen by someone who'd recognised it.

The method was admirable, the execution rapid, and when the weather improved they'd be away with their prize.

The carpet – and chart – had been loaded aboard *Providence* with Rebecca and Gavery. The only conclusion was that they were not only the thieves but had planned it all. *They* were the spies, at the same time biding their moment to seize the chart. Considered objectively, Rebecca had always been in a prime position to be toured around the warships, forts and defensive positions, guest of the many officers she'd strung along. She had probably gained a better picture of the Bermudian lines of defence than most general officers, and now with the priceless Hurd chart, she could name her price.

It was galling, but they should be in time to stop them.

'Hamilton – *Providence*,' he barked at a bemused carriage driver, just returned from there.

It was the same tedious drive through the scrub and thickets of the North Shore road but mercifully the storm had eased considerably and, apart from trees blown across the road and imploring villagers wanting help to put their wind-blasted cottages to rights, there was nothing to impede them.

Hamilton was in far better condition than St George's as it had no confined harbour and therefore no tangle of shipwrecks. But Kydd had eyes for one thing only – the brig *Providence*.

The Holt wharf was at the end of King Street. From his viewpoint on the northern slopes, Kydd looked down as they turned into it. A sizeable brig was visible alongside.

'Jarvey, your whip, man!' he shouted up at the coach driver.

He was ignored: the storm-water was fast sluicing downhill, gouging valleys in the poorly made-up road and the driver was forced to go slowly to avoid them. Kydd held his temper but then, to his dismay, he saw that the topmasts, now all he could see of *Providence*, were in motion: the ship had cast off and was being warped out.

When the carriage finally swept onto the wharf he saw

that the boats had made good progress in hauling the ship off. There were now fifty yards or more of open water between wharf and ship.

And it was indeed *Providence.*

'In the King's name,' he bawled, 'cease rowing this instant!'

Startled faces looked his way. Some stopped work, others scornfully persisted, and figures appeared to stare from the deck.

'*Providence*, ahoy! Return to your berth under penalty of arrest.'

More appeared aft and it was evident an argument was under way, but Kydd already knew he'd lost. The wind was offshore and all that was now needed was for sail to be set and, with no naval craft in sight to stop them, they were free to go.

Men raced up the shrouds and loosed sail on the foreyard. In the stiff winds the sail bellied taut in an instant, and as others caught, the brig was quickly under way, outward bound.

As a final insult its colours broke aloft. Flying free for all to see was the flag of the United States of America.

Kydd stood bristling with rage but only for a moment. He had to catch it.

If he took after it in *Thunderer*, spread more sail in the fading storm than the other dared, he had a chance. In fact, a good one in this blow.

He turned to Harris with a lop-sided smile. 'Oh, Edwin. I'm in rather of a hurry and—'

'You're off to *Thunderer*, I suspect.'

'As it happens. I'm going after *Providence* so if you'll excuse . . .'

'I'm coming with you, my friend. I want to be witness to the concluding act. You'll win, I know it in my bones you will, and I want to be there at the end. I owe it to my readers.'

'You can come, but I can't guarantee a victory at all,' Kydd murmured, touched by the man's faith in him.

A fast wherry ride out to *Thunderer* left them soaking wet with spray and Kydd took Roscoe's report while being towelled down in his cabin.

'Make it quick, Kit, we've got to get after that brig that left you a-lee just now.'

'Ah. Not possible, sir.'

'Tell me.'

'Fore-topmast sprung at the hounds. Can't send it down until the winds moderate further.'

This was a major spar structurally affected by split timber. He couldn't risk any kind of chase until it was repaired, which even with a nearby dockyard could take hours or even days.

It was over – the Hurd chart was on its way to America.

Kydd had to admit defeat to Roscoe and Harris. There was a vanishingly small possibility that *Weazel* would return in time. If the weather calmed further he could chance it in one of the Customs cutters, but once in the open sea *Providence* could take any course it chose and be lost in the vast immensity of ocean in a day.

'There's one plan as will give you best, I believe,' Harris said quietly. All eyes on him, he went on. 'None can outrun a Bermuda sloop. Fastest on the high seas.'

'Wasn't *Pickle* Bermuda built?' murmured Roscoe.

'*Pickle?*'

'Yes,' Kydd said heavily, 'Took the Trafalgar dispatches to the Admiralty in double-quick time – but she was schooner-rigged and we don't have her like in the Navy this side of the Atlantic.'

Harris grinned. 'Not in the Navy, but plenty to be had in these waters.'

'What are you saying, sir?'

'For the taking – hire a smuggler. Blinding fast, armed, a mite small but very handy I'm told.'

It made a lot of sense. Fore-and-aft rigged, it was said they could lie within four points of the wind to a square-rigger's six. But they were small – difficult to persuade a larger vessel to yield to a smaller. Unless persuaded by deadly aimed cannon fire, not the usual smuggler's strong point as they were unable to afford a top-class gunner.

'I know a Hamilton gentleman who for a modest fee might comply with your requirements,' Harris said.

'Whatever it costs!' Kydd blurted. 'Mr Roscoe, we're off to find ourselves a smuggler.'

He threw back on his damp uniform and turned to go. 'Oh, and tell gunner's mate Stirk that his services are required this hour, sea-bag and hammock, full gunner's pouch.'

Chapter 43

'Done!'

The owner tried to hide his delight at the bargain struck. A handsome fee, crew supplied but victualled, and paid *per diem* on a voyage charter by no less than this gentleman from the British Admiralty who would further reimburse any wear, tear or damage incurred.

Kydd took in *Pearl* as her crew readied her. A tiny thing really, but in Bermudian red cedar a fetching sight.

Her single mast – raked saucily, the main boom now on trestles extending wildly far past her stern. Sharp-lined, but with a dismaying lack of freeboard while leading from a full bow to a diminutive tucked stern, but a higher, narrow after-deck. As for rigging, there was an implied profusion of headsails on a monster-length bowsprit, at least three jibs, but it was the tall mainmast that dominated, with a short topmast and gaff-rigged mainsail. There were two modest yards crossed, comforting Kydd's naval soul; square topsails existed that could be backed and therefore he had the ability to manoeuvre aggressively in action.

She would do.

Stirk wasted no time. He was down on the maindeck, crouching over each of the eight six-pounders in turn using a mirror to peer intently down the bore. Kydd knew he was looking for kibes, shiny regions betraying where the ball on firing had rebounded ever so slightly on inevitable casting imperfections on its way out. Even a very small deflection would translate to a throw-off of tens of yards at range. He was selecting the piece that had the best chance at accuracy.

Kydd paced up and down, waiting while victuals and water were struck down into the diminutive hold, charts and inevitable naval paperwork sent aboard. A crew of sixty-five all told – the enormous sail area would need every one of them. The mate would take Kydd's orders on behalf of the crew, and for Navy presence, besides Stirk as gunner, he had seven Royal Marines.

He had no qualms about taking a direct commanding role. This was in essence a privateer turned smuggler when trade was slack, and he'd been a privateer captain himself at one time, a reasonably successful one at that.

Pearl slipped to sea, with her exceptional sea-keeping fore-and-aft rig easily able to stay with the buoyed passage to Five Fathom Hole, and then it was the open ocean.

The seas were still up, angry combers with spindrift curling from their crests, and the little sloop with her low freeboard saw green water over her decks, but gamely took it all in her sea-kindly way.

Providence was nowhere in sight but these seas did not favour a stout merchant brig, with bluff bows doggedly punching into the rollers. It was somewhere ahead, but with no tops aloft, *Pearl*'s radius of sighting anything would only be in the region of eight miles or so on either beam.

It was going to be a hard flog into the teeth of the blow.

The logical strategy was to set course for the American

coast employing a zigzag either side to give them the best chance of intercepting.

The day wore on, the winds marginally easing, and by nightfall they were seething along at an astonishing speed, perhaps some five knots faster than *Thunderer* in the same conditions.

They plunged into the night. The possibility of laying the brig by the heels was now slight. During that long period of darkness Kydd knew that with daybreak there had to be a decision.

But in the cold hours before dawn things changed. The wind veered more into the north-west and the bluster decreased to a fresh gale. Directly before them was the immensity of the North American continent. *Providence*'s captain would want to get his precious cargo securely into American hands just as soon as he could. The coast ahead had the two chief sea-ports of Savannah and Charleston. Charleston was the more attractive for it was where the United States Navy had its being and would most value their prize.

Kydd saw that he could claw an advantage by giving up the chase. He would take a direct course for Charleston, knowing that with his Bermuda sloop he could get there in one board while the square-rigged *Providence* had to make at least one tack about. As well, the three headsails on the huge bowsprit, with the balancing enormous length main boom extending well past the stern, gave her the soaring sail area that made her the fastest craft on the high seas.

A pallid dawn having broken, Kydd bounded on deck to see the mate lugubriously staring forward. 'I've a yen to see what *Pearl* can do, given her head, Mr Mate. All sail conformable, if you please.'

Astonished, the man gaped at him.

'Now, sir. And course – west b' north,' Kydd added. That

would take care of the considerable force of the north-setting Gulf Stream across their bows.

Kydd took in the sequence – jibs, the unreefed main hauled out to the boom end, lines thrumming with an exhilarating promise of power.

She flew. A cast of the log gave the phenomenal figure of fourteen knots and a whisker, an extraordinary speed. Mile after mile close-hauled in the flat, hard, driving blast. It was wet, uncomfortable in the unforgiving continuous thumping progress, but the most exciting sailing Kydd could recall.

There was no question: they would be off Charleston well before the brig, whatever her standing as a fast sailer. The legendary chart would be theirs, but *if*, and *only if*, Kydd's reasoning was correct and that was where they were headed. And *if* they could contrive the capture of a larger ship in sight of its refuge and safety.

Chapter 44

They reached the waters off Charleston in the early morning, giving them the opportunity to quarter the seas to see if *Providence* had by some phenomenon arrived, but she was nowhere to be seen.

Kydd laid *Pearl* out of sight offshore under easy sail and considered his position.

Unlike the chronometer-led precision navigation of the Royal Navy the merchant service often had a hazy idea of where they were in terms of longitude. Therefore the last miles before making landfall before a port were generally covered by proceeding in along the known line of latitude of that port. *Pearl* would be waiting along this line, a privateer trick he'd use for himself.

All day they cruised under reduced sail with no sign of their quarry. Dusk drew in, and with it all the anxieties of the night and despairing thoughts of how long he should stay, given that Savannah was a near equal prospect – and they could be landing their stolen treasure there at this very moment.

The night passed agonisingly slowly, with Kydd frustrated

but determined to see it through, to stand athwart the line for another three days. If nothing by then, he must return, defeated.

But as the grey seascape gained colour and the darkness retreated, his black mood was banished in an instant. Revealed by the advancing daybreak a sizeable trading brig was coming towards them, whose lines could only be those of *Providence.*

Catching his breath, Kydd roared the orders that saw men racing to quarters, while he took in the tactical situation. It had been a long time since he'd gone into action under fore-and-aft rig but it came back quickly.

First, the preliminaries. The brig would have no doubts about what was happening and would have to decide quickly whether to yield or fight. He would help them make up their mind.

'Helm down! Take us around and come up under her larboard quarter.' This was what he would have ordered on a Navy man-o'-war but with the mate looking at him, confused, he realised that under the present arrangement it was supposed he would directly command, not issue orders to some sailing master.

He corrected himself and *Pearl* fell off the wind to come in a half-circle to off the brig's larboard stern where he could hail their quarterdeck.

He nearly forgot. 'Get the ensign up, you lubbers.' No ship might fire on another without due display of its colours and soon they knew they had the King's Navy to face.

Aboard *Providence* they flew none, as was the usual practice at sea but after a pause a flag broke at the masthead, the Stars and Stripes of the United States of America. It meant not only an act of defiance but that the ship intended to fight.

'Ship ahoy!' Kydd bellowed, not bothering with a speaking trumpet. 'In the name of King George, I order you to heave to and be boarded!'

In response there was a ragged cheer and the crash of a gun, then several more, six-pounders, the same calibre as themselves. If it was going to be a fight the odds had considerably shortened.

'Mr Stirk?' he bawled down to the maindeck, where guns were being run out.

Stirk loped up, his expression unreadable. He was responsible to Kydd for getting a scratch crew he didn't know to fight guns he was not sure of, and against a bigger opponent.

He stopped before his captain and, without hesitation, touched his forelock. It affected Kydd. Uncountable years before he'd been part of Stirk's gun crew and to have this fine seaman make obeisance to him at this time was touching.

'Toby. Where's the best gun? We're not going to beat 'em with numbers, it'll have to be by accuracy.' And with Stirk at the firing lanyard.

'Number two starboard,' he said, without hesitation. 'They're most in dimber shape seein' they's f'r the merchantry, if'n ye needs a broadside.'

'Get there and be ready for me . . . cully,' he said quietly.

Now things were hotting up. A ball whistled within ten feet of him, punching a neat hole in the straining mainsail and a cry from forward was someone taking a hit. Kydd realised *Providence* must have a substantial crew to reload so fast.

At the same time he had to face that this was no savage one-to-one naval engagement between vessels of equal strength and endurance. His was a light and fast flyer, no ship-of-the-line. And, critically, here was where her fore-and-aft rig was to her distinct disadvantage. If her single huge mainsail was carried away in its gear they were instantly disabled and out of the fight. A square-sail-rigged ship, however, would carry forward with her several remaining sails.

But, gloriously, he was aware that he had a trump card that

could see *Pearl* the victor. He, Sir Thomas Kydd, was of the Royal Navy, heir to traditions and techniques of war centuries old – and he was matched against a merchant-service captain who, however courageous and astute, had none of it.

Raking, topsail backing, quarter boarding, the man would have no understanding or way of defending. Kydd would treat this as a naval engagement. 'Wear about,' he demanded of the mate, at which *Pearl* wheeled about in a determined pirouette that laid her squarely across *Providence*'s stern cabin ready for a fine raking shot. Stirk needed no orders, and along the deck her guns cracked out and rapidly made a dismal ruin of the other ship's stern-quarters.

Without pause, *Pearl* came to the wind on the opposite quarter of *Providence* where Kydd had his deciding manoeuvre ready. Sending word to Stirk, he carefully took up position and, after a considered pause, number-two gun starboard opened up.

One by one, precisely aimed balls slammed across the quarterdeck of the hapless brig. The pitiless shot slamming in caused the officers to fall prostrate. Those at the helm abandoned it and scattered. The ship was sent into a spiral of disorder that could only end in one way.

As *Pearl* came around for another pass the colours were jerked down angrily and it was all over.

Kydd took away *Pearl*'s boat with Stirk and five of his marines to claim possession. He was met at the bulwarks by a fierce and sullen captain.

'I am led to understand you have on board this vessel the persons of one Abe Gavery and Rebecca Holt. I demand you deliver them up to me in the King's name.'

The man stared back at him in astonishment.

'This moment, sir. Else I shall ask my men to make search and they are not disposed to be gentle.'

The pair emerged from the after hatch, and when Rebecca saw Kydd she threw herself at him, tears streaking. 'Oh, the good Lord be praised! I'm saved!' she sobbed, clinging to him.

He wrenched free of her but she continued, looking up at him in adoration, 'I've been abducted by this wicked creature and never thought I'd be rescued by you, Sir Thomas. If there's anything I can do for you, I beg ask it.'

There were baffled growls from Gavery, who tried to reach her, but Kydd intervened.

'There is indeed, Miss Holt,' he said, stony-faced. 'You have in your possession a remarkably figured Turkish carpet. I'd very much like to view it.'

As if a mask had been torn away her features turned venomous.

'Come, come, Miss Rebecca, we have witnesses.'

She did not respond, but the captain helpfully offered, 'We have it becketed up under the deckhead aft, keeps it out of the weather as they asks it.'

He led the way, and there, wrapped in the canvas of an old sail, was the governor's carpet.

'Take it down, if you will,' Kydd asked, hiding his elation.

It was lowered to the deck, its fastenings cut loose and carefully it was unrolled. There for all to see was the south-east corner of Captain Hurd's infinitely precious sea chart of Bermuda, neatly interleaved between the rolls of the carpet and further protected by a light cloth on both sides.

The shocked look on the captain's face was evidence that he'd thought only to be aiding an eloping pair but Kydd had no compunction.

'I'm taking this vessel in charge, sir. To return to Bermuda immediately.'

Chapter 45

Monte Rosa

'Do have another of these cakes, Kit. They're most toothsome indeed,' Bowden said warmly, pushing the dish towards Roscoe.

'Thanks, old fellow. Rather feel the need for something sweet and delightful that doesn't leave a sour taste for the acquaintance.'

Persephone hid a smile and dispatched the maid for more.

'So all is now square and, er, a-taunto, my dearest?' she enquired of Kydd, sprawled comfortably in a wicker chair in the sun.

'I think we may safely say it, Seph. They are the spies right enough, but it's not thought a good idea to make public the business with the Hurd chart, so we arranged that if they stand mumchance on the subject, they'll only face charges of theft of public property. We haven't any real evidence anyway on the spying but now they're known, they're harmless.'

'What about the villainous rogues who helped 'em steal the chart?'

'Shipped back to England, they'll be transported to Van Diemen's Land, I wouldn't be surprised.'

'Not so wonderful for some,' muttered Harris.

'How so?' Kydd said, opening one eye.

'Here in Bermuda nothing ever happens worthy to set in bold print and get tongues wagging. Now I've been privy to the most exciting motions this age and I'm told to hold fire with my quill. Vexing to a degree, is it not?'

'Have another slice of rum cake, Edwin,' Persephone said soothingly. 'I'm sanguine something will happen soon.'

'Here? Nobody ever—'

He was interrupted by the sudden appearance of the lieutenant aide of the dockyard commodore.

'Sir Thomas!'

'Come aboard, old fellow,' Kydd murmured, wondering what the devil he wanted.

His conscience was clear. *Thunderer* had been repaired and in a week or so he might consider another cruise, this time to the north. But Commodore Evans had no operational authority, so why the rather inconvenient interruption?

'Sir! Most urgent, um, and private.'

Kydd heaved himself out of his chair and took the anxious lieutenant deeper into the garden, where the jasmine and oleander were particularly fragrant.

'Well?'

'The commodore has had a communication direct from their lordships only this past hour. In it they desire him to discover where you may be and pass on their direct order that you proceed to sea within the shortest possible time for Portsmouth and orders.'

The urgency was plain – the reason for it was not.

'Do they say why?'

'Er, I'm not personally acquainted with the dispatch, Sir

Thomas, but I'm led to believe by the commodore that there have been grave developments on the continent involving Bonaparte.'

Kydd was being recalled.

It could only mean that the situation in Europe had taken a turn for the worse for some fearful reason. His time on this balmy paradise had suddenly come to an end.

Chapter 46

Dresden

'Gently, *mon brave*,' Jean-Baptiste Moreau grumbled, 'You're not fettling a warhorse.' The donning of dress uniform for an adjutant commandant of the Imperial General Staff, with its profusion of buttons, epaulettes and all manner of finery, was not to be hurried. Boyer, his valued manservant, obediently eased the tightening.

The elaborate toilette was for a formal appearance at the Grand Quartier Général Impérial, Emperor Napoleon Bonaparte's headquarters, as a member of his inner Military Household, as distinct from Minister for War Berthier's more field-oriented Army General headquarters. He'd been asked for by Bonaparte himself to head the *corps des ingénieurs-géographe*, the body under Général de Brigade Bacler d'Albe and his *bureau topographique* responsible for the vast folios of maps and field guides necessary for the planning and direction of campaigns. Although an engineer, Moreau's sense of fitness for the siting of guns and possibilities for the bridging of rivers had recommended him to the

Emperor, himself an artillery specialist, and a certain regard had developed.

At the moment an armistice was in place, that of Pläswitz, a near-miraculous achievement by Bonaparte to halt the tide of vengeful enemies flooding across Europe. This had threatened to overwhelm what remained of the army that had suffered humiliation and ruination in the disastrous retreat from Moscow. It had now held for close on six weeks and Bonaparte had not been idle, working himself and his staff mercilessly to make good the gaping deficiencies in his forces.

Although exhausted after the ferocious trials of the retreat, and aching to see his family with every fibre of his being, Moreau was impressed by the feat and grateful for his safe existence here in the ancient splendour of Dresden. Holding the line in Germany was now a barrier to the invading horde: could there be hope at last that under Bonaparte's genius the long fight back could be won?

The dinner was a commingling of the Military Household and Berthier's major general's headquarters, nominally hosted by the young Prince Eugène de Beauharnais, stepson of the Emperor, in his own right an able general.

It was a glittering occasion. Gold, scarlet, white and blue of the very highest brilliance, immaculately coiffured tonsures, rouge and fragrant salves in discreet abundance, and the most exquisite manners on display.

At one end of the long table the prince took his place, an affable and generous host, while Moreau found his halfway along, opposite a nervous senior aide de camp and a red-faced *général de division*. Light talk eddied about until the blare of trumpets outside announced their principal guest and there was a general scrambling to rise.

Emperor Napoleon Bonaparte briskly strode to his chair

and, after exchanging bows of acknowledgement, took his seat to the right of the host.

Moreau knew something was in the wind for without winsome ladies on hand Napoleon wouldn't spend his valuable time on mere entertainments. Soon after conversations resumed and wine had gone round, the Emperor raised his voice and theatrically hailed Berthier, seated at the other end of the table.

'Hey now, *mes vieille culottes*, what do you think of our situation now, then?'

It was clearly an offer to hold forth but Berthier took his time, wiping his mouth with a lace napkin and avoiding eyes until the table had fallen silent.

'Grave times, *mon empereur*,' he said ponderously, 'but not serious.' This brought small titters from around the table.

'We have the traitor Bernadotte with the Army of the North; all Prussians and Swedes trying to be useful to the Coalition; with Blücher and the Army of Silesia struggling to hold together a mixed circus of Prussians and Russians further south. The benighted Bennigsen and the Army of Poland are attempting to bring a horde of raw Russian peasants to the centre but, of course, the Army of Bohemia under Schwarzenberg remains the greatest mischief.

'All is of a tangle, however, for we have both Tsar Alexander and Frederick William of Prussia in the field with their troops and arguing loudly over how a war should be done. In numbers, not as if any true *briscard* might take fright.'

Moreau hid a cynical smile. There would be none at this table who would be unaware of the strategics. This recitation had to be for another purpose.

'Oh, talking of numbers, what's the latest figure you have for our own strength?' Bonaparte said easily, quite as if he hadn't before him the tally down to the last detail. 'Taking into account our recent and very effective recruiting measures.'

Berthier eased and looked about the table – a little smugly, Moreau thought.

'Our strength? As of the last three days and well into this very fortunate armistice we have an astonishing count. Gentlemen, I give you the grand total of over a quarter-million under arms and near a thousand guns – which at the present rate bids fair to approach our order of battle before the Russian campaign.'

There were gasps of awe as the news was digested. The extended conscription plan and a rapid transfer of assets from Spain, with a cunning scheme to move the National Guard wholesale into the regular army, had succeeded beyond expectations and now the Grande Armée was a continental force again.

'No wonder the Allies clamoured for an armistice,' chuckled a *général de brigade.*

'As not forgetting they were well stung at Lützen,' muttered another, lifting his brandy glass in salute. As in the old days, this recent battle had Napoleon rolling triumphant over his foes, sending the Russian commander, Wittgenstein, into a hasty retreat.

'It was Bautzen that did for 'em,' growled a moustachioed general. Even more recently, another battle in the old style took advantage of their increase in troops, now able to outnumber Blücher's Prussians and Russians combined. But for their acute shortage of cavalry, Bonaparte would have crushed and routed the fleeing allies.

Despite his weariness, Moreau felt a lifting of spirit – this was something like the old days of victories, not the grinding misery of endless retreat. He knew of the success of the recruitment campaign but to hear it spelled out before all made a glorious return so believable. Which was why Bonaparte had turned on this show for them, of course.

The mood lightened, the chatter resumed, but Moreau dared a response. 'Shall we hear what our most illustrious commander-in-chief has in mind for our future plans?'

It was preposterous to seek such openly, but Moreau suspected it would not be an unwelcome question, given the implied reason for the gathering.

Napoleon gave a good-natured start, as though he'd been caught out by the demand and, with a slight bow in his direction, began, 'You'll understandably keep this to yourselves but these are my thoughts. We shall have Germany as our shield and safeguard against the barbarians, using the Elbe and Main as our line of defence while we gather strength. I shall take Hamburg from Bernadotte, and as for the Prussians, we shall then crush 'em as we've done so often in the past. I'm not concerned with them. And the Russians will come to their senses before very long, recognising they have a supply train stretching across half of Europe and will start to feel isolated – they'll need to retire to their borders to recover.

'Austria is dithering as usual, Metternich doesn't know where to turn after our victories and still in alliance will certainly not declare war upon us, leaving just the perfidious Britons, who prefer to sit it out on the water, refusing to come upon the land to fight it out, man to man. Gentlemen, our destiny is to winter in Germany, gaining strength day by day, and when the time is ripe to resume the mantle of empire as is our sovereign right as Frenchmen.'

The room erupted into a bedlam of acclamation and joy. There was no doubting the warmth and admiration for the man. This was what it was to be part of the greatest military machine in history and Moreau was humbled and elated.

'Do excuse me, I have duties that may not be put aside.' Bonaparte stood, his aides instantly by him, and with gracious nods left and right, departed.

Moreau knew this would be an appearance before his soldiers, one that the Emperor set great store by, and he followed.

A company of infantry was drawn up in the courtyard, an officer waiting, an eagle proudly held, the ranks in open order for inspection. Each motionless, rigid.

Moreau recognised them as Grenadiers, the battalion elite, steadfast and reliable, who had seen it through at Bautzen and countless other encounters.

Striding out purposefully, Bonaparte came to a stop before them, his gaze sweeping the ranks. Without taking his eyes off them, he spoke briefly to the officer with drawn sword, his escort and in charge of the men.

Then he began, slowly, at one end of the front rank. Moreau could see there was no deceiving, a waggish realigning of a cross-belt here, a sniff at a musket lock there – the Emperor knew all the tricks.

Eventually he came to a slightly shorter individual towards the centre and stopped before him with a frown. The man visibly paled – then Napoleon Bonaparte spoke to him. 'I know you!' he said, after a considered pause. 'Now let me see, it was Marengo, was it not? I remember you, old fellow. As brave a cock-sparrow in the fighting as ever I saw that day! Tell me, did they ever notice your spirit? You wear no decoration.'

'N-no, *mon empereur*, they didn't.'

Napoleon gave a grimace, hesitated. Then his hand went to his own Legion of Honour, unclasped it and pinned it to the old soldier's chest. 'There now, and I hope my own will be sufficient to right the omission.'

The man was now openly weeping, and Napoleon clapped him on the shoulder. 'Brace up, *le géant*, I'll have much need of your sort before very long.'

Chapter 47

Thunderer, *at sea*

The beat across the Atlantic was unremarkable under the steady urging of the south-westerlies and a greying of the seas as the spiteful autumn weather of the British Isles set in. Kydd was robbed of Persephone's company by the immediate nature of his recall. Required to stay to see to the finalising of the lease of Monte Rosa, and disposal of domestic effects, she would follow later.

Over on the beam, plunging and rising, was *Weazel.* Kydd had given Bowden the opportunity to be escort over the nondescript five-ship convoy to England. He'd be shepherding them into Falmouth while Kydd went on to Portsmouth to discover why he'd been so abruptly ordered back.

The Lizard hove into view, after a long overseas voyage its welcome sight half hidden behind rain-squalls, a smother of white at its foot where Atlantic rollers found land at last.

After Bermuda the cold bluster was a shock and Kydd shuddered at the chill of the winds across the quarterdeck, but many of the ship's company had found duties that required them to be up on deck within sight of their native land.

There were scores of sail, a token of the unbreakable river of trade that was the source of England's strength.

On the other side of the peninsula a frigate of the Channel Squadron had the effrontery to throw out the challenge to *Thunderer*, quickly answered with the correct response.

Weazel parted company, taking her convoy into Falmouth, and the same brisk south-westerly saw *Thunderer* making good time to their final destination and anchorage, Portsmouth.

Until he'd made his number with the port admiral and claimed his orders, anything was possible, including a stern instruction to proceed immediately to strengthen the blockade squadrons off the French coast. This would imply no liberty ashore and also the hard work to victual and water first and would be unpopular.

Thunderer took in sail, the anchor plunged into the muddy grey waters and the big ship found her rest.

'Hands to priddy decks, no liberty for now,' Kydd told Roscoe, and without delay took his barge into the Signal Station landing, hurrying up the weed-slimed steps.

The port admiral, an officer Kydd did not know, was nevertheless effusive in his greeting and he wondered why.

'Your orders, Sir Thomas,' he said warmly, handing over a thin pack. 'Do you desire the privacy of my office to acquaint yourself of their contents?'

Even more unusual. 'Thank you, sir. That would be kind in you.' Was this so that the man would learn what they contained?

The orders were in the usual sealed packet, the Admiralty cipher in plain view. He broke the seal.

Behind the time-honoured verbiage was a simple direction. As of this date he was to assume the responsibility and dignity of the rank of commodore of the second class, to hold himself ready for a particular service that would be advised in due course.

Commodore! He'd been in the rank before, in the Adriatic, but that had been more or less an artifice to allow him to command a flotilla of frigates. 'Of the second class' meant there would be post-captains under him, but no ships-of-the-line.

It was certainly notice – a promotion, even, hoisting a commodore's pennant – but after the particular service he must inevitably strike his flag and revert to post-captain.

However, it meant that the spectre of dreary duty, being part of the blockade fleet in winter seas, was no longer to be feared. He wondered why he'd been chosen and just what the service was.

'There are no further orders?'

'None.'

The concluding paragraph required him to store to five days' notice for sea, implying some urgency in the matter. The service therefore must be important.

'Sir, you'd oblige me with your opinion. These orders appoint me commodore for a particular service without explanation. Do you think—'

'Sir Thomas, I'm as much ignorant in the question as you. I can only counsel patience. Your supplementary orders must arrive soon.'

There was a note of resignation in his voice, and Kydd realised he'd been aware of his elevation but had been hoping that the packet would satisfy his curiosity.

On the way back Kydd glanced around. Was it his

imagination or was the wartime drab of the port more grey and bleak than he remembered?

'Well, Mr Roscoe.' There was a marked stillness on deck as all strained to hear their fate. 'Two things. We shan't be here for long as we've been chosen for a particular service, but I will allow liberty for the hands on a daily basis. Have you a shilling?'

'Er . . . here, sir.'

'Then we shall toss for the first liberty. Come, now – are the larbowlines heads or tails?'

Kydd flipped the coin and hid the result.

'Tails, the rogues.'

'So it is, Mr Roscoe. The second: do you bend on a commodore's pennant and hoist it this hour.'

He turned and went below, leaving them to their excited babble.

The wardroom had already taken hold of a goodly pile of newspapers and eagerly absorbed the intelligence and gossip of the day. Kydd borrowed the *Morning Chronicle* and settled down in his armchair.

News – only a brace of days old, instead of several weeks and reading almost as if it were history. He turned to the first page. Napoleon Bonaparte. He'd been victorious in yet another encounter. Not having followed the Emperor's recent progress, its name and place on the continent were meaningless to Kydd. He would get more when he received the intelligence due a commodore.

Further in there was talk of failed harvests, bread prices out of reach, and riots in the north over the use of machinery to replace manual workers. Britain's survival and ability to conduct the war needed a robust factory system to ensure that the subsidy of arms and equipment that kept the Coalition supplied and in the field was continued, but at the cost of so much misery?

He'd noticed on the streets people were much less conspicuous in their dress, presumably out of wartime thrift but it was a saddening prospect. Even the newspaper he held felt more flimsy, makeshift.

He threw off the mood but one impression stayed. If Bonaparte was fighting back and succeeding, this war was going to last for a long time – with only one to prevail at the end.

His supplementary orders arrived two days later, but they only deepened the mystery. In terse phrases they desired his presence with all dispatch not at the Admiralty but at Horse Guards, its equivalent for the Army. A new-minted commodore to report to Horse Guards? It made no sense.

Chapter 48

Kydd posted to London, the immediacy of the summons reason enough for the expense, but he took the precaution of verifying his orders at the office of the First Lord at the Admiralty, close by Horse Guards.

The clerk, world-weary and short with him, suggested he follow orders and present himself as named and particularised.

And in the unfamiliar and exotic surroundings of the Army's highest situation, his distinctive naval uniform attracting unabashed stares, he was told that no one had any interest in him whatsoever.

His orders, however, were plain and unequivocal so he left for his club, with the understanding that he would be sent for when they'd discovered why he'd been summoned.

Even the august Brooks's was showing signs of malaise: peeling gilt here and there, fading draperies, worn furniture. And when his friend Prinker bustled up, he was uncharacteristically subdued.

'You've been away all year, Tiger, so you've no idea how low in the water we feel.'

'Why so, old chap?'

'Do recollect, m' good friend, it's now a whole twenty years we've been whanging away at the French and no result. Twenty years! As I was a green younker when it all started and now . . .'

He tailed off, leaving Kydd to recall that he, too, had been a raw youth when it all began, pressed into a navy at war and the old eighteenth-century certainties fast disappearing into the past.

The world was wearying of wars and the scale of carnage on a continental scale, armies of half a million locked in a mortal struggle one with another, and villainous taxation to support it all. When would it end for good?

Prinker grimaced. 'And now we hear Boney has conjured himself a mighty army again and is making ready to fall on the Ivans and the rest. Who knows? This time he might win!'

Kydd's mysterious mission must be connected with it in some way and he quailed at the thought of being swept up in some gigantic confrontation. 'Never mind, Prinker. While we've got a stout navy, we're sure to come in first.'

He didn't sleep well that night, and it wasn't just the thought of Persephone and Francis crossing a wild autumn Atlantic without him. He feared that the next few weeks would be hard and perilous – and who knew the outcome?

Chapter 49

Early the next morning Kydd had a visitor.

'Meares, lieutenant colonel, 91st Regiment o' Foot. Come to welcome and escort you to Horse Guards.'

He was shortly being ushered into an office of consequence, the dark walls well decorated with captured flags, frowning military portraits and campaign trophies of years past.

Several men were standing in a group near a long table, watching him enter. The individual in the centre was in general's full-dress uniform and wore a patrician frown.

'Sir, may I present Commodore Sir Thomas Kydd,' Meares intoned, and turned to Kydd. 'Sir Thomas, this is Lieutenant General Sir Thomas Graham.'

Bows were stiffly exchanged.

'My apologies for the misunderstanding, Sir Thomas. You see, we were rather expecting an admiral and staff.'

Kydd hesitated only a moment, then drew himself up importantly. 'Should there be need of extended capability at sea in this venture, it shall be made available as needs suggest.'

'Hmm. Then shall we begin?'

It was a planning council and Kydd was a latecomer. He was quickly advised of the purpose but given little time to digest it.

Once again, for the fourth time in these wars, the British were going to make an assault on Antwerp. Less than a hundred miles to the eastward – not more than a day's sail – the city had been called 'A pistol pointed at the heart of England'. Kydd knew from his clandestine reconnaissance not so long before that the French had made it a naval base of size and were still industriously building up an invasion fleet there.

The last attempt at reducing it, in 1809, had failed. Walcheren had gone down in history as the last time that Britain had landed troops on the mainland of Europe. The country had suffered a gross defeat, not from the French but as a result of deadly miasmic fevers. Kydd had not been involved and had only a hazy idea of what had happened. That he was to be part of this latest try was not what he would have wished for.

Graham intervened smoothly, 'I hardly think the Navy has any major purpose in this campaign but nevertheless it's comforting to know any evacuation contemplated will be attended to in the traditional way.'

The discussions moved on. Much was made of the order of landing, the seniority of commanders and the role of cavalry and artillery. Kydd, though, had seen service in both the Egyptian and Cape Town landings and had more than a little distrust of plans made in ignorance of the immediate position.

'And when in place at Willemstad we will—'

Kydd quickly took in the map of the Low Countries spread out before him. 'Sir, I'm in accord with your dispositions, but Willemstad? How will you reach this port – up the river, past the fortresses and in the lee of Amsterdam?'

'Damn it, sir! My orders are clear – get the boats there and land the regiments to set up suitable arrangements to supply my fighting battalions.'

'Sir, the Scheldt is notorious for its sandbanks and mud-flats. Should you add the complications of tides and contrary currents then—'

'Commodore,' Graham ground out, 'what is this to me? Your remit is to land us to time and place, not point out imaginary difficulties. I expect you to do so, sir.'

Kydd held his temper in check. 'General, these are no imaginary obstacles. They—'

'Sir, I was advised you were a senior and experienced officer, well used to conjoint operations – Egypt, the Cape were mentioned. If now you find this vital enterprise not to your taste, I shall approach the Admiralty for another. The times are perilous, and delay is not to be countenanced.'

'I am fully aware of my duty,' Kydd bit off, 'which is to afford the Army the means to achieve their goal – but only in so far as it is within my power to command same.'

'Then could I suggest you retire to consider your position and return a workable scheme to land our forces safely at Willemstad?' Graham said cuttingly. 'You would then favour Colonel Meares with an early presentation of your plans – say, some days hence?'

Boiling with resentment, Kydd took his leave. It was no use rebelling, however, for should the First Lord learn of his disinclination to serve in this position it would mark him for all time as an unsound choice for higher commands.

He became aware that someone had fallen into step beside him. It was Meares, wearing a comically anxious expression. 'Sir Thomas, I'll have you know our tribe is not all of his stripe, sir.'

Kydd couldn't help a smile. 'Colonel, and I'll have *you* know that this is not my first acquaintance with the breed.'

With a relieved grin, Meares added, 'My office? Quiet and nearby, we need to talk.'

It was small and crowded with drawers, maps and staff impedimenta but chairs were found and the orderly sergeant sent away.

'Sir, you'll understand that this bold venture is very important to us in all respects.'

'Why so?'

Meares laid out the politics of it all. Antwerp possessed sufficient men-o'-war and an invasion fleet and these were positioned within a day's sail of London. It unnerved the British war council, who tried to make it a prime objective for the advancing armies of the Sixth Coalition. The nearest army, Prussians under Blücher, refused, saying that it should remain as a besieged outpost in their rear to be left isolated as they swept past.

Until now the enemy had been on the run and the four separate advancing columns would compete to be the first to make the most direct lunge into the heart of France to the gates of Paris and weren't about to be distracted.

There were, however, rumours about Bonaparte's army being inexplicably swollen to near what it was before Moscow, which only made the Allies nervous at having to face a gargantuan fight to the finish with assets bled away on a difficult siege.

It all added up to one single conclusion: if the British wanted Antwerp so badly they were welcome to take it themselves.

Apart from Spain, there were no British troops on the mainland of Europe, bar a paltry showing with Bernadotte in Swedish Pomerania. It was a frightful thought to contemplate that in this landing they could suffer from the same curse that had damned all previous attempts.

Slowly, realisation crept in upon Kydd. He would be in charge of the seaborne assault, and if it did not succeed, he would go down in history as the man who had failed England at its time of greatest need.

Too appalled to speak, he heard Meares continue about the regiments and guns assigned and barely took in that there was apparently a shockingly small number for such an objective. The gunfire support for the landings was to be supplied by the Navy, as were the flat-boats and flanking gunboats and, of course, the all-important transports to convey Graham's forces across the Channel.

Kydd had heard nothing of this from the Admiralty, who seemed to think that this was naught to do with them. Graham was clearly piling all responsibility on him so that, in the case of a disaster, his would not be the blame.

It was the first armed assault on Europe since 1809 and, although a flag-officer, he wasn't even to have planning staff for an action to take place within a very short time. It was lunatic!

Kydd looked Meares in the eye. 'Colonel, which plans have you seen in respect of what happens after getting ashore?'

'Oh. Well, not so many. General Graham is very busy at the moment, I have to tell you, and—'

'I thought as much. This whole business is shamefully hurried, brought along to satisfy hastily conceived political objectives and altogether premature. Colonel, you and I must think hard on what can still be done.'

Meares rocked back in consternation. 'You mean . . .'

'I do. There have been neither instructions nor detailed plans given me by the Admiralty either. It's assumed, I believe, that I will make my own way in the matter of planning and execution.'

He deliberated for a moment, then asked, 'Your general. What's his nature? That is to say, is he a fire-breather in action or is he more, shall we say, contemplative in his motions?'

'I, er, would account him a more than ordinary man of honour in the article of courage and initiative, Sir Thomas. Until lately, in the Iberian peninsula, where he gained the entire approbation of the Duke of Wellington.'

Kydd leaned forward. 'Sir, you may tell me your feelings in full,' he said softly. 'I assure you, nothing will go further.'

Meares gave a brief smile. 'A difficult man to satisfy. Aristocratic and cool, he has many high-placed friends both here in Horse Guards and in Parliament.'

'An officer much given to trust that his subordinates will act in accordance with his orders?'

'If I might be frank on the question . . .'

'Pray be so.'

'He does believe his orders are carried out in their entirety in exactly the same tenor as those given to his servant, unquestioned and not requiring confirmation.'

'Then he will believe I shall follow his instructions and land his troops at Willemstad without troubling to know the details.'

'That would seem to be the case,' Meares said carefully.

Kydd gave a secret smile. 'Then I conceive we have a means to an end,' he said enigmatically. 'By the way, old fellow, why Willemstad? It's well in the north, Antwerp in the south . . .'

'Our gallant general is not one to provide reasons for his orders, but I'm of the opinion it's because being far from positions of strategical significance it'll be thinly defended, all the better than landing troops under heavy fire close to Antwerp.'

It made sense, but why not take a coastal town and have the Navy safeguard the flow of stores and supplies?

Kydd garnered as much information as he could about the magnitude of his task, numbers of fighting soldiers, their paraphernalia, where located and so forth, then made his excuses.

Chapter 50

Crossing to the Admiralty telegraph office in the next building, Commodore Kydd transmitted a direction to Roscoe to sail his flagship to Sheerness with all dispatch. In this fair westerly *Thunderer* should be at the anchorage in a day or two.

This would form his headquarters where he would have about him those of sound nauticals who knew what they should do in response to his orders, and blessedly, where he would have somewhere of his own to lay his head.

In the meantime as a matter of urgency he had to find some wise soul, who knew the Low Countries from the point of view of naval operations, to alert him of the hazards of wind, tide and the enemy.

He could try the Admiralty offices but a new-made flag-officer wandering around asking what he should do would probably not be in his best interests.

A name came to mind. Bazely. The salty brig-sloop commander had been one of his closest friends and had been centrally involved in the hopeless failure that had been the

Walcheren expedition. He would be able to tell in the smallest detail what he had to face.

But would he be in town? When Kydd arrived at his lodgings at the Albany, he found he was in luck.

The older seaman was much the same, his face now lined and fringed with grey and with it he was a trifle more corpulent but still strong-voiced and upright.

His features creased with pleasure. 'Well, I'm blessed if'n it isn't Tom Cutlass, now cap'n of his very own sail-o'-the-line! Come in, come in, ye're most welcome.'

Kydd had dressed in plain clothes out of deference to him, a mere unrated sloop commander. 'My dear fellow. So good to see you after all these years. Do I find you in health?'

'You do, you do.' He chuckled. 'An' I see one before me as is sleek as an otter, nothing t' do with wearing a collar, yes?'

'Collar? Oh, Persephone keeps me on a long leash, never fear.' Bazely, a long-time bachelor, valued his freedom too much ever to have succumbed to female wiles.

'It's not a-frolicking ye've come for, is it?'

'Not as who should say,' Kydd replied uncomfortably. 'More in the line of advice.'

'Certainly. A drop o' the right true sort?' His hand went to the bell cord.

'A small one,' Kydd said absently. Was it right to involve this uncomplicated and loyal friend in what amounted to political decisions?

'So fire away, then.'

'Well . . . for my sins I've been taken up as a commodore, for the nonce, of course, and the post is not one I'd choose for myself.' He took a long pull at his whisky and continued, 'It rather seems I'm to take the Army in a descent on Antwerp.'

'Good God – another Walcheren!' Bazely's expression hardened. 'Have they learned nothing, the witless simkins?' he rasped. He collected himself and went on tightly, 'Ye'd better tell me what they're serving you, an' all.'

Kydd explained events. Bazely leaned back and regarded him with hooded eyes. 'An' you're the loon who'd think it his duty to wander in an' die – am I right?'

'I have to go.'

'I thought ye would say that. So what's the plan?'

'None worth a spit,' Kydd said bitterly. 'This benighted general has his gaze fixed on a landing at Willemstad, which is—'

'I know where Willemstad is well enough, cuffin. And the rest o' the God-forsaken mud-holes. So why's he want to broach the length of the Hollands Deep, as is thick wi' guns all the way, and leagues from Antwerp? Why not—'

'Orders.'

'You'll not do it, Tom, m' friend. Nothing deep draught, can't fight y' way through. Shore never more'n a hundred yards off the navigable channel, easy targets for the Mongseer artillery.'

'I said, orders.'

'This is not to mention the waterways – currents shifting wi' the tide state, mud-banks changing position as they will, this time o' the year could be ice – don't do it, Tom, I beg o' you!'

'If I show craven, their lordships won't have any mercy, Bazely. I have to move on it.'

His friend gazed at him with an affecting look of respect and fondness, then briskly drained his whisky and slapped down the glass. 'Then let's see what'll fadge.' He looked away for a space, then turned back with an animated expression. 'He's left the details t' you. It has to include all measures taken t' achieve the object. So – we makes our own landing, an' it's miles from Willemstad as will cause 'em a sore distraction, callin' away their troops, thinkin' that's where we're makin' our assault.'

'Where?' Kydd demanded, seizing hopefully on the 'we're'.

'A place I've a right good memory of, on an island – Walcheren itself.'

'What?'

'Roompot, in the north, at the seaward tip, has a small wharf. It's where we evacuated when . . .'

Kydd said nothing, letting Bazely gather his thoughts.

'Give 'em a day or two to wake up and quit Willemstad then send in y'r boats.'

'Nothing deep-draught.'

'Plenty of flat-boats about. What the Hollanders call *schuyts*. Soldiery board from transports offshore under the guns o' *Thunderer* and proceed up the Hollands Deep with something like a well-handled sloop ahead t' test the waters.'

Kydd stroked his chin. It sounded reasonable and had the great attraction that it would be under his direct command at all times.

'Ye'll like it that any winds in the west is fair for a single tack to Willemstad. Jus' be sure an' ship a local pilot.'

That settled it. 'I do believe I'll do it,' Kydd said, almost incredulous that he had some sort of plan afoot already. 'I'm much in debt to you, old fellow. So much, I'm hesitating to ask a further boon . . .'

'Ask away, cully. I can always say no.'

It was to bear a fist with the hard part – transforming ideas into the reality of ships and guns, tonnage required, order of embarkation and therefore landing, numbers of horse-lifting gear and even ramped craft for getting heavy guns ashore. All in a context unknown to Kydd but all too familiar to Bazely.

He took Kydd's lists of regiments, infantry and cavalry

and, under his experienced hand, produced the necessary figures. And from these they had the requirements Kydd needed to make demand on the Transport Board and the Admiralty. It was then going to be rigorous staff work to translate the whole into a set of orders, one for every vessel and Army commander taking part.

That could safely be left for *Thunderer*'s arrival and her band of officers to lend a hand.

'Er, you said we're to make the assault. Does this mean you're desiring a share in the sport at all?'

'Thank ye, an' of a certainty I do. Excepting I'm to transfer to the Mediterranean at the end o' this week.'

'Ah.'

Bazely gave a rueful smile and said, 'To take up a ship. *Topaze* 32,' he added modestly.

'A 32 – then you . . .'

'Aye. Made post last month.'

Bazely: no longer the phlegmatic and utterly reliable brig-sloop commander, now in rig as a full post-captain, Royal Navy.

'Well, I'm blessed!' Kydd laughed. 'Tonight you'll sup with me and drink to your elevation.'

It gave time for him to scratch out communications to the Transport Board and the Board of Admiralty with solemn assurances that it was only in the press of some urgency that he was requiring immediate attention, making every effort to invoke the name of General Sir Thomas Graham, leader of the expedition. He took pleasure in further indicating that he might be reached in his flagship.

The next afternoon advice came by telegraph that *Thunderer* had anchored at the Nore, awaiting orders. Kydd lost no time in leaving the capital for the biting onshore winds of Sheerness, the scene of so much drama in his youth.

Chapter 51

Aboard Thunderer

'Mr Roscoe, I have my orders and they are to assist in a landing . . . in the Low Countries.'

'Walcheren!'

'Not as if it will be the same as before, sir. Do keep a countenance before the ship's company, if you will,' he said irritably. 'All my officers to muster in my cabin in one hour's time.'

It gave space for Binard to fuss over him and to lay out his workings. Thankfully the sailing master had adequate charts of Brabant and the Low Countries, which he inspected carefully while he could.

Bazely had been right – the Walcheren landing at Roompot was perfectly open to the sea and, on the opposite side of the island to Antwerp, would be lightly defended.

The officers began arriving, taking their places around the table and uncharacteristically quiet in the knowledge that very shortly they would learn why their ship had been so abruptly plucked from their ocean Elysium.

'It's Antwerp.'

At the stricken looks this produced, Kydd continued, 'More to the point, to land troops at Willemstad in the Hollands Deep.'

Roscoe, quicker than the others, spluttered, 'Why Willemstad? It's miles up shoal waters.'

Kydd had given thought to this. 'The main objective is Antwerp, well to the south. General Graham believes that to capture and garrison the town would allow it to be used as a staging point for supplies in the forthcoming siege of Antwerp.'

'Isn't Hollands Deep lined with guns as can pound any who trespass there?' Roscoe seemed unusually well informed.

'My plans include a diversionary descent on Walcheren which should draw them away,' Kydd said briefly, and held up his hands against further interruption.

In swift professional terms he outlined the objective, situation and plan. These officers had nothing really to do in the larger picture but they had the right to know how *Thunderer* would be handled and any unusual requirements.

Replies from the Transport Board were blessedly quick. He was to be allowed a total of nine named vessels, barely more than half of what he'd asked for, and they would be assembled in Yarmouth Roads, the traditional stepping-off place for overseas expeditions.

From the Admiralty Board came terse advice that he was to be granted only a sloop and three cutters, with voluminous instructions concerning their employment, storing and victualling under his signature. Expenditure of powder and shot was to be strictly accounted for, and all motions of his flotilla in support of the Army were to be recorded for later reconciliation in the table of costs relative to their appropriate departments.

As if in grudging recognition of the enormity of what faced him, it was allowed that he was granted to name which sloop he desired to sail under his flag, always provided it was both on his station and available for service.

At once, by the marvel of the Admiralty telegraph, Commander Bowden in Plymouth was receiving peremptory orders to proceed in *Weazel* at once to the Nore command there to place himself at the disposal of Commodore Kydd.

With his officers in frenzied labour producing the orders in fair, Kydd felt it time to present himself at Horse Guards once more.

'I trust this will not take long, Sir Thomas. I have much to do in the greater conduct of this expedition,' Graham said coldly, waving away his officers.

'Then very briefly, sir. An assembly of the transports at the Hinderplaat at the entrance to Hollands Deep. They transfer to flat-boats and, preceded by a naval sloop and cutters to discourage the enemy, will arrive at Willemstad within the same day, to disembark on the south shore.'

'Under heavy fire? I rather think it less than prudent, sir.'

'Sir, the other element in my plan is to provide a distraction – a landing at a place well removed from Willemstad but which will serve to draw away their attention.'

'Hmph.'

'Therefore I'm under the obligation to request you to furnish me with men for this task – say, half a battalion?'

Graham drew himself up, glaring. 'Am I to understand you to demand I reduce my own forces engaged in vital tasks by this significant amount? Preposterous!'

Kydd held back his temper. 'Then some three companies of—'

'No! This plan is your contriving, Sir Thomas. Yours is the duty to find the resources.'

'Sir, I must protest! Without we have a—'

'Where are your written orders? I insist my subordinate commanders do carry full instructions for the period they must spend under naval control.'

'They will be in your hands in two days,' Kydd said thickly, and marched out with all the dignity he could muster.

Outside, a sympathetic Meares explained that just at that time Graham was in negotiation with Blücher for a substantial detachment of Prussians to aid in the reduction of Antwerp and could be very short with those who distracted him.

For Kydd this was a catastrophe. Without a diversion, the entire length of the waterway would be in full array against him. Had he the moral right to send in essentially defenceless men against point-blank cannon fire?

There was nothing more he could do and he returned to *Thunderer* in a sullen mood. What a shambles of incomprehension and muddled planning, the like of which for haste and carelessness he'd never experienced.

He headed to his cabin to claim a measure of solitude. But then, in a jet of warmth that took him to the edge of weeping, he found waiting for him a little package of his favourite currant jelly and a hurried note from Persephone that assured him of her safe arrival, with Francis, in England.

Chapter 52

The orders were nearly finished and the transports assembling in Yarmouth to where the regiments were marching to board their ships. If he was going to stop the madness, time was running out – but at what cost would it be to his reputation and career?

In time for the evening tide he sent off the orders and *Thunderer* quietly put to sea, the gentle heave and muffled splash of her wake in the stillness of the night doing wonders for his spirits. Even so, he knew that by morning as he entered the anchorage he must have an answer to his dilemma and he slept badly.

In the early hours he woke groggily to hear the sentry outside his cabin door in a coughing fit yet again. He needed every scrap of rest before he faced the next day and, flinging open the door, demanded of the shocked man that the marine sergeant-of-the-watch present himself.

In his sleeping wear he snapped at the astonished sergeant, 'This man is not fit for duty. Relieve him this instant!'

He slipped into a forty-fathom sleep, and when he awoke

he had the answer. It had everything to do with his loyal body of Royal Marines.

'Captain Clinton,' he enquired amiably, over his morning toast. 'Do you ever yearn for action ashore at all?'

Thunderer could command the services of ninety-one marines, and with something like the same again as reinforcements from local sources, he was in a position to make a noticeable fuss in the dock area and inland with the Navy close in to effect any rescue needed. He trusted Bazely that Roompot would be as sketchily defended as he remembered.

He was being required by the leader of the expedition to find resources for the diversion and this would be his authorisation to lay claim to his reinforcements. After all, it was only a temporary deployment and under Navy control, and would be attractive to Royal Marines officers craving distinction.

The transports were there, busily engaged in taking in stores, and the first echelons of the expeditionary force were encamped in fields.

Kydd found time to meet them all and to take measure of the army command, who he decided, as far as he was able to judge, were capable enough and he left them to it. They assured him that they were ready in all respects to embark in three days' time.

That meant he should begin his diversion the required two days before – it was perilously soon.

As flag-officer of the expedition, he had one more crucial duty. The Royal Marines added to his forces came from ships of all rates and establishments. Were they now to be carried on the books of *Thunderer* for pay and victualling? Or should the larger budget line for the expedition be invoiced?

In the last two days before sailing his time was spent

dispatching worried pursers and junior lieutenants in every direction. Long experience told him that to be amiss in accounts was far worse for an officer's career than any blunder in the face of the enemy.

And then General Graham named the day.

It was all now passing inevitable. Two days before the Willemstad assault went in, Kydd must set the diversion in train so in consequence his own sailing order went out.

At last *Weazel* arrived and the welcome but mystified features of Bowden graced his cabin as he outlined the shape of the action. It would be only *Thunderer* and *Weazel* attending at the landing; if it required more, it had turned into a fleet engagement and the entire venture would be brought into question.

The landing party of marines would be accommodated in both vessels, the discomforts of the passage ameliorated by its brevity.

With no further delay the two ships raised anchor and proceeded.

It was a heart-thumping time: who knew what was waiting for them? But also it was an exciting and emotional moment for Kydd. Lowly and temporary commodore he might be, but he was in command of a fleet bent on nothing less than an assault on the continent of Europe.

The weather was boisterous, stinging spray and flat, hard winds, which in the blackness of the night drove all military passengers below deck. But Kydd found it bracing, token of the mastery of man in not fighting the sea's might but harnessing it for his own purposes.

He slept well, long familiarity telling him that whatever was in store for them in the morning nothing could be done at this time to alter it.

The morning saw them some miles off the eastern estuary of the Scheldt, and as the light improved, *Thunderer* prepared to close in. The land was utterly flat in every direction, scrubby sand and mud, and barely inhabited until Roompot was sighted on the northern side of the island: a small, somnolent village with a modest steeple, a haphazard waterfront but with a long breakwater and jetty.

It was just as Bazely had said – insignificant, no fortifications observable and no swarming troops forming up to deny them the landing.

Kydd's heart calmed at the sight, but it was only the beginning. There was indication of deeper water on the southern side on the chart and he was relying on this advantage to come within gun range of the little town. But in prudence he had men in both fore-chains chanting the soundings.

They drew nearer. Figures could be seen running between buildings. There would be little doubt what the big ship intended.

'Mr Clinton, it seems we're not to be greeted by Napoleon's finest this hour. I desire you should show our disappointment with an appropriate display, making foray inland every so often as will set them to flight.'

The Royal Marines captain smiled thinly. 'As they will believe we are an advance party to an invasion. I understand, sir.'

Anchoring as the shallows approached, *Weazel* close by, boats were launched and quickly filled with red-coated marines.

In an orderly procession the long-boat, cutters and pinnaces headed in with Kydd anxiously following them with a telescope. The first marines scrambled up to the jetty and at the double formed a perimeter guard to allow the rest to land.

A feeble sputter of muskets broke out at one end of the waterfront but the disciplined crash of marine firelocks brought an instant silence.

Then, at the eastern end of the town, three horsemen broke cover and furiously galloped away. Kydd allowed a satisfied smile to surface. It was now time for the main performance.

The return to Yarmouth was rapid but uncomfortable in the increasing bad weather. Kydd became uneasily aware that forces other than the enemy's might lead to the confusion and ruin of the best of his plans. If the winds veered yet more into the east it would be foul for Holland and the expedition.

When he finally made Yarmouth Roads through driving rain he saw that columns of men and their baggage were assembling and taking boat for a transport. Already five of the transports had taken up their position in the convoy assembly anchorage offshore.

It was idiocy of the first order. Storming ashore, Kydd found the camp headquarters tent. 'General, are you aware that this entire expedition may well be stood down in the next few hours?'

Graham stared at him as at a lunatic. 'Kindly explain yourself, sir.'

'If this fresh gale continues to veer more to the east we stand to be headed – a foul wind cannot be commanded to step aside by man or beast. It would have been more prudent, sir, to embark your troops to my advice and—'

'I take no instruction from you or the highest in the Navy, sir! The timing of this motion on Europe is critical, and I'll have you know that delicate negotiations with the Prussians are set fair to bear fruit if we keep our word that our army will be in the field on the date specified.'

'Sir. I appreciate your position but at the same time—'

'The expedition will proceed.'

Kydd drew a ragged breath. 'General. It will not. Weather conditions will physically prevent it. As senior naval officer responsible for the safe conveyance of the military, it will be my word that sets the expedition to sea – and only mine.'

It sounded arrogant, but he knew he had the authority and the power to do it – and he must.

The general's nostrils flared dangerously. 'Sir Thomas, you are abusing your position in base ignorance of higher affairs. You can be assured I shall be laying the whole matter of your obstructing a duly constituted military operation before your superiors. Dammit, you're not even an admiral.'

Kydd felt himself reddening but held back. 'And I do strongly suggest, sir, that you disembark your men while you can.'

'I shall certainly not. They'll stay aboard ready to put to sea the instant the weather moderates – providing Commodore Kydd in his wisdom deigns to allow it,' he finished acidly.

Chapter 53

Aboard Montrose

The elderly vessel, once a fifty-gun fourth-rate, was now *en flute* and emptied of guns. In their place, four hundred soldiers of the 33rd Regiment of Foot were crowded with their kit, making shift to create some form of under-deck camp in the absence of tents and campfires while the ship jibbed and heaved to her anchors with the onrush of seas.

The old hands, like Sergeant Jeb Hoskins, knew better than to complain. As he was at pains to tell the men of his platoon, sheltered from the icy wind and rain, and even provided with a table and bench, they were infinitely better off than in bivouac in the open, even if the worn timbers of the ship leaked and ran with water.

They had been aboard all morning, hours with nothing to do. The occasional seaman passing through would grin, and in the knowledge that the gale was strengthening from the east, would assure them that they'd be there for a long time yet.

It was gloomy, the dark relieved only by odorous rush dips

that flickered in the cold air currents as the gale plucked at their refuge. They sat huddled in their greatcoats, told campaign stories, and threw dice.

'Platoon . . . *hoh*!' Hoskins thundered, spotting the legs of the officer coming uncertainly down the ladder. The men got wearily to their feet. This was only Reeves, the junior lieutenant commanding the platoon, but was a break in the tedium for all that.

'Oh, er, sit down again, men.' Lieutenant Reeves was absurdly young-looking to be in command of a platoon of line infantry and probably grateful for the services of the platoon sergeant, Hoskins.

'I've come to tell you some unwelcome news. It appears that the weather is against us and as a consequence we shall be staying here until it improves. I'm sorry but we can't go back on land because the waves are too big for the boats. Um, do make yourselves as comfortable as you can. That is all.'

The buzz of talk after he departed was not complimentary to Reeves, the Army, or the Navy, who, it seemed, was scared to get them to the continent at any point soon.

Hoskins slumped back and closed his eyes but jerked them open at the sound of scuffles and a high-pitched squeal.

From forward, in the direction of the manger, which was filled with livestock to be taken ashore later, several men were dragging a small figure, struggling furiously.

'What's this, then?'

A ragamuffin of a child glared up defiantly.

'Found 'im at the sheep's tucker, like.'

Hoskins didn't need to be told – this was a stowaway. 'Who are you, y' cheeky younker?' he demanded. 'Explain y'self.'

'You're off t' fight Napoleon,' the child said proudly, 'an' I want t' be with you.'

'Name?' he growled. The little scamp was probably all of twelve but it was difficult to tell as he was so undernourished.

'Simon, sir.'

'Well, Simon, we got t' throw ye overboard, not having room t' keep you.'

'I wan' to join y' colours.' There was a stubborn lift to the chin that softened the sergeant's manner.

'What? How old are ye, Simon, if'n I can ask it.'

'Fifteen,' came a reply.

'So. Twelve is a mite young to be humpin' a musket, don't y' think?'

'I been a maltster's apprentice, knows about humpin' things. Sir, why can't I be your drummer boy an' march with you?' The eyes were shining and Hoskins supposed that the lad's village must recently have been visited by a recruiting party with fife and drum. And he'd been refused on account of being too young.

Hoskins stroked his chin. 'Well, now, an' we don't jus' take men on without they're trained up properly. See, we'se off t' war, I'll have ye know.'

Reeves would not be sympathetic, quoting endless regulations. But on the other hand the boats had stopped running and the stowaway would be stuck with them for the foreseeable future.

Then, in a rush of warmth, he saw a way. The company had had to ship with only a single drummer available. Stationed at one end of the line, he was often not heard at the opposite end in the clamour of battle. What if he asked the drummer to teach the youngster the rhythms and calls to be able to perform at the other end? If Reeves was then approached it might be a different story.

It would need the connivance of the whole platoon as well

as Searle, the gawky drummer, but the result would be satisfactory for all concerned.

'Jake, get off y' arse an' ask Joe Searle t' give ear t' me.'

It was arranged. In the ship's bows there was a space called the forepeak, now given over to the stowage of odd seamanlike articles, but it was well out of hearing of any on deck. This would be Simon's classroom and hiding place.

The child was ready and willing, and the platoon soon took to the boy, smuggling meals to the hungry creature and at night allowing him to sleep among them.

Things were looking up for the little runaway.

Chapter 54

Two days later the barometer was on the turn – twenty-eight inches and rising. Kydd sent word to the general to prepare to sail. The seas were still white-capped, rolling in with undiminished energy, but the wind had veered further, allowing the military convoy to claw off under reduced sail and begin the enterprise.

By the usual means the enemy would have notice of an invading fleet, and spies in taverns and brothels could be relied on to find out where it was headed. They would now have had days to bring up reinforcements and Kydd's expectations were turning to dread.

Out into the cold wastes of the North Sea the gaggle of gale-tossed ships laboured, a stirring vision for any artist but one of worry and care for Kydd. Graham and his staff had quartered in *Thunderer*, the largest vessel, but the general kept to his cabin with no interest at all in the sight.

If the French wanted to contest the landing with naval forces they would be waiting at the Hinderplaat, the broad shallows at the entrance to the Hollands Deep. To oppose them, Kydd had his trusty *Thunderer* but nothing else of size.

Ordinarily a flag-officer would have his orders and instructions issued to his fleet for just such an action, but with only *Weazel* and a scatter of lesser craft it would have been ludicrous.

That morning as he peered into his mirror there was a betraying tinge of grey at his temples. Taking a man-o'-war into a mortal fight was one thing, the worry and nerves of fleet command and responsibility, however small, quite another.

The land came into view a little before midday without the fearful sight of an enemy squadron, but another decision slammed in. Willemstad was some twenty-five miles up the fairway and it would take the best part of a day even with winds in the right quadrant for the clumsy transports to make it there. And given the foul ground and treacherous mud-flats, it had to be in daylight. If they began the transit now they'd be only halfway when night fell and the consequences could be disastrous.

'Signal to anchor,' Kydd croaked, to the signal lieutenant. It could be only himself who told Graham that they could not proceed until the next morning, another delay and this time in full view of the enemy.

It was reaching nightmare proportions, this whole hastily conceived, ill-executed and under-resourced venture. The first to take place under his flag – and probably the last.

As he prepared to go below to bury himself in his cabin he spared a thought for the soldiery trapped in their wooden prison: they'd been led to expect only a day of hardship. There would now be five in all.

In the extravagant comfort of his personal accommodation he contemplated the morrow. On the Hinderplaat, *Thunderer* was about as far as she could go up the waterway. If he wanted to go further he would have to ship in another –

Weazel. And he did want to, if only to be in the lead when, as planned, the Navy penetrated up to Willemstad, revealing enemy gun positions and ensuring no surprises lay ahead.

Whether they could suppress point-blank fire from the banks with the puny guns *Weazel* possessed was another matter. It was a major concern: safe passage of the transports was critical and one disabled by enemy fire in the narrow waters would block the others, leaving them open to a concentrated battering.

Before dawn he shifted to *Weazel*, politely welcomed by Bowden, who effusively assured him of the honour he was doing his command by hoisting his flag in her. There was no need to point out the towering hazards to the young man: they'd been together for years of active service and he calmly prepared his ship for the trial ahead without undue discussion.

At the first glimmer of daybreak the little brig-sloop went to general quarters, manning all her eight six-pounders on both sides; astern of her, the three cutters did likewise.

'Carry on, sir?' Bowden asked neutrally, standing loosely on the quarterdeck in a creditable imitation of Kydd.

'Please do, Charles,' Kydd murmured, and the final act began.

The light had extended to take in both sides of the chill bleak flatness as *Weazel* got under way with cautious sail. In the shelter of the channel the seas gradually diminished but thankfully the winds stayed steady from the south-west.

Occasional buildings, huts and villages came into view but Kydd could see no horse artillery galloping up to take aim. He glanced astern – the cutters were demurely in line and, well beyond, the transports were beginning to make sail.

The two sides closed in, less than a mile apart now and shortly they would be up with Hellevoetsluis, a small port with roads inland and very likely to be defended.

The brig nosed forward, gun crews still and tense, the boatswain in the bows ignoring the shore, eyes on the muddy waters ahead, not trusting the chart. The little town drew closer, merchant shipping alongside at its waterfront and a modest fort without a flag abroad waiting on the far side.

They crept ahead, no sudden activity ashore as a prelude to a storm of gunfire. Closer still, there was the thin smoke of cooking fires above the town but the fort seemed still and undisturbed.

Within gun range Kydd eased. It had to be accepted that they'd achieved something of a miracle in catching the fort asleep and off guard.

He threw a glance astern. The transports were beginning to enter the channel. When the drowsy sentries awoke it would be to a terrifying sight before them: an invading fleet of ships. No doubt the bad weather had persuaded them that no commanding admiral would ever risk entering shoal waters in those conditions.

The habitations fell away, which was a relief as the chart indicated that the shipping channel was close to the southern bank as they sailed to one side of an island. But then to pass a larger island on the opposite side the channel narrowed rapidly, which brought them to within less than a hundred yards of the muddy banks – and Haringvliet, a small but well-placed town that was sure to boast many cannons, with every target obliged to come within an unmissable range.

Their only chance was to press on as speedily as they could to minimise time under the vengeful muzzles. Without being told, Bowden had more sail shaken out as they came up to the deadly narrows.

The light had strengthened – with the sunrise behind them the unknown gunners had the best possible conditions in their favour.

Kydd couldn't see them but he knew they would hold their fire until the last possible minute to keep their positions out of sight, matches burning, tensed to unleash their storm of death.

Nearer and nearer – the discipline of the artillery companies was superb, for *Weazel*'s own guns could not be trained until they revealed themselves.

A deadly tension descended on the brig and as the edges of the town came up Kydd braced himself ready for the shocking blaze of shot . . . which never came.

Without fuss *Weazel* made her way past, further still and then Haringvliet was safely behind them without a shot having been fired.

Kydd shivered. It was unaccountable. Why had they not opened fire? Then the channel widened, this time in the final stretch – to Willemstad.

He couldn't rely on whatever had held the fire from Haringvliet. His task now was to discover the gun positions around Willemstad and group his ships to try to suppress the holocaust of fire that would inevitably greet the landing troops.

The obvious place to attack was the Fort de Ruijter. It was an earthen but substantial fortress positioned to dominate the Hollands Deep and access to the town of Willemstad. It could clearly be seen on the southern bank with colours a-fly but they were difficult to make out.

He signalled the cutters to lie off while *Weazel* made a first pass across the line of fire. The brig lay over and under more sail swashed past without any response from the enemy.

Before Kydd could try to reason why there was a shout from forward. 'Quarterdeck, ahoy! I see a cutter inshore wi' English colours.'

As Kydd picked it up in his telescope he could see it was making its way out to him.

'*Curlew*, four guns,' was the reply when challenged.

'Come aboard, *Curlew*.'

The lieutenant-in-command, taken aback at coming upon a full commodore, obeyed with speed. 'L'tenant Richards, sir.'

'Why are you . . . What is the situation hereabouts? I have a convoy of transports for the reduction of Willemstad and have met no opposition of any kind.'

'Willemstad? I beg you will stay your hand. Matters are not as you might think.'

'Lieutenant,' Kydd began dangerously, 'I have command of an expedition of extreme importance for the capture or destruction of Willemstad and—'

'Sir! I implore you! Do not or—'

'You have ten seconds to explain yourself, sir.'

'Um, has no one told you? The Hollanders have been in revolt! The Stadtholder Prince William of Orange has taken authority to call out the citizens to overthrow Boney. Now the French have fallen back to their fortresses, like Antwerp, and we hold the countryside and the fort here besides.'

So that was why there'd been no firestorm. And so like Graham not to have deigned to take notice of local intelligence. The whole expedition should never have been mounted.

Nevertheless, in a stab of regret he recognised that, as the operation was now over, he must haul down his flag and revert to commonplace sail-of-the-line captain and take *Thunderer* to rejoin the fleet. It had been an unsettling experience.

Chapter 55

Willemstad

Before he left Kydd decided perhaps he should pay his respects to the general commanding. Graham was now ashore in Willemstad as the military disembarked and would be occupied with taking the enterprise further but he had an obligation of sorts.

Graham was busy, papers in his hand and surrounded by his regimental staff. He glared at Kydd. 'Be damned to it, sir, and I fail to understand you.'

At a loss to find alternative words to express that he was merely paying a polite leave-taking Kydd stayed silent.

'Sir Thomas. I distinctly heard you to say your intent is to cease support for the expedition and sail away. I demand you explain this unwarrantable abandoning of your duty.'

'My orders . . . Your requirement was to see your transports safely to Willemstad. This has been done, sir,' Kydd said tightly.

'This is not why you and your fleet have been seconded to me, sir. The principal intent of the expedition is to reduce

Antwerp, or has your Admiralty failed sufficiently to explain this to you?'

Kydd's orders emphasised the safe passage to Willemstad but in their scribbled brevity made no mention of a larger mission. 'It has not been made clear to me, sir. I shall need written authority to extend my deployment in these waters.' It might have been understood at Horse Guards but they didn't underwrite the expenses.

'Very well, sir, you shall have it. So now can we get on with our war?' Graham paused then turned to Meares. 'Draw up the necessary for signature.'

Outside, Kydd rounded on Meares. 'Have you no conception of what the tasking of a fleet involves? Stores, water, powder . . . We have no lines of supply at sea, sir!'

'Sir Thomas,' Meares said soothingly, 'if you'd indent our quartermaster-general with your wants it'll be taken up and accommodated, have no fear.'

'And what does the villainous redcoat want of the Navy, pray tell?'

'Ah. Nothing in any particular – I rather sense only that he feels safer with the Royal Navy at hand. You see, he must now push into the country for it's been agreed that the British will descend on Antwerp from the north while Field Marshal Blücher has been persuaded to send a like-numbered column from the east, from the interior. Who knows what we'll find waiting for us?'

Chapter 56

'Platoon will countermarch in column! Right about – *tuuurn*!' The sergeant major's stentorian bellow echoed effortlessly across the parade ground of the Willemstad fort. Rank and file obediently turned and wheeled before the stand where General Graham was taking the salute, the military band energetically crashing out the quick-march air of the 33rd of Foot.

And at the near side of 2 Company, nearly bursting with pride, a small figure marched with slung drum and all the impedimenta of a full regimental drummer.

The ranks processed around and then once more before the ceremonial march-off. In the barrack-room cheerful jabber broke out – this was what it was to be a front-line soldier of the King, not stuffed below decks like a parcel of chickens in a coop.

Lieutenant Reeves had told them earlier of their charge, and after their days of confinement they were more than ready. It was intended to make a quick thirty-mile march across country to Antwerp where, with the aid of the Prussians, they would lay the French under siege until they surrendered.

It should be straightforward enough, particularly as it was said that the Frogs had, in terror of their advance, retreated into their strongholds. And, as the older hands were saying with relish, there was nothing like the prospect of a fallen city to provide entertainment.

'Won't we have a battle, sir?' Simon said, disappointed.

Sergeant Hoskins gave a grim smile. 'We could have an' all,' he said knowingly. 'On the road they'll want t' slow us down, do us a mischief afore we gets to lie outside their walls. An' as well I wager this poxy weather'll get worse before it gets better, lad.'

A day later they had reason to remember his words. At dawn, bugles summoned them to form up in marching order in their campaign uniform of red serge with stiff shako and stout shoes, tightly laced, full knapsacks, ammunition pouches, powder flasks, blanket and greatcoat. Not forgetting razor, canteen and spare clothing, in all adding up to the weight of a fair-sized pig.

Hoskins was liberal with his advice to the platoon. The mess tin was absolutely necessary but the regulation brushes and blacking could discreetly be left behind. Every pound carried would be felt in spades at the first hill and priority was to be given to powder and ball – and the heavy, nine-pound musket.

They stepped off to a rousing quick march along a good road. The bitingly chill winds caused a halt: every man found his greatcoat and gratefully donned it.

'No, Simon, ain't good to be out in th' cold, younker,' Hoskins admonished Simon.

The young lad glowered. 'I has a redcoat uniform an' proud of it!' he protested.

'As won't be o' use t' a frozen stiff,' Hoskins murmured, and helped the lad into his oversize greatcoat.

They moved off again, the rougher road with its stones and holes felt only too tenderly underfoot.

Another hour past the first road intersection, the direct route south became harder – and the first drifting snowflakes fell.

The cold was intense and raw. By now there were no sprightly regimental tunes – little Simon found himself in turns with the other drummer, Searle, providing a marching beat, a monotonous loud tapping.

By midday the soldiers were finding that the roads were giving out to cart-tracks, each side mud-slides to be avoided, and nothing but cheerless, perfectly flat scrub further out.

The noonday halt afforded a measure of relief. Tea, hard biscuits and rum gave them heart to continue and they marched off in good spirits.

They moved into another realm. Mud. The autumn rains had ensured that the lower reaches were near liquid, not yet cold enough to be frozen hard. The regiment marched on, a treacherous winding way, ever onwards to who knew where.

The ground squelched and slid under their feet, the marching rhythm broken up into individual slipping and skating, and still the day wore on. Early in the afternoon a drifting rain squall chilled each man to the bone – then turned to the freezing misery of sleet.

No one spoke, trudging forward while their burdens burned their muscles, and always the cloying, pulling mud. In some places mud pits swallowed limbs to the knees and in the struggle to wrench free, shoes were torn off and the march for those men would turn into the agony of bare feet on near-frozen ground.

At four a halt for the night was called. Any hope for surcease was crushed when it was found that the baggage train, with encampment gear and the field kitchens, was hopelessly mired far in the rear.

'That's what the rations ye carries are for, lad,' Hoskins said sympathetically, seeing the pinched face of the little drummer-boy with all the ravenous hunger of youth. 'Here, try some o' mine.' He rummaged in his knapsack and found some strips of dried meat in a cloth.

'Th-thanks, Mr Hoskins,' the grateful, shivering boy said, gingerly taking one and gnawing at it. 'Um, where do we sleep, then?' he mumbled, his eyes dull with exhaustion.

'Bivouac.' At the child's hesitation he explained, 'Under the stars, like, seein' we haven't any tents.'

Overhead grey clouds scudded and an icy evening breeze began whipping in spitefully. New recruits were dismayed, then appalled. Told to find the least sodden mud to lie in to sleep under a single blanket and greatcoat only, it would be a trial of endurance. Endless night hours of unimaginable cold and wet, sleeplessness and fear were all that could be expected.

After the first few hours there was whimpering in the darkness. Hoskins reached out and pulled the child to him.

'Stow it, young man,' he whispered. 'This is all a test for ye,' he explained sternly. 'Them as can't take it are no use to King George an' they gets sent back, thrown out o' the Army, like. Now, you doesn't want that, now, do you.'

The noise stopped and a little voice answered meekly, 'No, Mr Hoskins. I want t' be in the big battle with th' others.'

Chapter 57

In the morning there was no rain, but a dank, raw mist lay in a dismal blanket while they formed up, dragging on their mud-soaked wet garments in a paroxysm of shivering and swearing.

Manfully humping his drum, Simon stepped it out with Sergeant Hoskins, managing a smile at Reeves's enquiry of the night and ignoring the gripes of hunger that were taking centre place in his thoughts.

'Are we getting closer t' Antwerp, Mr Hoskins?' he asked respectfully. The sergeant knew everything, of course.

'I'd think so, younker,' the man answered, not meeting his eye. 'An' you should—'

He stopped in his tracks. Somewhere in the mists ahead there was a flurry of harmless-sounding pops.

'Hey, now, an' the Frogs know we're about.'

An urgent order to cease line of march came down, and while they were halted a section of the light infantry and the few riflemen they had with them urgently sloshed and squelched past, disappearing on the way to the head of the column.

A little later there was a concentrated outbreak of musketry, then nothing. The order to resume the march came and they stepped off once more.

After some time, the mist thinned and they passed a peculiar sight. In the polder field next to them, there were one or two of what seemed to be discarded bundles of clothing.

'What's that, then, Mr Hoskins?' Simon said, puzzled.

'Ah. That there's what's left o' the Frogs who thought t' get in our way.'

'You mean . . .?'

'Aye. Won't bother us any more.'

Simon couldn't take his eyes from the sight and was silent for a long time afterwards.

'Are there any more, d'you think?'

'Might be some. But they're up agin the 33rd and I wouldn't want t' be in their shoes, young man, would you?'

The slow tramp mercifully got easier as the ground firmed. Now the glutinous mud was infused with sand and the firmer going told, the pace picking up to something like a regimental stride.

It ended, surprisingly, with a halt halfway through the morning. Rumours swirled and then it became clear that Antwerp was not so very far distant and their first action in earnest might soon take place.

Reeves made it clear to them. 'The Prussians are in sight. We're to reduce the town of Merksem as a preliminary to the bombardment of Antwerp.'

Hoskins interpreted for the sake of the less experienced: 'He's saying as we has to take this Merksem if we're goin' to have somewheres to lay our heads while we sieges Antwerp.'

Word came back from the two probing companies of light infantry that not only were the French absent but the Dutch villagers were more than happy to see them. In short order men were grounding their knapsacks and feeling the warmth of a kitchen fire as they were welcomed in.

'What about the battle, Mr Hoskins?'

'Ah, well, we see about that'n in the mornin'. Light along some more o' that cheese, lad.'

The contrast between the pain and hardships of the march and the warmth and shelter of the village was marked and they gathered strength and recruited the spirits. There was no way the regimental rank and file could know of the larger picture or even what it meant. Boney was turning on them with a big army and that was all they were told.

In the morning they found out a little more. During the night the Prussians marched stolidly on to take up their designated positions for the bombardment. By halfway through the day it was evident that all was not as it should be – riders in odd-looking hussar costume were galloping this way and that and their own officers were shouting at each other.

Later in the afternoon the reason became clear. Their bitterly cold march had outstripped the progress of their guns by a wide margin and any talk of a bombardment of Antwerp was ridiculous.

Another day passed and there was movement. The impatient Prussians were lending the British some of their guns, horse-drawn rather than massive siege artillery but better than nothing.

It was time to close with the enemy. Excitement swept through the men. Kit was laid out and inspected, weapons sharpened and polished. In a short space they would be called on to risk their lives in the crucible of mortal combat.

A parade was called and General Graham said wise and strong words, none of which were heard by 2 Company in the whipping icy winds, but when the parade was dismissed it was not back to their billets, but to be sectioned off for their opening place on the battlefield.

Reeves seemed to have a difficulty to resolve with the colonel and he returned with a scowl. 'For those looking forward to an honest mill with the enemy, I'm sorry to disappoint you,' he said woodenly. 'Our company has been chosen with others to stand out on our inland perimeter to guard against any outflanking manoeuvre the enemy thinks to make behind our backs. A valuable – no, essential responsibility if the assault is to be made without interference.'

Hoskins gave a twisted smile. 'Last into the city is us, lookin' out f'r their arses while they gets the frolics an' the loot.'

'None o' that talk in front of the men,' Reeves said sharply, but strode off quickly with a humourless smile.

From that point on the 33rd maintained the sentinels, videttes and patrols on the outer periphery of the lowland scrub and woodlands about Merksem, a tedious and uneventful experience, especially as the continual low grumble of guns told of the opening of the battle for Antwerp.

It was not an exciting time for a drummer-boy, whose day now consisted of endless waiting for the order to fiercely beat out the 'Stand to your arms!' to repel an attack on their rear.

Those not on watch and ward were aimlessly talking and gaming, theirs not to concern themselves with matters strategical.

After three days the rumble of guns tailed off. No man needed telling – this was the moment when the Allies rolled forward through the breaches and took to the foe, hand to hand, in a brutal finish to the siege.

'What's happening?' Simon asked anxiously. 'Tell me, Mr Hoskins, please!'

The sergeant said nothing, vacantly looking away from his little friend as the hours dragged by.

Then, as if it were the most normal thing in the world, a squadron of Prussian cavalry appeared. Trotting easily with a festive jingle, they passed through the closely defended positions of the 33rd and on into countryside.

They were followed by the tramping of several columns of the same green-dressed infantry as they'd seen before, their faces set and unreadable.

Several soldiers of the 33rd called out, trying to make sense of it all but the continentals knew no English, and apart from the odd meaningless shout, trudged on.

After a period, the procession petered out, with headquarters staff and officers on horseback, followed by the baggage train, well stowed and immaculate.

Hoskins watched the proceedings with increasing concern. 'Don't like this, Simon lad. They shoulda been gettin' well rorty b' now. Where they off to?'

Chapter 58

'I can't believe it of 'em!' Meares said, aghast.

'Believe it, old fellow,' Godden, the quartermaster-general, grunted, looking up from his papers. 'Our hook-nose friend in charge had no guns to speak of. What could he do?'

'He must have known Blücher is hell-driven to take on Bonaparte directly. He's never going to be interested in Antwerp.'

Godden tried to hide a cynical expression. 'But he talked the German round, made him see his way clear to give us a covering force for the bombardment.'

'And a few guns, yes, I know, but to take 'em all back after three days, well . . .'

'Politicking, m' fine friend. Has to impress his king. Frederick always did like to stay close to the front line and give advice to his marshals.'

'Well, where does this leave us?' Meares said, in dismay. 'He took back his guns as well, and ours are days away still. With our pathetic forces what's Antwerp got to fear of us?'

A sudden hush fell in the headquarters tent as Graham entered.

'Officers. All here at four,' he snapped.

'The Navy as well?' Godden asked neutrally.

'Yes, yes. Get the fool here, too.'

Kydd had taken quarters in *Weazel*, which was moored handily the other side of the neck of land separating Brabant from Antwerp.

Meares intercepted him on his way to the meeting. 'Be warned, sailor, His Nibs is in a fine rage, the Prussians having folded their tents and quit the land.'

'Why did they do that?'

'By previous arrangement. Blücher gave Graham three days to force a breach but the guns he had didn't have either weight of metal or the range to do the job. So the beggar pulls out, leaving our man alone to contemplate his future.'

'So. The siege of Antwerp is a failure. The whole expedition is a failure – the reason we're here is . . .'

'Yes. Shall we go in now?'

It was nearly evening when Graham returned, with several other officers, grave-featured and, as it seemed to Kydd, somewhat defensive.

The general began belligerently: 'Some here would say that our motions before Antwerp have not met with the success they deserve and therefore we must retire whence we came. If there are any of that persuasion at this meeting they will make themselves known and I will without delay find their replacements.'

There were stony looks but no offers to resign.

'Very well. This meeting is to inform you all that I do not intend to skulk cravenly away while the enemy is in the field.

Far from it – my intent is to strike at the biggest prize short of Antwerp and reduce it to impotence.

'Bergen Op Zoom. At the eastern extremity of the Scheldt and a valuable supply port for the French.' He paused impressively then snapped, 'Map.'

Spread out over the table, officers crowded around to peer at it.

'As you know, since the Dutch revolt, the French have withdrawn into town garrisons, leaving the countryside to us. I intend to take full advantage of this.'

He looked up sharply. 'A two-pronged assault. One from inland to isolate and take Fort de Roovere to landward here in the north of the town and . . . and the other from the sea.'

His gaze pierced Kydd. 'The Navy will land a strong force all along the seafront, which will draw the attention of the defences while the actual assault will take place from inland.'

Kydd swallowed hard. He'd had no warning of this plan, no consultation. And it was complete nonsense.

'Are you clear about this, Commodore?'

'Er, without a glance at my charts I cannot say, General.'

The map was a marvellously detailed production, down to the smallest windmill, but not one depth sounding or offshore shoal was marked.

Graham gave a loud sigh. 'Why is it when the Navy is asked for some trifle they're able to find every reason why it'll be impossible? All I desire is a substantial distraction to the south while we get busy in the north. Are you saying this is beyond the powers of the Royal Navy?'

'Sir. The inner reaches of the Scheldt are at present iced in,' Kydd said, with as much control as he could muster. 'This, and the fact that spring tides will expose mud-flats to strandings and worse, gives me severe misgivings that any force can be expected to close with the land. If I'd been consulted at—'

'So we cannot count on the Navy, it seems,' Graham said, pained. 'Therefore we will have to finish the job ourselves.'

The looks thrown at Kydd were more sympathy than hostility but he felt his face burn with the injustice of the demands. All the essentials of conjunct operations were being ignored – timings, reserves, order of landing, covering fire. Even without consideration of natural impediments, this was a hasty and ill-thought-out exercise.

He stayed. There was always the eventuality that the Army would have to be evacuated. He would place himself offshore for the duration of the operation, and needed to know the shape of the action.

Graham went on ponderously. There would now be a pincer movement into the streets of the town from each side but the big earthen Fort de Roovere would be their main objective. To this end it would be taken under assault by no less than four divisions. One from the north to divert attention inland, a main centre division directly at the southern gate and two wing divisions, who were apparently to swarm up the slopes and, mounting the ramparts, trot around either side, meet in the middle and be in position to descend into the body of the fort to complete the subjugation.

When Kydd heard that this was to be in the pitch dark of a moonless night, in the teeth of pitiless winter weather, he wordlessly shook his head.

Leaving, he drew Meares aside. 'My dear fellow. Tell me he doesn't mean to proceed with this lunacy.'

The officer, his face drawn, looked about him carefully before he spoke. 'I fear we must accept that he does.'

'Why? Is this lonely, Godforsaken place worth the blood and lives?'

'If you understood . . .'

'Tell me.'

Meares dropped his voice to a near whisper. 'He's had communication from London. In view of the failure of the Antwerp siege he's to hold himself and his regiments ready for a transfer to America. He desperately needs a quick victory, on the one hand to show he's yet capable, on the other that he and his command are still needed here, where there remains a chance for glory.'

Kydd's resentment was swept aside in a rush of feeling. Out there in the frozen slush were redcoats who had volunteered for the King. In trust of their leaders they were now going to throw themselves into lethal combat under a flawed plan of action.

'I pity the poor devils with all my heart,' he murmured.

'I'll remember that, my friend.'

'You mean . . .?'

'I'm to command the left division on the ramparts,' Meares said simply.

Chapter 59

'I'll go over it once more for the simkins among you,' Lieutenant Reeves said peevishly, not at all sure himself of what was expected of the company.

'We march into the town under cover of night. Stay in close order and don't stray. Then . . .'

The company let him drone on.

'When do we start, Mr Hoskins?'

'Shut y'r jabber, younker.' The sergeant was not in a good mood. The orders were clear enough. The main thing was to get across the dry moat and up onto the ramparts without being heard. He'd been in enough actions to know it was asking a lot. Still, the talk of an outside diversion taking place while they scrambled up was encouraging, as was the promise that a main central charge at the gate was timed to go in as they circled the rampart walkway to meet up with the other wing.

What was disturbing Hoskins was the lack of detail. It would be brutal out in the winter dark. How could they make out friend or foe when circling to meet the other wing? If they came across the enemy, they had only one shot in their firelock. After that it was going to be close in with the bayonet, and the top of an earth rampart in the dark with driving sleet was not the place to be doing such bloody work.

And passing orders – no affair went precisely to plan. This was not the usual battlefield, there would be no company drummers, and bugle calls would have no meaning in the circumstances.

'So, I wish you all good fortune and we shall meet again after the engagement.'

Reeves looked as troubled as he felt, the sergeant realised, so he loudly set to inspecting kit and sniffing out any who thought to drown their fears in grog.

There were to be no drummers but young Simon had a part to play, a vital part. He was to be company messenger. Unarmed, but fleet of foot, he was given the names of the four division commanders and a stout leather satchel. The old sergeant knew that the lad would be a much-changed creature after he emerged from this night.

At length the word came. They left the shelter of the town meeting-place and formed up outside. The cold was bitter and drove into their vitals. In the utter darkness it was impossible to see very far into the distance, the essence of winter misery.

After what seemed an endless wait while others joined, they moved off, in broken step to muffle their progress. For an hour or more they moved through deserted streets and fields until they reached the northern town boundary.

Somewhere ahead was the fort. They halted and waited but almost immediately out in the gloom came the sudden stabbing of gun-flash, a distant rapping of musketry.

The diversion had begun.

'Company – fix bayonets.' A storm of clicking sounded. 'Port arms. To the fore – march!'

It was a relief in a way to be moving. Hoskins walked up and down the line, ensuring their heading and pace before falling back to where he could keep them under eye. And be close to young Simon.

'Stay by me, tiddler,' he growled, proud of the way his charge was taking the hideous cold and late hour.

They found themselves crossing a muddy field but crackling frost kept the going firm, then out in the gloom, darker shadows, angular and long, showed the location of the fort. There was still a spirited engagement continuing on the far side and they pressed forward with nervous energy.

Even more heartening was a nearer paroxysm of fire. This had to be the centre division, as the diversion drew away defenders, now moving to the opposite side as planned.

This was the outer glacis and still no opposition. They were very close now – down into the dry moat, stumbling and catching in the rubbish-strewn bramble growth.

Shouts and death cries came, unidentifiable sounds of battle. Then the steep slope was before them. They slipped and panted up its frozen sleet-covered side, bracing for a sudden eruption of hostile figures at the crest – but there were none.

As they emerged onto the top of the ramparts a feeble cheer was heard, then another, stronger. Hoskins waited for Reeves to give the order. They had to move, now, but the man seemed strangely tongue-tied.

'T' go t' the left, sir!' he prompted. That was the direction given to make contact with the unseen other division circling in the opposite way.

Reeves was staring into the chaos that was developing in the pit below the ramparts, each moment of death and drama pitilessly lit by a gun-flash.

Seeing his sword hanging limply, his features blank, Hoskins guessed it was probably his first lethal combat.

A sudden squeal was a man dropping, writhing and kicking uncontrollably. They'd been seen from the pit of the fort where a group of French were coming together to bring the invading redcoats under fire.

'Sir – sir!' Hoskins cried. There was no response. The sergeant threw a glance down – the numbers were increasing but if that part of their company on the rampart came together they could give the French as good as they gave.

'Sir, please . . .'

Another man took a ball, dropping his musket and falling to his knees.

Reeves turned to him as if to speak but Hoskins saw that he was all a-tremble and knew he'd have to do something to head off a looming disaster. Get the company together and take on the French?

No! Their orders were to circle around to meet the other division, not delay to deal with a situation. What if the other side was waiting for them and they didn't appear? As well there was no point in using up their only shot – reloads in the wet blackness were unthinkable.

Simon stood beside him, clutching his satchel as if his life depended on it, the white of his eyes vivid in the darkness but bravely waiting to be told what to do.

'Company . . . to your left, advance!' Hoskins bellowed, and obediently the men turned. At not much more than an awkward lope they followed the ramparts.

The main charge against the gate seemed to be reaching some sort of crescendo and waves of the enemy ran to the inside to take on the assault. It would be their job to fire down from above, then descend to finish the job with bayonets.

He noted that the diversion had petered out, and with it indication of the midway mark on the rampart where they should meet the other wing to face inward and begin a close hand-to-hand fight. Hoskins tried to estimate the point – it was his decision. Reeves was jogging along with them, almost in a trance.

They came to where he guessed was the right spot but with a sinking feeling the sergeant could see no figures lurking ahead in the dark – no movement of any kind. Should he wait for the far division to arrive on the scene to meet them or push on further until he found them? If they'd run into trouble was it wise to blunder into it themselves?

One thing was certain. They couldn't stay where they were, stationary targets. They were already taking casualties and—

'Sergeant!' A tall figure with drawn sword was thrusting through towards him. 'Where's your l'tenant?'

It was Lieutenant Colonel Meares with three others.

'Er, here, sir.' He indicated the limp figure of Reeves, bowed and vacant.

Meares took one look and strode over. He delivered a resounding slap across the man's face, and again, the other way.

'Get a grip, you revolting shab, or I swear I'll have you shot.'

Reeves looked up, his eyes dull. 'Yes. Yes, sir.'

Meares wheeled on the sergeant. 'What's the situation?'

It was quickly explained. 'Very well. We must find them. Your company messenger?'

At the sight of the young lad he didn't hesitate. 'Listen carefully, messenger. Double on ahead, keep going on until you find the other division. Tell 'em to come here at the run. Do you know the password?'

'"Up the Orange"!' piped up the child. 'Reply, "God Save the King."'

'Very good. Off you go.'

Before Hoskins could say anything Simon was racing away into the darkness and was quickly lost to sight.

'The company to lie prone – that's fall down, you fool!'

At least they were now no longer easy targets.

Chapter 60

It seemed an age before there was a scurrying in the darkness and Simon came running towards them, panting. 'Sir, can't find 'em! Went all the way round like, they's nowhere.'

'What did you see, lad?'

'Well, a lot o' fightin' and pother down at the gate – but it's hard to see in this'n. Nothin' on the ramparts.'

'Ah. Well done, Mr Messenger,' Meares said thoughtfully.

'Um, I know it's not much sense in't,' Simon added hopefully, 'but I swear I saw Joe Searle down in wi' the others, maybe Colour Sergeant Roberts, in some kind o' mill.'

'You mean, down in the pit going against the French?'

'Don't rightly know what the Frogs look like, sir, but they were at it somethin' cruel.'

Meares drew a sharp breath. 'Damnation. If that's true, then that's Carleton, who's disobeyed orders for whatever reason. We've got to find out why and be prepared if necessary to descend and join up with him.'

He hesitated but then went on firmly, 'Messenger. I want you should get down to where you saw your friend and see what the position is. Right?'

Hoskins pushed forward. 'Sir, it'll better be me. No place f'r a younker.'

Turning to him Meares said kindly, 'You're right, Sergeant, it's not anywhere a youngster should be – but I believe he has a better chance in dodging about down there than you, don't you think? Every Frenchman will want a piece of you, but a child?'

'Sir, it's—'

'Off you go, m'lad.'

Simon returned, his tunic stained with powder-smoke and the tails of his coat slashed, but determined to say his message.

'It was them, sir. Colonel Carleton took 'em off the ramparts to look f'r the fort magazine, t' finish the assault in one hit, like. Joe, he thinks he's mad an' it's true, they're hard set b' the Frogs.'

He opened his satchel and took out a roughly scrawled piece of paper. 'Colonel says t' give you this'n an' he's not s-sanguine he can resist f-for much longer.'

Meares took it and read it by the light of gun-flash.

'Yes,' he said, slowly folding it. 'He does appear hard-pressed. Sergeant, prepare your company. A sharp volley, all aimed shots, then we go down with the bayonet. Clear?'

'Yes, sir.'

Chapter 61

Aboard Weazel

'You really should be below, sir,' Bowden said, but Kydd was having none of it. Raw and bitter it might be on the open water, but this was nothing compared to the suffering of the soldiers in the winter countryside.

'Think on the redcoats, Charles,' he said quietly. 'I'd not change places with any of the beggars for the worst the north Atlantic can show.'

He'd sent a midshipman ashore every day to keep informed so he knew that this night was the scheduled time for the assault.

What could he do to contribute to something he didn't believe in? Or even if he did, in the face of conditions like this?

Moodily, he paced the ice-slimed surface of the tiny quarterdeck, taking care to be in seizing distance of the lifeline. He glanced at the low-rimmed, near featureless land. It was a drab, white-blotched vista and the ice extended out to the best part of a mile under the ugly solid grey of the clouds low above.

'Sir – there's nothing you can do,' Bowden said, his teeth chattering. 'Only lie off and let events befall as they will.'

'Yes. They're on their own now, poor gullions. If it were in my power . . .'

But they were being held clear of the coast by the ice.

For the hundredth time under the slightest show of sail they slowly slid past the distant town. It was a nondescript drab, the wharves of the cargo working area clearly in view. In deference to the ice approaches there were no ships at the berths.

And they could not think to take their own ship inshore to an alongside berth, dashing any thought of being on hand to evacuate in the case of a retreat.

In the normal course of events a rescuing ship would lie out, her sails set but doused while boats were sent in to pick up the Army, but here it was never going to be feasible to send in boats to attempt to smash and pull oars into the ice.

Could they tell the men to go out on the ice to the outer edge to clamber aboard in free water? Kydd knew little of ice, how thick it must be to bear weight, how many men at a time . . . It was probably more certain than less that the ill-planned enterprise would fail and a withdrawal was on the cards. Beaten soldiers, crippled by cold and exhaustion, desperate to get away from such a hell.

He had to do something. 'Charles. Take us up to the edge of the ice.'

He quickly saw it was utterly unfit for the task of taking a boat up to it and bringing the men in. Wind-driven, a jerking and surging welter of floes of differing sizes were pressed up to the fringes. It didn't thicken and consolidate until a hundred yards or more further in. It was simply not possible to contemplate any kind of evacuation.

Cast down, Kydd continued his pace up and down. He took out his pocket telescope and swept the waterfront. It was bleak, still and deserted from end to end.

If only he could bring in the ship as usual, smartly alongside. He could then run out the brow and the fleeing soldiers could quick-march straight on board, no complications with boats – but he knew he was wasting time thinking about it. He'd seen it was not possible.

It would be dusk in not so many hours. At some time before midnight the regiments would march away to their destiny and the Navy would be unable to help.

Binard came on deck, almost comically clad in a mountain of clothing, bearing a steaming flask and tankard, which he offered with a bow and a pained expression.

The hot whisky toddy flooded Kydd's being and, holding it in his cupped hands, he let his mind wander.

Almost immediately he came to an intriguing idea. It was madness, of course, and he'd never heard of it before, but . . .

'The boatswain, if you please,' he asked the huddled officer-of-the-watch, obliged to remain on deck as long as Kydd was there.

'Sir?' *Weazel*'s boatswain was a bluff-featured Welshman, wary and careful before a full commodore.

Kydd didn't mention what he had in mind for he had to make sure of the facts first.

He closely questioned the mystified sailor. Anchors. The cathead and working tackle forward. The mechanical advantage of a three-fold purchase. Weights. The age when this particular kedge and sheet anchor had been forged. Where they were stowed.

As far as he could see it was all looking quite possible.

By the time he'd inspected the run of deck going aft from the foredeck on both sides he judged that it was in fact very possible. Energised, he wheeled on the officer-of-the-watch. 'Turn up the hands, sir. The watch below included – clear lower deck.'

It was extraordinary – was the commodore taking leave of his wits?

The young officer stuttered an acknowledgement and soon a boatswain's mate was pealing 'All hands on deck!' at the hatchways.

In the uproar and confusion Bowden's first lieutenant came aft to the quarterdeck and, after a quick glance at his captain and saluting Kydd, carefully demanded, 'Sir Thomas, and you'd oblige me by telling me your intentions.'

This officer would be ultimately responsible for their carrying out, whether an operation of war or merely a senior officer's idle whim.

'I wish the kedge anchor bent on to a three-fold-purchase at the larboard cathead, the sheet anchor to starboard. The deck to be sanded for thirty yards aft. Compree?'

He saw that the boatswain understood, then glanced at Bowden and his first lieutenant, who clearly did not.

'Why are the ship's company all turned up? Er, sir.'

'Mr Bowden. Are you aware there's an action afoot ashore as will be a hard-run thing? If the affair goes against us we shall be obliged to take off the lobsterbacks. How do you propose we do this, sir?'

'Um, the boats?'

'I don't think so.'

'Then . . .'

'The ice. We can't get to the wharf where we can take 'em aboard at the trot. But I have a notion how we can.'

His plan involved a cunning use of *Weazel*'s heavy anchors of the old sort, forge welded in the traditional way with the two flukes joined at the base of the shank instead of the more modern style with one piece bent around and hammer-welded in a regular semi-circle. The older ones were recognisable by a sharp V shape at the base.

And the cathead, a timber projecting over the bows, normally used to assist in bringing aboard and stowing the anchor when putting to sea, would be fitted with a three-sheave block and tackle from which would be suspended on each side the two heavy anchors.

'How . . .?'

'I noticed the wind's fair. We nuzzle the bows into the ice until we're brought up all standing. Then we let go our suspended anchors on both sides and they plunge into the ice and break it in pieces, allowing us to surge forward. All hands heave the anchors back up – it's only a few feet – and we go on in the same way.'

Kydd addressed the resentful men, spelling out the situation facing the redcoats, and then he had them.

The hardest part was to orient the ship to enter the ice crabwise, which was achieved by judicious trimming of the fore-and-aft staysails, but then the calvary could begin.

'Two, six – heavy!' The crew ran away with it and the anchors were poised once more.

'Let go!' The anchors plunged down, their base V easily piercing the ice-shelf, splintering a hole.

'Well! Heave away!'

And so it went on until *Weazel* was miraculously up with the deserted wharf in the last of the daylight.

They were in – they had kept faith.

Chapter 62

Ashore

Lieutenant Colonel Meares raised his sword so all could see, then bellowed, 'Fire!'

In a shattering fusillade muskets crashed down from the encircling rampart out of the darkness with shocking effectiveness.

'Battalion – *to the fore, charge!*' Meares yelled, waving his sword.

A fierce roar arose but the sergeant snatched back the little messenger. 'Not you, younker!' he shouted. 'Stay right here t' be ready to do y'r duty or be buggered to it an' I'll have yer liver for breakfast!'

He then disappeared into the running, stumbling blood-mad tide that made for the pit below, bayonets to their front in a lethally gleaming, medieval death charge. Few Frenchmen stayed to test their courage: they fled for the safety of the stone casemates, securing the doors and hatches.

'To me!' Meares called hoarsely, his sword held high.

Men came at the run and he quickly made dispositions.

'Sergeant,' he threw at Hoskins, 'find your messenger. We must get reinforcements.'

'Sah!'

Panting hard, Hoskins made the top of the steep incline to the ramparts. 'Simon? Where are ye? Needs t' send a message, mate.'

'Here I is, like y' said, Mr Hoskins.' The lad raced to his side, unconsciously clutching at his uniform coat.

'Go an' report t' Colonel Meares and—'

He was interrupted by a near simultaneous crash of musketry from down in the pit. The fleeing French had made it to their casemates – dry, warm but with the most precious article of all: lantern light.

Some quick-thinking French sergeant had got them reloading and they had then burst out into the open in a rage of fire that had torn mercilessly into the bayonet-armed British, who'd not been able to reload.

It was slaughter. Men fell, scrabbling to find shelter behind the bodies of the dead; others were picked off as they tried to clamber up the incline out of the pit.

Meares crumpled, hit by several bullets simultaneously, his blood mingling with that of those he'd led into battle. It couldn't go on.

A trumpet brayed and the fire fell away, followed by a raucous, hectoring shout.

'What are they d-doing, M-Mr Hoskins?' Simon whispered, his small frame trembling under the sergeant's protecting hand.

'I don't rightly know the Frog lingo but I reckon it might be tellin' us t' surrender.'

It seemed to be the case for, one by one, the survivors rose to their feet, throwing aside their useless muskets and making off to one side where a French trooper pointed.

The sergeant snorted. 'An' it's them down there that's givin' it in, lad. Not us.'

He jerked the youngster to his feet and in the darkness they plunged down the slope the way they'd come, into the brambles and filth of the dry moat, then up the other side where they found the same open muddy field as before. There was a hint of general lightening, a gradually extending vision of distance that would lead soon to full daylight and their discovery.

Squelching forward, it seemed to take an age before the denser shadows of woodland came nearer and the welcome shelter of tree and scrub.

'Now let's be scratching our noddles – how's to get away an' all.'

Choose the wrong direction and it could be the end for them in a very short time and if—

'Leave off, lad, you're hurting me.'

But the desperate grip on his arm didn't loosen. 'Mr Hoskins – behind you, th-there's . . .'

Wrenching about he saw uniformed figures spreading out as they approached and tugged frantically at the heavy German sword he favoured in place of the bayonet.

'Skewer the bastard, quick!' someone called.

They were English!

Throwing aside his sword, Hoskins swore loudly. 'Y' shonkers, an' you nearly did m' heart in. What regiment?'

'Fifty-fifth, Colonel Morrice, an' you?' It was a ragged corporal without a shako.

'Thirty-third and on the rampart wings. Didn't go s' well cos we couldn't reload and the Mongseers could.'

'Aye, same as we. Main attack an' they had men hid away, got all around us, dropped the colonel and adjutant both. No one t' take us under charge and when the Frogs called for surrender most did, like.'

'So . . .'

'So we gets out. At the double.'

'Where?' demanded the corporal, distrustfully.

''Ow long have yez been wi' the colours, y' ninny? There's always bin the Navy t' take us off 'n' they'll be there now, waitin' for us, my oath on't.'

'Down at the docks – maybe. I'm havin' none of it, cully. Th' only sure way for us'n is to go back the way we came – to Willemstad where we know there's barracks and—'

'That's a gooney notion – Willemstad is two, three days away. Docks are just over the hill.'

'An' you think the Navy's goin' to bother f'r a crew of redcoats?' jeered the corporal.

'O' course they is. S' let's be havin' you – all t' muster here.'

'Not us, you're on y'r own.'

The sergeant bellied up to the younger man and tapped his chevrons meaningfully. 'See these? They're sayin' as how you're followin' my orders or ye'll be explainin' y'self before the colonel.'

There were, astonishingly, forty-eight, most still with their arms, and it was likely that more would emerge as they progressed. They set off south-west, in the general direction of the waterfront and through the hostile but quiet town.

Chapter 63

Aboard Weazel

In the far distance all sounds of war and battle had faded into an ominous stillness. The two officers stood together, straining hard to make out what was happening.

'Don't like that we're not hearing anything,' Bowden said diffidently.

'Could be the fortress has already dipped its rag.'

'We'd be getting runners telling us to stand by for prisoners.'

'Mr Bowden. Turn out your Royal Marines with muskets and ball.'

'Aye aye, sir.'

It was little enough, and all they'd seen of the enemy were one or two astonished early risers, but they were ready for anything.

A short time later and still with the disconcerting quiet from inland there was a sudden flurry of shots a street or two away. It could be French escapers or British pursuers . . . or was it the other way?

They waited tensely and then, without warning, a flood

of soldiers in red coats stumbled forward, beseeching, desperate.

'Send down your marines,' Kydd snapped, 'to give fire if they're molested.'

The Royal Marines spread out and took up position as the fleeing soldiers found sanctuary. They were in the hundreds but made nothing of being prodded into each and every space *Weazel* could afford.

Kydd looked around. 'Bring the marines back aboard. That seems the lot and we have to get to sea.'

There was now the question of where he should take his exhausted passengers. Roompot was where it had all started and where there'd been a military presence since. It had the value of being on the same stretch of river, but at its estuary and the blessed open sea.

Decks crowded, *Weazel* found her way back the twenty-five miles to the windswept tidal mud-flats and the field cantonment where the Union Flag still flew.

A supply depot, it had a plain but serviceable landing stage for stores transports, and the brig-sloop was able to come alongside to discharge her human cargo.

They filed ashore, most still with their muskets but in a sad state. That British arms had come to this!

They seemed cheerful enough, though, and Kydd was touched when, as a grizzled sergeant shepherded a ridiculously young child soldier down the brow, both of them bedraggled and muddy, the youngster determinedly came to a stop and turned to give a shy wave.

A lump in his throat, Kydd waved back and watched them go.

It was the end of the enterprise in which he'd done what he could in the face of military lunacy. He supposed he should report to Graham. The general might well have some other ill-thought scheme that could be brought under the umbrella of an action against Antwerp and he'd be bound to be involved.

'Call away a barge, Charles. I'm off ashore to see what's taking shape.'

He was taken to a tent in the headquarters complex. A weary Lieutenant Colonel Williams offered sherry.

'Rather not, old fellow. Lot on my mind.'

As to the whereabouts of General Graham, Williams was quickly forthcoming. 'He took ship for England as quick as maybe.'

'Who's then in charge of the Antwerp expedition?'

'As far as I'm aware, there's no expedition any more.'

'Then who do I . . .'

It was no use asking. The entire business was a shambles. His way ahead was clear: he must haul down his flag and return with his ships to England for orders. Sheerness, and the Nore Command, was nearest.

Bitterly, he realised that Graham's rapid departure was to ensure he was in London when the news broke of the failure of his operation and give time for the blame to be shifted elsewhere. That the Navy had been unforgivably late in sailing would be a prime excuse and his brief time under a flag of his own would undoubtedly be his last – and Persephone had never even seen him at the head of a fleet at sea, however modest.

Still, there was one blessing. He'd be quit of the extreme folly that was the Low Countries.

He went back to *Weazel*, relishing the neat, clean and uncompromising warlike world he knew so well.

A worried Bowden asked him of their fate.

'We're going home, Charles!' Kydd said, with the broadest of smiles.

Chapter 64

Sheerness

The Nore was in the grip of a winter misery of raw, icy winds. Kydd, now returned to the spacious comfort of *Thunderer*, slipped the ship into her assigned berth where without ceremony his commodore's pennant was hauled down for the last time.

Their arrival would have been telegraphed to the Admiralty but it would take a formal request for orders to result in his destiny being made known.

His dispatches would be of key importance in the decision. Which could be anything from an immediate attachment to a blockade squadron or, with Bonaparte showing every sign of recovery and revival, it could be at any one of a number of trouble spots.

Or, if seen as an ineffective commander, their lordships at the Admiralty might decide to retire him and relieve him of his ship.

He gulped, dismissed Roscoe and the others to their

jollifications, and bent to the task of rendering details of the recent events. It had to be as speedy as he could contrive, or decisions would have been made that could not be unmade. His quill flew across the paper.

By early morning his report was ready, and as soon as he could he sent it on its way. It was done and he could only await his fate.

In a way he was relieved that it was all over and he accepted a dinner invitation from the sympathetic port admiral to find that Bowden was one of the guests, a kindly meant gesture.

He didn't send for Persephone: until things had resolved one way or the other he didn't want to worry her.

On the third day it came by Admiralty messenger, a slim pack that contained within it his future. In the privacy of his cabin he broke the seal. Two papers – the first the standard orders for deployment of His Majesty's Ship to the North Sea squadron. This was the closest to the bitter fighting where the Allies were confronting a snarling Napoleon Bonaparte. It would do very well.

The other was a personally written note from the secretary to the Admiralty, the legendary and feared Croker. '. . . and their lordships desire me to convey their full approbation of your conduct while acting under your flag as Commodore. In particular their express approval of your actions in relation to conjunct operations in the late expedition under the direction of General Sir Thomas Graham . . .'

It couldn't be plainer. They had known the whole truth, the difficulties he'd been under, and the impossibilities he'd been faced with, and were not only in sympathy but were approving the decisions he'd made in what could have been a delicate situation.

That Croker himself had penned the piece was significant. It was proof positive that he'd been noticed, this as a notable leader and presumably safe pair of hands in the future.

Happiness burst in on him in full measure.

Chapter 65

But Kydd's joy was short-lived. It was as if the entire world was holding its breath while titanic forces were rising to a climactic resolving of a clash of empires, of destinies. Napoleon Bonaparte had been in ignominious retreat but had recently miraculously held the line while he conjured into existence a new army. Now he stood ready to take on the combined wrath of the Allies – and, quite conceivably, as in the old way, go on to win, to crush.

To be part of the fleet of wooden walls that held the tyrant prisoner in continental Europe was a crucial role. The Dutch fleet, for instance, was very much alive in the Texel, and Kydd knew from personal experience that the invasion fleet, building in every harbour from France to Holland, was no idle threat. It existed and at any time could take to the sea.

With a vast and growing empire in far parts of the world, paradoxically Britain was more vulnerable than it had ever been, needing precious naval assets in those remote places at the expense of home defence. The North Sea Squadron was stretched to the limit. It was tasked with responsibility for the entire coastline of the continent from the French border, on to the Netherlands, Germany, Denmark and the Baltic approaches through to Norway and the Arctic north.

This enormous distance must be held unceasingly, in long weeks of ferocious weather or fog-clamped calms. Even days of slackened vigilance could allow a fatal sally by an alerted battle-fleet. Kydd expected *Thunderer* would be placed in the forefront of such a contest, and in the last few days at Sheerness he had the old ship made as trim and battle-worthy as he knew how.

The North Sea Squadron rendezvous was to seaward of the Hook of Holland. There, a solitary ship-of-the-line, *Culloden*, wearing the blue ensign of Admiral Cotton lay off, and coming to, *Thunderer*'s barge took Kydd aboard.

His accession to the squadron was brief. The admiral was clearly exhausted, out of humour and not impressed by his recent actions. A pack of fighting instructions was handed over and words on signal discipline and weekly accounts delivered. Without further ado Kydd was told he was to attach himself to the northern element of the squadron under Rear Admiral Cole in Swedish Gothenburg.

The war with Sweden was over, and in fact, although ruled by a Frenchman, the country had been persuaded to side against Napoleon. Now it could be relied on to take care of the Baltic. This left only Denmark, near helpless after the bombardment of its capital and loss of its entire fleet, and Norway, its dependency, both of which, as Bonaparte's allies, were under blockade.

With neither possessing any ships of size there was little prospect of any kind of action, let alone a full-blown fleet clash-at-arms and Kydd's spirits fell. There would be no appeal – he had been deployed in accordance with how Cotton saw best use of the latest addition to his force.

On the other hand, if there was an irruption of the enemy invasion fleet he was near enough to be called to the fight in hours. He wouldn't miss any great conflict. Clutching dispatches for Cole, he returned to *Thunderer* and, quickly disabusing the fire-eating Roscoe, set sail north without delay.

He knew Gothenburg. The naval anchorage, called Wingo Sound by British seamen, was well off the city, a dozen miles or more at a desolate windswept outer island that was nevertheless excellent shelter and well placed for a quick dash to the open sea.

Within the bay were two ships – one wearing the pennant of a rear admiral had to be *Theseus* and Kydd lost no time in making his way over to her.

The winds were chill and northern and, despite his well-quilted boat cloak, he was soon shuddering with cold. How distant was the memory of Bermuda and its wafting tropical scent.

He was piped aboard with all due respect but Kydd was immediately struck by a certain listlessness, a blank-eyed acceptance of the daily round. No vigorous movements, no curiosity at the new arrival. Was it the boredom of blockade or did it have a deeper rooting?

'Do sit, Kydd.' Rear Admiral Cole gestured.

'Sir.' He lowered himself into an old, well-creased leather armchair. It was singular perhaps that he wasn't intimidated by his surroundings, but *Theseus* was in the same class as *Thunderer* and the cabin the same size as his, with the same appointments. And, as he had to admit, his decorating was superior in most respects, Kydd having been lucky with prize-money.

'A roborative? The wind is cruel on the bones in these latitudes.'

Cole was the most advanced in years of any flag-officer he had known, bent, wizened, his uniform drooping from a shrunken frame. Nevertheless, his manner was watchful and shrewd.

'You've served in these parts before, I believe.'

'I have, sir.'

'Then you'll know the natives. When was that, pray?'

'With Admiral Saumarez and a little later.' Before the retreat from Moscow.

'Then be advised, matters have advanced since those times.' Cole looked at him gravely, his eyes tired and rheumy.

'I fancy there are not so many threats left to our maritime well-being, sir.'

'There are not, true, but we have another duty that takes our full attention.'

'Sir?'

'In this northern element I have no less than five ships-of-the-line and a strong show of supporting craft, both rated and unrated. Why do you think I've been granted such a bounty in these waters?'

It couldn't be blockade – Cole had a larger force than that off Brest, whose duty there was to confine anything up to twenty of the enemy ships-of-the-line. And in these distant northern waters there was nothing to blockade – no enemy naval bases, strategic anchorages, military strongholds.

As for any deadly threat – he couldn't bring to mind any that could pose a hazard to a single frigate, let alone a battleship. Yet the Admiralty in a time of the highest peril for the nation had seen fit to concentrate what amounted to a battle fleet in this part of the world.

'Sir, I stand at a loss for words.'

'Then please to pay attention. Should you fail in this duty, there will be pother at the level of nations.'

'Sir.'

'What do you know of the Sixth Coalition?'

'Er, lately brought about to combine against Bonaparte. Wherein we find Prussia, Austria, and Russia, um, and Portugal, Sweden—'

'Yes. And Sweden. Why did Bernadotte desert Napoleon and go over to the Allied cause?'

'Sir, my task—'

'Kindly answer my question, if you will.'

'He sees us as the eventual winner in the longer term?'

'No, sir. And I cannot emphasise this enough. It is because delicate negotiations gave him cause to do so and in the form of a treaty inviolate, that of Stockholm these few months ago. It was signed under two hands – Sweden and Great Britain.'

'To commence hostilities against the French Emperor?' It seemed Cole needed to make talk of high strategy – to underline his impotence in this backwater?

'To enter into the Coalition of nations, yes.' He leaned back and regarded Kydd speculatively. 'You wonder why I waste your time with this maundering.'

'Well, sir, it did—'

'Then hoist this aboard. The price for Sweden's commitment, as quietly mentioned in the lesser clauses of the treaty, is Norway.'

'Sir?' Kydd tried to make sense of it.

'Norway. Bernadotte – or Prince Karl Johan as we must now refer to him – has come in with his not inconsiderable army and fleet, on the basis that he be given a free hand in the annexing of Norway to the Swedish throne. Presumably at the victorious conclusion of the war.'

'As I understand it, Norway is ruled by the Danish,' Kydd said carefully.

'It is at this time, but their king, Frederick, in siding with Bonaparte in pique at our action at Copenhagen, did choose wrongly. Without a fleet, he could not defend what was his, and Norway has therefore been cut off by our sea-power and is helpless. But at the same time they must be accounted an ally of Napoleon, and therefore an enemy of Britain.'

'Sir, how is this to me, if I might be so forward in the matter?'

'Simply this. Your employing here is to one end – the blockade of Norway. That, and nothing more.'

Kydd was incredulous. 'With so many other line-of-battle ships? If Norway is isolated and deprived it'll be poor and no threat to any man.'

'That is not the point and is why I've been at some pains to give you a full appraisal. The main objective is not the subjugation of a minor kingdom but the satisfying of a formidable power.'

'Sweden.'

'Just so. To draw them into the immense encounter that's looming over us we must show by our actions that we're truly in full sympathy with their object – the detaching of Norway from the Danes. The only means we have at hand in this is to let it be seen that the reduction by sea of the country, while our loyal ally prepares to take it by land, is an unquestioned fulfilling of our promise.'

'I see.'

'So, I do require you to undertake a close – no, a tight blockade on Norway in the waters I shall assign you. Know that the contraband list is extensive and complete, including foodstuffs and clothing.'

Kydd remembered the desperate conditions of the people in Iceland those years ago, cut off in the same way from their motherland. This was the same, writ large.

'I shall expect a keen and active attention to duty, sir, as does not allow a single bottom to make port. As will convince the Swedes of our genuine interest in their objective.

'I'm sure I make myself clear and am equally certain of your faithful adherence to our formal obligation.'

'Aye aye, sir.' There was little else to say. A sad and pathetic duty for a noble and war-tested sail-of-the-line.

'You shall be assisted by a number of sloops of various rates under your command as I shall endeavour to find as soon as I may.'

'Sir.'

'Do bear in mind at all times our ruling principle – that this is entirely in support of the Treaty of Stockholm as concluded by His Majesty's Government and any failure to prosecute its provisions is presumably a treasonable act.'

'I understand, sir.' The satisfying of Sweden as an objective seemed to indicate a degree of importance that was extraordinary.

Chapter 66

London, the townhouse of Lord and Lady Farndon

'I see the Austrians under Radetzky have been doing well in Silesia,' Nicholas Renzi, 5th Earl of Farndon, murmured, his newspaper rustling.

'If you say so, dear,' Cecilia said primly. 'You know I can never remember all those heathen foreign names.'

'Says here that with forty thousand in the field, before he—'

'My lord?' It was Jago, the dark-jowled and inscrutable under-steward, bearing an envelope on a silver tray.

To his wife's frustration, Renzi had insisted the man accompany the rest of the servants here for the season.

He picked up the single folded sheet and saw immediately what was afoot. It was from Congalton, the high-ranking member of the secret service with whom he'd had dealings in the past on matters of national importance. In his crabbed hand he expressed a polite wish to renew their acquaintance at Lord Farndon's leisure, covertly letting him know that a mission awaited, should he feel suited to it.

*

Congalton rose and with a polite bow desired Renzi to sit. The room was familiar – so many exciting and dangerous episodes in his life had started in this plain, windowless space, the austere and all-knowing shadowy figure always the instigator.

'My lord, so kind in you to visit.'

Renzi knew better than to bandy small-talk and waited patiently.

'It would appear that there is a matter in which their lordships are much exercised in reaching a conclusion.' Their lordships were the mysterious beings to whom Congalton answered.

'Do explain, dear fellow.'

'Then do you know aught of the Swedes, in particular the Treaty of Stockholm, my lord?'

'I have heard of its singular provisions, yes. For Great Britain to deliver up Norway when asked?'

'In fine, yes. In return, however, we have secured the military services of the dominating Nordic power. Not only that, but particularly the services of their regent, Karl Johan – Marshal Bernadotte that was. Some would say the most able field general in Europe short of Napoleon himself. And with his accession to the Coalition they've given him command of the Army of the North to guard the northern flank of the Allies as they advance on France.'

'Indeed. I'd heard that if Bonaparte were ever to be toppled his name would be foremost in those to be the new Emperor of the French empire.'

'Yes. A prize indeed for the Allies, and all as a result of your Treaty of Stockholm.'

'Then?'

'There is a . . . difficulty.'

'Which being?'

'We have enacted the treaty and it has brought results. But we are now bound by its provisions – we have agreed to the acquisition of Norway.'

'But?'

'Their lordships have determined that at the same time this is not altogether in our national interest.'

Renzi waited.

'The war of Napoleon will not go on for all of time. There will be a new world afterwards and they fear that we may well be disadvantaged in it as a result of actions of convenience carried out now.'

'Norway?'

'If Sweden possesses Norway it has as well its dependencies in the north. That will not be enough for them. With the combined forces at hand it will feel emboldened to seize both sides of the sound into the Baltic, simply by invading Denmark, a weak, bankrupt and beaten nation.

'This will place the Baltic and the entire north from Greenland to Russia in the power of the Swedish. You will understand that no domination by a single power can be contemplated.'

'I see,' Renzi said thoughtfully. 'But the treaty is inviolable, internationally ratified. We have no choice now.'

'Quite.'

'Then?'

Congalton fiddled with a dog-eared quill and looked at Renzi directly. 'This supposes that when the Swedes move to take Norway it will be in the nature of an unopposed annexing. In other words, Norway will be diminished in its existence to become merely a province of Greater Sweden, and Sweden will therefore run from the Baltic to the Atlantic as one nation under one king.'

'An unconscionable upsetting of the balance of Nordic nations.'

'Indeed. There is, however, one condition that will give pause to our Karl Johan. That is, if instead of annexing a province, Norway is in truth a kingdom – a nation with its own king and parliament. A swallowing of such in the style of Emperor Napoleon would not be tolerated by the Allies, who are sworn to fight together against such behaviour.'

Renzi could see it. 'Ah – but it does not possess same. When the country is wrested from Denmark it will lose its king in the process. Any authority for a parliament as well. Sweden will no doubt provide both – to its own advantage, of course.'

'You are right. But we have a small margin of time before the Swedes take possession.'

'To what end, pray?'

'Before the Swedes take possession of Norway, should there be an uprising of discontent against Danish rule, which has been woefully impotent these last years, and should this result in their acclaiming a king of their own – which they did have some four hundred years ago, I beg to remind you – we have a nation in being. And the condition is fulfilled.'

'Surely, old fellow, you don't wish me to—'

'Not at all, my lord. All my masters require is a species of reconnoitre that will reveal whether there exists in Norway any such desire or even a credible formed body that has this objective.'

'And?'

'I speak with delicacy and circumspection, you'll appreciate.' Congalton's voice lowered as if to hide his words from listeners. 'For if there is such a movement they have a decision to make. To render support privily of a material kind while at once openly affirming the Swedish position or . . .'

'Or?'

'My lord, you will appreciate that the stakes are considerable. To this end it would necessarily be the objective of His Majesty's Government to force the issue at the highest diplomatic level, engaging various national obligations and so forth. This they would much rather not be seen to be doing.'

Renzi sat back in something like dismay. This was an almost impossible task – the discovery and assessing of a revolutionary band with the capability of bringing into existence an entire nation, such that the powers-that-be would take him at his word and stay their hand from extreme measures.

'This is a hard thing, sir. I have no knowledge or acquaintance with Norway. How might I be trusted to discover its true allegiances?'

Congalton became businesslike as in the old way. 'You will go in your customary character as a rich noble looking to tinker with an investment, this time in Sweden, our ally. This will be the prospect of a recently discovered iron-ore deposit, which, as it happens, is close to the Norwegian border. Naturally, you will want to see for yourself and will disappear into the interior for a month or so before returning to England.'

Having slipped into Norway instead.

'Will I have friends? That is, are there those who will guide me at all?'

'We have some names,' Congalton said guardedly. 'This part of your enterprise requires little or no baggage and therefore establishment. Perhaps a well-trusted companion – I seem to remember you have made profitable use of such in the past.'

'Yes. Er, when . . .?'

'Your passage to Gothenburg is arranged for a week hence, my lord.'

Chapter 67

At sea

'Er, my lord . . .' The captain of the Swedish packet hesitantly entered Renzi's cabin, cap in hand, and waited.

Renzi groaned under his coverlet, prostrated by a pitiable state of sea-sickness. It was well pretended and the perfect cover to allow him his privacy. While on the voyage he avoided questions and studied all he could of the Norwegians. As a naval officer in another life he had long since conquered the malady but he knew that, further forward, Jago hadn't that advantage.

'Yes?' he answered weakly.

'Happy t' say, the Buskar light is under our lee.'

'Pray what can that mean to me?'

'As we shall be alongside before the day is out, my lord. That's t' say, there'll be no more moving as that we can rely upon.'

It had been a quick and uneventful passage to Gothenburg but the hardest part was the immediate future.

He stayed out of sight as his sea senses told him that first one, then a second boat had touched while sails were backed, and now it was the smoother waters of the entry to Gothenburg.

It wouldn't be easy – if the authorities were watching him what chance did he have of slipping into Norway and making contact with revolutionaries?

At the least they'd be interested in him: what he was doing in Sweden, why the noble lord was visiting unannounced.

As expected they were boarded as soon as the lines were ashore and he found himself politely but closely queried, Jago's presence being of no account.

They were told he'd been approached in England by a projector who'd learned of a large iron-ore deposit and was seeking backing for its exploitation; he was in Sweden simply to satisfy himself of its existence.

The reason for his discretion was obvious. Should his presence become known, he would lose his commercial advantage. Therefore his reasons for the visit and the source location hc was keeping to himself.

And then he saw a way forward. Renzi knew how the official mind worked and had no doubt that he would be only half believed until they had some assurance of his innocence. So he'd play along to just that end.

Would the gentlemen he saw before him arrange for him to be taken discreetly by some official means to a place near the location? It would thereby ensure no undesirables would be involved while of course he would recompense the government.

It would suit their purposes indeed to be able to see at the first hand what he was about and where, and at the same time provide for Renzi a reliable means to get to where he wanted to go without hindrance of any kind.

Chapter 68

In the small but comfortable aviso, they made Strömstad by late afternoon, a charming town set among myriad islands, each white-streaked with snow. Its nestled buildings were in bright Scandinavian colours. Renzi was escorted to a snug inn of the old style. Would my lord require later further escort to the site of the iron ore?

Renzi felt it not appropriate, meaningfully consulting his map while keeping it shielded and letting it be known that he would be hiring a local guide, who would not be told the exact location until the last moment.

The officials left with every wish for good luck in his prospect and, sipping an akvavit of remarkable herbal presence before a handsome fire, he and Jago set to making plans.

Jago was to use his talent for passing among the underworld to find a means of entering Norway. Congalton's two names were both in the same town – Fredrikstad, not more than thirty miles inside the border.

He was back within the day with the answer. A fishing boat. Small, local, of the kind the English blockaders left alone as not worth taking in prize, and able to make use of thc maze of islets along the coastline.

There were complications. The most disturbing was that he was crossing into a country that was at war with Britain and he therefore risked being taken up as a spy.

Consequently it was too dangerous not only for the fishing-boat crew but his lodgings in Fredrikstad to be aware he was English, but what else could he be?

French.

The Denmark-Norway kingdom of Frederick VI in Copenhagen still nominally ruled Norway and they had chosen to ally with France. A Frenchman therefore had every reason to be in the country and need fear nothing from a Norwegian.

A certain Monsieur Laval thus eased out of the inn before dawn, leaving behind a satisfying quantity of evidence that the English lord had quietly left for the interior and his iron-ore trove.

The boat was a small half decker with a three-man crew, all of whom were gratifyingly silent and uninterested in their passenger. They were under way as a wan light stole across the seascape and its multitude of skerries and islands.

There was no point at which it could be said they'd crossed a border. Norway appeared just the same as Sweden and the islets just as numerous. But it brought with it unwelcome attentions. A brig-sloop flying a red ensign sent away a boat with the obvious intention of making their acquaintance.

Instantly a stinking fisherman's smock was thrust at Renzi, with a pair of decrepit leather sea-boots, which he hastened to throw on. Then a keg of fish was shoved at him and a gutting knife slapped into his hand.

A fresh-faced midshipman sent one seaman to rummage the half-deck while he poked about the usual raffle strewn around the deck of working fishermen. His glance fell on Renzi, who casually took a still-wriggling fish and began slitting it open.

The rest of the crew stopped working to stare at the revolted midshipman, who coloured and declared loudly, 'Nothing here, you men. Back aboard, then.'

Chapter 69

Fredrikstad was at the head of a lengthy lead, a pretty town with a small waterfront set about with warehouses and official buildings of another age. As the fishing boat passed by on the way to its berth Renzi surveyed the scene surreptitiously.

He sensed a quiet, somewhat morbid air, an almost total lack of activity that could only have been caused by the near demise of meaningful trade by the close blockade. If it were ever known who he was, his would probably not be a pleasant fate.

Followed by a wordless Jago hefting their luggage – a single sentence of English between them would be all it needed to betray them – Renzi headed for the largest tavern he could see.

His French only brought incomprehension and suspicion but he dared use no other language and played the perplexed Frenchman until a drowsy clerk was roused out.

His grasp of the language was execrable but Renzi was able to establish himself as a harmless businessman in the timber trade wanting to stay for a few days to look over local prospects.

In the morning he sent Jago off to make communication with the names he had. A reply came back quickly: Renzi was to wait until dark before calling alone at the address specified.

This turned out to be a derelict house towards the edge of town and the meeting took place in darkness.

'*Qui ai-je le plaisir de rencontrer, m'sieur?*' opened one of the dimly seen pair. The accent was not native, the delivery more of the recent imperial style, but at least they were spared the need for an interpreter.

'*Laval, facteur de bois navale*,' he answered easily.

'What is your interest in the independence of Norway, M'sieur le facteur?'

Could it be so easy?

'My sympathies are with any who value liberty and justice, sir. Do I understand that you represent those who believe Norway must seek her own way in this world, her own anointed head, her own assembly?'

There was a low exchange between them and then a careful reply.

'You must know we so believe, sir. Do you come to our land to offer assistance in this precious goal?'

Renzi could hardly believe his luck.

'It could well be possible, *mes braves*. First you will tell me about your band.'

'*M'sieur – d'où viens-tu?*' This was the previously silent one of the pair, from his accent undoubtedly a French native, asking Renzi of his origins as a Frenchman.

In a flash things had changed. Why did he need to know this?

'*De Guadeloupe*.' He'd play safe as an overseas expatriate until he understood what was going on.

'*Une espèce de fadaises*,' spat the man venomously, rejecting the notion.

'Er, let's not be too hasty, Bertrand,' the first said quickly. 'Sir, you said you came to make contribution to our struggle. Is this so?'

'As I need to assure myself of the ardour of your striving.'

'The Emperor has every indication of our loyalties,' the second came back suspiciously. 'Why is it so necessary to repeat ourselves?'

'Emperor?' In his astonishment Renzi couldn't help the slip.

The gleam of a pistol suddenly appeared in the shadows. 'If you are not sent from *L'Empereur* then who are you, spy?'

Renzi froze. His pretence at being French was no longer in any way possible. Should he instead make appeal to their patriotism?

'Do, I beg, first explain to me how a true son of Norway who craves independence and liberty can feel able to call on the name of the Emperor of the French?'

'Ah – so you are English. I guessed so. Well, Englishman, I would have thought it self-evident. We do so yearn for liberation from the Danish yoke, but we will not receive it from your hands. Only the world-conquering Napoleon is in a position to offer this, which he will do the moment he recovers from his late reverses.'

Renzi could say nothing. He'd found his clandestine independence group – but they were siding with the French and were never going to be of use to Congalton's lords.

'Bertrand, we must—'

'I know. He's an embarrassment. What shall we do with him?'

Chapter 70

Thunderer, *off the coast of Norway*

Kydd's blockade station was easily defined – Oslofjorden, the fifty-mile long narrow inlet leading to the Norwegian capital, Christiania. It was, of all the thousand odd miles of the country's coastline, the most lucrative. Half of the eastern side was Swedish, and smuggling and other illicit activities were common, but the blockade was merciless. Little traffic still attempted the run after five years of war.

Kydd knew the opposite side of the fjord from not so very long before. Admiral Saumarez had tasked him to destroy the last warship of size the Dano-Norwegians had at sea, a frigate. He'd been successful but only after a heart-stopping fight among the iron-hard skerries and islets of the inner leads there.

Now he was to clamp a hold on everything that moved at sea, after relieving the 74-gun *Ganges*.

Thunderer's purpose was to lie offshore to be on call for the boats that were doing his bidding as the front-line labour inshore.

It would be dreary and uninspiring work and more than a little distasteful. The admiral had mentioned that contraband included food and clothing, as these were the articles an army needed, quite as much as guns and powder, but consequently common people would see hardship. For the task he had two brigs and four cutters. He was pleased to note the name of one Commander Bowden and *Weazel* in their number.

On sighting Kydd's little command, *Ganges* and her brood wearily set sail for Gothenburg and an overdue fettling.

Under easy sail Kydd placed himself squarely in deep water across the seaway to Christiania while he sent his hounds in.

Day by day it was the same. Grey, cold and windswept, the seas unwelcoming and desolate, the land distant and unattainable. It had to be done – while *Thunderer* and her sisters kept the seas the Norwegians would never be able to prevent the Swedes eventually taking their country for their own.

Kydd had no particular feelings on the matter. Like many Englishmen he regarded events on the continent as largely distant, meaningless affairs. There'd been ebbs and flows of military successes and reverses up and down Europe ever since he'd first been to sea.

His duty was to make it possible for an ally to receive due recompense, in territory, for their blood and gold in the service of the Coalition. Not for him to dispute any moral standing. As far as he was dimly aware, the Norwegians had been under a Danish crown for centuries and all they were doing was exchanging that crown for a Swedish one.

Of much more concern was that there was every chance Napoleon Bonaparte would very shortly recoil like a snake and, with his miraculously produced army, throw the world into full-scale conquests once more.

But meanwhile Kydd would do his duty to Admiral Cole

and the faceless others, make certain Norway was deprived of everything, and bow to Fate.

The gloomy Swedish pilot they carried was not helpful. Apparently there were countless tracks through the islands and passages where a modest-sized merchant ship could slip on its way north into Christiania. This would be by routes known to the centuries and perilous in the extreme.

The best discouragement for tempted blockade runners would be appearances at random by his men-o'-war, the risks then considered by them too great to run the gauntlet.

Thunderer would ply a central position on the ten and a half degree meridian going north to fifty-nine and a half degree latitude and south again, always on hand if needed. The brigs and cutters were equally spaced on either side of the fjord, reporting regularly.

So time passed.

Chapter 71

In a little less than a week the grey seas bore a brig-sloop towards them out of a mist-laden horizon. It was *Weazel* and a set-faced Bowden hailed to request he see Kydd on a confidential matter.

Both ships heaved to in the calm sea and Bowden came aboard, in full dress and sword, an ominous sign. He was ushered below.

'Why, Charles, dear fellow. No need for full fig. Or is it . . .'

'It is, Sir Thomas.' Bowden was stiff and formal.

'Do sit and tell me.'

He remained standing and spoke woodenly. 'Sir, it's with the utmost regret I have to ask you for a court-martial on certain members of my ship's company.'

'Good God, Charles! Are you in jest, man?'

'Sir. Contrary to my express order three men broke ship and took a boat ashore. In it they carried goods of a contraband nature, which they then passed to the enemy.'

Kydd could hardly believe his ears. That English seamen should seek to profit in such a blatant manner meant that most of *Weazel*'s people must have been involved, the ship and her crew rotten to the core.

Bowden's features were haggard.

'This needs dealing with at once. If it was known in the fleet as a whole that they had got away with such acts . . .'

'Sir.'

'Are they taken up?'

'In irons.'

'Good. Tell me now precisely what happened.'

'I was cruising the western shore as per your orders, sir, with no sightings of any kind. I then had occasion to anchor for the night, those parts being particularly hazardous in the hours of darkness. I chose the shelter provided by the entry to an inner lead – a place by the name of, er, Årøysund.'

He paused as if to recruit his memory, then pressed on. 'During the night when sea watches stood down, apparently we were visited by a person from the village who spoke with one of my people who was himself a Norwegian. He it was who became the ringleader to persuade a number of others to take the pinnace ashore with the goods.'

Kydd, with his first-hand knowledge of the lower deck, was suspicious. Subversive things didn't happen so quickly – and with a non-English ringleader?

'What goods did they take, pray?'

'Sir, I have to report that the galley was plundered of its next-day victuals.'

Kydd jerked back in surprise. 'Salt pork and such?' he replied incredulously.

'Just so. And it seems the seamen gave up their evening meal of hard tack and cheese to go with it.'

'I see. Charles, you did right to bring this before me. There's injustice here and I'm not sure in all charity where it lies.' He stood and declared briskly, 'I'm to look into this serious matter myself. I'll trouble you to take me back to where the offence took place.'

Later that day, with Roscoe as his witness, Kydd stepped ashore at the rickety landing stage at Årøysund, a tiny village set on a slope, near completely surrounded by low forested islands.

The first thing that was noticeable was the deathly quiet. Nothing stirred.

Although the nearest houses were close no one came to see who had visited. And heavily on the air was a sickly sweet stench that caught in the throat.

Kydd posted three marines at the boat with its crew and he and Roscoe set off.

The houses showed decay, weathered timbers, miserable gardens. At the first Roscoe shied back with a muffled cry, his sleeve across his mouth.

Laid neatly side by side were four bodies. They had been dead some time, the skin shrivelled and discoloured. It was clear how this had happened. The horrifically sunken skull features, grossly distended stomach and spindle-thin limbs showed they had starved to death.

At the next house it was the same. Old people, children, babies – all were taken. The last to live had only the strength to drag them from their homes where they'd died. No burying or last rites had been possible.

Kydd and Roscoe stared at each other in horror, unable to move. The implication was plain. As if before the muzzle of their guns, they had brought about these heart-wrenching scenes of death of innocent folk whose only offence was to belong to the wrong side.

Kydd knew that the other extent of Oslofjorden, with its border with Sweden, flat countryside and roads, was much more prosperous. Here, rugged, impassable mountainous spines and poor soils meant the only sustenance possible was by sea trade, and when that was cut off by blockade there was no hope.

'Sir?' Roscoe mumbled, gesturing up the slope. One or two ghost-like figures dodged sideways out of sight. Those who still survived.

They turned and stumbled back to the boat. Without a word the crew put out and they left the tragedy behind them.

Chapter 72

On the way back to *Weazel*, Kydd wrestled with his thoughts. The suffering he'd just witnessed tore at his reason, questioning the sturdy pillars of his existence that were demanding such a price. He'd always done his duty, usually a comfort to cleave to in the worst situations for its calm, unequivocal demands that assured him by its certainties.

However, in the final analysis there was no question, no argument. Whatever he felt – and he'd been much affected – duty demanded that he follow his orders, which in this case came from Admiral Cole, insisting that the blockade be as tight as it could be. He'd even gone so far as to say that anything less was nothing short of treason.

But when it resulted in this?

More pressing was what he must face back aboard *Weazel*. His instincts had been right. The lower deck had known of the strict orders behind the blockade but had learned of the situation ashore when a local man had gone out to the anchored vessel to beg for something to eat.

The seamen's impulsive act had been to lay hands on all the victuals they could readily find and send them ashore with their no doubt agonised Norwegian shipmate. Only Bowden's unexpected late-night turn around the decks when he noticed the pinnace missing had done for them.

Both his own flotilla orders and *Weazel*'s captain's orders had been clear and unarguable. The three in bilboes had been lawfully taken in charge but the entire ship's company had been complicit in the act. Should the three suffer while others were allowed to go free?

And what of the future, should the blockade continue its cruel progress? If Kydd was seen by other members of the Norway Squadron condoning contraband smuggling he would quickly find himself before a court-martial. His duty was straightforward. And if he was going to do his duty he had every right to expect that those under him do the same.

So where did that leave the men in irons? The charge of direct defiance of orders at three levels was too serious to overlook – and in any case a court-martial was not his to summon. The awesome weight of naval justice demanded he took Bowden's unanswerable evidence and recommend them for court-martial.

This would not be possible until the end of their spell on blockade and then they would have to await the day when five post-captains were free to sit on the trial. The unfortunate prisoners would languish an unknown length of time in irons to finally meet their fate. It was brutal and piteous, with only one possible end.

As he climbed over the brig-sloop's bulwarks Kydd was suddenly struck with an idea. Lifting his eyes to meet Bowden's, he intoned before the watch-on-deck, 'Ah, yes. You were indeed right, Commander. I shall therefore see the prisoners before me in one hour.' It would give him some small time to collect his wits.

'Master-at-arms, this is not a trial. Strike off their gyves, sir.'

The three, blinking in the sunlight, watched him as though he'd taken leave of his senses. Soon he had *Weazel*'s entire company crowded on deck and in the rigging, straining to hear. Bowden and his lieutenant stood behind Kydd and the lectern.

'These men.' He let the words hang for a space before going on: 'I'm minded to congratulate you for your late initiatives, performed in the best traditions of the service.'

He struggled to control his amusement at the chase of emotions across their features.

'Yes, your captain has let me know everything. To seek to gain valuable intelligence by bribing the enemy with foodstuffs they're unable to get for themselves, and that out of your own pockets, so to speak.'

He paused impressively, looking around him at the confused and puzzled faces, and went on ponderously, 'It was a well-meant operation and I can understand your desire to carry it out in confidence, seeking to earn unshared distinction for yourselves. However, I should make it clear that these actions should rightfully be left to those whose business it is – the winning of notice will already be yours in the event of a famous gun action, you may well be assured.'

The silence hung, so he continued in a light tone, 'As to your offences – breaking out of the ship is not lightly to be ignored but I beg your captain will be good enough to overlook it this once. Contravention of orders is another matter. You men, this must never happen again or the outcome will be very different.

'Carry on if you please, Commander.'

Chapter 73

Kydd returned to his ship in a black mood, a pall of feeling remaining after what he'd seen and could do nothing about. It was no good reasoning that, in the chaos of war, worse things were happening on the continent to his south as the Allies grappled with Napoleon in a climactic struggle for mastery or defeat.

Thunderer took up her easy sail in the centreline of the fjord and he could sense that something of what had passed had reached her company. They'd been considerably cast down at this evidence of their hideous war on the common folk.

With a start he recollected that, apart from their side-affair in Spanish Florida, they had smelt no powder in the entire year up to the present. For a ship-of-the-line this was not unusual, these days, but it was not what his ship needed. And the chances of any fight worth the name in these waters were vanishingly little.

Then, out of a bank of drizzle, an aviso cutter emerged, clearly searching for them. This was no run-of-the-mill delivery of dispatches for *Thunderer*'s pennant numbers were in the signal. It shortened sail and came alongside. A line finished with a weighted monkey's fist was flung down from *Thunderer's* quarterdeck, and shortly hauled back aboard with a canvas bundle bent on.

Kydd's hail, wanting to know if anything had newly happened in the south, was answered with an apologetic reply that indeed there had but the lieutenant-in-command had been too busy, occupied in his errands, to take on board just what was going on.

Presumably the canvas pouch would yield the answer and, knowing every eye was on him, Kydd hurried to his cabin. It was from Colston, the rear admiral commanding the much-diminished Baltic Squadron now that Saumarez had struck his flag and returned home.

A hurried, even perfunctory note ordered that, with the utmost expedition, he was to detach himself from duty and, with the other sail-of-the-line, proceed south to rendezvous in the western Baltic north of Rostock, leaving his minor vessels to continue the Norway blockade.

No reason was given but Kydd's pulse quickened. Ships-of-the-line were not snatched from their station without good reason and this had to be a concentration of force for an action – presumably on a fleet scale.

A fleet action! The last he'd seen had been the miniature battle at Lissa, fought between frigates. And before that . . .Trafalgar?

There was nothing about resupply, stores, watering – these he had to assume would be made available at the rendez-vous.

When he thought about it more, it seemed odd. That it had not been a summons to the traditional battlefield of the North Sea, on the other side of Denmark, was a puzzler. Where was the threat in the Baltic? But it was no good wasting time in speculation. They would learn soon enough.

He emerged on deck as casually as he could manage. Instantly all activity stopped. 'Mr Roscoe.'

The first lieutenant hurried over, watched by a hundred eyes. 'Sir?'

'I want to be under way, all plain sail, by the end of the watch.'

'Aye aye, sir. Er, the course?'

'As will take us through the Sound.'

It said it all in one. Dead south through the Kattegat past Denmark, then the narrow and dangerous passage between it and Sweden before emerging into the Baltic. The rendezvous required hooking around its southern islands to end off the north German shore.

That night, as they swashed south in the full moon, the wardroom was ablaze with excitement. A stirring action would undeniably bring opportunity for distinction, and who knew what advancement after the fighting and possibly gun money, head money, even prize money?

It was tantalising – and bewildering. Who was the foe? Where were the strategicals?

Kydd could do nothing to settle the arguments, being in much the same perplexity, but he suspected from their frowns that they thought he was holding something back.

Chapter 74

In the morning light they passed Helsingør, Shakespeare's Elsinore, the narrowest part of the Great Sound, with nothing more than a token rumble of guns. The Danes, without the navy seized from them, had no means available of doing much more and *Thunderer* stretched south, past Copenhagen and out into the Baltic.

In the evening light they raised *Theseus*. Several other 74s were visible hove to beyond her.

Not delaying, Kydd took boat for the flagship. It was a scene of confusion and disarray.

He was kept waiting along with two other captains before he was summoned. Admiral Cole was distracted, almost to the point of flustered.

'Little time to explain, Kydd. There's a move against Boney afoot as requires our immediate support and I'm vexed to find ways to do so. Do forgive if I ask Flags to lay out the essentials – and good fortune in what's to come, old chap.'

Pryce, the smooth and urbane flag-lieutenant, took Kydd aside to fill him in. While Bonaparte gathered his forces in the heart of Germany for the grand fight-back, the Army of the North under the new-minted Swede, Bernadotte, had made secret plans to invade Denmark. This involved swinging around and thrusting up from the south to effectively seal off the peninsula of Denmark isolating them from events on the mainland and hopefully bringing about their capitulation. The stakes were impressive: the Danes and their entire armed forces would be prevented from joining the coming Armageddon on the side of Napoleon.

Pryce drily went on to point out that many were of the opinion – rightly or wrongly – that the Swedes were simply accelerating their time-line for taking Norway. Irrespective, the British government had promised every assistance in this initiative and hence here they were, being very visible at the stepping-off point for the invasion. What the Navy could achieve was not made clear and their presence in the area was if anything an embarrassment.

Kydd's hopes of a great fleet action died. Yet again, political forces at the very highest were determining what was happening on the battlefield.

His orders, when they came, were terse and to the point. In the absence of higher direction, the ships-of-the-line were deployed equally along an east-west line ready for any call that came.

Thunderer was allocated the furthest west in consideration of Kydd's experience in these waters earlier and she duly entered the confined seaways off the ancient Hansa ports of Rostock and Lübeck, the nearest to the point of invasion. It was galling to know that world-changing events were about to unfold under their lee but their orders were to await any cry that came.

Kydd did what he could. He sent Roscoe ashore to find out what was going on. He returned the same day with a major of the King's German Legion, a British formation, with news.

The invasion had started well and the combined Swedish and Russian forces had stormed in – but then the Danes had fought back. At a place called Sehested they'd even won a face-to-face battle against the Cossacks and Prussians and looked to hold the line and even drive the entire invasion to a standstill.

The major gravely explained that unless the reinforcements the Danes were pouring in from the north were stopped, the outcome was severely in doubt.

Kydd glanced at the map the man had produced. It was a landsman's work and made very clear the hazards and obstacles facing any army advance. What it did not show were the opportunities – such as a substantial inlet less than a dozen miles above the fighting.

He examined the map more closely. The Eckernförde Bight: not only was it positioned to advantage but the entire advance of the Danes passed by its inner end. Their route was constricted by a lake further inland, thereby forcing them to within cannon-shot of the sea. Cannon-shot!

'Major, should I move quickly I do believe I shall be able to relieve the situation.'

The hard-bitten officer looked unconvinced. 'I have no authority to authorise any actions you might propose and—'

'*You* have not, but I may act under my own initiative.' This was true – if he saw a chance to punish the enemy he had every right to move on it. 'Expect your reinforcements to cease as of the morning,' he said confidently.

Chapter 75

The Eckernförde Bight

The long stretch of water between the two shores was no more than a couple of miles across. It was peaceful and uncluttered and Kydd saw that what he had in mind was more than possible: keep out of sight for the remainder of the day, then during the hours of darkness, quietly close with the pinch-point on the coast to arrive at daybreak when armies begin to go on the move.

A gentle north-easterly was useful for both entry and leaving and it was pleasant sailing weather, which saw them at dawn at the sleepy far end. Reed-fringed, quiet, there were many fishing boats at their moorings. And military activity was clearly visible to each side of the inland highway.

For them it must have been a sight for disbelief – a two-decker battleship settling to moorings right off their camp, her size and lethal beauty having never been seen before in this remote backwater.

'A kedge bow and stern,' Kydd ordered crisply. This way

a cable led to the capstan could allow the whole ship to be aimed, the shots sweeping half a mile of the bank and preventing a drifting away under the concussion of her broadsides.

It started well, the crash and thunder of her first ripple broadside echoing shockingly in the early-morning light, the balls slamming and skipping into the confusion ashore. At this angle, with the lake at their rear, there was nowhere to hide from the onslaught.

After an interval horse artillery was brought forward to pop impotently at the great ship and the next broadside took most of them out of action. However, it was not long before some quick-witted leader had the camp retire and go to ground, out of sight.

Thunderer ceased fire and the officers scanned the desolation. 'Where are the beggars?' Roscoe said, aggrieved. The spell of gunfire had clearly been relished.

'I rather thought they're lying low over that rise,' the diffident third lieutenant, Martyn said, pointing.

The slight inclination was enough to keep those on the far side of the ridge below the trajectory of the slamming shot.

It was a disappointment but then Kydd remembered that he'd been this way before. 'Get me the gunner's mate,' he ordered.

Stirk appeared promptly. 'Beyond that rise is an army. Can you rouse 'em out with reduced charges?'

'Aye, sir. Better the thirty-twos, I say.'

'Very good. Make it so.' A whole charge in a gun sent the shot flat and hard at high velocity, a reduced charge a higher, curved trajectory. This was what was wanted to loft over the ridge and descend in an unchecked rampage on the other side.

The balls of the biggest guns, the lower-deck thirty-two pounders, were massive. Each one five times the weight of metal of standard army artillery, they would cause stupefying mayhem as they came unstoppably out of the sky.

By mid-morning there was no more movement inland. Rather than risk passing the giant slaying machine along the narrow way the battalions had fallen back in disarray. There would be no reinforcements going south today.

Thunderer had nothing to fear from retribution in the form of any enemy ship-of-the-line and her might would deter any other.

Staying where they were would intimidate the Danes from going on the march once more but it couldn't last. Sooner or later it would be calculated that to pass the long way around the lake and then south would be safer, even at the cost of days' delay.

Kydd's duty was plain. The major had been at pains to point out that circumstances in the south around Kiel were to be measured in a matter of days, if not hours. He'd stay, perhaps keeping up a random deterrent fire during the night, and quit only when it was clear the enemy had departed for the longer march.

Through the day they remained at anchor, the breeze backing more to the north and easing. It was not worrying Kydd, for there was nothing capable of causing them trouble, and when it died to a calm they were securely at anchor. It would pick up later, acting with the usual Baltic contrariness.

As the dog-watches approached, the officer-of-the-watch was presented with an uncertainty, a mystery. The approaching dusk was accompanied by a mist that lay low on the waters, and one of the lookouts swore he'd glimpsed shadows within it.

'Fishing boats comin' home, o' course,' the master said, not deigning to use a telescope.

'Local folk wanting to set their peepers on what's behind all the noise.' Roscoe chuckled.

But for Kydd, no stranger to these waters, this brought back painful recollections. Not so far from here in Danish waters he had nearly lost *Tyger* to gunboats. And in these same conditions of calms and no manoeuvrability.

Suddenly, almost together, six of the beasts emerged, under oars and with an immense gun flaunting on each foredeck. The Danes were masters of this kind of naval warfare for they'd had no other means to contest the seas. At one point in the Great Sound the sail-of-the-line *Africa* had barely escaped being taken by a swarm of the vermin.

Low, beetling craft with huge ensigns that raced to close, they were shaping up for an attack, coming up from right ahead and astern where no defending guns could bear.

The breeze was frustratingly dull and fluky but in the tensions of the moment Kydd noticed something that could be their saving. In these island-studded waters currents were complex and sometimes difficult. Kydd, though, had served in the Channel Islands, probably in this aspect having the worst in the world. There, he'd learned how to read the whorls and shadows in the water that betrayed their presence. And he'd seen how here an offshore current was sweeping in a half-circle along the shoreline. 'Buoy and slip the stern kedge,' he snapped urgently.

Freed at one end, *Thunderer* slewed ponderously around her forward anchors under the influence of the passing mass of water, her guns inexorably coming on to bear at the nearing gunboats.

They shied aside but it was in vain – the heavy guns of the battleship smashed out, the balls skipping and slamming, leaving two damaged and settling in the water.

It was the last throw of the dice for the Danes, and *Thunderer* settled back to her deadly watch.

Chapter 76

A day later all visible movements ashore tapered off into a desolate stillness. It was time to leave.

In this passing strange atmosphere there was little Kydd could do except take up his place off Rostock once more and await developments.

He was not there long before the same aviso cutter brought to and the same transfer of instructions by canvas pouch was hauled in. Kydd learned that he was to assume he was no longer under detachment and therefore free to resume station, an armistice with Denmark-Norway being now in effect.

Who knew what had happened to the Swedish invasion of Denmark? His duty now was to report back to Admiral Cole in Gothenburg.

An uneventful passage saw him pick up moorings at Wingo and take a boat to *Theseus*.

'So a quiet time, hey,' the admiral said, a little wearily Kydd thought.

'Sir. Might I know what has occurred lately, sir? The armistice and such.'

'The Danes did not get their reinforcements to the south

in time and Kiel was taken. This being so they thought it proper at this point to seek terms. These are now being negotiated.'

A surrender? 'So . . . ?'

'There is no hope for Denmark, cut off from anything Boney can do for them. There remains only the question of whether Sweden will complete the invasion and swallow the country whole.'

'And we?'

'We, dear fellow, are in the hands of the politicals who have decreed that we are on the side of Sweden and will not interfere.'

'Then do I ask what shall be our concern now?'

'I can tell you that – and it's directly from London. We're to maintain the blockade until the Swedes have full possession of Norway.'

'To apply pressure on the Norwegians to concede quickly.'

'Quite. Unpleasant, goes against the grain, but this is what we're told. There does seem to be some sort of treaty afoot but how long it'll take I've no idea.'

Their arrival back on station was not met with jubilation, even less so with the news they were carrying. Kydd called his captains aboard to explain.

'Denmark has to capitulate. This means that it loses Norway. But not yet – there's a deal of jawing still. Meanwhile we've got the task of maintaining the blockade, same as before.'

'Sir,' Bowden said carefully, 'if the blockade is to continue, does it not imply that we're still at war with Denmark? How will the prize courts deal with such without a timely act of reprisal?'

'Denmark-Norway you should say. And I cannot answer

you, sir. All prizes to the Gothenburg vice-admiralty courts and the best of luck,' he added cynically.

They readied to leave but Kydd held up his hands. 'Gentlemen – I'd rather you were in no mystery regarding my views on blockade. The contraband list remains the same but . . .' he paused significantly, catching eyes one by one '. . . should you come across a cargo of grain or foodstuffs and your vessel finds it cannot forereach on it, bring the business to a conclusion, so to speak, I will perfectly understand.'

There were methods to simulate a low speed – a bucket streamed astern, a sail doused underwater, a mis-streamed topsail – and the chase would escape, allowing its cargo to make port while witnesses would swear the hunter had done all he could to seize the victim.

Kydd was saying that if his captains chose to let certain of their prizes go free and feed the population he didn't want to know of it.

HMS *Thunderer* then loosed sail and got under way.

Chapter 77

Frederikstad

Renzi heard voices outside the musty room in which he was confined. Raised, irritable, they were in a tongue he had no hope of understanding. He lifted his head in the darkness and tried to guess what was going on. There was a newcomer, his voice young, forceful. The two original captors responded in low growls of resentment.

This was the most hastily prepared venture he'd ever undertaken for Congalton, in a part of the world he knew next to nothing about. His captors were amateurs at clandestine dealings but it didn't stop them being dangerous – the quickest way to resolve their problem would be to get rid of him.

There was a lull in the conversation, then a bad-tempered mutter and the sound of a chair being pushed back. Without warning his door was thrown open by the one answering to Bertrand.

'Come out, show yourself whoever you are.' It was in English.

Sitting at the table was a young man, by his dress probably a student.

Renzi stood blinking, uncertain of the situation. On the table was a well-thumbed newspaper.

'You are English?' the young man said in amazement, his accent nearly flawless.

Renzi paused. Any kind of admission could be taken in a number of ways.

'Oh, don't worry, you're free to go,' he added.

Outside, to his death?

'You see, I've brought them news.' He tapped the paper. 'Things have changed and—'

'The world has changed, and for the worse,' Bertrand moaned. 'We've lost our chance, our only hope.'

The young man gave a twisted smile. 'It looks bad, I'll admit, but for you people there can be no future.'

He looked at Renzi curiously. 'You've fallen in with a crew who believe Napoleon Bonaparte is going to hand us our freedom. A foolish notion but now of no account. Holstein has been invaded by Sweden right up to Jutland. The Danes have been beaten – there's now a treaty signed in Kiel. It's all over – Denmark is cut off from France entirely, and for all time.'

He raised a lazy eyebrow. 'Bertrand and his fellows must find something else to do.'

Renzi's bondage had no more meaning.

'Get out while you can,' Bertrand said, with a scowl, 'before we change our minds.'

Renzi swallowed; he was free. With a short bow he crossed to the outer door, hesitated and, when no move was made to stop him, stepped out into the sunshine.

He hurried away but after some time he heard footsteps behind him – it was the young man, who quickly caught up with him.

Renzi turned, ready for anything.

'Might we talk?'

Before Renzi could reply he said, 'You're English. I know, as I studied these last three years in London.'

'Might I ask it, why should this concern you?'

'I'm taken why an Englishman dare show his face in Norway at this time. And profess an interest in our desire for liberty? Could it be that he's sent by his government to ensure the annexation by Sweden will take place smoothly?'

'A spy? I think not, sir.'

'Then?'

There was no shaking off the young man whose manner nevertheless was impeccably respectful.

'I am an Englishman who has much sympathy with the desire of Norway to seek its own ways, free of domination by foreigners.'

'Why are you here, then?'

'To shake the hands of any who will stand in the cause of independence.' He stopped. 'Do I see such a one?'

There was no hesitation. 'You do, sir. Øyvind Gundersen, student of law at Det kongelig Frederiks – our university of Christiania.'

An intelligent and connected young man. Renzi's spirits rose – if he could win his friendship, an entrée into what served as an independence movement was more than possible.

'I'm happy to make your acquaintance Mr, um, Øyvind? Nicholas Renzi of Wiltshire in England.'

They solemnly shook hands.

'Mr Renzi, I'm not at all certain why you're here but it can't be as a spy. Not to discover if there's disagreement with the Swedish plan – they can find out that for themselves. You're not here to parley trade, you haven't the cut of the jib if I might make bold to say.'

They reached the corner and, holding up his hand, Øyvind checked first.

'It does not signify,' Renzi said. 'Accept, I beg, that I wish Norway only the happiest outcome in what must lie ahead.' He knew as he spoke that the sincerity was not pretended.

The student regarded him closely. 'Do you know? I'm inclined to believe you, Mr Renzi. And that you are on some mission that bears on my country's future. Am I right?'

It was a crossing point. Dare he trust not only his life but his vital task to this unknown university student?

'You are right, Øyvind. Do believe that I need to find a band of patriots who have a good chance to secure independence for the interest of those in England who support the same – and there are many.'

'In logic there are but two conditions: you lie, or you do not.' He gave a shy smile. 'I choose to believe you, Mr Renzi.'

They walked on.

'It does cross my mind, Mr Renzi. Do you have somewhere that you may trust to lay your head? If not, my own home is available to you wherein you'll hear more than one opinion of what vexes us.'

Renzi gave a small bow of thanks. This was perfect: Øyvind would seek out the likely insurgents and at the same time he would be giving ear to what the people themselves were saying.

The only disadvantage: a three-day journey north from Frederikstad to his family home, Råholt, in the countryside some thirty miles north of the capital. At least he need have no concerns for Jago – he'd send him back to England with a quick note for Cecilia.

Chapter 78

Råholt, northern Norway

The scenery was picturesque with the last snow of winter on the upper reaches, the boreal wilderness beyond a magic land of trolls and witches. At the edge of the village next to a crystal stream was the smithy where Mr Gundersen had his being.

Renzi was welcomed into the family home, the mother fussing over his appearance, but the beefy blacksmith glared suspiciously. A shy but entranced girl appeared briefly and a younger version of Øyvind came to scrutinise their visitor while he was shown to his room, neat in its Scandinavian spareness.

In the evening around the dinner table introductions were made.

'I've told them you are my friend who must also be accounted a friend of Norway.'

They sat in stillness in the low-beamed kitchen, regarding him gravely.

'My father, Yngvar.' The bushy-browed older man opposite

stared at him with open suspicion. Renzi inclined his head politely. The man reluctantly rumbled something but pugnaciously held a spoon vertically in his fist.

'My mother, Kirsten.' A lined but soft-featured woman took her cue and made a curious shy bobbing of her head.

'Brother Björn.' A handsome Nordic lad, frowning his importance. As their eyes met he folded his arms defensively and looked away.

'And Dagmar, my dear young sister.' Not much more than a child, she smiled demurely and dropped her eyes.

'Ah, do inform your family that I'm delighted circumstances have allowed me to visit Norway, a most beautiful country indeed.'

An ill-natured grumbling emanated from Yngvar.

'He says that if you think our land so wonderful, why do you starve us so?'

'The Treaty of Stockholm binds us to a blockade.'

'So you've let yourselves be beholden to the Swedes.' The blacksmith's look of contempt was impossible to miss.

'As a nation we bind ourselves to our promises.' He turned deliberately to Kirsten. 'Might I be allowed to compliment you on the soup? It's most warming to the soul.'

'What do you do in England that you must come here?' the boy interrupted.

'I am a gentleman of means,' Renzi said smoothly, 'and my business unhappily is not for the public ear.'

Dagmar eagerly asked him how the London ladies were wearing their hair, these days, and Renzi tried manfully to oblige. The atmosphere began to lighten as talk flowed to and fro. Country folk, they had eventually decided that if this was Øyvind's friend, they would therefore extend the civilities.

The next day came news from Christiania that set the house to buzzing. The provisions of the Treaty of Kiel had been made known to the people and they'd taken to the streets. And then the thunderbolt – a personal letter sent by the King of Denmark-Norway, Frederik VI, to his Norwegian subjects.

In it was the shocking revelation that, after more than four hundred years, the King was releasing them from their sworn allegiance and thereby relinquished all and any authority over Norway and its peoples. No longer would the Danes have the power to direct the destiny of Norwegians – but on the other hand, no more could Norway depend on Denmark to defend, support and take its part.

But a worse fate awaited. The Swedish had always coveted Norway, and with the connivance of the rest of the world, the way was laid open for it to annex the now headless country as a province of Sweden.

'I'm going to Christiania to find out more,' Øyvind declared forcefully. 'Do you come with me, Mr Renzi?'

Chapter 79

Christiania

The student quarters were much as they would be in any university town and, from his cheap straw mattress, Renzi smiled into the darkness. He'd laid his head in vastly different surroundings over the years, including the fo'c'sle of a man-o'-war and a sultan's palace, but this took him back to his wild youth, travelling around Europe.

They were up early, Øyvind and his friends desperate to take the pulse of the citizenry as rumours flew and strangers burst in to pass on the latest news.

In the monthly market the commotion was at its height with arguments between strangers, open tears in some, the occasional scuffle. And a restlessness that made Renzi glad he was part of a pack.

A shout went up at the end of the street, followed by more. Breathlessly, Renzi followed the running students to hear them cheering.

'It's the prince!' Øyvind shouted above the din. 'He's declared for liberty – freedom!'

There was another burst of cheering and Renzi was just able to prise from him the essence of the matter. It seemed that one Kristian Frederik, until yesterday the governor of Norway, the representative of Danish rule, had made it known that he opposed the annexation by Sweden and instead was advocating full independence for the country. 'He's the Crown Prince and heir to the Danish throne – turned Norwegian!' Øyvind told him proudly.

Renzi grasped the implications at once. If there was any chance that the people would follow him, here indeed was the kind of thing to stay their lordship's hands.

'Come – he's talking to the crowd. Let's go to hear!'

It was nothing formal, little of the hustings about the arrangements, merely a cart drawn up in the corner of a square.

In it a well-dressed young man, open-faced, a mop of tightly curled black hair setting off pleasant, well-meaning features, spoke strongly, persuasively.

Øyvind was clearly taken with what was being said and Renzi waited patiently for a translation. It turned out to be nothing less than a bid for the Crown of an independent Norway with the prince as its king. The details he would learn later, no doubt, but for now the young students were ecstatic.

'Dare I ask it, my friend,' Renzi asked, when he had the chance, 'why the fever?'

'The Swedes – we beat them in the field not a handful of years ago. Tell me why now we should be made their slaves?'

In the tiny, smelly taverns there were endless discussions. Renzi sat in one with an agreeable expression for any who looked his way until, thoroughly bored, he made his excuses and left.

In the morning, Øyvind, red-eyed but elated, let it be known that he was of a mind to follow the man he'd heard. And he would find others by his side. It was not difficult for Renzi to go along, and all those with a hankering for independence would now show themselves.

The next meeting was under cover, in a church hall with wooden benches. Øyvind wanted Renzi to make acquaintance with one Georg Sverdrup, a professor at Øyvind's university, and Kristian Falsen, another scholarly-looking gentleman.

The meeting apparently proved successful, the earnest propositions put forward by the prince received with surprised acclamation.

Caught up in the moment, Renzi saw that if one of such an eminence was preaching independence this movement needed watching. And the prince himself – was he a figurehead or had he a real chance at snatching a kingly title?

That night he heard of what was being promised: while the regent of Sweden, Bernadotte – Karl Johan – was occupied in the mortal struggle with Napoleon, there was a fleeting chance at independence, the establishing of a nation with king and country that could never be a provincial appendix to another state.

The way forward was to make a move to independence, then go on to create a constitution that precluded external interference.

The odds against such were colossal: if it was carried off, however, it would meet everything that Congalton's masters required.

He had to speak to the prince.

Chapter 80

The following night the meeting place was an imposing theatre. Afterwards, Renzi made it his business to stroll with Øyvind in homage past the prince's borrowed lodging. It was a respectably sized mansion of a fashionable presence with stolid figures about the building guarding the person of the prince.

Renzi duly noted their presence for he had a plan.

Begging off his attendance at the next meeting, he hurried back to the mansion and saw with satisfaction that, in their amateurish enthusiasm, the watchkeepers had all dutifully followed the prince, leaving the building unguarded.

Experienced in clandestine matters as he was, it was the work of moments to slip down the side and find an entry point. Servants were concentrating on the kitchen and dining rooms, and the big front drawing room was, as he had expected, deserted.

He found what he needed, a large chesterfield sofa, and lay full length behind it to wait.

After an uncomfortable age he heard the noise of the

prince's return, fading upstairs as no doubt the man went to change after his public appearance. Then – as Renzi had hoped – he entered the drawing room to unwind alone.

There were weary words, a servant left, returned to a clinking of glass and, leaving the prince to his privacy, departed.

Cradling brandy, Frederik was in an armchair gazing into the fire when Renzi stood up noiselessly behind him, and moved to the door as if he'd just entered.

He coughed discreetly.

Turning sharply, the prince stared at him and rapped out something unintelligible.

'*Mon seigneur, pardonnez mon intrusion.*' French was the courtly language, which such as he would be sure to possess.

'*Que diable se passe-t-il?*'

Yes, he had French.

'Sir,' Renzi said mildly, spreading out his empty hands, 'you will see I'm quite unarmed and mean you no harm.'

'Then explain yourself, sir!'

'I am Nicholas Renzi and I do ask that you believe me a true friend of Norway – and to Danes as well.'

'You're English!'

'Sir, not so very long ago I ventured at my peril to the court of King Christian VII in Copenhagen. In fact on three occasions, as I recall, we two dined together in the Amalienborg.' It was in a vast banqueting hall, and he did not remember the young prince being present.

'So?'

'I was there on a most confidential mission of advice to the regent at the time of the seizure of the Danish fleet. We spoke at some length, and it is to my great regret the advice was not taken. If it had been . . .'

'Confidential? Who is this?'

'Those in Great Britain wishing the best of fortunes to your people, sir.'

'And you want to ply your advice on me, now?' Frederik said shrewdly. 'If so, allow me to inform you I make my own plans and decisions and will not be dictated to by a foreigner.'

'Sir, this is as it should be. If I speak, it is only to confide facts and views of a serious and privileged character that will assist you in your deliberations.'

The prince put down his brandy and regarded Renzi frankly. 'Sir. Would you be so good as to tell me who you are? You say you attended on the King, Christian VII. Pray, what was your impression of the good king?'

'I sincerely feel for any afflicted by such a malady. It's to the credit of the palace attendants that he was afforded such comforts he enjoyed. I flatter myself that I—'

'And the prince regent then, what colour eyes has he?'

'Sir, blue eyes, his features fine-drawn and—'

'So, I can trust that you know my family. And you're here on a like errand. What is it you want me to hear, supposing I'm inclined to listen?'

With a knot in his stomach Renzi took a breath. Now was the time to either speak generalities or something like the truth of the matter. Only the second would give him the credibility for anything more, but at the risk of disbelief.

'Sir, I'm neither an accredited diplomat nor military. This is a marked advantage for you, for if on the one hand I cannot be held literally to anything I say, on the other you will be made privy to matters the powers-that-be would not be happy to be made known in an official capacity.'

'Go on.'

There was no indication of how it was being received, so Renzi proceeded as if at a favourable cue.

'You will know, sir, that under the provisions of the recent

Treaty of Stockholm Great Britain is bound in supporting the Swedish claim to Norway.'

'Of course.'

'What you will not know is that while the British must be public in their support, within they are not happy to see Norway fall entirely under Swedish rule, as it must if annexed as a province.'

'Then why do they not object – repudiate the treaty?'

'Great Britain must stand by the treaty, as with a promise its honour forbids it to break.'

'What is that to this country, then?'

'There is a dire problem it faces.' That Britain should have a problem clearly roused his interest.

'And it is in this wise: that in the future, be it in few or many years, Napoleon Bonaparte will be beaten and a new world shall begin. It's feared that by then the Swedes, with all the resources gained from direct rule of their new territory of Norway, will turn on Denmark, by then a desolated and defenceless land. The combined weight of all three, with control of the sound to the Baltic, will enable it to turn on Finland as well. Britain cannot allow that a single country shall dominate the region so comprehensively.'

'Then?'

'Sweden begins its march on the north by first annexing Norway. This must not be permitted to happen – and it cannot, should there be a particular circumstance in place.'

'Oh?'

'If Norway becomes a nation of its own with king and parliament both, Britain will bring to bear a fury of moral indignation among the members of the Coalition that Sweden desires to conquer a people without recourse just as Bonaparte has done, the Emperor they have spent twenty years and more in opposing for actions such as that.'

'You're saying that Norway as an independent nation will be enough to thwart the Swedes. What assurance have I that the English will act in the way you say?'

'There is none – but what you are declaring to your people concerning your design to become King of Norway is well noted. Should this be strengthened by the creation of a parliament as tempered by laws of the people, then no man may say Norway is not a nation among equals and cannot be trodden underfoot by Sweden or any other.'

The prince rubbed his chin thoughtfully. 'Your words are singular and well-advised, Mr Renzi. I shall think on it.'

'As time is the enemy – we cannot know when Bernadotte, or should I say Karl Johan, will return from the battlefield to claim his due.'

'I said, I will consider my position.' He resumed his stare into the fire.

There was nothing more Renzi could do. It was, as he must accept, in the prince's hands now.

He bowed and made to go but the prince stopped him. 'Mr Renzi, do linger in Christiania for a space – I may have need of an ear on occasion.'

Was there any future in the man's dreams? To achieve what was needed, his desire to be king must come behind the wishes of the people, and was he capable of so stepping down?

And just how long did he have? Karl Johan would be hearing what was afoot and would move fast to crush an upstart claiming his promised throne and the figurehead of a leaderless independence movement.

Renzi could not see much of a future for Frederik or for any rising in his name. The question he had to face now was how long he should wait on the sidelines for the inevitable.

Keeping his despondency to himself, he tried to enjoy student life but with the wisdom of his years he found their careless optimism wearing.

Chapter 81

Several mornings later Øyvind came to Renzi, confused and mystified. 'Frederik – they say he's fled Christiania,' he mumbled.

It made sense, keeping out of the reach of the Swedes, but where did that leave the cause if the focus had disappeared?

But then rumours began emerging. He had not fled: rather, in a bold stroke he'd gathered about him a meeting of leading figures in a mansion somewhere in the country. There they would confer on the best course to lead to independence.

What, if anything, would come of it all? A fractious, divided discord was most likely: how could there have been a tradition of politics in a Norway ruled by a remote and powerless Denmark?

Days followed. And in an astonishing development things changed.

Kristian Frederik reappeared suddenly and made a dramatic announcement that set the entire town alight.

It was nothing less than a formal declaration of independence.

On a principle of self-determination Norway was taking up the sovereignty the Danish king had relinquished, irrespective of foreign claims. Further, an assembly was to be immediately convened of elected delegates from all over the country to forge a constitution agreeable to the people – even to the point that the head of state, be it king or commoner, would be elected by the same.

As regent, Frederik would continue until the conclusion of the process, but for now he asked that the citizens of Norway join him in an oath of fealty to the cause of their sacred independence.

Delegates? An assembly of the people to create their own destiny?

For hours on end bells sounded, the comfort of church assembly in a time of national need driving the masses in their thousands to the ancient cathedral of Domkirke to gather and to begin the process of electing their delegates.

Renzi took it all in as the crowds seethed and shouted around him, excited and noisy.

Then he joined Øyvind on a grinding cart to the family home to share their news.

It was received in wonder and hope. Could it be what was needed – some sort of release from the grinding despair of war? As an independent nation could they not negotiate a peace with Great Britain that would lift the endless misery and hardships of blockade?

There was much discussion. Then Yngvar opened the chest of best clothing and was rummaging through it.

'What are you doing?' Kirsten wanted to know.

He didn't speak until he'd found a green velvet coat, which he held up.

'Good enough?' he grunted. It looked as if it would be a tight fit, Renzi thought, but kept it to himself.

'*What for*, Yngvar?'

'Tomorrow. I'm going to the church to get my name down as this town's delegate to the prince's meeting.'

No one looked less like a constitutional lawyer than the lined, granite-faced, powerfully built smith, but his sincerity was obvious.

There was a moment's shocked silence. Then Dagmar threw herself at her father with an adoring shriek, and Björn, not far behind, came up to stand in awed respect before him.

'What party do you represent, Father?' Øyvind asked gravely.

'Party? What are you talking of, boy? I'm there to see common sense wins.'

Chapter 82

Råholt

In the morning Yngvar was off, with a jaunty wave, on Raskt, the second best horse. Back before dark, he was brimming with news. He'd been duly elected by the people as their delegate to the meeting, which was to be dignified with the title of Grunnlovsforsamlingen, the Norwegian Constituent Assembly. It was significant that the assembly was to be conducted not at the chief town, Christiania, but at a mansion in the country, where peace could be found, lent for the occasion by one of Frederik's wealthier friends. This was in the township of Eidsvoll, not far distant, which would allow him to return every so often with tidings of important events and descriptions of the dignitaries he met, a heady experience for a humble blacksmith.

In only a very few days it was time for the formal opening of proceedings with, who else, Prince Kristian Frederik himself to perform the honours.

Renzi arrived with the proud family on the due day at a

modest but attractive white-finished timber-built manor prominently situated on rolling slopes. It was besieged by a sizeable crowd. They were found by Yngvar, bursting with pride, who told them that only notables such as himself could be allowed inside but that the prince would be making his opening speech in full view from the steps.

At eleven, Kristian Frederik made his appearance. Arrayed in sashed and silver-laced finery over scarlet with a fashionably high collar, he acknowledged the wild cheering with bows, then called for silence.

Øyvind was riveted by his words and Renzi had to do without his customary interpretation. It was not hard, though, to make out the tenor of the speech from the cries and shouts of his enthusiastic audience.

They died away, heads turning at a disturbance at the rear. Frederik stopped as it resolved into a carriage trying to make its way through. Murmurs of irritation and shouts broke out from the crowd.

Øyvind, leaping up to catch a glimpse, gave a smothered gasp. 'It's – it's a Swedish state carriage of some kind.'

It came to a halt and four dark-clad men descended, pushing their way through the audience to confront the prince. One waved a document and shouted forcefully.

Frederik waited until he'd finished. Then, in a voice intended for the crowd, replied. It brought on angry responses and an altercation seemed inevitable.

The document was forced on the prince, who, without reading it, threw it down. Sweeping the man aside, he took out a paper of his own and addressed the gathering in ringing tones. This brought on a tempest of cheering and the Swedes stormed off.

Only in the delirium of the evening's entertainments did it at last become clear what had taken place. This had been a mission sent by the Swedish government to protest in the loudest possible terms to Frederik's actions, which were interpreted to be a reckless and illegal repudiation of the Treaty of Kiel.

But for the fact that Karl Johan and his army were absent, locked in fighting with Napoleon Bonaparte, there would assuredly be a massing of troops on the border in preparation for a punitive invasion and occupation.

The four envoys had brought with them a personal proclamation that promised forgiveness if Norway would submit to the provisions of the treaty but Frederik was having none of it. Well prepared, he'd made plain that he had not been the one to sign the treaty, or any other Norwegian, and therefore, in his view, its validity was very much in question. In any case, by the solemn invocations of the Lex Regia of 1665, the Danish king had no right unilaterally to change the nature of his dynasty or cede portions of his territory to foreigners. In the event Norway was taking up its own destiny and, until the wishes of the people became known in the course of this assembly, he was acting as regent.

The die was cast. Here was open defiance of Sweden and, indeed, the rest of the world. Who knew where it would all end?

There were feasting and celebrations, but under it all the realisation that if the French had needed a bloody revolution and ten years, the Americans a seven-year full war to achieve their independence, how long would it take Norway?

Yngvar returned home after five days, dog-tired but exultant. To a full table of eager listeners he told of how history was being made at the packed main assembly room, bare of near all decoration except draped fir branches, fresh and fragrant. There were few chairs and the delegates were wedged together on hard benches. There, he, Yngvar Gundersen, had met and argued with the great of Norway. Men like the scholarly Falsen, whose ideas on the form of constitution were much talked about; the rich Peder Anker, who'd studied under Linnaeus; and the calm and insistent president of the Constituent Assembly, Professor Georg Sverdrup, who'd wrangled with Nicolai Wergeland over the mandate of the gathering and the legitimacy of Frederik to be regent.

He'd been there when the noble principles underpinning the constitution were established and voted upon: the right of the people to determine their own form of state, with the right to property and equality at its heart.

Proudly he explained that as the delegates had found themselves with differing positions on the varying subjects and formed themselves into parties he thought it proper to declare for himself. It was to be either the Independents who believed that nothing short of a Norway standing proud and alone on the world's stage would serve, or the Union cause, which thought that some kind of association with a stronger nation would be a safer course – Denmark or Sweden?

'So you're a Union man then, Pappa?' a wide-eyed Dagmar blurted.

'No, he's not!' Björn spluttered. 'Nothing but glorious independence. Now's our only chance and—'

'Be quiet, child,' Yngvar scolded. 'My ears ache from such words all the day long. No, if Count Wedel Jarlsberg himself decides we must have friends in this hard world that satisfies me. A Union fellow I am.'

To Renzi it was precisely what was wanted. A practical, well-led and effective independence movement that, if it moved quickly, had every chance of success. It wasn't the details of the form of government that were important, rather that there was a case for nationhood. He couldn't say yet, but all the signs for a successful conclusion to Congalton's mission were there.

In the weeks that followed, progress was rapid, touching on a range of important matters. In the framing of the constitution there was to be no involvement by a foreign power or external authority. The structure of the state was to be of a completely independent status headed by an elected monarch advised by a two-chamber Storting but the country would not be having aristocrats or a noble class in any form.

On his visits home Yngvar spoke gleefully of arguments and confrontations long into the night and delegates falling, asleep, off the benches. He summarised the general drift of the assembly by quoting Frederik, who'd said, 'These people want to be Norwegians, not Swedish.'

One by one details were settled and a draft constitution was drawn up by the patient secretary and the learned but persuasive Falsen.

Despite himself, Renzi sensed the rising excitement and readily fell in with Øyvind's suggestion that they take advantage of his father's position and see where it was all taking place – if only to tell of it in later years.

The mansion without the crowds looked even nobler. They passed through the rooms in awe, stood outside the biggest listening to the drone of voices and were jostled by distracted delegates as votes were cast and records taken.

It wasn't a striking or magnificent scene but a nation was being born and Renzi gave it due reverence, while Øyvind seemed struck dumb.

'Aha – isn't this Mr Renzi?' Kristian Frederik boomed, coming out unexpectedly from a side room. Øyvind bowed and moved to one side to let Renzi be led away.

'You've come to see how we're progressing, no doubt.'

'Sir. To be here when history is made is not to be missed.'

The prince beamed. 'I rather think that the end is not far – days only. The constitution agreed, signed and, upon the election of a king, it might be said that the independent kingdom of Norway duly exists.'

Renzi smothered a sigh of satisfaction. His mission had not been easy and he'd done little to contribute to its fruition, but in a short while he'd be back in London with the evidence needed to thwart the Swedish bid for northern dominance.

Chapter 83

Eidsvoll

The maid, clutching fresh linens, went to the door of Prince Frederik's chamber to make up the room. It was not an onerous task – the prince was the only one of the assembly granted accommodation in the manor. The others had to find lodgings in surrounding farms and villages.

She tapped lightly, her strict instructions to allow the future king his rest in the morning, but it would not be long before the assembly met and he would need to complete his toilette.

There was no response, so she tapped again. Still no sign of life. It must have been a late night, but all had their duty so she gently opened the door with a soft morning greeting . . . and stopped.

The bed was in immaculate order – exactly as she'd left it the previous day. It had not been slept in.

This was puzzling. She'd seen him when serving at dinner in the evening and, as she was always informed of his arrangements, knew he'd not gone out. She hesitated – should she tell someone?

He might well be somewhere else, which was unfair of them not to tell her, so she decided to go to the top, the president of the assembly, and let him know.

Professor Sverdrup was gathering his papers and looked up with a frown.

She bobbed a curtsey and informed him that the prince was missing.

Sverdrup stared at her in bewilderment. 'You haven't . . .?'

'No, Professor. I've not seen *Hans Høyhet* since last night.'

'He's due to address us on suffrage at ten. Stop what you're doing and go and ask about where he is. Oh, and keep this to yourself, won't you, my dear?'

She was back in minutes, flustered and worried. 'I was careful in my asking, but no one at all has seen him this morning, and it's not like him not to let us know.'

The professor sat slowly. Was Frederik absent-mindedly out visiting? Not very likely as too many people relied on being able to get hold of him at any time.

It was a most disturbing event for within days the final draft of the constitution would be ready for signing and then the King's election. Without his presence they would have no valid instrument to bring the new kingdom of Norway into being.

He had to be found. The more Sverdrup pondered, the more uneasy he felt. The prince was no philanderer, given to secret night assignations, and particularly at this time was most assiduous in his duties.

There was however an explanation that met the situation fully. The same imperative that made Prince Frederik indispensable in the final creation of the kingdom might well have occurred to the Swedes or possibly extreme members of the Union faction. Remove the prince and the kingdom could not come into existence before Karl Johan could complete his annexation by military means.

In a chill of fear Sverdrup, a peaceful academic, could nevertheless see how easy it would be to carry out – unless it had been achieved already.

He pulled out his fob watch. Just after nine o'clock. This was far more important than anything they were doing in these closing stages. He'd call a lay-day for further deliberations or, better still, swear that Frederik was ill and had taken to his bed. Above all, if it got out, there would be dismay and consternation and any number of rumours that could result in catastrophe for their cause.

How best to look for him? He'd gather together a dozen or so of his most trusted delegates and, after swearing them to secrecy, send them out on search. The abductors could not have gone far in the time and with Frederik, after his tour of the country probably the most recognisable figure of their age, they would need to move carefully.

Yes – to start instantly!

Chapter 84

Råholt

'Øyvind, get Raskt fettled, watered and fed. He needs it, worthless beast,' Yngvar ordered, as he slid from the lathered horse that evening.

'Father, she's in a state. What have you been about?' The grey mare was trembling and wild-eyed.

'So don't ask, boy. I'll take Sterkt.' Their best horse, slower but strongly built.

'But what have you been up to? It's only a few miles to Eidsvoll.'

'Explanations! I've not the time, been out all day and need a belly-full of your mother's rice porridge.'

Now truly alarmed, his son persisted. 'Something's gone wrong – I've every right to know, Father.'

In emotion-charged tones Yngvar told him that the prince was missing and an all-day inconspicuous search had thrown up nothing. The hunt would continue at night when it could be expected the kidnap party would be on the move.

A pall of helplessness descended as the news was relayed to Renzi.

Despairing at the ruin of his mission, he took Øyvind aside. 'I have to agree, it seems the Swedes have achieved what was wanted and we have so little time to do anything about it.'

'We? This is not your affair, sir.'

'Let us say it is for now, my friend. Now, if I was the chief of the band I'd think my main worry was to be discovered with the prince. Therefore he'll do his best to keep clear of the roads both in daylight and even at night when there are so few people abroad.'

'I know – that's why we've men out in all directions, and—'

'And the longer they're holding their captive the greater risk it is of having him stumbled upon. They've to get him to Sweden as soon as they can. Their difficulty is that the distance to the border is long and this increases greatly the risk of discovery, there being only one of a pair of roads they can use.'

'In disguise they can—'

'The risk is too great. There's only one action they can take.'

'I was wrong,' Øyvind replied slowly. 'You are too knowing of these dark ways. You are more than you seem, sir!'

'For all that, do hear what I say, I beg. You have men out on every road – but one.'

'Oh?'

'The sea. A quick sail of several hours only finds them at the border and a day or two later to Gothenburg and on to Stockholm.'

The young man caught his breath as the thought sank in. 'Ah – Oslofjorden is only twenty, thirty miles from where we stand. We may be too late.'

'We may, or may not. There is one sure way to find out.'

'Ask the fisher-folk?'

'No. We ask those whose business it is – the British Royal Navy.' Renzi gave a half-smile. 'On blockade, they must know precisely who is upon the waters off Norway, that it does not pass.'

'Those devils! You can't just—'

'I'm English, they will hear me, I believe.'

Chapter 85

Aboard Thunderer

The officer-of-the-watch eyed Kydd from a distance. With essentially little to do, his captain had taken to impulsive growling at perceived sins of seamanship or slackness in the execution of gunnery practice and the like.

Kydd, however, had his reasons. From routine dispatches he knew a climactic struggle was being fought not that far distant to the south and *Thunderer* was not part of it. The work she'd been given was demeaning and in many ways could be seen as amoral. If only the Swedes could put an end to it by marching in and taking their prize, the better for all.

Day followed day, the seas swept clear, and the only sail abroad his own little squadron on their endless flog up and down the coast.

He glanced at *Firefly* cutter just emerging from the coastal mists. If anything it was better to be aloof as the reigning ship-of-the-line than to be at the hard edge of the punishment served out to any challenging their blockade.

'Sir. *Firefly* cutter. Wishes to speak,' the officer-of-the-watch reported formally.

'Very good. Carry on.'

Thunderer's foresail was backed and the little cutter rounded to under their stern. Kydd watched as Roscoe bellowed irascibly at them from on high.

If this was a weak excuse to make Gothenburg or somewhere civilised for a break in routine they'd be quickly sent on their way to a place much less congenial.

The salty lieutenant-in-command cupped his hands and hailed back. 'Sir, I've a gent wants a word wi' Sir Thomas. Says as how it's urgent an' all.'

Kydd glanced down at the heaving vessel but couldn't make out anything of the two figures in the cockpit space aft, both in foul-weather gear.

Roscoe came over. 'Sir. One wishes to—'

'Yes. In my cabin.' Anything for a diversion.

There was an apologetic knock and the officer-of-the-watch poked his head around the door. 'A Mr Renzi, sir, as would like—'

Kydd shot to his feet as, impossibly, his oldest and best friend showed himself. 'Nicholas! What the devil . . .?' he said delighted, holding out his hand.

'Dear fellow – I do wish it that we could meet in more languid circumstances but for now I do beg you to hear me out.'

Kydd indicated a chair. 'Refreshment – running a mort shy of a full cupboard but . . .'

'Your sympathetic ear to my difficulties would be more appreciated.'

'Of course,' Kydd said, moved by his grave manner and taking the armchair opposite. 'I'd not thought to see you in these benighted waters, but you'll have your reasons.'

'I do, but be aware that they are of the most confidential nature, which I find I must wrestle with my conscience to divulge to any beyond my authorised intimates.'

Kydd, by now aware of Renzi's clandestine activities at the highest level, murmured his sympathies.

'Yet unless you know the whole, my request will appear, er, eccentric.'

'It shall be copper-bottomed safe with me, as you know, Nicholas.'

The crucial secret then: that despite the public signing of the Treaty of Kiel the British government had no desire to see the Swedes own the north and if there were any way to prevent it they would.

And if there was any kind of group or cabal capable of declaring independence and turning this into a credible form of government it would make the act of annexation indigestible.

'Have you found such a one, Nicholas?'

'I have, led by a prince with the most admirable principles.'

Kydd couldn't see where this was leading. 'So, this is in some way an anxiety for you?'

'If the prince is taken from the equation we have no king, no head of state, no kingdom. And now we find that he's disappeared, feared held by the Swedes.'

'I see. Um, then how can I help you, old trout?'

'Have you any report of a suspicious boat or ship putting out for Sweden?'

'None. I can be very sure of that – an empty sea to thrash up and down, a sail of any kind is a joy to see.'

'Dear fellow. I must then ask it. Should I desire you to set your entirely estimable armada to the task of looking for Prince Frederik would it be at all to your liking?'

Kydd froze, then looked down. When he raised his eyes

Renzi could see his features were set and uncompromising. 'Nicholas. Your same government has caused the Admiralty to set me afloat for the one reason. To exert my force in the cause of furthering the King of Sweden's lawful claim to Norway. Should I go cruising about to find one who stands to be the greatest threat to this end and tenderly convey him to do his worst then . . . then I shall most certainly be as much guilty of treason as Guy Fawkes.'

'I was rather afraid you'd see it in that light.'

'Besides which, all those who follow will likewise be complicit. I cannot in all conscience order them to treason.'

There was a bleakness in his tone that told Renzi he was not to be moved. Nevertheless he had to try. 'This I can understand, dear fellow. Yet dare I claim it that the higher duty is to the Crown itself that desires his being and that of his cause?'

Kydd's tight expression did not ease. 'No, Nicholas, that does not fadge. I have my orders and if others observe my flouting of them for no grounds that can be revealed I shall be crucified in short order, and rightly so.'

It was Renzi now whose face became dogged and set. 'Old friend, do recall what you saw on Årøysund. Will you betray that monstrous vision for—'

'Nicholas. As long as I bear myself in the King's uniform nothing will serve that will persuade me to play Judas to my orders. That is my firm and steadfast position.'

Several minutes passed, and Kydd at last softened his expression. 'Dear fellow – you can see my difficulty, can you not?'

Renzi looked away bleakly.

'Accuse me of selfishness but do accept I have a loving wife and young son whose future is so dear to me that I must place them first in my obligations.'

Still Renzi remained mute.

'As I can't readily see how . . . Um, well, perhaps there is . . . Yes, I believe there is!'

'Pray tell.'

'Should I doff my rig as naval officer and act the plain man, possibly there's things I can do. Who's to say precisely how I should occupy myself when stepping ashore in a private fashion?'

'I thought to ask more in the line of a fleet search, Thomas. There's little a single man however noble can do in this case.'

'Hmm. That wasn't what I plan, m' friend. Let's take a look at our charts.'

They had good charts, well proven by months of blockade and he pored knowingly over them. 'Where's your prince?'

'As it happens I've a one who can give us a good steer on that.'

Øyvind would be somewhere forward having followed Renzi aboard, no doubt being shown around the wonders of a modern battleship.

He came quickly. Properly respectful of the captain, he spotted the charts laid out and saw straight away what was needed.

'Eidsvoll,' he said positively, pointing inland some distance. 'The road to Sweden goes here, and here, past Christiania, about a hundred of your English miles.'

Kydd kept his silence for a few minutes, then said, 'If I had charge of those villains, the roads would not be my choice, too long with many chances to be caught. Sea – but only in a Swedish ship.'

'Why?'

'Gets him through our blockade without searches, they being our treaty friends. So he's had to get word to send a ship to pick up them and their prize.'

'So . . .'

'They've flown overnight to the nearest deep-sea coast to go to a lonely island to await the Swedish ship they've summoned.'

'Which island, pray?'

'Ah. That's the question. We have to go in quest of it.'

'With your blockade fleet.'

'I said I cannot involve them, Nicholas. No, a little work with the head-piece will go far in easing the business.'

His brow furrowed for a space then cleared. 'The deep-sea approaches to Christiania narrow suddenly here at, er, this place.'

'Ingersløkka,' Øyvind said helpfully.

'Only a mile or so across the narrows, the ship will not be willing to go in further than there. Just twenty miles or so out – is there a coast road?'

'There is.'

'So we look for a fisher village or such that has a small island or two offshore from it. They won't want to go further than they have to, so we start from your Inger place and go on.'

He traced the coastline until he came to a first cluster of islands. 'I'll wager he'll be in among these.' He looked closer. 'And here's your village on the shore. Sonskilen. Does it have a road inland as will connect it to your Eidsvoll?'

'It does.'

'Then that's where I'll look first.'

'You?'

'In a local fishing smack – in plain clothes, needless to say.'

'Alone?' Renzi said, aghast. 'Those knaves! You don't know how many there are, and they're like to be armed.'

'We'll see. Do you both go on deck for a space.'

He summoned the gunner's mate. 'Toby. I'm stepping ashore – on my own.'

Stirk's weathered face broke into a frown.

'I'm of a mind to have a boat's crew as I can trust but there's complications as needs them to make a choice for themselves.'

It was explained and Stirk chuckled. 'We'd give a bucket o' cobbs t' be out on some pranks while th' rest is flogging up and down like, an' we never pays mind t' the politicking anyways.'

The manner was easy and assured but Kydd knew that, behind it, there was a touching faith that Stirk's captain knew what he was doing and for some reason had to go about it in this furtive way.

A little later Captain Sir Thomas Kydd told the first lieutenant that he was going ashore with his two recent guests and to call away his barge but with a boat's crew he'd already selected.

With Sonskilen discreetly out of sight in their lee *Thunderer* sent away the boat under sail and good time was made to the tiny fishing port.

There were few to see them slip into the diminutive market and waterfront. With his Swedish captain's coxswain Halgren to assist, the languages being so similar, it was not long before they'd been able to hire a local fishing craft – a *seksæring*, thirty feet in length with a spritsail and gaff and capable of six-oared progress into the wind. Just what was required in these waters.

They found their places, Stirk at stroke, Kydd opposite, Renzi and Halgren at main, Doud and Pinto at fore. Without comment Øyvind slid in to take the tiller and they shoved off.

It was a well-found boat with a high sheer forward to take the respectably sized seas of the Skagerrak but caulked by tarry moss in view of the blockade's efficient seizure of contraband pitch.

The boat-keeper in their buoyed barge gave a restrained wave to see them off, at a loss to see their noble captain take an oar, but for those in the boat it was memories – of the days when Kydd had been one of them, even under the same iron-built gun captain.

Taking stock of the situation, Kydd knew the theory was good but did they have the time? Each island would have to be circled and then the next across, and at any moment the Swedish ship would arrive. If he didn't call it correctly they would lose.

Catching a fitful south-westerly they stepped the mast and hoisted sail, so close to the water that their hissing progress seemed satisfyingly fast and Kydd, relieving Øyvind at the tiller, shaped course for the nearer of two.

It came up rapidly, an anonymous-looking lumpy island, well-covered with conifers and a pale beach at one end.

Kydd took a clockwise circuit, going in with the dark, rocky shoreline as close as he dared, peering into it with as much concentration as he could muster.

'Um, sir, an' jus' what exactly are we lookin' out fer?'

Kydd cursed under his breath, not at Stirk's question but that he'd not given them an idea of their objective. He'd thought about it, of course. The island would need to be small, devoid of human presence. If there were buildings or settlements it would have been avoided and they wouldn't be there.

So a pristine islet, possibly with an old fishermen's landing stage handy, but most revealing, some sort of temporary shelter, a tent perhaps at a place where there was otherwise nowhere to lay the head. It would also serve as a signal to seaward for the arriving ship so should be visible to them as well.

When it came, the actual release of the prince should present no great difficulty – brawny sailors against a few wharf-rats, it should not take long.

If they found their quarry.

They completed their circling and moved to the next, more open to the sea. It had a sandy bay on the inland side with two or three fishermen's huts, which if they were a naval searching party would be the first place to be turned over. Without delay they left the island behind and made for the next and furthest out to seaward.

A little larger but seemingly more remote, near triangular and with an odd central rise bare of trees, this was Bevøya, it seemed.

The afternoon was approaching a Nordic dusk and Kydd was anxious to complete this initial cluster of islands before dark and made straight for its fir-clad flanks. Only half a mile in length it didn't take long to complete the north-east side but as they quartered its featureless shore Kydd had a twinge of apprehension.

As they reached the finality of that side and prepared to round it for the run to the south that marked the open-sea-facing length, he felt a frisson of excitement as the last piece of the jigsaw fell into place.

Along this side there were no further islands or land to seaward – no one therefore who could spy any ship that came in directly from the sea. The prince's disappearance from Norwegian soil would be guaranteed not to be witnessed and even Kydd's own squadron would have no power to prevent a Swedish flag vessel from proceeding on its mission.

'Keep a bright lookout, you men,' he growled.

The light was low but it was good enough to make out the jumbled grey boulders at the water's edge, the pines that covered the lower part of Bevøya, like a blanket, and at near a third the way along – a small, rickety boat jetty.

And beyond, up in the woods, a scrap of pale that might very well be a canvas shelter.

'We're going in,' he said softly, not at all sure what they would meet when they set foot ashore.

As they approached the jetty figures appeared, descending to meet them.

'We're fisher-folk,' Kydd hissed urgently. 'Be like 'em!'

Innocently they doused sail and under oars headed for the jetty as if with fisher-like intentions. The figures stood still and waited.

'*Stå ved siden av*,' called Halgren, at Kydd's prompting.

The menacing figures stiffened and shouted something – and Kydd saw, with a lurch of the heart, that all were carrying muskets.

'Says as we should go away, this is not our island.'

Proof positive.

'We're all a-scunnered,' Kydd said, in a low voice. 'Terrified. Back-water starboard, heavy up larboard.'

In all fear the fishermen scrambled to get to sea again, but out of sight shipped oars and came to a confabulation, the bobbing motion of the characteristically Scandinavian craft oddly reassuring.

'It's them,' Kydd said, with a satisfied finality. 'We've found your prince.'

His tone was firm and encouraging but it was bluff. Here he was, at the impossibly lofty height of the captain of a ship-of-the-line with whole decks of heavy guns ready to bellow their rage at his sole command, surely the monarch of all he surveyed upon the seas. And for reasons owing to matters political far away he was now leading a party on a foolhardy effort to free some sort of captive in the face of armed opposition. In effect he had to recognise that this was a petty officer's job and his reflexes were no longer at that level.

'Toby,' he asked, in a low voice, 'what's your thinking, if I might ask it?'

Stirk's expression gave nothing away. 'The beggars'll be all together, no sense in 'em ramblin' away on their own. An' that'll be where the prince is – in that there tent.'

'So?'

'We got t' get 'em out o' there. Out in the open – good targets, then.'

'Can't fire on our friends.' And in any case what had they to fire at them with? For that matter what else had they in hand to go against armed men?

Suddenly all the odds had stiffened against them. Decisions had to be made of a very grave nature.

For some reason the situation didn't seem to trouble Stirk, who felt about under the thwart and pulled a stout bundle into view. 'Sir?' he said simply, holding out a mariner's sea-bag. But it didn't hold sailors' gear. Instead, there was the unmistakable oily sheen of combat steel – cutlasses of the trustiest sort, each swaddled in rags to deaden their give-away clanking. Under these were a trussed clutch of boarding pistols.

Kydd's heart warmed to the tough old seaman but it didn't change a thing. 'No guns, no firing.'

Stirk must have smuggled them into his barge and then here. He was only doing what a good petty officer should do, ensuring his boat's crew were properly equipped with barkers and slashers even if it appeared the officer in charge had unaccountably forgotten to give the necessary orders.

Seeing the weapons, Renzi brightened. 'As saves the day! They won't be expecting this and—'

'Didn't you hear me, Nicholas? I said no firelocks. These

may be vile scrubs but might be Swedish. We leave bodies and it'll be hell to pay whatever we finish with.'

'If we don't take these pistols we haven't a prayer against them.' And if they failed to recover the prince before the ship came it would be catastrophic for the young Norwegian democracy.

'No guns.'

'So the venture is over just when we know where he is?' Renzi bit his lip but Kydd was not going to be swayed, staring forward without a word.

Minutes passed. The boat bobbed cheerfully but there was no sound from any of its occupants.

Then, unexpectedly, Kydd spoke. 'So we take 'em with blades – making sure they yield before harm's done.' It was asking a lot – to ignore musket and pistol fire to close with what amounted to an enemy with cutlass alone and fight them to a standstill to force a conclusion. But if the stakes were as fraught as Renzi made out there was no alternative.

In a moral sense Kydd had no compunction in using force – the Swedes had been caught out in a sordid diplomatic ploy and would not want to make a fuss at its thwarting. It had merely to be done without bloodshed.

'We make the assault at first light,' when a collision of lethal weapons had a chance of ending in other than bloody stumbles.

The night stretched ahead. The hours dragged. The cold bit deeper.

Kydd had had many an endless night shot through with fearful imaginings during his years of naval experience, but this was among the worst he could recall. It was the helplessness that was so galling – the meaning of combat for him now being the command of heavy cannon and manoeuvring a great ship. But, here, he was trapped in a situation where the possession of a few muskets could turn the battle decisively against them.

In the last bitterly cold hours before the dawning Renzi coughed meaningfully. 'It does cross my mind how we might even our odds, gentlemen.'

'Say away, Nicholas. We're all listening.'

'No guns. We've a half-dozen pistols with nothing for them to do. Supposing we land a man with them at the end of the bay to conceal himself. He fires one – in the air, naturally. The odious parcel of villains rushes out to see what the alarum is. Our man fires the rest into the air, they believe they are under attack and the undisciplined rascals blaze away promiscuously, leaving them in short order with empty weapons. Then we—'

'Well done, Nicholas!' Kydd snorted. 'This then is our signal to rush 'em from behind with naked blades and—'

'Convince them to drop their weapons. No blood, no bodies.'

Light was promising in the east. If they were to make their placements it would have to be soon.

'The one at the pistols. A volunteer?'

He would be firing harmless shots into the air while his shipmates were in peril of their lives. There were no glad shouts.

It would have to be a direct order but Kydd hesitated. 'Mr Stirk. These are your pistols and the honour is yours to choose who shall fire them.'

'Aye, sir, an' I chooses . . . Doud.'

'Be buggered to it, Toby!' Doud spluttered. 'An' miss the frolics?'

'Either you or . . . Pinto.'

'Me? Y' knows I c'n handle a blade better'n any!' The

Portuguese was indeed deadly with his razor-sharp knife as Kydd well remembered from *Duke William*.

'Well . . .'

Kydd felt in his pocket and came out with a Norwegian rigsdaler. 'Here you are, Toby.'

'Sir?'

'A coin.'

'Oh, aye. Best o' three, then.'

The rest was straightforward. Kydd recalled the bay had at one end a useful tumble of rocks that would be within sight of the camp and, as the first light crept in, Pinto was landed out of view to take up position.

His would be the responsibility of judging the daylight suitable for sword-play and opening up with the first shot – the practical definition used since medieval times was the ability to see a grey goose at a mile.

For the rest it would be challenging. There was only one way to get into position and that was to land unseen around the point before easing around the shoreline to a spot below the tent – in the knowledge that if they were spotted it would bring down a fusillade of musketry.

They noiselessly brought the boat in, heaving it up a tiny fine-gravel beach. 'Øyvind, stay here,' Kydd ordered quietly. It might be his prince but the fight was all theirs.

In the uneasy calm of the morning they crept along, heads well down, conscious of the seeming crash of their footsteps in the shingle and that without scabbards their naked cutlasses must be carried at point.

A pair of seagulls made a deafening fuss of departing at the intrusion but there was always the comforting soft hiss and return of wavelets.

Kydd signed for them to crouch and carefully lifted his eyes above the line of the topsoil edge. There was the tent, perfectly still and strangely menacing. As far as he could see no guards were posted; right at the moment they would be feeling very secure in their isolated hideaway.

He eased down and they settled in to wait.

The light strengthened, banishing the sea-mists and extending the horizon seawards. When the ship appeared it would be clearly visible. Would they be in time?

It was now in Kydd's judgement quite clear and sharp enough for lethal combat but it had to be Pinto's decision and—

A sharp rap – to a band of warriors it was unmistakable. A shot, and grinning faces acknowledged it! Kydd warned by sign for them to keep down and peeped over the edge once more.

One by one, in varying degrees of disarray, figures boiled out of the canvas, gaping out at the morning, then into the distance to where another two gunshots cracked into the stillness, the smoke eddying up from the rocks. The two with muskets got off their shots, others diving back to re-emerge with their own, hastily buckling on sword-belts.

Last to come out was a short but voluble figure plainly bellowing at them to retaliate. The muskets went up and the morning was rent with the crash of guns, all of them.

Kydd counted. Seven – with their five they stood every chance!

Rising to his feet he scrambled up the rough slope, sensing the others with him. Seeing startled faces turning to them he felt a rising lust for combat, roaring out a battle-cry.

Next to him he heard an even louder, elemental howling as Stirk pushed past. Halgren and another added their fear-some shrieks.

Their foes rallied quickly, wrenching out their swords, and in moments they clashed together.

Their leader went for Kydd, a pistol going off wildly before he threw it to one side and raised his sword to fall on him. It was a heavy, cavalry-type sabre and Kydd smiled with satisfaction. A good weapon with the weight to slash down at unprotected infantrymen but sadly slow for skilled sword-play.

He took the first blow with an upraised blade, noticing the snarl of scorn at the sight of his primitive sea-service cutlass. The man was military-trained but had clearly had little combat experience.

Kydd parried and faked a thrust at the chest to keep him at bay. The man recoiled, waving his sabre wildly – in a mortal confrontation he would be spilling his life's blood by now.

It gave Kydd time to look about.

The massively built Halgren smashed out his weapon at his terrified opponent, who could think only to wave his hanger in the Swede's face.

With an irritated grunt his left hand, now a hook since an honourable wound years before, reached out and, with a sharp jerk and a wrench, plucked the blade from the man's grip. He turned and fled.

Doud, in full view, was enjoying himself. His opponent was bigger, his sword of a curved Moorish kind but Doud's heavy cutlass flicked effortlessly in snake-like jabs and parries, forcing the man to the defensive at every move.

He was tiring, leaving himself open to Doud's merciless onslaught, which stopped inches before a mortal blow. He was playing with his foe who suddenly, panting and heaving, threw down his blade.

Stirk was in the centre, dominating all with his piratical presence – the red bandanna, glittering dark eyes and brass earrings, and an expression of ferocious glee as he pressed his man back with great crashing hits.

And then – an unearthly howl from behind – it was Renzi, but not the cultured gentleman Kydd knew. A whirling cutlass in one hand and, snatched from somewhere, a dagger in the other. Like a Renaissance *condottiero*, he was holding two adversaries to something more than a draw.

It was too much for Kydd's man who, transfixed, dropped his guard and in a flash the grey steel of Kydd's blade pricked at his throat.

'*And gentlemen in England now abed shall think themselves accurs'd they were not here!*' Renzi joyously sang, but it was all over. In the face of the Royal Navy's practised bulldog boarding, the villainous kidnapping crew had dropped their weapons and now stood about wretchedly.

And from the tent emerged two figures – one was Øyvind but the other was Prince Kristian Frederik, rubbing his wrists and blinking in the early-morning sunshine.

Renzi bowed politely. 'Sir, I believe your presence at Eidsvoll would be missed, were we not to return this hour.'

'Mr Renzi,' the prince replied in French, 'you are known to me, and Mr Øyvind Gundersen has explained himself. Do kindly introduce these others to whom I owe my freedom.'

Kydd allowed himself a smile of satisfaction. Despite untold limitations, he and a handful of *Thunderer*'s men had brought deliverance to the future King of Norway and thus the chance for a new country to win its independence.

He met Renzi's eye but before they could share the moment there was a muffled gasp and several cries of dismay. Kydd saw where they were gazing and spun around to look out to sea. And there, shockingly close, a ship glided around the point. Backing sails, it heaved to, and clear above, the colours of Sweden floated out.

By the narrowest of margins they had lost the race. And if they had any idea of fleeing in their stout *seksæring* they could forget it. Not only was this a Swedish ship but it was a frigate – no doubt sent to make it diplomatically ill-advised to be subjected to any kind of search – and they would be run down in less than a mile.

It was check-mate. With a snarl of satisfaction the leader of the kidnappers turned on Kydd.

And then the world changed once again. As if in a dream a vision firmed from the morning mists beyond the frigate. A ship far bigger came on, nothing less than a ship-of-the-line. Huge, magnificent and powerful, it loomed majestically above the lesser, which lost no time in loosing sail and leaving the scene.

It was *Thunderer*, come to her own in their need.

Chapter 86

The carriage ground off, the coachman driving the horses fast on the road to Eidsvoll. In it Prince Frederik sat with his deliverers, talking in a low voice to Øyvind.

Renzi looked at Kydd. 'Old fellow, why do you think it was that dear *Thunderer* should make her appearance when she did? It does seem a mort more than a coincidence.'

'No mystery, Nicholas. Just Mr Roscoe doing his duty.'

'You ordered it?'

'In a manner of speaking. If he sees a strange frigate his standing order is to follow it until proven a friend. A flag is easy enough to flaunt, and proper coxcombs we'd be if he let past an enemy.'

Renzi chuckled. 'So the frigate decides to depart without ceremony, not wanting to be seen as party to a plot to abduct a prince.'

The other two finished their exchange and Øyvind respectfully turned to Kydd. 'Sir, Prince Frederik is at a stand to think how he might reward you for your gallant act. A public address and decorating at Eidsvoll or something of a more tangible value? He will be honoured to meet your wishes in the matter, whatever is decided.'

Kydd was horrified. If ever it became known that he had had a central hand in the frustration of the Swedish desire for Norway against the strictest orders of the government his career was over. 'Oh, er, tender my warmest regards and so forth, but do strongly convey that I am excessively modest and any such display would do violence to my sensitivities. At a later date a personally written letter would be more than appreciated.'

It took some considerable discussion to extend this to the confidential bestowing of the Grand Cross of the Order of Duke Peter of Oldenburg, following the prince's crowning. For the boat's crew there would be a purse of silver to share among them and Øyvind might look to interesting employment after his graduation.

Professor Sverdrup was nearly overcome when summoned to the carriage to receive the prince, who was soon smuggled back into his lodging quite as if he'd never departed, leaving Øyvind to convey Kydd and Renzi back to the bosom of his family, neither wanting to miss the conclusion.

'Naught to worry on,' he said airily to his weary father. 'Just a message that wasn't passed on, is all.'

'As it may be, boy, but tomorrow we votes on our constitution as will be binding on us all,' he grumbled. 'An' I can tell you, we has in it that we're to be a kingdom, and Kristian Frederik is like to be king of it. If he's not here to be king we doesn't have a constitution, now do we?'

Kirsten broke in breathlessly, 'When he gets to take the crown will we common folk be allowed to see?'

'With soldiers in red coats to march up and down, like they do in England?' Björn wanted to know.

'There'll be plenty to celebrate,' Yngvar said, recovering his humour. 'Did I tell you we'll be clapping eyes on our new flag at the signing?'

In the event, when the constitution was adopted and signed by the president of the assembly it was a quiet affair, none but delegates present.

The following day Yngvar was uncharacteristically quiet when he returned home not far short of midnight. 'It's done, by God, the words fair written an' all in one for us to see.'

He sighed and reached for the akvavit bottle. 'Each one of us, called by muster, signs our name. Some has to be helped, not having had much use o' quills before, but it's all there.'

Renzi knew he meant that the document was now an irrevocable shout of defiance against the Swedes who would now make of it what they would.

'And tomorrow we've a body o' assemblymen as will be going to the prince to see if he'd accept the throne should he be elected king. If he does, well . . .'

It was never in question, and when Yngvar returned the next afternoon it was with the news that indeed the prince had been duly elected and had accepted the crown as King Kristian Frederik of Norway.

In the Gundersen house the moment was bewildering, wonderful and historic. Of course there had to be some sort of celebration.

Their guests were shooed out and a feast set in train. There were difficulties – the blockade for the humbler sort had effectively cut off all that could in any way be described as extravagant.

As they sat down in the gaily decorated dining place Captain Sir Thomas Kydd and the Earl of Farndon were handed a mug of beer, with generous splicings of cognac-tinted akvavit, which drew snorts of appreciation.

Dishes arrived, the first of which was *finnbiff*, reindeer meat pieces, fried in bacon fat, with mushrooms, and doused in sour cream, served with an astonishing caramel-sweet brown cheese.

But nothing prepared the foreigners for the final course placed before them. It was *lutefisk*, a dish of a jelly-like consistency served with potatoes and coarse mustard. A blank-faced Øyvind informed them it was really dried and aged stockfish well cured in lye.

Then the table was cleared and a delightfully light and delicate mousse made its appearance, *trollkrem*, or troll cream, a celebration of the toothsome forest lingonberry, which went far to settle the stomach.

Glasses were charged with akvavit once again, and Renzi wanted to know more about the trolls.

All eyes turned to Yngvar, who sat back expansively, then began to tell of them. How if he were to go north through Viken and penetrate the mountainous wilderness of the Vestlandet it would be to trespass on the very lands of the troll peoples, fiends and demons that lived among the rocks and caves and occupied themselves gleefully in tormenting hapless travellers. In a breathless stillness he went on to explain that it was necessary to keep a sharp eye open among the desolate crags for odd-shaped formations because, who knew, a man-eating *troldfolk* might be lying in wait, motionless.

'So why haven't we seen any hereabouts, Father?' Øyvind asked.

'And after all that learning at your fancy university?' Yngvar snorted. 'Everyone knows it's because they're scareful of all the church bells ringing, sees 'em off back to the mountains.'

*

The next day Yngvar was back early. He said nothing, sitting by the fire and staring into it. At length he glanced up and harrumphed something that only Kirsten caught.

'Today is your father's last day as a delegate. The prince – that is, the King – wants to say farewell and thank you before he goes to Christiania to be crowned. Yngvar says he must go, but would be honoured if we all come too.'

The dray was prepared and, decorously, all the family installed themselves, the ladies in their traditional *bunad* – long dresses in magnificent colours and ornamentation – and the gentlemen in dark velvet coats, knee breeches, buckled shoes and low-crowned black hats.

Feeling very much the outsiders, the Englishmen kept quiet, and when the new King made an address from the steps of the manor they kept well to one side. Øyvind found them and, in some embarrassment, explained that there was now to be a church service of thanks but that the ancient Eidsvoll Kirke was too small to take all who wanted to attend. The pair decided to take a stroll around the little township.

They returned to find the manor once more surrounded by the delegates' families, looking on as if they were expecting something.

Øyvind hurried up to them, clearly excited. 'Do come with me, my friends!' he demanded, beckoning.

The Eidsvoll manor was thronged by men who seemed to be at a loss but also exalted by the occasion. King Frederik had apparently expressed a desire to meet the delegates for the last time on this moving occasion.

It was to take place in the largest room and Øyvind ushered them around it to a small doorway.

'Wait here,' he instructed.

The ceremony proceeded apace with more than a hundred

delegates packed into the room, and when the King reached each one he was not sparing in his particular thanks.

And then it was over.

Or was it? A shout arose and then another, and in an impulsive gesture every delegate grasped hands in a continuous chain. '*Enig og tro til Dovre faller!*' they bellowed together in high emotion.

'What was that?' Kydd whispered to Øyvind.

'They say, "We will be united and loyal until the mountains of Dovre tumble down." In Norway, this means for ever.' Øyvind's eyes were moist and some of the delegates were openly weeping.

It was a charged moment. Sombrely, Kydd turned to his friend. 'Nicholas. You and I have seen our share of war and destruction, but this day we've witnessed something else – creation and hope.'

Renzi's eyes took in the room. 'And a country that goes forward with destiny in its own hands.'

Glossary

Alcalde	mayor of Spanish *barrio*
Bermoothes	Shakespearean term for the Bermudas
bowline-on-a-bight	a bowline with two elements, used in life-saving
break bulk	open the hold, begin removing cargo
Briscard	Napoleonic military veteran
bum-boat	small open boat trading with the shore
chigger	native to Florida, insect parasite
chivvy	urge on faster
conjunct	military operation involving both Army and Navy
Cousin Jonathan	friendly British term for Americans
crepuscular	relating to twilight
dicked in the nob	taking a blow to the head
diligence	a public vehicle with duties similar to a taxi
dimber	fine, attractive
El Soberano	chiefly in charge, sovereign ruler
fettle	to fit and repair as required for battle
gibbous	the moon when greater than a semi-circle
glacis	a slope before fortifications
godown	oriental term for a warehouse
gullion	worthless person
gyre	powerful whirl of water
Hansa ports	referring to cartel of ports in the thirteenth-century Baltic
huachinango	variety of red snapper
invest	in a military sense, to besiege
Irish pennant	odd ropes hanging about aloft
keckling	rope wound on a cable to protect it from exterior abrasion

ketureen	a light Jamaican carriage
killick	anchor
larbowlines	the larboard watch
Mongseer	lower-deck term for a Frenchman
noggin	a splash of something cheering
parbuckle	method to haul weights up steep rises
pinchbeck	cheap alloy of copper and zinc resembling gold
polder	Dutch, marshy land reclaimed
priddy	to prettify, Scots
ravelin	an outwork protecting the bastions of a fortress
rorty	in a state of careless exhilaration
rummer	a rum-based noggin
rutter	routier, plotting ships' tracks for others
scunnered	in a state of acute irritation
shabbaroon	an ill-dressed shabby fellow
shonky	a useless person
slow-match	a gunpowder line burning at an inch an hour
squib	a newspaper piece expected to explode on the public
strake	a plank of a boat that stretches fully fore and aft
vidette	sentinels mounted on horseback

Author's Note

In my books I've sent Thomas Kydd to almost every part of the globe that saw the Royal Navy in operations. As the conflicts with Napoleon Bonaparte progressed, it became a full-scale world war, with all that that means, in far-flung locations.

Our hero's been at the summit of a live volcano, at the pirate's lair of Port Royal and even to the ends of the earth – Van Diemen's Land, the Tasmania of today. In this tale I've plundered events of the time to take him to some relatively little-known but intriguing spots where affairs of consequence were unfolding.

Bermuda, for instance. Never a place for stirring fleet battles, its very existence off the American coast and as a southern station for the North American Squadron ensured its place in naval history. A place of calm and peace in a world gone mad, I don't grudge Kydd's spell in its embrace.

It retains a delightful English feel with a great deal of what met the eye in his day still to be seen. While the dockyard is where cruise ships now tie up, much of the original area is visible and greatly to be recommended to explore. There is also a world-class museum right at hand, whose excellent monographs I have taken full advantage of in this volume, as I did from the unstinting help and advice of students of Bermudian culture and history, Edward Harris and Edwin Mortimer.

The Bermuda sloop was indeed famed for its celerity, a consequence of its lightweight local cedar construction and vast sail spread. *Pickle*, one of its class, was picked by Admiral Collingwood to rush the Trafalgar dispatch to England. It could be said that the rig is the ancestor of most yachts afloat today – single fore and main extending to the masthead, mainsail luff secured full-length but probably without the lengthy bowsprit.

For me, Bermuda has a poignant significance, for buried in St George's cemetery lies Vice Admiral Andrew Mitchell who, like Kydd, made the awesome journey from pressed man to admiral – but Kydd did not suffer the brutal flogging-round-the-fleet Mitchell received as a young seaman.

On the continent nearby, America was in its energetic infancy but under the burden of war with the British and therefore confined to its shores by the inevitable naval blockade. It could be said that this circumstance triggered the change of perspective from the Atlantic and its seaward ports to the unfettered westward and unlimited opportunities – so thank you, Royal Navy!

It was a time of characters and adventurers of every stripe. In my research I came across a young army scout, by the name of Davy Crockett, and mention of skulking desperadoes in Cape Canaveral. There were also wicked English agents tempting the scalp-hunting Creeks, led by Red Eagle, and the Seminoles under the redoubtable Bowlegs to make a strike against Georgia and the southern American states. As it happened, President Madison had to renounce his boots-on-the-ground move but within half a dozen years Spain saw Florida east and west both proudly flying the Stars and Stripes.

The other side of the Atlantic was where the big guns had their say. I'm still in awe of Napoleon Bonaparte who, after his calamitous retreat from Moscow, in a matter of months had pulled together an army of a quarter-million to menace the fractious Allies with another twenty years of war.

For the Allies, and particularly the British, the action against Antwerp was nothing short of a catastrophe: the French still had possession at the very end of the war. Had it come off, it would have been a major blow against Bonaparte, but it didn't, and the engagement at Bergen Op Zoom recounted in this book goes down in British Army history as the worst rate of loss of any military operation in the whole of the Napoleonic wars.

At their best, conjunct operations of Army and Navy were world-beating. Earlier in this series I've described actions in Egypt that led to Napoleon fleeing and abandoning his army; the landings at the Cape that began the British empire in Africa – and not forgetting that the entire Peninsular War began with a landing by Royal Marines. Antwerp, though, was at the opposite end of the scale.

The expertise built up in these empire-building operations was largely down to the unsung efforts of the Transport Board, who organised the shipping, often in the hundreds, that was necessary to place the soldiery ashore. Tasked with finding these resources the practice was to contract at very short notice with merchant ships under escort of the Navy – expertise that continued right through the long Victorian century all the way to our own time. The Falklands War, for instance, saw ships at the sharp end that were STUFT – Ships Taken Up From Trade, something Kydd would have recognised.

In his day conditions could be hideous. Little imagination is needed to conjure what it was like from icy seas to land with but a single shot and bayonet, then, half blinded with snow, to face mortal combat on a hostile shore.

Incidentally, the crossed-anchor insignia I wore as a petty officer was of Kydd's eighteenth-century pattern with the two flukes coming together at the end of the shank in a pronounced sharp point at the crown. I'm happy to say that to this day seamen in the Royal Navy still sport this easily recognised pre-Nelson form.

Several years ago a Norwegian reader, Even Andersen, alerted me to a painful episode in naval history. He quoted Henrik Ibsen from his vivid and harrowing poem '*Terje Vigen*', which throws into stark relief the effects on the population of the Royal Navy's blockade on Norway. Andersen also recounted details of the Norwegian response that gripped my admiration and set the creative juices flowing – and a determination to have Kydd involved in some way.

To consider the second oldest working constitution in the world was created in weeks under these conditions, and has subsequently never had significant amendments until 2014, is astonishing. The Norwegian Syttende Mai, their National Day held all over the globe, commemorates the signing at Eidsvoll, and kings of Norway have been elected ever since.

The town itself, charming and rural among the low boreal juniper and spruce, is much as it was, and Carsten Anker's manor house has been preserved, with knowledgeable guides at hand to explain the events of those times.

The island of Bevøya is now a yachting destination, setting out from Kydd's Sonskilen, which still has its seagoing heart, the Norwegians being as much born sailors as the English.

The Swedes do not come out of this story well for, as predicted, the Allies, once at peace, would not tolerate a

Bonaparte-style annexation of a sovereign nation. A fitful occupation gave way, to their credit, to a compromise that allowed for a continuation of the constitution until full independence.

As ever, my deep appreciation must go to Team Stockwin – my agent Isobel Dixon, my editor Morgan Springett, graphic designer Lary Rostant and copy editor Hazel Orme. And a BZ for her contribution throughout the whole process, to my wife and literary partner, Kathy.

As a postscript, just before I began writing this book, I signed a new contract for four further Kydd titles. The adventure will continue . . .